FLOODS OF SPRING

By Henry Bellamann

SIMON AND SCHUSTER · NEW YORK
1942

To My Friend

James Thornton Gittman

FLOODS OF SPRING

BOOK ONE

I

IT WAS a morning in early May and a heavy white mist covered the river and obscured the hills. The flood, now past its crest, rustled and whispered along the banks. Farther out a deeper sound came through the clinging mist. It was a sound compounded of many small sounds, the multitudinous voices of many waters—many currents breaking on the surface in an infinity of small patterns, each one sighing, and murmuring—all merging into a muted clamor, felt rather than heard, as if the air itself moved and sounded in unison with the complex river flow.

A small river packet, the *Charles Edward,* made its way slowly upstream, avoiding the mighty onrush of the main current, but being equally cautious of dangerous shallows and newly formed sand bars.

The *Charles Edward,* out from St. Louis, was calling at various small river ports. It might proceed as far as Jefferson City, or even farther, depending upon river conditions. It was a dingy boat, crazily decorated in imitation of the palatial Mississippi craft of an earlier date. Its engines were almost as crazy as its decorations. It crept along, crossing and recrossing the river, dropping a passenger here and there, taking on others, unloading occasional heavy boxes and crates with much noise and confusion and a minimum of efficiency.

Today, at this early hour, the decks were almost deserted. The

Charles Edward seemed to struggle in a world of its own—a world of pearly mist above, with now and then a distant gleam of fabulous emerald trees rising terrace upon terrace to touch a luminous strip of gray-blue sky, and below a world of waters making furtive sounds as it swept dizzily alongside.

In this uncertainty of earth and sky there was something illusory and dreamlike, something dangerous and indifferent.

Savina Kettring looked fearfully at the river. From where she sat, she could see nothing but sky and water. The morning mists were thinning but the banks were still shrouded. The land was dim and uncertain.

The boat seemed scarcely to move. Almost imperceptibly, it toiled in a wide curve, and Savina saw a long, straight stretch of the river that seemed to flow out from the horizon itself. She had not believed there was so much water in the world.

She leaned toward the rail to look at the wild water which turned and twisted, thrust sideways and backward, and boiled upward in sudden wide circles as if things, desperate and huge, were drowning there.

Savina thought of the bright and friendly Susquehanna in her own Pennsylvania. She sighed. It was a long sigh, deep and tremulous. It sounded like a small, stifled sob. But Savina was not crying.

Passengers seeing her on the narrow promenade looked at her with open curiosity. It was evident from her clothes that she was not one of the "emigrant crowd" that was coming out from the Eastern states.

Savina leaned back and closed her eyes but she could still see the dreadful currents of thick, muddy water. No use trying to shut out the sight. Better to look at it. Nevertheless, she tried not to. She smoothed the wide folds of her brown alpaca dress and straightened the many rows of black fringe that circled the skirt. Someone passed, and she folded her hands quietly on her lap. The gleam of a broad new wedding ring shone through the mesh of the lace mitts which left her slim white fingers free. The fringes and the mitts and the row of tight rosebuds edging her close bonnet were vanities. Savina

[4]

knew that, but she treasured them. She looked out again at the riverbanks, clearer now. She could see trees and tangled vegetation over backwaters that reached into savage darkness.

It was a wilderness. What good would her pretty bonnet and her new lace mitts be in a wilderness? It would have been nice to wear them on Sundays when she went to church in Martinsgrove. She sighed again. It was not to be, and so there was no use thinking about it. But her heart beat hard and fast when she thought about home, and her throat tightened so that she feared she might be ill.

No trace of emotion showed on Savina's face. The bands of pale, blond hair lay straight and smooth beneath the confines of braids about her head. Her mouth, fresh and firm, was slightly compressed in its habitual control. But faint waves of pink passed now and then across her face, normally as creamy white as pear blossom. Everything about Savina· was expressive of physical and spiritual purity.

Once, as the morning wore on, she heard a shout from what seemed to be a dilapidated landing. There was an answering call, loud and incomprehensible, from somewhere below. She had no idea what it meant, but there was the sound of a bell, and a change in the rhythm of the paddle wheel. The boat veered away from shore. Savina arose and went hesitatingly to the rail. She shaded her eyes with both hands and tried to get a better view of the land. Her eyes, smoky gray and shy, had an expression now that was oddly mixed and contradictory—as if she looked eagerly for something she did not expect to find. It was a new look in the eyes of Savina Kettring.

An elderly woman with a figured shawl draped about her shoulders came out of a door near by. She paused beside Savina and nodded. "I think it's going to be a fine day after all." The woman spoke with a rising inflection as if she were asking a question. She looked at Savina with interest that was clearly sympathetic.

Savina smiled a bit uncertainly and flushed. Her lashes fluttered in evident embarrassment.

She spoke softly. *"Ich schwetze englisch gar net."*

"What? Oh—I—excuse me! I thought—well, well, excuse me."

The woman hurried away. Savina looked after her, wondering

[5]

a little, and returned to her seat. She did not know what the stranger had said. At home, miles from the frequently traveled roads, few of her people spoke English.

Her gaze returned to the river. The sun was shining brightly, and the turbulence of the great yellow tide plunging toward her was clearly visible now, and terrifying. She was not feeling well. Maybe, she thought, she might be hungry. She wondered what Peter had done with the lunch basket. It had been restocked at St. Louis. She would ask him as soon as he came back again to this—this—she wondered what they called this part of a boat. A porch, maybe. She wished very much that Peter would come and sit beside her and talk. He had been standing up there at the front of the boat all morning, just looking. He seemed to be fascinated by the river. He stood so straight and so proud, she thought, as if he were running the boat himself.

Savina sat very still, looking hard at that straight figure in the long black coat. Peter was her husband, but she did not really know Peter. She knew now that she had never known him at all.

And Peter . . .
Peter was not thinking about Savina. He had not thought of her since he had taken his stand up forward where he could have a wide, free view of the river.

A curious happiness filled the breast of Peter Kettring this morning. A curious happiness because it was compounded of so many colliding and contradictory elements. Liberation, a sense of immeasurable, immediate freedom, the approach of strange, new experiences. With liberation went an almost eerie feeling of emptiness. The old had not yet been replaced by the new, and with the certainty of new experience went the uneasiness that always accompanies the unknown.

Nevertheless, Peter was enjoying one of the rarest of human experiences. He had abandoned a way of life he had disliked. He was adopting a new way of life he desired. He was free to do this without regret or hindrance.

Peter Kettring had money in the bank.

[6]

Now and then fellow passengers paused to speak to Peter but no one stayed to talk. He replied courteously and immediately turned to his absorbed contemplation of the scene.

"Curious fellow," one remarked to another.

"Yes. Looks like he's got something on his mind."

"Came on at St. Louis, didn't he?"

"Yes. He's from Pennsylvania. He did tell me that much. Talks like an educated man."

"He's got a good-looking wife. D'you see her?"

"Yes."

"Well, lots of 'em coming out here from the East now that the war's over."

"Yes, and mark my words. The Yankees will overrun this country."

"Well, we need somebody in here with git-up-'n'-git."

"I don't like 'em."

"No use talkin' like that. This country in here was half Yankee all the time. War's over. Might as well forget it."

"It'll be a long time before that'll happen."

"What's that fellow going to do out here?"

"Couldn't find out. Close-mouthed."

"Looks like a lawyer, or something."

"Looks like all the Easterners I've seen lately. Standoffish."

"Yep. They're like that."

"Well, Clem, it suits me all right. I don't want to talk to 'em any more'n they want to talk to me."

The one addressed as Clem squinted at the motionless figure of Peter. "Fine-looking man."

The other nodded. "Yes, he is. Must be over six feet."

Peter stood stone still and erect. He was controlling a rising excitement, hoping that no one might notice. Only a close observer would have sensed that an extreme alertness—an alertness of the whole man—was there, quick and tense beneath the carefully maintained poise.

He unbuttoned his coat and took off his hat. He did not relax.

His eyes, black and brooding under heavy brows, did not suggest youth, but the clear firm line of his profile did. Peter Kettring was only twenty-seven.

When he thought of himself—and he was thinking intensely of himself at this moment—he had a strangely mixed feeling of being both old and young. As he recalled the past few years with their dreadful tumult and hardships, he felt very old. When he thought of the immediate future he felt his whole body thrill with youth and expectation. The future! His future—*his*—with no one to interfere. He was free of every slightest trammel that life could lay upon him. He held his world in his own hands. He would make of it what he wanted.

At times some recollection of the four hideous years of war passed across his mind like a transforming shadow. The image of a face would flick into his consciousness, the sullen face of a prisoner, or the white set face of some desperate young rebel sighted along his rifle barrel. There were so many of them rising from the recollections of that long nightmare. He had come back. So many had not.

Whenever Peter thought of these things his eyes froze stony-still and he would not speak to anyone. Savina knew the moods but she did not understand them. She did not recognize the terrible reticence of a man who has killed other men.

Peter Kettring was born and reared in Philadelphia. His mother had died when he was a small boy. There remained only a dim memory of her. He was an only child and his father, Jonathan Kettring, had devoted much time to Peter's education. Dr. Jonathan Kettring was a Presbyterian preacher. Peter had often been puzzled by the contradictions in his father who had swung from extremes of fanatical severity to moods of melting gentleness. But he understood now—the explanation was fairly simple. His father's stern and uncompromising traits were straight out of his theology—hard, cold thinking carried to its ultimate conclusions and applied directly to life. His gentleness came from his literary tastes and preoccupations, which had been wide and unorthodox.

Dr. Kettring had planned a career for his son which should in some way have to do with letters. Just what had never been decided, but in preparation for European study, he had given Peter a substantial grounding in languages. The intellectual relationship of father and son had been rather close. Their emotional relationship had been tenuous.

Then the Civil War. Peter had not understood the issues very well, but he was caught in the excitement of marching men, and bands, rallies and flags, and violent arguments on every hand. Dr. Kettring had been furiously partisan. All that followed happened quickly. Peter enlisted. He found himself suddenly bereft of his familiar world of thought and feeling and plunged into an insanity of blood and fire, of pain and disease and dirt. He could not summon ordered recollections from the daze of those experiences.

Early in 1864 Dr. Kettring died, and at the end of the war Peter returned to the empty house in Spruce Street. For weeks he did nothing. It was as though the whole machinery of thought had been rusted out of existence. He picked up books and looked at them. The words were dead and dusty.

It was not until the summer of 1866 that he realized he must begin to plan his future. He rejected the idea of further study at present. Perhaps he should try to find a teaching post. The suggestion came from some of his father's old friends. He agreed, rather apathetically. Some small college, maybe, out in the state, or even in Ohio, they said. But the educational world, too, was disrupted. There seemed to be few college posts for a young and inexperienced man, no matter how much he knew about Latin, nor how well he spoke German and French. The best that inquiry produced was a village school in Martinsgrove far to the west of the state. Peter accepted it, and found himself, late in August, the master of a tiny village school in the heart of the Pennsylvania Dutch country.

Peter had never seen anything like this beautiful and peaceful region. When he looked out from the neat little village to the smooth rolling fields, the thick-foliaged trees, and the blue dreaming hills beyond, he felt the pulse of new emotions. He did not know what they were.

The school did not interest him. He went through the routine of teaching, only half aware of what he did. His pupils ranged from beginners to big husky boys and girls of sixteen or seventeen. They were orderly, respectful, and obedient. "Teacher" was an exalted personage and his word the ultimate authority. Instruction was given in both English and German, although the children habitually spoke the quaint and sometimes weird dialect known as Pennsylvania Dutch.

Peter boarded with the family of Anton Hummelfelder. Old Anton was the richest man in the region, and the most respected.

The Hummelfelder house was big and comfortable. Mrs. Hummelfelder and her two grown daughters, Sissy and Edie, seemingly cooked from morning to night. The three big sons sat in a row at one side of the dining table, eating in glassy-eyed silence. At first Peter was uncomfortable. The boys seemed never to take their eyes from him. He soon discovered that they were simply overawed at actually seeing a person—a professor, too!—from "Philadelphy."

There was never any mention of the war. Evidently it had concerned the Hummelfelders but little. When the sons had been drafted, Pop Hummelfelder had simply bought substitutes for them. Now that the incomprehensible conflict was over they thought no more about it.

When Peter mentioned having fought through the four years, Anton said: "Think now!" and Mrs. Hummelfelder clucked, "Tchk! Tchk!" The subject was not referred to again.

Peter was aroused from these recollections by the deep whistle somewhere back of him. The magnificent bronze sound was out of all proportion to the size of the *Charles Edward*. Peter smiled a little. The boat sidled toward the right bank and edged up to a landing. He walked back and stood at the railing beside Savina. On shore, a dozen men in dirty, ragged clothes stood about listlessly. A few Negroes, almost naked, looked pleased and happy.

"Peter—*die Schwatze!*"

Savina had seen Negroes for the first time at St. Louis.

Peter looked at her. Her eyes were wide and horrified.

"Yes, yes. There will be many of them here."

[10]

"Oh, Peter. They look terrible. So wild!"

"They're not wild. They're like children."

"They must be so poor—in rags like that."

"Worse than poor." There was a trace of bitterness in Peter's voice—something that echoed oddly in his own ear of his father's voice. "They have nothing."

"They live in the woods, maybe?"

"Anywhere. In huts. You'll see."

"I think I am afraid of them."

"No need. They will not hurt you."

"There will be many black people, like these, at St. Stephens, where we go?"

"They are everywhere out here."

"So? Think now! Everything is so strange here."

"You must not be homesick, Savina."

"Homesick?" She considered the word as if she had never heard it before. "Homesick? No, of course not. But—"

"What?"

"St. Stephens. What will it be like?"

"Like any one of these places you've seen today."

"They're so dirty, Peter, and so falling down. The people must be lazy."

"They had slaves. They don't know how to work."

"Think, now!" This was the favorite Pennsylvania Dutch expression of wonder, amazement, regret, or incomprehension. "Think, now!" she said again.

"We won't be in such a place. We will go immediately to a farm."

The boat was moving. Peter went back to his place, but Savina remained staring at the huddle of unpainted houses. Her eyes were wide and her breath came and went quickly. She raised her hands a little, slowly clenched them, and then beat softly on the flat wooden rail.

The mists lifted by eleven o'clock and the broad river was a maze of light. Peter half closed his eyes against the glare, but the kaleidoscopic movement of sunlight and water was hypnotic. He leaned against the rail. The shuttling pictures of recollection began to move again, to impose themselves on the moving water, vaguely at first, then more and more clearly until the view before him disappeared.

This kind of retrospective meditation was not entirely new to Peter. He had felt the same way during those first autumn months at the Hummelfelders'. Then, too, he had been turned in on himself in a way that was unsettling and uncomfortable. He realized that the Hummelfelders respected him as the teacher, the stranger "from off," but not in the way that they respected John Wauckman, or Albert Fischer, or Maas Haltiwanger—men no older than he, who owned big farms and who were somebody in the countryside. He saw, too, that it was not only because of property; it had, somehow, to do with emphasis. They lived in a certain way. That way was respected in the valley. It had to do, first of all, with material things—acres, houses, livestock, and implements—but it also had to do with something one did with those things. That something was elusive. Peter thought a great deal about it, and as he thought, many of his own values showed thin, unsubstantial, and trivial.

He remembered that evening when he had said, casually, that he might buy a farm. There had been a brief moment when the clatter of knives and forks stopped. Then Pop Hummelfelder said: "Farms cost a lot of money."

Peter recognized the implied question. "I think I could manage it."

Pop speared a slice of bread with his fork. "Herman Ringstreiter is thinking about selling out since his boy died last summer. He can't work the place no more by himself."

"Is it a good farm?"

"It's a good farm. Herman knows how to take care of a farm."

"I guess a man could learn to run a farm." Peter spoke a shade stiffly. Pop's quick ear caught the tone.

"It's nice to own something under your own feet," he said.

"I have a house in Philadelphia. I want to sell it. I have no kinfolks. It's a big house."

"A big house, eh? I looked at the houses once in Philadelphy. Tall, straight up, right against each other. A house in Philadelphy is worth a lot of money, I guess."

"More than enough to buy a farm."

Pop looked up, half incredulous. "Just a house, without even a yard? Think now!"

But Peter sensed that he had won a sort of consideration which he had not had before.

"The Ringstreiter place has got awful good outbuildings on it. It's a good place," Anton remarked as they left the table.

Through that winter and into the spring Peter followed the life of the valley with absorbed attention. These people lived comfortably in big houses, they took extreme care of horses and cattle, they worked with furious energy from four or five o'clock in the morning until suppertime; they seemed to have no interest in any life other than this and no notion of change. Their farms and their work made up a way of life and this way of life was an end in itself.

Peter watched and listened for any sign or word which might suggest an interest in ideas. But the Hummelfelders and their neighbors seemed to be wholly given over to the seasonal rounds of action. One task followed the other in a rigidly prescribed order. The simple action of beginning a piece of work without hesitation and continuing with it until it was finished had all of the aspects of ritual and religion. To work on one's own land with one's own property summed up all of the necessary attributes of living.

Peter felt that there was something in the nature of these people that escaped definition. They were not peasants driven by a force outside of themselves. Their impulses came from within. Much was custom and habit, but custom and habit fell short of a full interpretation.

If there was any sort of mysticism here—some deep, pagan devotion to the soil and the cultivation of its fruits—it was never revealed. Still, Peter wondered. There might be something like that, something very old and from very far away—older than history. Certainly, no matter how scornful he might feel of the igno-

[13]

rance and self-imposed limitations of these people, they had deep wells of strength and peace to draw from which were inaccessible to him. With each passing month he was more and more determined to discover what these sources were, and to find his own way to them.

He moved gradually into the rhythm of the farm life. He found himself going about with Anton, or with the boys, who had long since dropped their uneasy reticence, helping a little here and there. The Hummelfelders accepted Peter almost as one of their own.

There was something about Peter's fire-eyed intensity that drew comment from old Anton.

"He ain't easy-like," he said to his wife.

"I noticed from the first." She nodded vigorously. "I minded once maybe it was a girl, maybe back in Philadelphy, but I guess ain't. He don't give notice to girls."

Anton looked quickly at her, his eyebrows making ever so slight an interrogation. She shook her head. "No, no. I wasn't thinking about Sissy or Edie. They don't give no notice to him, either. I think they look further away."

"So?"

"Maybe."

"Peter Kettring is a smart young man."

"He likes it here. You think?"

"Yes, he likes the things—everything, I believe. It's funny, too, for a town boy, that way."

"He ought to settle down."

"I guess he's got enough money, but it'll take him a long time to learn."

"If he married a good girl, now."

"Yes. He ought to settle down. He could learn."

Peter was learning. He was learning far more than Anton guessed. His quick intelligence organized his observation, and he saw the whole, neatly dovetailed system of the Hummelfelders' efficient farming as logical and right. The logic and rightness of it blurred into another estimate—it seemed in its rounded completeness to be fundamentally good.

When the school term was finished, Peter returned to Philadelphia. He sold the house and rearranged some financial matters at the bank. He was somewhat amazed when he added up his resources. He was well off. He surprised himself and the Hummelfelders by returning almost at once to Martinsgrove.

"I want to board with you this summer and help on the place."

Anton scratched his head. "Want to learn, eh?"

"Yes."

"All right. You can piddle around and I guess that will earn your keep."

"I don't want to piddle."

"Can you keep up with the boys, you think?"

"I'm strong."

"All right. I'll pay you ten dollars a month and **your** keep. But we work hard. You know that?"

"Yes, I know. It's a bargain."

And so began a strange apprenticeship. It was not an apprenticeship to Anton, or even to a technic of farming; it was an apprenticeship to the soil.

Anton and his sons, like all of the valley farmers, worked with a kind of desperate haste. They were paced by the swift seasons, and there was never a moment to lose, but even they were astonished by the ferocity of Peter's efforts.

"*Der Teifel kann mir holen* if he don't do the work of two men, that Peter."

"He learns?" Mrs. Hummelfelder wagged her head as if she were confirming something she already knew.

"It looks like he knows beforehand. You don't have to tell him much. He catches on right away."

"Tchk! Smart like that in books, and works smart, too! It ain't often."

Peter had brought several boxes of books with him from his father's library. In spite of back-wrenching work and aching fatigue, he read a great deal. He was looking for something, though he was not quite sure what it might be. He dragged his rusty attention through difficult and crabbed books. The more he read the more he was certain that these printed papers were explanation of the ills of the world. Word spinning! Ideas made up in the air with no root anywhere. It was this that dried up the blood in men's veins and made fools of them. Science, yes, that was all right, science and —and what? He was not sure there was anything else worth putting down in books. He thought he understood his father better now. His father and all of his father's fathers had been preachers and lawyers and teachers. They had lived on printed pages—fed on them until they were pale and unreal. They went away from the living world—the world you could touch. Parasites of print— all of them!

He remembered how angry his father could become over a difference of opinion about something of no practical importance. Predestination! Foreordination! The election of souls! All of that snarled and tangled thinking! He—Peter—had been in battle. He had seen men die. He had killed men—seen them stagger and clutch at the air and fall on their faces. And men had made that war because they could not agree on ideas. If everyone worked in the world as these simple people here in the valley and attended to their own affairs as these people did, they would not have time or the wish to make a war.

Here—here in this valley, he thought, was some sort of solution to all the questions which vexed the minds of men into writing difficult books.

He closed the last of the musty volumes with a gesture of finality. He wanted to learn. Yes. But something that Anton could teach him—Anton and these green fields and quiet streams. He was going to school to the earth itself.

The blaze of light from the water was uncomfortable. He turned away from the railing, crossed his hands behind him and walked slowly around the deck.

"There's that sour-looking feller again. Shore looks troubled in his mind."

"I've seen fellers look like that when they was runnin' away. Might be the law's after him."

"Naw, he looks too straight and hard at you. He ain't afraid of anything, that feller ain't. He's got a go-to-hell look in his eyes."

Peter did have a go-to-hell look in his eyes, but he was not troubled in his mind. He was merely impatient—impatient even of the introspection and remembering which engaged him. He wished to be getting on with his plans—with his world. He was sure of what he wanted his world to be, and sure that he could create it.

Back there in Martinsgrove Peter had reached all of his important conclusions. He thought he had reasoned well, but Peter's mind had never been well enough organized to reason well. He had only learned to use his memory when he was a student, and then when he might have gone on intellectual explorations, he was in the army, forced to mechanical obedience. Hunger and cold and illness and enormous fatigues congealed all streams of thought. The intellectual and spiritual injuries were deep and lasting. He did know that the ways of other men had been imposed on him and that they were ways of disaster. Now he would think for himself, reach his own conclusions, and abide by them. With this assuring of himself came a lightly concealed arrogance—the direct, small, secret heir of Jonathan Kettring's theological hardheadedness.

Peter was too proud to take anyone for an actual model, but he had realized early in his stay at Martinsgrove that Anton Hummelfelder had some qualities that he desired for himself. That aspect of completeness—yes, that was the character of Anton's relation to the world, completeness.

Anton was not made by the land—not entirely. Anton made his farm, his "place" as he correctly called it, and it in turn acted upon him. Anton and his place fitted each other like two halves of a single growth. Peter did not interpret it quite correctly. He saw Anton as the master of his world. But Anton, deeply in harmony with some elemental instinct for the truth of life, was the partner of his "place," in complete communication with it. Peter had seen him scoop up a handful of soil and hold it, peering closely at it, fingering it, and letting it spill slowly from his slanted palm. Perhaps he was only making a practical examination of the thoroughness of the harrowing, but Peter thought there was a look of communication in the old man's eye. He was always touching things, laying his hand on the smooth limbs of trees, patting the cows and horses—all with a manner oddly mixed: possession, inquiry, approval. Affection, too, Peter wished to add, but a compound of possession and approval was about as near to affection as Anton could reach. The more Peter considered Anton the less obvious he seemed to be. Not mysterious or enigmatic. Just a way of being—so close to his earth and the things growing out of it that he was a moving part of it.

Peter envied him.

At the same time he was becoming aware of the valley's conventions. Everyone seemed free, but it was freedom within a rigid frame, understood and accepted. He found it difficult at first to understand Anton's adjustment to these restrictions. But it was simply that Anton lacked imagination. So did his sons and daughters. This was the way of life—and that was all there was to it.

Peter began to press against these hard boundaries, a very little at first, then, as he felt the familiar old theological rigidities beneath the casual-seeming manners of the region, more and more violently.

It was not until the Umholz family came to the Hummelfelders' on New Year's Day that he saw his way. Even then he did not see it all at once. Gabriel Umholz was a rich farmer from the southern part of the county. He had one daughter, an only child. This fact alone was sufficient to set the Umholzes apart. Savina lived an easier life than other farm girls. She did her work well, but Mrs. Hummelfelder said she was spoiled.

Savina did not look like the other girls Peter had seen. She was prettier and gentler. She had almost the demureness of a Mennonite girl, or a Quaker, but the Umholzes, like most of the people in the valley, were Lutheran.

After the stupefying New Year dinner the girls went upstairs, and the men sat talking. Gabriel Umholz told about his younger brother, John, who had gone West, to Iowa. He had a farm, an unbelievably big farm, and he was getting on very well. Land was cheap and good. You could raise anything out there. The nearest neighbor, though, was several miles away. John's wife did not like that, but Gabriel's tone suggested that this was not a matter of any moment.

"If I was fifteen years younger, I'd go out there myself."

Peter tingled. He felt as if someone had called his name from far away—a clear and imperious summons.

Presently the girls came downstairs again. Peter arose and offered his chair to Savina. This piece of city manners struck the whole room dumb. Savina flushed scarlet. Peter saw Mrs. Hummelfelder wink at Anton. Mrs. Umholz drew herself up a little proudly. She knew all there was to know about the young teacher, and Savina was no common child.

One Friday afternoon—Peter remembered it well—not more than six months ago, he had been sitting at his desk in the little schoolhouse. The air was warm and honeysweet with spring. The room had become suddenly unbearable. It closed in on him. He arose and took a deep breath.

"That will be all for today. You may go home now."

The pupils were too astonished at first to move, but in a few minutes they were outside, whispering to each other as they watched the tall, black-clothed figure striding away up the hill.

Peter had never gone far into the thick woods on the slope back of the schoolhouse. He did not know if there were paths or not. But he made no effort to find one. He struck straight up the stiff rise toward a rocky point he had often observed from the valley. It was harder going than he had guessed, but the air was cool there among the young leaves, and intoxicating. It was nearly an hour before he reached the thin shrubbery that grew in the scant soil above the jutting rocky point. The wiry stems of huckleberry bushes made a tangled snare for his feet, but he did not pause. He stumbled and thrust his way to the bare gray rocks. He caught his breath, and some tension inside of him broke. He sat down quickly. He was too dizzy to stand.

The whole world seemed spread out before him. The trees billowed downward in waves of young green, pink, and pale yellow. Far down the brown plowed earth lay velvety in the sun. Faraway sounds, confused and mellowed by distance, floated toward him. To the north the young foliage faded and shadowed into blue and violet. The haze of spring sun lay over the whole landscape like a gold and silver net.

And then Peter did something he had not done since childhood. He began to cry.

He cried hard and for a long time, making choking sounds and pounding on his knees with his fists.

If anyone had seen him, they would have thought he had gone crazy. He still wondered why he had done so.

But in that hour all that had tormented Peter from within himself was swept away. He even allowed himself a measure of self-pity. He felt that his whole life had been made up of harshness —hard lessons, severe discipline, a complete lack of warmth from anyone, and then the war with its corroding and destructive action.

At the Hummelfelders' he had known the first feminine ministrations of his life. Just the simple matters of good cooking, of being urged to eat more of a dish he liked, of having his clothes attended to. A gentler feeling stole over him.

Then he pounded on his knees again.

The violent surge of rebellion arose again, sweeping every reasonable thought before it. He must get out of this—away from here! He arose and shaded his eyes with his hand. He could see across the valley and across the first line of lower hills to what he guessed was another valley almost like a river of light, and then to a deeper blue contour of a farther range of higher mountains. His imagination ran like light—Ohio, Indiana—Illinois and the Mississippi— Iowa, and to the west of Iowa where John Umholz lived, *miles from any neighbor*. There a man could live, could shed every restriction of these old crystallized forms, there he could construct from a beginning, there he could be entirely free, free to be as lonely as he wished, or, he amended, as he might have to be. Lonely. He thought of that again. Why should he be lonely? He could choose someone—someone to go with him and—and well, just *be there,* while he made around him every aspect of life as he wished it to be.

Gabriel Umholz said . . . Gabriel Umholz! *Savina!*

The name was like a flash of lightning blazing suddenly across the tumult of a storm, holding it for one instant in the rigidity of complete illumination.

Savina!

He saw her in that blinding inner light as clearly as if she stood there before him. He had no need of introspection or question. He saw her as if she already belonged to him. The fiery wave in his brain burned away the whole confusion of these weeks and months of question, leaving a clear skeleton of purpose, of imperative necessity.

Old habits of thought tried to make logic of what he felt. All of these weeks since he had seen her—yes, yes—her image had been growing into its place in his life—her warmth into his blood. He tried to ask if this were just another kind of fury, kin to all that had surged beneath the surface of his mind, but he could make no answer to the question. All of this had grown back of his attention.

He still looked upon the inner vision: Savina, small and soft, willowy of motion, gentle of speech. About her and over her a sense of blossoming orchards . . .

He took an uncertain step forward and with his recovered attention the landscape came again into focus. Wide blue shadows lay across the fields. The foot of the hill was already darkening. He started down the steep rocks, jumping from one boulder to another. Then he plunged into the dense undergrowth and fought his way through.

The next day he asked Anton for the horse and buggy.

"I'm going to see Savina Umholz."

"Um, so? So it's like that, eh?"

"Yes; it's like that."

"She's a fine-looking girl."

"Yes."

"Savina is a good girl."

Savina's mother said the same thing the next afternoon when they came back from a buggy ride, and announced that they were going to be married.

They were married the day after the little school closed. Peter did not know what Savina felt about going to the West. She said nothing. She listened to him exactly as a child listens, and said, "*Ja,* Peter."

On the day of their departure Anton called him to the kitchen.

"I tell you something, Peter, and don't you forget it. You'll find a lot of new ways and a lot of people to tell you how to do things. Maybe you'll have to learn little different ways, but it won't be much. The land is always the same." He wagged his finger. "Everything that grows on top of the ground you plant in the light of the moon. Everything that grows down under, like potatoes and turnips, you plant in the dark of the moon.

"And remember this—plow deep and use plenty of manure. Work like the devil was after you, too, but first of all, plenty of manure!"

Now that he was actually on his way Peter knew that he had surprisingly begun to take root in the life of that valley. Ever so little, perhaps, but still . . .

The little cluster of houses that made Martinsgrove had come nearer to being home than anything he had ever known. When he left he felt for the first time the tug of human relations. He was a little lonely. But there was Savina. He had to look at her repeatedly to assure himself that she was really there. She was so quiet that it was difficult to believe in her.

Peter felt emptied of his entire past—of his whole life. Everything that had lain heavy and hampering in his brain and heart was gone—swept out and away as on a flood. He came back to himself at this moment with the occurrence of the image in his mind. *As on a flood.* Yes. All of those troubling and interfering things—gone like this driftwood and weedy waste that went swirling by the boat.

That flood was subsiding now, just as they said this flood here on the river was falling hour by hour. Peter could see marks of the devastation along the bank, but there were places where already a brilliant new green was beginning on the far edge of a field. The flood swept away debris, carried away old things and left a new richness where its whirling waters had spread.

And now . . .

This was the magnificent adventure that he had dreamed that winter afternoon when Gabriel Umholz spoke of Iowa. He was glad, however, that he had not chosen Iowa. The land agent in Harrisburg had not drawn an attractive picture of Iowa. Then, too, John Umholz was out there somewhere. A relative of Savina's. Sooner or later they would have been bound to meet. Heaven only knew what complication could arise from that. No: better Missouri, where he knew no one, and where he could actually begin at the beginning. He liked the idea of the river, too. Water was something moving and alive. He hoped he would be able to find a place in sight of the river. This river—the majesty of it! This was indeed a river measured to the grandeur of this vast new country. It was a symbol of free expanse. Peter felt that it matched his dreams, his sense of himself in this new world, and his certainty of what he could make of it.

All afternoon he had been watching as the packet drew in to various small ports, on the lookout for river-bottom farms, and perhaps farms set up a little, looking down on the river as so many farms in Pennsylvania looked down in dignity on the Susquehanna. But he saw only sprawling places, outbuildings falling down, poor fences, or none at all. And not one fine barn! It was strange.

Savina was watching, too. She was hoping to see precisely the same thing Peter was looking for—a well-kept and prosperous farm. She knew that they were not far from St. Stephens now. Surely she would begin to see land and houses like—like home.

As she watched, greater and greater disquiet gathered heavily about her heart. She peered anxiously at the thickly wooded hills and the unkempt bottoms. It seemed to her that the region appeared more and more neglected. Wasteland! That is what her father would call it. Surely Peter would not buy wasteland. It would take forever to make anything out of such a place.

The interminable day wore on. The vast hollow of midafternoon passed. The silver light altered subtly. It was that strange hour of late afternoon which has so marked an effect on human beings. Perhaps it is the sense of fading sun that warns of the night. The sense that warned primitive man of the dangers of darkness, and which turned his straying feet back toward his cave in the hillside.

Savina felt it in a sudden onslaught of homesickness. Peter felt it, too, but less strongly. He turned from his daylong vigil and sat beside Savina.

"Well, we'll soon be there." Peter spoke in his careful, meticulous German. Savina admired this clear and beautiful speech. She thought that she must be at pains to learn to speak that way, too. She could read German well enough, but her daily speech remained the dialect of her valley. She knew only a few words of English. So far it had not occurred to her that she would be among people whom she could not understand and who could not understand her.

"Yes," she said. "I'll be glad to get off the boat once."

"Yes. Well, we'll soon see what it is like out here."

"It won't be like—like this?" She gestured toward the hills.

Peter hesitated. "Not very different, I'm afraid."

"It looks so wild. Even the people—"

"You see the worst kind around a river landing, Savina. There will be nice people."

"The black people! They look strange to me. And all day I haven't seen a new house, or a fresh-painted house anywhere."

"You're not likely to. There's been a war, Savina. The whole country was torn to pieces. Backwoods places such as Martinsgrove never knew what was going on."

"Backwoods? Martinsgrove?"

Peter smiled. "Yes, Savina, Martinsgrove is somewhat out of the world. You didn't hear much about it, but it was a big war. Thousands and thousands of men died. The men of this country killed each other."

"What really for, Peter? I never understood."

"So that those black people you see out there would not be slaves."

"Slaves, yes—" Savina said the words vaguely. Then she turned suddenly toward him. "Peter! Did you—did you—" She stammered and swallowed hard.

"What?"

"Did you kill anybody in the war?"

Peter's face set. "Don't be foolish. That's what we had to do."

"You shot people?"

"Yes. Lots of them. God knows how many."

He looked at her. She was white about the mouth.

"I saw pictures—" Her speech was muffled. "Things like knives on the end of guns—"

"Bayonets."

"Peter, you never—"

"Oh, God, yes! Everybody did. When you got close enough you either stuck him with your bayonet or he stuck you."

Savina was staring.

"Listen, Savina. Listen to me!"

"Yes, I'm listening."

"We won't talk about this again. I don't want ever to mention it another time."

"I don't want to talk about it, Peter. I don't ever want to hear about it, either."

"I was just telling you what is the matter with this country. It will pick up again, I guess. I don't know what it was like before. But a lot of the Southern country was pleasant before we got hold of it."

"And then?"

"There wasn't anything left of the places I saw—not when we had finished. But I don't want to talk about it."

[25]

Savina did not reply and they sat for some time without further speech. Peter leaned forward, his lids drooped. Peter was thinking hard. In this nostalgic hour he had spoken more of his feeling than he had supposed he ever would. It was, perhaps, that surprising happening which led him to say more. He had seen Savina shrink from him. He was not sure that he was hurt by it. He was sure that he was annoyed. It was irritating that Savina should not understand more clearly, and—and see into things a bit deeper. He wished to shake her out of it, but some more reasonable impulse recalled Martinsgrove, the Umholz household, and all of the factors and forces which so circumscribed Savina and her ways of thinking. He softened. She was so pretty, and—he turned to look at her again. He narrowed his eyes slightly as he gazed hard at the clear, lovely face and the deep, steady eyes. Savina was a real person. One could see that. She stood firm. *"Savina is a good girl."* The words echoed in his mind. Yes: Savina was good. There was no doubt about that. Uneducated in his sense of the word, but certainly thoughtful, and, yes, certainly intelligent.

"Savina."

"Yes, Peter."

He looked straight in her eyes for a moment, then he turned his gaze to the rolling hills beyond the widening level land.

"It's going to be hard for us. You know how to work. I know that. But here it will be harder. I don't mean you must work like a field hand, or anything like that. But here we begin at the beginning. We will not have things to do with as you have always had at home. It's new country—it won't be anything like the life you are used to."

She nodded. Any talk about work—that she could understand. She waited for him to continue.

Peter looked slightly embarrassed. "Perhaps I should have told you more about it before—before we were married."

"I was willing to go with you—wherever."

"Well, then, so it is. We will soon see."

"Why did you wish to come here, so far?"

"To be free. I will try to explain a little. Back there, in Philadelphia, and in Martinsgrove, life is all set—one way. You can't do just anything you want to."

"What would anybody want to do but just the way—well, the way everybody does?"

Peter started to smile, and then was all at once serious.

"I want to be my own boss."

"Isn't everybody his own boss who has got a place of his own? Pa was his own boss."

"I don't think so, Savina—I mean this: in Martinsgrove and around there, everybody acts and behaves just like everybody else—because it is the custom."

"How else would anybody want to act? I wouldn't want to act any way that would make people talk."

"Now! There you are! *That's* what I mean. Suppose you were —as you *are* going to be—in a place where no one will talk—"

"*Ach!* People always talk."

"But where no one sees us, or knows us, to talk about us?"

"Where no one sees us?" Savina said the word slowly, with a kind of dismayed wonder.

"Yes. Where you can dress as you like, or stand on your head if you want to!"

"Peter. Should a woman stand on her head anywhere? Shame on you!"

"Suppose I wish to plow on Sunday?"

"Nobody plows on Sunday, Peter, nobody. Sunday, that is different. You rest a little and go to church."

"I shall never go to church again as long as I live."

"Why do you say that, Peter? You should not speak so. Your father was a preacher!"

"Yes; he was a preacher. And I read his books."

Peter straightened up, and laid his fist firmly in the other palm. "Yes. I read his books; I remember his sermons, and I tell you all of that is foolishness. It's just word-making. The church he was always talking about—somebody just made that in a book. People always have done that. All the evil in the world comes out of books."

Savina sat very still. She did not know what to say.

"I—I thought—"

"Yes, Savina. I know what you thought! You thought just what Pastor Helmeyer told you to think."

"Isn't he a good man, Peter, Pastor Helmeyer?"

"Savina, there is much difference between being good and being right."

She turned her head to look straight into his eyes. At that moment she reminded him of his little pupils in the school at Martinsgrove. She waited.

"People who are *right* go by rule. People who are good make their own rules."

"Pastor Helmeyer—"

"He is a fool."

"I misdoubt me that he is a fool, Peter. But I think—maybe—do you mean that right is out of the head, and good is from the heart?"

Peter looked at her. She thought he was about to smile at what she said—her opinions must seem so childish to him—but he seemed hardly to have heard her.

"There is good in books, too, Savina—in some of them, but people read and read and read and they lose reality."

"Die wirklechkeit?—what does that mean, that word?"

"Reality. Just what is, what actually, really is, like earth and sky and water—like this bench here."

"Isn't everything reality then?"

"No. But you don't need to think about it."

Her eyes were searching his face, a shade anxiously. "So much I don't know, and you are so smart."

His eyes crinkled as he stood up and looked down at her.

"I would not be dumb, Peter."

Peter's eyes darkened. *"Betend dass Gott dich erhallte, so rein und so schön und so hold."*

"What did you say?"

"Nothing. Don't bother yourself trying to think."

"One has to think—all the time. How can that be helped?"

"Do you think all the time, Savina?"

"Yes, always—when I am awake."

"What do you think about?"

"About what I have to do, and how to do it, and what I have to do tomorrow, and to make plans for it all. There is always so much to think about, one is never finished thinking."

He nodded gravely. "I believe you."

She glanced quickly at him—suspiciously. She was not sure that he was not making mock of her, but his face was serious. She felt closer to him than she had at any time. Maybe she was getting used to him—acquainted with him. That was what she had had to tell herself over and over during those first frightening nights with the deep alarm of lying beside a man—and so strange a man to her as Peter was—in the long hours of the night. She had not been able to sleep at first. Now it was already different.

Peter walked back and forth, but only a few steps each way. He had an uneasy look in his eyes. Now that St. Stephens was only an hour distant he was doubtful about the impression it might make on Savina. It was a new experience for Peter, having to consider anyone else in any way. He was not at all sure that he was comfortable about it. Perhaps it had been a mistake to marry before he had had a look at this country. Perhaps he should have waited, or, even, married someone here who already knew the life of the region. He missed a step in his walk. He was surprised at the strange emotional reaction he felt in himself at this last thought. Something arose in instant denial.

That something denied even the right to make question, and having denied went singing into obscure places of his being. He held himself very still that nothing of this should reveal itself.

Another side of Peter's mind came instantly into action—the familiar behavior of his reasonable mind. It swept critically in transview of these disconnected, emotional waves of feeling. He was immediately his usual controlled self. He had made his plans, he had seen his way, he had sensed the difficulties, he had counted the cost, he had weighed the gain—his mind tagged each platitudinous echo of his father's moralizing talks. He was sure he was right.

He must, above all else, not be sentimental. In the second of thinking so, and in measuring his decisions, he wondered if something of this hardening was directed against Savina.

Inconsistently, he sat down and said, "Don't be afraid, Savina."

"I'm not afraid, Peter."

"I just don't want you to worry."

"Why should I worry? Is there something else—something you have not told me?"

"No. I'm not hiding anything. It's just—well, you see, when your people came to America a long time ago, they left their familiar ways, and had to face hard conditions, and hard times. Did you ever stop to wonder why they did that?"

"I have not thought about it. But—to get along better, maybe."

"Better? Better in what way?"

"*Ach,* you are being schoolteacher, now."

"No, no. They came, Savina, to be free."

"Free—you say that again."

"But that's why they did come."

Savina thought for a moment. She nodded. "Yes, I guess all of our people like to have their own way." She smiled a little. "You are like that, too, I think."

"Yes, I am. But you should remember that when they came to Martinsgrove, they found things rather wild, too. Like that." He pointed to the shore.

"You are afraid of something, Peter—something you think maybe we will find out here?"

He flushed. "No—I'm not afraid. I—I just don't want you to be disappointed at first. Wait until we have been out here for a year or so, and everything will be all right."

"We'll make out, I guess, Peter. I know how to do."

He felt comfortable. Maybe he had been a little weak to let any shadow of discouragement touch him, and more, to say anything about it to Savina. But perhaps it was well they had talked it over so there could be no misunderstanding. It was all right now. It might be a little rough, even "out-and-out wild" as Savina had said. He would be able to manage.

A sudden thought startled him. Perhaps Savina thought they were going to be poor.

"Savina, there's one thing I forgot to mention. We've got some money. We won't be poor."

"I know. I'm not thinking about that."

"But of course you don't really know. I sold out everything I had. We've got plenty of money to get started right."

There was a glint of amusement in Savina's eyes. "Don't you know Pa found out all about that?"

"Found out?"

"Of course. He wanted to know if you were able to take care of me all right."

"But how did he find out?"

"Oh, everybody in Martinsgrove knows just about what you are worth."

"I see. Maybe I ought to have told you myself."

"There was no call to do that."

"I—we've got about fifteen thousand dollars, Savina."

"So? That's nice. Pa thought it was about twelve."

Peter was half annoyed, and for a moment amused. He knew the cautious ways of the Pennsylvania Dutch people. He just had not thought of their taking any interest in his affairs. So Savina had known all the time. He had not needed to be so concerned.

"Of course, Peter, you know that—that I did not marry you for that reason. Not just because you had some money."

Peter stared at her anew. Savina was uncomfortably full of surprises.

"I would have married you if you had not had anything. Pa and Ma were poor when they were married. But now, I guess things are different. People would talk if you had no money. The Fischers especially—they would hurry around saying Savina Umholz did not do so well when she married. I'm glad they can't say that about us."

Peter was surprised that Savina could be so talkative.

"Anyway," she continued, "Amy Fischer didn't do so well herself. She married Abel Prentner, he was an Amisher and they live in a house with two rooms. Think! You can't hardly turn around in such a place. I don't like the Fischers. Still I wouldn't care if we didn't have anything at all. We could make out. You are smart, and I know how to work. Ma saw to it that I learned everything. It's nice, though, to have things so it's not so hard—"

The deep whistle above their heads sounded three long blasts. Peter jumped toward the rail. "That must mean we're getting in to St. Stephens!"

They peered ahead, but could see nothing. The river was a blinding sheet of gold.

"I can see nothing at all, Peter. Where is it, you think?"

"Must be around the bend just ahead. I know it's on the north bank."

"How big is St. Stephens? I never thought to ask."

"Just a stopping place, I guess, like all these others we've seen."

"I think I see a church steeple. Up that way, Peter."

Peter squinted. "No. That's a tree."

Fifteen minutes later the port of St. Stephens was in sight. Peter and Savina strained their eyes for details. Savina held to Peter's arms as the boat drew in toward the landing. St. Stephens stood back from the river—perhaps a quarter of a mile distant. It was hardly more than a huddle of gray, dirty-looking houses.

The landing was in a dangerous state of decay.

"Stay here a minute, Savina. I'll see about our things."

A group of men lounged against boxes and barrels. They looked exactly like the ones Savina had seen at all of the stops. They stared openly at her. One man, wearing a wide black satin tie folded under a flaring collar, said something to a group near the boat. All of them laughed. Savina felt her color rise. She turned and walked away. In a few minutes Peter came for her.

"All of the things are together, Peter? The valises?"

"We'll look when we get off. Come on."

The short gangplank shook a little, and Savina clutched at Peter. It felt queer to be standing on something stationary again. She drew a deep breath.

Peter was pointing out his boxes and pieces of baggage to a tall, bony man in dingy clothes. The man nodded, counted the pieces over again, and pointed to the road that led from the landing to the straggle of houses that was St. Stephens.

"Come on, Savina, we'll have to walk up there. It's no distance. Feel good to stretch our legs a little."

"What do we do first, Peter?"

"Find lodgings. That man back there said there was a kind of boardinghouse—not exactly a hotel, I guess—where we can stay while we look about. We might want to go on farther—somewhere or other. There's nothing tying us down. We can go anywhere we want to."

Peter spoke almost jubilantly. His voice shook slightly.

Savina had been so excited she had forgotten to look around. Already the road had lifted so much that they could look down a little on the river. It was a casual sort of road, cut deep with wheel marks in the soft blackish soil. Peter and Savina walked single file along a narrow path next to a rough board fence. The sloping field was uneven and thick with weeds. Two or three cows stood looking at them. Savina stopped and gazed at the hills which rose in a huge semicircle above a wide stretch of uneven and overgrown bottom land. The hills were pretty, very pretty—not so high or so evenly green as the mountains near Martinsgrove, but like everything she had seen out here, wild-looking.

Such a lot of uncared-for land! So much waste!

They came into the village. There were no sidewalks, just sandy strips on both sides of the road. Some buildings were boarded up. The whole village had an abandoned look.

They passed a wide-open door. Savina sniffed the familiar odor of a general store. It looked dark inside, but under the shed roof built across the walk stood a number of barrels with lids.

"There. I guess that's the place. Right there at the next corner."

He pointed to a signboard nailed high on two posts. Black letters on a background of scaling white paint. RIVER HOUSE. BOARD AND ROOMS.

"That's it." Peter quickened his step.

The door stood open. Peter and Savina walked in.

"Yes, sir?"

A husky-looking elderly woman sat in a rocking chair near the window.

Peter removed his hat and bowed. "I want to engage a room."

"Just for the night?"

"No. For some time, maybe. I'm not sure how long."

The woman's glance traveled slowly over Savina's costume.

"Your wife?"

"Yes."

"I'm Mrs. Miner. I run this hotel. I can give you a big room on the corner, southeast, best room we've got."

"All right, I am sure that will do."

"Don't know how long you'll stay? It's cheaper by the week, a little."

"We'll take it by the week in any case. I'm thinking of settling here."

"Oh, that so? Is Mort Savage bringing your stuff up?"

"A tall man with red side whiskers?"

"That's Mort. I'll show you the room. Two dollars a day, with meals, for both of you. What's your name?"

"Kettring. Peter Kettring."

"Twelve dollars a week, if you want it by the week."

"That'll be satisfactory."

Peter stopped at the foot of the stair. "Where's the dining room?"

"Right there. That door. Want to see it?"

Peter looked into the room with its long table.

"Could we have a table, just for the two of us?"

"A private table? Well, I guess so. Nobody ever asked for one before. What for?"

"My wife does not speak English. It would be less awkward for her at first."

"Oh! Oh, I see. What is she? French from down to New Orleans?"

"No." Peter spoke curtly. "From the East. I'm from Philadelphia."

"Philadelphia? That's a long way. So you're city folks, eh?"

"I guess you'd say I am."

"What you count on doing in Missouri?—if you don't mind my asking."

"I think I'll buy a place out here."

Mrs. Miner looked steadily at Savina for a moment. Savina smiled, her short white teeth showing in an even row. Mrs. Miner nodded to Peter. "You picked a good one, even if she can't talk English. Pretty as a picture. Come on, I'll take you to your room. We have supper at half-past six. If it's ready on time."

Peter opened his wallet and handed Mrs. Miner two ten-dollar notes.

"For the first week," he said.

"I ain't used to my customers paying in advance. Not that I got any objections. Wish they would. Say, I haven't got any change up here."

"Let it go on next week, or give it to me later."

"Take off your hat, Mis' Kettring. Say, Mr. Kettring, how long you been married?"

"A very short time. Just a couple of weeks."

Mrs. Miner regarded Savina again with open but friendly appraisal. Then she unlocked a door leading to the next room.

"This ain't a room. It's hardly more'n a big closet, but it's got another washstand in it." She pulled aside the oilcloth tacked about the stand, and looked underneath. "An extra washstand," she repeated, "and—and things. Maybe your wife would like the little privacy." She laughed. "I know how it is when you're just new married, and all."

"Thank you, Mrs. Miner. That's thoughtful—and kind."

"Oh, it's all right. Place's just standing there. Nobody using it. No extra charge, of course, Mr. Kettring."

Mrs. Miner looked around the room once more. "Well, make yourselves at home. There's a kind of parlor downstairs. Make use of it when you want to get out of your own room a little. Whole place's wide open. I'll get on downstairs now. Remember, supper's at half-past six. We ring a couple of bells."

[35]

Peter closed the door. Savina lifted inquiring brows.

"What all did she have to say?"

"Nothing in particular. She's just goodhearted."

"It's bare-looking, this room."

It was a big, high-ceilinged room with whitewashed walls. The narrow windows had heavy brown-paper shades which rolled from the bottom and were tied with tasseled cords. The windows were clean and the bare floor was freshly scrubbed. There were patchwork quilts on the high four-poster bed. The chairs were hickory, with laced splint seats, evidently of local handiwork.

It was bare, as Savina said, but not uncheerful.

Savina rolled a window shade higher and looked out. There was nothing to see across the roofs, but some very green young willow trees and the river. The river seemed surprisingly near.

Peter moved uneasily about the room. He raised a window and leaned out.

"I think I'll walk for a little while before supper. I'd like to get the lay of the land."

Savina said nothing. She was still gazing out across the young willows to the river.

"You don't mind being by yourself for a while, do you?"

"No, no. Go ahead."

"I'll tell Mrs. Miner what to do about the baggage."

Peter hurried down the narrow uncarpeted stairs. He found Mrs. Miner outside talking to a woman. He guessed they had been talking about the new arrivals, but Mrs. Miner nodded heartily and he felt that the comment had been favorable.

"Mr. Kettring, I'd like to make you acquainted with Miz Pawling. She lives just up the road this way. Rhoda, this is the gentleman I was talking about from Philadelphia."

Mrs. Pawling looked at Peter with shrewd good-humored eyes. "I'm glad to make your acquaintance. I could tell right away you don't belong around here."

Peter bowed, and could not think of anything to say.

"Well, I'll be goin' on up the hill, Dolly." Mrs. Pawling nodded several times as if in belated agreement to something that had been said earlier in the conversation. She turned to Peter. "Tell your wife I'm coming to see her. If you pass by my home—it's the only brick house up this road—bring her in to visit. Be glad to see you. Good-by."

Peter lifted his hat again, evidently with more courtliness than was customary here, since Peter saw the two women exchange glances.

"I thought I'd look around a little before supper, Mrs. Miner. I guess the baggage will come before I get back."

"I'll attend to it. You won't find much to look at here, after coming from a big city."

"It will be different, and new to me."

"Well, I hope you'll like it, Mr. Kettring. We got some good people here. Some not so good." She smiled, and Peter smiled, too.

Mrs. Miner watched him as he rounded the corner. "Covers ground," she said to herself, "with them long legs of his."

Peter shivered with excitement. He was actually here—here in St. Stephens, the place where he could begin at once to make out of his life and his "place," as soon as he found one, anything he wished to make.

The street was narrow and sandy. Some halfhearted attempts had been made at graveling. Shallow drainage ditches were damp and grassy-green on both sides, and narrow walks, fortified with ashes and cinders, hugged the paling fences. This street was parallel to the river. A number of the houses were somewhat below this level. They looked as if they were sliding downhill.

Lilac bushes were blooming, somewhat belatedly, and a few snowball bushes were still hung with fading blossoms. The half-grown grass was sharply green and stiff. A few trees had leaves so young that the crinkle from the bud still showed. A faint smell came up from the river edge, a mixed smell of moist earth, water, and young vegetation. It was a heady smell.

There were few people about, but smoke was rising, blue and straight, from many chimneys. Supper was in preparation from one end of St. Stephens to the other.

The little street wavered now in accommodating curves about some large vacant lots, and was about to become a country road.

Peter went up a sloping alley to another street. There were larger houses and larger yards here. There were fruit trees and bee-hives everywhere. But even at its best it was untidy. Peter wondered.

He remembered the smooth, groomed look of the valley above Martinsgrove. The branches on the trees, the leaves themselves seemed to grow in more orderly fashion. It was a controlled land, disciplined by man.

This—this was shaggy, and rough, and untamed. He looked up at the great curve of high hills that swept back and around St. Stephens. Wild and arrogant. To Peter there was something of challenge in their look; and something very deep in him arose ready to shout in answer to that challenge.

As he stood there, his head thrown back and his intent gaze sweeping the long range of wooded upland, he was certain that in that seeming challenge and in his ready response some sudden kinship had been established. The spirit in him that was homeless set its wings for landing.

In these first tentative looks about him he was making note of his bearings. These rudimentary notations were the signature of a beginning possession.

There, he found himself saying in a fashion almost childish—there on my right is the river, running fast and hard to make way for yet more river to come. There on my left are the hills. Here—here where I stand—is the town of St. Stephens, and here am I, Peter Kettring. That is East, up there is North, and over there is South. The south bank, he said to himself, and he looked at it through the blue that was deepening over there. *The south bank:* it had a strange sound as if already by comparison this, the north bank, was an explored and known country. He identified himself with *this*. *That* was distant and strange. The first little thread of a root turned downward in this soil, this north bank a whole river's breadth away from that veiled and mysterious south bank. By these swift leaps of feeling *this* was established as something known. One was already here, standing in this place, noticing the sand and

gravel underfoot, the mullein stalks and burdock growing in the
ditch, the many shades of green along the hill. His feet seemed to
set themselves all the more firmly on this north bank as he walked
slowly along looking at the ground before him, the hills and sky
above him, and the vivid growing things.

He tried to be sober, and to hold his mind to steadier pace, but
his imaginings, like hounds free after long confinement, were leaping and running here and there, up and down and across the brilliant landscape.

2

The next day Peter went to see Carter Day, the president of
St. Stephens' new little bank. Mr. Day was respectful: Peter had
just doubled the deposits of the St. Stephens Exchange Bank.

Peter reached for his hat.

"Keep your seat, Mr. Kettring. I'd like to talk to you a little."

"You are not too busy? I'd like to talk to you, too. I was just
going to ask you where I could get some advice on buying a place."

"Are you in a big hurry to get settled?"

"Well, yes. I want to look around, though."

"I would, I would if I were you. How much of a place do you
want?"

"Big enough to—" Peter hesitated and a look came into his
eyes that puzzled Mr. Day. "Well, big enough so I won't have
neighbors too close to me."

"I see. I see." Carter Day looked keenly at Peter. He didn't see
at all, but he repeated the words absently.

"I guess I want a pretty big place."

"You'll need help with a big place."

"Not after I'm settled."

"Farming out here, Mr. Kettring, isn't the same as it is in the
East. The land—well, I guess you'd say the land isn't tamed. It
takes more—handling. Everything's pretty much run down. The
war. Were you in the army, Mr. Kettring?"

"Yes."

"I see. Well, we had right smart trouble around here, first one way and then another. Still lots of hard feelings on both sides, mostly by people who didn't do any fighting. It'll take time to smooth over. But, as I said, everything's been neglected. You can buy land dirt cheap. If you go in a little distance from the river, they'll just about give it to you."

"I'd like to stay on the river."

"Well, there's fine land in the bottoms. Then, there's something about the river. If you've been raised near to it, or been used to it for a long time, you miss it when you can't see it."

"I think I can understand that."

"Would you like to be close to St. Stephens?"

"Not too close."

"Don't go up in the country too far whatever you do. You can't get out in the winter. Roads are terrible."

"Who'll I see first about looking at places?"

"Well, now. Let me see. You could talk to Lawyer Phillips, but there's some people think he's just a mite too sharp. Of course, I'm not advising you against anybody. But I believe I'd talk to Niles Tipton. He runs the store just off to the left of the landing as you come up from the river. He knows every foot of the country like he knows the palm of his hand. He's been handling some places. You can count on what he says."

"Do you think I could see him right away—today?"

"Why yes, of course. Just walk down there and ask for him. He's a big fat fellow. You'll likely see him outside hollering at the top of his voice at the niggers."

"I've wondered—how is it with them, now they're free?"

Mr. Day looked out of the window, then back again. "That's a big question, Mr. Kettring, and a hard question. Now, I don't mean to step on your toes any, but there's a lot of people think the Yankees didn't know what they were doing. Tore this country all to pieces—all to pieces. The niggers are free, but they don't know what to do, or how to do for themselves. They're pitiful."

"They look so to me. I don't understand it."

"You'll see after a while for yourself."

[40]

"Well, thank you, Mr. Day."

"Not at all. Drop in and talk any time you're passing along." Mr. Day walked out from the small office in the rear of the bank and stood at the front door.

"Fine day. By the way, Mr. Kettring, I don't mean to ask too many questions, but—have you had experience in farming?"

"A little. Not on my own farm."

"I wondered. You don't look like a farmer."

"I was a schoolteacher."

"Oh, I see, I see." He was mystified, and showed it. Peter saw that he was but he did not wish to talk about himself. The past seemed as long ago as it was far away.

"Good morning, Mr. Day, and thank you again."

"Not at all, not at all. Don't mention it."

Peter found Niles Tipton sitting on the raised platform that ran across the front of his store. Peter explained his wishes.

"So you want to buy, eh? Well, I guess I'm the man can help you. Want to git in my buggy and ride around now? We could look at a few places before dinnertime."

"That would be fine."

Niles Tipton talked much, but asked few questions. That pleased Peter.

"I guess places out here look purt near like a wilderness to you."

"Well—not exactly."

"I was back there through your country one time, before the war. Places was awful neat. But I don't think people out here'd be willing to work as hard as the farmers I saw. 'Course, they got smaller places. Most places out here run two, three hundred acres."

Tipton's talk was rambling and casual, but Peter realized that he was shrewd. They saw nothing to Peter's liking that day, or the next.

The third day they drove all the way to Dawson's Point, the next landing below St. Stephens.

"This is Burton County. That road there—" Tipton pointed to

a sandy road that wound into the hills—"that road goes to Kings Row, the county seat. That's a town is going to grow. 'Tain't as big as Camperville—that's our own county seat—but it's a pretty town. Old settlement. Lots of our people do their trading there in preference to Camperville. You'll have to buy a lot of your stuff in Camperville, or Kings Row, or else get it sent down from Jeff City."

The buggy twisted from side to side in the sandy ruts.

"Getting on toward three o'clock, Mr. Kettring. I guess we better be heading for home."

"I'm taking a lot of your time, Mr. Tipton."

"Thunderation, that's my business. I'll make my pay when you buy, don't you worry!"

They rode in silence for half an hour. The afternoon was warm and sleep-provoking.

"Is that a house up there, Mr. Tipton?"

"Where?"

"Up there on that rise." Peter pointed.

"Oh, yes. Just a cabin. That's—why, of course, this is quite a place here. It's just been standing so long, I'd about forgotten it." Tipton reined in the horse. "Place belongs to a man named Nelse Adams. Left here right after the war broke out, and never came back, but they'd know about it at the bank, I guess. If not, somebody in Camperville would."

"Isn't this in—in Burton County?"

"No, we passed the county line a while back."

Tipton looked speculatively at Peter. "This is a bigger place 'n you'd want."

"How big is it?"

"Must be several hundred acres. Runs way up the hillsides back there. Now let me see—as well as I recollect it begins back there about where the bottom narrows. It's kind of half-moon-shaped. This whole bottom belongs to it, then around and back of that hill where the cabin is. That's the way you come into the place. In high water the river's likely to cover this road altogether."

"Is there any way of getting up there from here?"

"Nothing to see. It's just a log cabin."

"It would be a good place for a house."

"Wonderful. Sight of the river for miles."

"It's for sale?"

"Yes. I know that much about it. Say, we could walk up there. No ways at all."

Peter was already out of the buggy. Tipton pulled over to the side of the road. He took an iron weight from the back of the buggy that had a short rope attached to it.

"I'll just let old Billy eat a little grass, I guess." He snapped the rope to the horse's bridle, and the two of them started through the thick weeds toward the house.

"It's good land, Mr. Kettring, if you'd be interested in this big a place, but there's nothing here any more. You'd have fences to build, a house, and barn—well, just about everything."

"Land that can grow weeds like this must be rich enough to grow something else."

Tipton laughed. "You're right."

It was rough going. A network of vines tugged at every step. Presently they came out on the elevation where the cabin stood. Tipton looked in.

"All gone to rack and ruin. I don't guess there's been a soul here except hunters since Nelse went away."

The cabin had been a two-room structure originally, square rooms with "dog-run" between them. Later, apparently, a third room had been added. Solid enough, Peter thought, but the windows were gone, and the doors sagged. Some pale vines were struggling through the cracks in the floor. The house made a desolate picture. All at once he thought of Savina. Well, he thought, they might build another house right away. This could be used for something. He turned away and walked to the highest point of the spur that ran straight out toward the center of a wide crescent-shaped sweep of level bottom land. Shaped like a half-moon, as Tipton had said, the curve against the hills, the straight edge bordering the river.

Peter felt a sudden return of the excitement he had experienced that first evening when he had walked through the streets of St. Stephens. It was a choking, uncomfortable excitement.

"It's a pretty place, all right, Mr. Kettring, but—I always thought it had a kind of funny feeling about it. Spooky-like."

"It seems a lonely place. I like that."

Peter surveyed the great length of river that came into view far up beyond St. Stephens, and grew in light and in breadth, rolling in immediate majesty before him, and dimming again and shadowing in blue and violet until it disappeared. Across the river the undulant blue green lay still, dreamlike. Back of him the hills—he turned and looked at them. On all sides this place was cut off from intrusion.

"How far up the hills does this go?"

Tipton squinted at the dense woods above them. "I used to know in a general way, but I can't say right now. It would all have to be surveyed again anyhow."

"Could one buy it on up to the top of the hills?"

"Why, I'm sure you could. I guess that's still owned by the government. Buy it for most nothing. Are you sure enough thinking about this place, Mr. Kettring?"

"I'm sure it's what I want if the price is right."

Tipton took off his hat and wiped the sweat from his brow with his bandana handkerchief.

"Tell you what, Mr. Kettring. Let's get on back to town. Keep your mouth shut about this, and I'll find out everything about it. I expect there's a lot of back taxes. Have to find that out up to Camperville. But if you want to put it in my hands, I'll do all the preparation before anybody gets wind of what we're doing, and I'll get you a fair price. Folks down in St. Stephens already got the idea you're a rich Yankee. Somebody or other'd try to skin you sure."

"I'll leave it to you, Mr. Tipton."

"Reckon you want the whole of it?"

"Yes, of course."

"I'll get it for you. Just say nothing and leave it to me."

"That's agreed. If there's anything I can do to save you trouble—"

"No, no. That's my business. I'll charge you and Nelse both plenty. Count on that. I ain't working for my health." He laughed.

Peter felt that he already owned this land, and a fierce sense of proprietorship arose in him.

Savina waited. Peter was out every day. He took long drives with Niles Tipton, acquainting himself with the country. He talked more than was usual with him, and Savina listened eagerly. She wanted to go with Peter and see for herself, but he never asked her to. Waiting was painful for her. She felt guilty. Not to be busy at something was disgraceful. At home work was a gospel.

Mrs. Miner did her best to relieve this loneliness but even her best was not very effective. She invited Savina down to sit in the "front room" every day. Whenever visitors came, she introduced her with great politeness, explaining carefully that Savina was just learning English. But Savina was shy, and reluctant to try English words. She supposed she should learn but she was not interested in the idea. It still did not occur to her that she would need English to live comfortably in this new country. She did not visualize herself speaking to anyone except Peter once they were settled. Visiting had not been usual at Martinsgrove.

"She's an awful nice young woman, I can tell that much." Mrs. Miner was talking to a passer-by at the door. She dropped her voice almost to a whisper, thereby telling Savina that she was the subject of the conversation. "She's got the ways of nice people, well brought up. But it seems strange for anybody to be born in this country and not know how to talk English."

"Well, there's the Janeks up the hill there—"

Mrs. Miner interrupted. "Not the same kind of people at all. The Janeks are foreigners."

"They're learning English fast, I notice."

"Well, I guess Mrs. Kettring'll learn, too, but she doesn't seem interested much. I guess she lived off from things back there. Mr. Kettring explained that but you wouldn't think there was backwoods in Pennsylvania, would you?"

In the days following the first inspection of the Nelse Adams place, Peter, too, waited, but his was a consuming impatience. Nearly two weeks passed before he was assured that the place was actually for sale and at a far lower price than he had expected. There remained only details of settlement which Niles Tipton was attending to.

Tipton came to River House one morning just after breakfast. He wagged his head portentously. "Come on out here. Got some news for you."

"Well—"

"We got the place."

"Sure enough?"

"Yes. Just got to find out about the back taxes. Won't be much, but it'll come off the price. The place's good as yours. You can go ahead and buy up some stuff."

"You're sure I'd be safe in that?" Peter spoke with a consciously repressed voice. He was afraid he would sing if he did not hold himself in. He was realizing how great his fear had been that he might not be able to have this place. He reached out impulsively and shook Tipton's hand. "I don't know how to thank you, Mr. Tipton."

"Sho' now. It's just business, Mr. Kettring. I don't mind saying I've taken a liking to you. I'd be glad to do what I can for you even if it wasn't business. Had a little prejudice against you at first because you were a Yankee but I forgot that right away."

Peter drew back into himself somewhat, but he smiled. "Well, I guess we've got some wrong ideas about you people, too. But the war's over; we should have done with it." He looked away suddenly. Tipton had already come to know that habit of withdrawal.

"You're right, but people are awful pigheaded."

"I don't know much about people, Mr. Tipton."

"I guessed that much. You're a young man. We all got to learn, and there's just one way."

Peter nodded. "We hear that all through childhood. Experience. But we don't believe it."

"I know. When I was young I thought I knew all about everything."

Peter sensed much in Tipton that was not being said, and felt a beginning of something that was warmer than acquaintance. Something near to friendliness. It was not until Tipton had driven away that Peter wondered at himself. He had so impressed himself with the need for solitude—to make a life free of personal relations—to keep his own counsel and ask nothing of anyone. Was he weakening in that resolution? He was determined that he would not, but the recollection of Niles Tipton's words remained a spot of gentle warmth in his consciousness.

He started briskly up the slanting street, taking longer and longer strides. He must see the place, now—without delay. The Adams farm was to be his own. He did not have to say "the Adams place" any more. It was his now.

The street narrowed at the edge of the town and became a rutted road. It turned east and continued along the hillside. It was apparently little used. Here and there it had been badly washed by spring rains. It was heavily shaded now, and damp underfoot.

As the road went deeper into the woods all sense of the nearness of a town vanished. The air was moist and cool, the murmurous stillness of deep woods fell upon the ear, and Peter was aware of a sudden and curious sharpening of all his senses. That ancient and primitive instinct of watchfulness in the forest was instantly alive. Unconsciously, he walked as quietly as he could, and looked keenly into the shadowy green depths about him.

Two miles from St. Stephens to the farm, Tipton had said. Perhaps as the crow flies, Peter thought, but certainly much farther by this twisting hill road. Up here St. Stephens seemed far away. Peter realized that even to take one's bearing in a place was to identify one's self with it. He had begun to move familiarly about the little town. He was on speaking terms with a number of people, and on nodding terms with everybody. That familiarity with St. Stephens slipped away as a mood fades from consciousness.

He paused for a moment, listening. There was not a sound of

human beings or of human activity. Bird notes echoed with surprising loudness. The bluejays yelled as they swung their bold flight from tree to tree. Faint tinkles of hidden springs came to hearing after a while. But there was no glimpse of the river or the bottoms. A dense wall of green shut him in on every side.

The almost complete lack of underbrush surprised Peter. It must be characteristic of this region, he decided. There was a lush growth of flowering weeds and great areas of thick fern, but the lack of small growth provided short vistas through the great trees. It appeared to be virgin forest. The road itself seemed a surprising presence in this wild setting.

Peter experienced a thousand minute awarenesses as he stood among the ancient trees. It was as if innumerable small nerves were receiving new and strange sensations. That might even be true, he thought, and not an illusion of heightened senses.

Smaller birds and insects came one by one into the ear's ken. The wood was becoming in these few minutes infinitely populous.

Man had not so long ago come out of a habitation such as this, he thought. Perhaps he had, in his hard transitions, forgotten much, but perhaps there was much, very much, that man could recall with small effort, or with no effort at all given the right conditions. Perhaps that was why he was suddenly hypersensitive to these faint sounds, to furtive movements among the ferns, to barely perceptible wing flicks high in the trees, to the slight stir of air, and to the multitudinous drifts of smells which made up a complex impression of their own.

And so he stood there, watching—watching until he felt that he could almost see time itself go by. He listened more and more intently.

Points of perspiration came out on the backs of his hands, gleamed for an instant and dimmed, leaving a faint tingle as they dried. Each breath he drew was different. Now he took in a drier air as the currents were touched by sun falling through some high opening—warm and aromatically sweet; now a breath stirred up from the soft black earth, woody, leafy, a queer mingling of moldering stems and fresh new shoots. Minutes were varied and rich with sequences of light, sound, and sensation. It was the essence of the life of the woods and of time itself seen through a startling magnification, separated into elements, each one perceived as by some special organ of reception. Each segment of an instant, each recognition of each special impression filled Peter with a certainty that here were all the manifestations of life itself poured into his soul with an amplitude and a richness almost beyond endurance.

He walked on again, more slowly, with a different step. He made scarcely a sound. There was a slight give to his knees as he made each step, imperceptible even to his own eye, but exaggeratedly present to sensation. He had never seen an Indian, but he was walking like one.

He turned aside where a gray lichen-covered rock jutted out over a slope still brown with the spring fall of oak leaves. A shaft of sunlight brought every detail of rock and tree into shining relief. He sat down and swung his feet comfortably over the edge.

A round, black-and-white-spotted bug paused on a tiny fragment of stone. It opened its wings as if it were splitting itself in two, closed them again, and remained still in the sun. Peter looked at it curiously. Just like himself, he thought. Clambering to the top of a rock and sitting in the sun. But it was, he thought with his long habit of seriousness, a very symbol of this forest, maybe even of life as it should be. Its own world, its own way, its own habits, its instincts in happy place of troublesome and doubtful choice, its freedom from the travail and errors of thought. It knew no words, and must live in a scheme of signals, definite and unmistakable. That was it—signals. Sure signals from the earth itself, without confusion or equivocation. Surely if nature had anything to tell, it was just here in such small instances that it could speak clearly. *If nature had anything to tell!* He said that over, listening to the sound of it rather than perceiving the meaning of the words. Of course nature had everything to tell. He knew that now. He had not known it when he listened to his father's preaching, or to tutors from the theological school.

The ideas and teaching of theology and philosophy—that was a matter of words giving birth to words, an endless procreation growing more and more bloodless with the centuries, a science of words with a dry logic begotten of lifeless abstraction. And these had become the tyrants of the life of human beings who had come so far without them. He thought with a shrug of distaste for even the thinking of it, of the unending war of opinion—opinion that turned sometimes upon little more than the shadow cast in the mind by the shape of a word!

All that had been good came up straight from the earth itself, from—Peter stopped in the speeding track of his musing. He had been about to say from *pagan* participation in the earth's own law and logic. Then he wondered why he should recoil from a word, such as *pagan*. For the moment it seemed unintelligent to confound one's self in this fashion, to identify one's self with a destructive and alien way of thought. Alien? Alien to what?

Again he shrugged. This time he swept away a dancing little cloud of gnats. He supposed his thinking was a good deal like them. Maybe as senseless and confused.

Had he not told himself long ago that Anton Hummelfelder and the men and women of the valley of Martinsgrove had found out sufficient simple truth to live by? With such negations and refusals they had escaped the errors and turmoils of others who were supposed to be intelligent and thoughtful. It was all very well to call these men ignorant and primitive. Had not the philosophers and the religious of the world been confounded by events and overthrown again and again while the simple harmonies of such men as Anton survived the wrecks of civilizations?

Peter was not sure that maybe he wasn't underestimating or maybe omitting altogether the factor of old Anton's religion. But he shook this from his mind. Anton really had no religion. He was merely going through form—Anton's religion was like his belief in planting in the dark of the moon. It was wearisome to think about. He would buy his land and he would work his fields, and he would think no more. An intrusion of grisly images from the war burst into his attention. Those things, now! All he had seen, all he had been obliged to do. If he thought, he would have to consider them, do something about them in his mind. And he knew there was nothing to do. He must forget them. He must overlay them with something sane and sweet, as they had had to bury shattered bodies under the kindness of soil.

He looked again at the spotted bug. Well, maybe one could learn from a bug!

Peter arose, brushed clinging bits of leaves and dried moss from his trousers, and resumed his way.

He knew that his intellectual training had not been of the best if for no other reason than that it had not proceeded far enough. But he also knew that it had been too good for him to deceive himself about the character and quality of thought. He knew he had not done more than juggle some fragments of doctrine in the previous few moments. But, he said to himself, he was not trying to make an argument, and certainly not a philosophy. People who sought some simplification of existence were usually fanatically determined on changing a world, or upon burdening others with their own way of thinking. He was not changing anything for anyone else. He was not founding anything. He was merely shedding something. He was clear what it was he was discarding. He would firmly do that, for himself and for whatever might be his own—place, or family.

He went over the subject again in his mind, reiterated it, simplified it, and summarized it. He was free; he could afford a conduct of his own choosing; he was not beholden to anyone—family or friends: he had neither.

In all of this Peter was honest and clear. But for the moment he forgot something of importance.

He forgot Savina.

The day was becoming warmer. Waves of damp-smelling freshness still arose from the slope but there was an increasing heaviness in the surges of heat that seemed to press closer and closer. Peter removed his coat and carried it over his arm.

Everywhere—on every side of him—things were growing. Peter felt that every leaf and stem was busy with that one purpose. He liked that. He liked the intensity of it, as he imagined the process

—its fury and singleness. He had read something somewhere—he refused the intrusion of literary recollection. He did not wish to see through any medium other than his own eyes and his own mind.

Peter assumed a state of mind not far from make-believe. This was the wilderness—a far, unexplored place of the world, a nameless place, and he the explorer. A faint reminiscent tremor coursed along his nerves, some momentary happiness of childhood came to the surface of consciousness and gleamed for an instant, exciting him for that instant to a pitch of forgotten joy. The hills and the woods and out there the river! A whole world, indeed. Now, more truly, it seemed to be his own, because he was sure no one else felt about it as he did. He flung his arms out in a gesture that was like a claim.

He watched ahead through the trees for some sign that he was nearing the spur of hills bordering the old Adams place.

He smiled and nodded his head. Yes: the "old Adams place." That is what people would say now. No longer just the Adams place, but the Kettring place that was the old Adams place!

Presently he saw ahead of him what seemed to be much denser woods. It was a long hill that crossed his view. He tingled over the whole of his body. This was it! He walked faster; he was almost running.

Then he heard the sound of water. He paused and listened. A quick-running stream, evidently near. He came to it in a moment, a surprising, deep and narrow ravine separating him from the sharp rise ahead. This was just over the Adams line. He remembered that Tipton had told him of it. He looked a bit dubiously at the steep banks. It was the certain mark of wild and sudden spring torrents. Exhilaration leapt in his blood. Spring torrents! Gusty waters plunging down the river. These were the very pulses of this living land.

He stood listening. The small, varied clamor of the water hidden among ferns and overhanging lush new green magnified in his hearing until it seemed to fill the woods. This stream was his. Even the sound of it, moving through the trees like a chorus of running voices, would be his!

He walked along the bank looking for a crossing and came shortly to a foot log.

Peter half expected some special manifestation of his senses when he stepped on what was so soon to be his own domain. He was a little disappointed that he experienced no such thing. He had been feeling too deeply possessive of all he had seen, he decided, even of the day itself, to achieve more in that direction. He went on through the woods—he had lost trace of the road once across the ravine—looking and looking with all his power of sight as if he would command his eyes to see as they had never seen before.

Presently he stood beside the decaying log cabin.

The wide panorama of hills, the stretch of bottom lands, the river and the hazy outline of the south side were just as he had been remembering them. The place seemed bigger than he had thought, the thrust of this declining hill toward the river was longer, the neglected orchard on the east from the house extended farther.

There was a well. He examined it. It would need a good cleaning out and the curbing would have to be raised. The cabin could perhaps be used as a tool house. The barn could be built back of it toward the high woods maybe, facing east and west. The house, a good new house, as big as the Hummelfelders', out there on the last rise of this hill overlooking the bottoms and having a magnificent view of the river.

His planning was swift and comprehensive. He had observed the farms of Martinsgrove well. The house, the summer kitchen, the smoke house, the chicken house, the barn, a tool house out of the cabin, maybe a spring house if he could locate a proper spring near enough—swiftly he placed them in their prospective places. He would build and build fast. By fall . . .

Peter looked up toward the long ridge of the hills, a little bluish, under this clear hard sky. Overhead great clouds moved eastward. They moved faster, he thought, than clouds ordinarily moved on such a calm summery day. The high trees on the ridge were in constant motion too, as if stirred by agitated winds from the other side. These and the hurrying river gave to the whole landscape a restless, vivacious quality. A windy country, he thought.

Yes, he had heard that said. But here, where he stood, there was little stir. In winter, too, this would be a sheltered place.

Peter loved those hills at once. He saw the river before him as a giant barrier set against all intrusion. It would protect him and his thoughts from anything that might wish to come too near. Between him and all that he had determined to keep away was this—this beautiful living guardian of his peace and security. Up there—the winds might pour across, but the hills stood between him and their winter sharpness, as they also stood between him and whatever might encroach from that direction. Yes: he must buy all the way up to the ridge.

He stepped up on a boulder at the edge of the hill and searched the wide view before him. He could see no living soul. There were other farms, he knew, on down the river, but they were out of sight. There was not a boat in sight. He stepped down again. He might be, for all that could be seen from here, the only man in the world. A deep content spread to every nerve and muscle. No one had ever seen Peter Kettring look as he looked now. The tenseness, the aloofness, the forbidding severity disappeared. He looked young, and eager, and happy.

The sun was directly overhead when Peter concluded his exploration of the orchard. A fine big orchard with good trees, ideally set sloping to the southeast, sheltered from the north and west winds, tilted to the morning sun, but spared the savage heat of afternoons, steep enough for proper drainage—he shook his head; it was in bad state, though. No pruning for years, clusters of suckers about the trees—the whole place taken with a tall wiry grass and many weeds. A big job here—just in this one place. He would add peach and cherry trees, pear and plum . . . what other kinds of fruit trees were there? Anyway, he'd have some of every kind that grew in this climate.

He descended to the wide level of overgrown bottom. It was oppressively hot here. Not a breath of that moving air which still stirred the trees along the hilltops. No hint of the cool damp of the woods. It was hot with a steady, businesslike heat. He nodded approvingly. Fine growing weather. Work in these bottoms would be hard and exhausting. Tipton had said it was. No matter. That was what he wanted. Work on his own farm, in his own fields, with his own tools in his hands—that could never be a hardship. He would like to be at it now.

He thrashed through weeds waist-high in many places. He kicked at a few spots of exposed soil. Soft, rich, dark, with a mixture of sand and loam. He recalled what Anton Hummelfelder had said about plenty of manure. He would write to Anton someday and tell him about this soil of an almost inexhaustible richness. This sticky, clinging air, this broiling sun—these were kin to such a soil. A great richness, a great fecundity.

A mighty land and, as far as he could see from where he stood here in the bottom, his own.

He must go back up to the hills now, all the way to the top. He must cover this place of his today—walk over the whole of it.

It was hard climbing. The soles of his shoes became slippery, there was no path, and it was hot, even in the dense shade. He stopped at a spring and ate the lunch Mrs. Miner had given him. Bread and several pieces of fried chicken. He lay down beside the spring and drank.

There were giant trees all about him. A few of them he knew, but many of them were strange. A sprightly tree growing on a stony bank in a half-clear spot attracted his attention. It was a gay tree with a silvery trunk and rather thin foliage, and the leaves danced at the slightest breath of air. He thought it might be what Niles Tipton had said was rock maple, but he was not sure.

Farther on in a ditchlike depression he came on a small dark red blossom that smelled like watermelon. He wondered what it was. It had a name and habits. He realized that he knew practically nothing of such things. Maybe he would buy a book on botany and learn about them. Instantly he flushed with a kind of anger at the thought. Books! Books! Would he never be free of the thought of books?

Why must he go to books to discover what lay here before him, at his own feet, for him to read, and to read in its own terms—in its own language? The flush faded: he was pleased with that thought and with the near poetry of his own words. Yes—certainly! *In its own language.*

Yes, by God, he would find out about things, about everything on his place, but he would find out about them at the source—from the things themselves. What did he care if that were a rock maple or not? He knew it now—he was acquainted with it, its look and its manner. And this three-leaved flower—he would name it himself. It was his. He would—or better still, he would simply remember it as it looked, it would have a place in his memory and in his mind from that appearance. It would need no other designation.

He knew that he would never forget the look of anything. Now in this moment of exultant possession it never occurred to him that he would ever need to speak to others of what he saw. Like Adam in the morning of his first day in Eden, Peter was making the acquaintance of his world and assigning places and importances to each detail in the fresh catalogues of his attention.

That night Peter talked with Savina until late. Savina listened with two minds. She listened carefully to Peter's account of the place. Yes; a wilderness as she had feared that day on the boat, but now she was not dismayed at the thought: she had done some thinking while Peter was riding about over the country. Even with her limited English she had understood from Mrs. Miner much of the condition and manner of life here in St. Stephens and in the country around. Peter's version of the "wilderness farm" did not sound attractive to her, but with Peter, and with all she knew, they would make out. But to all of this she listened mechanically.

Peter did not wish to take her out to see the place just yet.

"You couldn't walk around for the weeds—and all."

"It is so wild as that?"

"Neglected."

She shook her head at the slothfulness and waste.

"I'm going to put some Negroes to work first—"

"Black people!"

"Yes. To do the first general clearing up."

"And we stay here then, with Mrs. Miner?"

"For a while. We'll have to."

"It is so lonesome. I don't know what to make with myself when I have nothing to do."

Peter nodded absently.

"Never in my life have I been so good for nothing. I guess I could knit some maybe."

"Yes." Peter was not listening.

"But still it is the wrong time in the year to knit. I have always been busy with other things."

Peter stirred in his chair. "You'll have a big house."

"I will like that. It is nice to take care of a big house. Lots of places to put things away. How big, Peter?"

"Say, like the Hummelfelders'."

"That is nice."

She sat, as always, very still. Now she had quite the manner of being "company." Her hands were folded and lay motionless in her lap.

Savina was very restful to look at, Peter thought absently.

Savina listened through the evening for something other than Peter was saying in description of what he had seen that day.

She knew that somehow, in some way, Peter had been hurt and turned back on himself—long before he had come to Martinsgrove. She did not wish to say that he was peculiar, not even to herself, because the word had unkind meanings in her way of thinking, but she almost admitted that it was true.

Just a little peculiarity, she went on in her careful, precise thinking, had a way of becoming downright crankiness later on. She recalled some cranky people she had known and heard of.

"*A' gute fraw kann fiel mit ihr mann dhu dass er nett wase, wenn sie scharf is'.*" Her mother had dropped the indirect piece of advice with the casual shyness that was characteristic of her own dealings with Gabriel Umholz.

Yes. Savina was sure her mother was right: "a woman can do a lot with her husband that he doesn't know about if she's clever."

Savina was not taking secret counsel of herself against anything

[57]

in Peter, or that he might wish to do. She was Peter's wife, and anything she might do would be wholly for Peter—for their "place," for their life. Once a girl married she was completely set to a clear purpose.

Occasionally she had heard of people who did not "get along well together." This seemed monstrous and unnatural. Moreover it was not sensible.

Savina would never consciously choose a higher criterion for feeling or action than just being sensible. Sensible. It was the best thing anybody could be and all good flowed straight from it. She did not know that being sensible was not the brooding and tender feeling that she was spreading over and around her thought of Peter. Affection and love, as words, had rare existence in her thinking, and made still rarer appearance in her vocabulary. One *liked* people, one *thought a lot* of one's family. So spoke the undemonstrative people of Martinsgrove. And extravagantly on occasions: "she can't think of anything but her man." But such lack of balance was not mentioned kindly.

Savina would never know how deeply she loved Peter—certainly not through conscious use of such stranger words. What she felt for him would find expression in a lifetime of service—cooking, washing, cleaning. Peter would expect nothing else and no other course would occur to her. It was the way good women lived and behaved. And when a good woman died people spoke quietly of her afterward, saying: "She always was a good woman."

"Yes, she kept a nice house."

"She took good care of her man."

"Her children were always well behaved."

"Yes, yes. Tilly worked all the time."

"Tilly was always *gescheidt.*"

And when the good women of the neighborhood said *gescheidt,* they had paid all the tribute to Tilly that was possible.

And so Savina . . .

Or so everyone thought in Martinsgrove, except Mom Fischer, who had not liked Savina anyway.

"She's too quiet, that Savina. You mind my words. You'll see yet. Still waters run deep." And Mom Fischer had not meant that the depth was to good purpose.

Savina was not quite the even continuance of the ways of the older generation. She had never done heavy work as most farm girls had. Family discipline at the Umholzes' was light. And in that greater freedom some measure of fancy had grown in the mind of Savina. She was a freer soul than most girls of her time and place.

That was why tonight feelings arose and commanded place in her heart—feelings that were a little frightening, a little *wild*. It was unsettling—such a fierce and overwhelming protective urge as she felt at this moment. There was, surely, no call for such violence. She would not like to be one of those women who "could think of nothing but her man."

A rush of pink spread over Savina's face. She glanced cautiously at Peter to see if he noticed. But Peter was leaning forward resting his elbows on his knees, lacing and twisting his fingers. From time to time he talked, always of plans. She listened, but each time her attention divided.

It was a strange feeling that came to her when he spoke. Peter planned as if he were preparing to go on a journey to the ends of the earth. Now, when he had actually arrived at the place of all his planning, his talk gave the impression of—of—she hunted vainly for an exact description of what she felt—maybe as if he were just setting out on a long and solitary march to a place where he was to be wholly alone. It gave her an uncomfortable sense of not being a part of his plans.

He used the word *alone* so often. She smoothed out her slight frown of perplexity. Maybe it meant nothing. Maybe it was only Peter's way of speech. He had been alone so much of his life that perhaps he hardly realized as yet that she was with him, and was to be with him always.

A wave of complex emotions arose chokingly. There was so much to do! Such a world to make! A sudden impatience flamed up in her mind. She wished to be at work. For the first time she forgot that she disliked and feared everything she had seen of this new country.

Peter went at the work of reclaiming and restoring the old Adams place with a high heart.

The first week was a chain of rebuffs and disappointments. He could not engage anyone to work for him. The Negroes were shy and uncommunicative on first approach, and later sullen and muttering. A few told him openly they would not work "fur no Yankee man." All of Peter's efforts to start clearing and building met with obstacles.

He went to Niles Tipton. Niles listened to his story.

"Come on, Mr. Kettring, git in my buggy. Let's drive up the road a piece. Talk better out in the open."

They drove for a few minutes along the sandy road, the heat quivering and dancing in glassy waves ahead of them. Peter was irritated and impatient.

"Well, Mr. Tipton, what's it all about? Why can't I get anything done?"

"Cool off, son, cool off. We'll talk about your troubles directly. Here, take the lines a minute while I clean out my pipe. Smoke?"

Peter shook his head.

"Too bad. Chew?"

Peter smiled. One could not maintain annoyance in Tipton's company.

The buggy ground along in the loose sand, weaving from side to side as it followed the twisting ruts. Niles Tipton wabbled with the motion. His mountain of fat seemed to shake inside his skin. He took up three fourths of the seat and his thigh was hot against Peter. Presently he finished his deliberate preparations and lighted his pipe. The sharp smell of the sulphur match stung Peter's nose.

"Now. Give me the lines." He drew with satisfaction on his corncob pipe. "Y'ought to smoke, Mr. Kettring—hell, I'm going to call you Peter. We've been polite a long time now. Mind?"

"Certainly not—Niles."

"That's better. Now listen, I know what you're up against. I kinda suggested to you once you might have trouble, but you didn't catch on."

"But why? All I want is some work done. I'm ready to pay for it."

"Well, son, you're a Yankee." Tipton grinned broadly, and laid his big hand on Peter's knee. "We're kind of divided up around here, too. You know that. I think Mr. Day at the bank was more Yankee than he ever let on."

"The war's over. I was on my side—they were on theirs. It's settled."

"Things don't settle so easy, Peter."

"It wasn't easy."

"Well, no, I guess not. I mean things don't just stay settled. Lots of soreheads."

"But—"

"Let me talk a while, son. You're from off. We always lived here. We know each other. We kinda accept each other's opinions because we know everything there is to know about everybody. But when a stranger comes in all we know about him is that he holds different ideas. He just represents a difference of opinion and nothing else. You see?"

"No, I don't. A man's opinion—"

"Is his own business, you're going to say. Maybe 'tis in heaven but it ain't in St. Stephens. Your opinion and mine and everybody else's is everybody's business, and you can bet your bottom dollar that's one kind of business everybody's going to 'tend to."

Peter squirmed in his seat. "Nobody even knows what my opinions are."

"You're a Yankee. You represent an opinion. Son, I don't know where you've been living, but you appear to me not to've lived very close to anybody or else you'd know more about people in general."

"Well, all I want is to get my farm cleared and my buildings up so I can run the place myself. Then I won't care what anybody thinks about me."

"I don't say you're not in your rights, but you can't make people work for you if they don't want to."

"Do you mean to say I'm not going to get anybody to work for me?"

"Not the way you're going at it."

"How else could I go at it? I just offered jobs and nobody would take them."

"They don't want to work for you. The white people want to show you they don't like a Yankee coming in here—"

"From the looks of this run-down country they could do with a few more Yankees, I'd say."

Tipton nodded patiently. "Yes. But nobody wants you to tell 'em so."

"Excuse me—Niles. I'm not criticizing you."

"Oh, shucks, I know that. I was going on to say the Negroes are actually afraid. They've heard curious tales about Yankee employers. White people fill 'em full of ideas. Poor devils—"

"What is going to become of them?"

Tipton twinkled. "Well, out here we kinda thought you all in the East and North knew the answer to that question."

Peter flushed. "I never heard much about Negroes, except that they were oppressed."

"And that we beat hell out of 'em every morning before breakfast!"

"No, I didn't hear any such nonsense. But slavery was oppression."

"Let's don't get on that subject. Of course it was, and awful bad for the white man. But that ain't our problem this morning. You want to get your work done, don't you?"

"Certainly, I do."

"All righty. There's lots of ways to kill a goose. Want me to tell you how to get it done?"

"That's why I came to you. You've been friendly to me, and—I'm grateful."

"Tch! Tch! Stuff! Well, now, I got a scheme. You've bought a lot of stuff through me, and I aim to see that you keep on doing the same thing. Tell you what you do. You come on back with me and set down on paper exactly what you want done, all your plans for your buildings and everything. Then you let the contract to me and I'll get it done."

"Well—"

"No, don't misunderstand me. I ain't after any money at all. This way you'd have to buy everything through me—"

"I intended to do that anyway."

"But I'll save you a stack of money in the end—I can get cheaper help than you can. You'll have to pay a boss, though."

"I don't see why I can't—well, be boss on my own place." Peter stiffened again.

"Well, son, it's just a *leetle* finagling, that's all. People'll work for me and they won't work for you. That's the long and short of it. I hate to say it to you, but it's the truth. Quicker we get these things said and understood, the quicker you'll get your work done. After a while people'll get used to you. They'll get to know **you** and they'll like you fine—same's I do."

"Thank you for that. I appreciate all you say, but outside of you and Mr. Day I don't care what anybody in this Godforsaken hole thinks about me."

"What'd you come here for, son?"

Peter flushed. "You've got a right to ask that question. I didn't mean to be impolite. I had good raising—"

"You don't have to tell me that. But you've got a mighty hot head. It'll get you into trouble sure's you're born."

"I don't really think of St. Stephens as a Godforsaken hole. I came here to—well, I wanted to shed everything and start new with a place of my own. That's all."

"That's all good enough. Nobody can say anything against it."

"I'm willing to attend to my own business."

"And you want everybody else to attend to theirs? That's about the size of it, ain't it?"

"Now you're getting me into a corner again—but that *is* about the size of it."

"Well, Peter, it just don't happen in this world. People won't 'tend to their own business."

Peter made an impatient gesture.

Niles continued. "Son, that's why people get together in droves the way they do." He chuckled. "Tell you what we'll do, now,

Peter. Let's turn around and drive out to your place. Let's make the plans, and I'll get you some men out there first thing in the morning. We'll have everything all fixed up so quick you'll wonder what you were worrying about. We don't want you getting in a huff and going off somewheres else. We need some good Yankee money around here."

Peter was somewhat mollified, but back in his mind lay a heavy dark spot of resentment.

Even later on when the farm was rapidly emerging from its shabby neglect, he was still angry. He found himself going about on his own place like an outsider. Niles Tipton had delegated direction to Tom Jewett, a tall, thin, gangling man who looked both indifferent and incompetent. Peter judged him badly. Tom Jewett could get more work out of a gang of Negroes than anybody on the river. Jewett consulted with Peter, but he was too casual about it to make Peter quite happy. There was something nearly contemptuous in his reception of Peter's ideas. The fact was that Jewett knew very well what to do, and did it without permission. As it was, Peter got some good retaining walls and better drainage than he could have devised for himself. He saw this before long and kept out of Jewett's way. He made great ado over his own projects, and spent weeks at the hardest kind of work, digging a cellar, laying foundations, and gradually his industry and his independent intelligence commanded the respect of the foreman.

"You can tell sense when you see it at work," Jewett remarked to Niles. "That Yankee's got brains. No doubt about it."

"Yep. Most of 'em have. Plus git-up-and-git. That's why they git on better'n we do."

One day Peter walked up through pasture land where a rail fence was being laid. A Negro was preparing to cut a tall tree.

"Don't cut that tree," Peter ordered peremptorily.

The Negro looked at him stupidly. "Mr. Tom, he say cut hit down."

"But I say don't cut it. That's a fine tree."

"Yassuh. Mr. Tom, he say cut hit out de way."

"I heard you. But I don't want it cut down."

"Hit's right in de line of de fence."

"Run the fence around it, fool."

The Negro swung the ax lazily and sank it in the trunk of the great chestnut.

"Here! Didn't I tell you not to chop that tree? Can't you hear?"

"Yassuh, I heah." The Negro looked sullen. "Mr. Tom, he say—"

"I don't give a damn what anybody says. I'm telling you what to do."

"Mr. Tom, he de boss."

"You fool! Don't you know this is my place?"

"I'se workin' for Mr. Tom."

"You're working for me!"

"No, suh."

"Stop all this talk. Do as I say."

The Negro reached for the ax, but before he could lay hands on it, Peter had knocked him down.

Peter stood quite still, wondering dazedly how he had happened to do that. The Negro got slowly to his feet. His head was lowered like an angry animal. Slowly he reached for the ax, his half-closed eyes on Peter.

Peter was about to step back when Jewett's voice rang out loud behind him.

"Here! Bob! God damn your black soul to hell, what do you think you're doing?" He came up quickly. "What's the trouble here?"

"He was about to cut that tree. I told him not to, and he was going ahead anyway."

Jewett nodded shortly. He turned to the still lowering Negro. "Get out. Get on back to town. I don't want you around here!"

"Yassuh."

Jewett waited until the big Negro had shuffled out of earshot.

"Now, Mr. Kettring, we'd better understand each other. I'm the boss here, and I give orders."

[65]

Peter's face turned a dark scarlet. "I'll have you remember that it's my place and I'm paying for this work."

"That's all right. When you want anything done you just tell me. That nigger would have killed you."

"I'm not easily killed, Mr. Jewett. A lot of people have tried."

"What do you mean?"

"I was in the Union army for four years." Peter stressed the word Union slightly.

Jewett's eyes narrowed. He took a twist of tobacco from his hip pocket, cut a section from it, and rolled it into his cheek. He snapped his clasp knife shut, returned the tobacco to his pocket, and then looked Peter straight in the eye.

"You want this work done, don't you, Mr. Kettring?"

"Of course."

"Well, then, let my niggers alone. I'll talk to 'em myself."

"I don't understand you. You discharged the man!"

"White people stand together here, even when they're different kinds. How do you think we'd ever keep niggers in their place if we didn't? But I'll do the bossing of my gang as long as we work here."

"I'm not sure how long that will be, Mr. Jewett."

"Suit yourself."

Jewett turned carelessly and walked down the slope. Peter found that he was shaking. A curious chill rested at the back of his neck. He looked at the ax still stuck in the tree. He knew that he wanted to kill someone.

He stood there looking to the right and left as though he sought some way out of the cage of wrath that pressed in on him. It seemed as if a blighting shadow fell over everything. He began to compare this moment with all that he had been dreaming these past weeks. Yes: he had been dreaming. And this was the ugly moment of waking.

Why had he come so far in search of something that had perhaps lain at his hand, and among people whom he knew and understood? He realized he had had the hope back there in Martinsgrove that far away among strangers he would remain a stranger himself, that he could live alone, that life could be made a self-contained and self-sustaining process. Now, already, he knew many people here. Bitterness and scorn arose in him. Yes: he knew people; and he did not like them. Clearly, they did not like him. And what had he done to deserve that? He had asked nothing of anyone that he was not ready to pay for in cash. Of course he did not care whether anyone liked him or not. He was not sure but that he might prefer their dislike. Dislike—that was stimulating. He would . . . what would he do? He felt suddenly limp. There was no one on whom he could unleash the rage that still shook in his veins.

This—this was to be the perfect answer—this place. He felt now that the collision just experienced would not be easy to forget. The thought of it, the memory of his own humiliation at having to accept it, would lie over many days to come. It would have to be wiped out by a sterner independence, a tighter isolation.

He walked a few steps downhill, turned and looked back at the hills. A grayish, silvery haze of this midsummer heat dimmed them a little. Above the line of trees the sky had almost a violet look. Maybe up there he might be able to think better. He would be alone, and quite out of sight of anyone.

In a few moments he was in the muffled atmosphere of the woods. There was a look of coolness but it was hot. Spiderwebs touched his face and hands and clung irritatingly. There were few sounds save the strident yell of a bluejay—that arrogant, contemptuous, jeering freebooter of the woods. The tense look on Peter's face relaxed at once. He almost smiled. He had heard bad things about jay birds, but he was sure he liked them. Never, he decided, would he allow anyone to hunt here or to kill a living thing. Maybe there were marauding creatures who would have to be discouraged, but other things—here they would find welcome, and the right to live free from threat and intrusion.

The powerful spell of the woods fell on the tumult of his spirit. Here among his trees—his—everything in sight, all his. Every stone, every tree, every stick and leaf. In this moment of rising exultation his sense of possession was less arrogant. Rather, it was pride, and a pride of partnership. He believed that he and his trees, he and his birds, were destined to understand each other.

He continued on his way. He had never gone all the way to the top of the ridge. Today, he decided, he would see what the country-side looked like from the height. But he was disappointed. The trees shut out the view. Glimpses of sky and a tantalizing suggestion of a wide valley were all he could see.

Peter walked along the ridge looking for an opening in the heavy foliage. He was about to give it up and start downhill again when he saw a rocky mass ahead of him. It loomed among the trees, dark and forbidding—almost purple, in contrast to the sun-streaked green about it. He hurried on, clambering over scattered boulders, coming out finally on a small plateaulike area where a few tall hickory trees stood straight as a group of columns. All at once he had a view of the country on both sides of the ridge. His own place lying far below him like a huge amphitheater, the miles and miles of river shimmering in the light, the distant gray-blue south bank, and on the other hand a broad sunny valley with pastures and fields, and a group of buildings half hidden in a grove of trees. That was the Sandifer farm. He had heard about it, but he was not curious about it. It was a safe distance away. He leaned against a tree and his head drooped a little. He played with a thin switch, wondering vaguely what kind of bush it was that it came from, and absently broke it into tiny pieces.

Today and its difficulties together with the annoyances of the preceding days made hard contrast with the luminous dream he had had before coming to the West. He had not taken into account any notion of the kind of people he would find here. If he had thought of them at all, it had been as a vague notion of individuals in no way related to his own projects. One had to deal with people, of course. But he had not in any way anticipated these open dis-likes and hostilities. He had tried to crowd out thought of the war, and had had no conception of its aftermath of prejudice.

Well—he would have to tolerate just so much of people as he was obliged to. Once his buildings were up, and the work which he could not do alone completed, he would retreat from acquaintance.

The day was swinging toward afternoon but he was not aware

of it. His head sank lower and his face grew darker as he pondered his relationship to St. Stephens.

Peter had been scarred and outwardly aged by the war, but inside he was still something of a boy—the boy whose development, posited on unworldly lines, had been checked that day when he marched to war. Inside he was sensitive and expectant. The shock of his recent encounters here had been greater than he realized, perhaps, certainly the extent of his recoil was out of all proportion to the events. He was trying to say this to himself now, but as his reason so counseled him, his sense of confusion, of injury and dismay deepened, and with it his resolution to keep out of people's way.

So, standing there, that summer day in the rich silence and beauty of the hilltop Peter began to lay the foundations of his life as it was to be. Out of the persistent miseries, the dogging resentments, and the disillusionments, he laid his foundations wide and deep—and dark. But on those foundations he would build, stubbornly. These were not the plans of a man in any harmony with the worlds of other men, or of a man who had any care or love for other men. It was the planning of a stranger in a strange place, half hating, half fearing—a man choosing a lonely way, and a shadowed one. His first steps might be uncertain, but he would proceed with increasing confidence. His turning away from the common pleasures of acquaintance and casual exchanges would become as pride.

Thus began at last his life here on his own place, shut away from the past and the present by the river and the hills. The beginning was not what he had dreamed, but its dark and its solitude touched his spirit with a curious comfort—not healing, but grateful relief.

3

Snow was flying over the hills before Peter and Savina moved into the new house. Before that the fall had swept the hills with such a conflagration of color as neither had ever seen. To Peter that amazing spectacle had seemed deeply in accord with his feeling about the place and with his own mood. When it was over and the fires had died down to a deep glow in the lowland oaks, leaving the hills ash and brown, he felt that his own resentments and sudden flaring hatreds had died down, too. A little of the season's quiet fell on his troubled spirit.

Savina saw in this same violent passing of a season a symbol of all that she had come to think and believe of the region. Nothing that she saw here in the happenings of nature or the behavior of the people reassured her. Savina's vocabulary was limited and so she was not able to express even to herself her own variations of thought. She had only one word for everything: wild. It was all so wild, and wildness was the antithesis of all that she had ever seen or believed to be right and proper. But she made no outward complaint.

The house was big and for the time and place rather fine. It was built in a strict Pennsylvania Dutch style, severely plain, no porches, two front doors, and with broad brick chimneys on both sides. It was painted white, and with its freshly polished windows it glistened handsomely among the bare trees surrounding it.

Inside it smelled of new timber, and of wood fires.

Savina laid the bright new rag carpets she had brought with her, and spread the gay patchwork quilts on the beds. She was proud of them. They were the choicest patterns and quilted in the most elaborate and feathery designs. Her painted chests were disposed among the more ornate furniture bought in Kings Row. Now that it was all finished, set in order, and shining, she wished a little for someone she could show it to.

"It's very fine, isn't it, Peter? I like it."

"That's good. It is comfortable, and it's yours."

"I guess I think of it as ours."

Peter nodded. "It's funny, I think of it as yours, and of the fields outside and the barn as mine."

"Yes, that is a funny way to think."

It troubled her a little, this remark of his. It was as if he had divided the place and set her and himself just that much apart. The thought hung heavily for a while in her mind, then settled away in her unconscious uneasiness.

Almost at once the two of them fell into a routine as like as possible to that which they had known in the East. Peter arose early, started the fire in the kitchen stove, and went out to attend to his stock. An hour later he came in to a breakfast of sausage or *panhass,* eggs, fried potatoes, homemade bread, and strong coffee.

He worked hard all day, preparing the place for next season's farming. Savina baked and cleaned, churned and busied herself until night. After an early supper they sat in the kitchen until nine o'clock when they went to bed upstairs in a cold bedroom. Bedrooms were heated in Martinsgrove only in case of illness. It was so as a matter of course to Savina, and Peter adopted her ways of living without thinking. His mind was wholly set on building a circumscribed independence, and as quickly as possible.

Even in those first months his visits to St. Stephens were made at increasingly long intervals, and then only to purchase equipment. It seemed to him that he would never have done with this, but it was Savina who suggested needs and told him what he must have. Savina was concerned, too, in making the place independent of outside help, but for wholly different reasons. She understood this as a practical economy. It had always been done that way at home.

It was late in November that Lena Janek came to visit Savina. The Janek farm, a small one, was in a sort of cove near St. Stephens. Peter met Lena just before she reached the bridge he had built across the gully where the foot log had been. Lena smiled broadly and spoke to Peter in a dialect German.

"I guess you're Peter Kettring, heh?"

Peter stiffened. He instinctively disliked this peasant familiarity. He saw that she was pregnant, too, and that embarrassed him, all the more that she seemed so unconscious of it.

He bowed slightly, and took off his hat. "That is my name."

"*Ja.* I already knew that. I'm going to visit your wife. I brought her some little things." Lena pointed to her basket and wagged her head as if to say she were not one to come empty-handed; she knew what was proper.

"I didn't know my wife—er—knew anyone."

"Oh, I don't know her. I'm just making a neighborly visit. *Ja.* Seeing we're both foreigners, and land folks, too."

Peter wanted to deny these statements, but he pointed across the bridge and said, "The house is up that way."

"Thank you. You must come to see us, too, Mr. Kettring. Your name is Peter, not?"

"Yes."

"Well. I call you Peter. My man is named Michael. Michael Janek. I'm Lena."

Peter bowed again.

Lena regarded him shrewdly. "You don't act like a landsman. You have manners like city people. And you speak high German."

"I'm an American. I happened to learn German."

"*Ach,* so! It is not your own speech, then, German. We're Bohemian. I thought—I heard down in St. Stephens that you were foreigners, too, like us."

"We're American."

"Your wife, too, heh?"

"Yes."

"But I hear she cannot speak English!"

Peter saw that Lena meant no harm. She was like the people of Martinsgrove and the valley. He spoke more gently when he answered her.

"My wife's people, in the East—in Pennsylvania—"

"Where is that?"

"It's a state—like Missouri—but East."

"*Ach,* so! That I never heard. We are not so long in this country, Michael and me."

"And so, she speaks like her people—a kind of German."

"Lands-people talk, heh?"

"I suppose that's what you'd call it."

Lena swung her basket to the other arm. "I guess we'll understand each other, somehow. I go on now. I'm a little heavy on my feet." She laughed heartily. "I think maybe I got more than one child in there."

Peter colored, and she laughed again.

Savina saw Lena as she came out of the woods. She was instantly in a flutter. Hurriedly, she changed her blue apron for a white one, smoothed her hair before the small wavy mirror that hung over the washpan, and put the already neat kitchen into stricter order. She opened the door into the west front room, raised the curtains, and lighted the fire that was already laid. By the time Lena reached the kitchen door, Savina was ready to receive her.

"Good day, Mrs. Kettring."

"Good day."

"I'm Lena Janek. I live up close to St. Stephens."

"Come in and take off your things. It's cold today."

"Not when you're walking. But I'm pretty heavy on my feet, as you can see. It was quite a walk."

"Yes, of course. Now take a chair. We'll sit in the front room as soon as it's warmer in there. When I'm all by myself, I don't keep fires going in the rest of the house."

Lena proffered her basket. "I brought you some cookies. I just baked them this morning. I thought maybe you and your man would maybe like them for supper. They're nice to dip in your coffee."

"Oh, they look good! I don't bake such good cookies myself, as that."

This was a formula that Lena understood perfectly. She nodded.

"These didn't turn out as good as usual. I've got some new flour."

"They look—just perfect. And this?"

"Oh, that!" Lena was elaborately casual. "That's just some watermelon rind I pickled last summer."

"Watermelon rind?"

"Yes." Lena spoke proudly. "I learned to make it since I came here. It's like a kind of sweet pickle."

"It looks very good."

"I'll tell you how to make it. It's easy to do."

"Oh, thank you. I'd like that. Now, just a minute while I put some water on to heat. We'll have coffee."

Savina opened her big kitchen cupboard. She was glad that Lena was sitting where she could look into it and see how orderly it was. She set out cups and saucers, coffeecake, butter and jelly, and laid out a blue fringed cloth and napkins.

"Oh, you don't have to go to so much trouble for me! Just a cup of hot coffee in one of those plain cups from the bottom shelf."

Savina laughed. She liked Lena at once.

"No. You're company—at least for this first visit. Next time maybe you'll get the everyday cup!"

Lena laughed, too. She was quite at her ease. "My, my, but you're awful pretty, Mrs. Kettring."

Savina blushed, and Lena clucked. "What's your name?"

"Savina."

"Savina? That's nice. How long have you been married?"

"Just since this spring."

"But that long already! Ain't nothing happened yet?"

Savina looked inquiringly at Lena, then she flushed a bright red.

"*Ach!*" Lena went on easily. "You don't have to blush when it's just us two womenfolks talking. I was married a whole year before anything happened. Michael was afraid something was wrong with me, but I just laughed. I told him to keep trying, that maybe he wasn't any good himself!" Lena leaned her head back against the high-backed chair and roared with laughter. She showed all of her white, strong teeth when she laughed. Savina half turned her back to hide her embarrassment but this frankness and laughter were too contagious, and she found herself laughing, too.

"That shut him up, you can believe me." Lena wiped her eyes. "Now look at me! I guess I'm making up for lost time, I'm so big. It's maybe twins."

Savina tried to join in this unseemly talk. She had never heard such matters discussed except in quiet whispers. "Would you like that?" she ventured.

"Twins? Oh, yes, I guess so. They could soon look after each other, I guess."

She looked speculatively at Savina. "Still and all, it's maybe just as nice not to have children right away. When you're new married —well, it's nice just to have fun for a while."

This was too much for Savina. She rushed into the front room and made great ado about the fire. When she returned to the kitchen her face was still warm and pink. Lena smiled, half to herself. She considered Savina more carefully. So little, and so slender! Like a little girl, sure enough.

"Are you healthy?" she asked abruptly. "You're right thin."

"Yes. My mother was always thin, too."

"So? Your parents are living?"

"Yes, both of them."

"It's hard, isn't it, to be so far from them?"

"I guess so. I try not to think about it."

"Yes, yes, I know. Once we're married, we go where our man goes."

"You came from across the water, didn't you?"

"Yes. How did you know that?"

"Mrs. Miner told me."

"So? She knew. I have never spoken to her."

"She's a nice woman. She was good to me when I stayed there. You see we didn't have a place to live."

"Yes, I know all about it. Everybody said your man was a rich one."

"Oh, no. He's not a rich man."

"He spent a lot of money. Did you sell your farm in—in that place you came from?"

"My husband didn't have a farm—he was a schoolteacher."

"And now he makes a farmer of himself?"

"Yes. He loves land."

"It's good, that way. My people were always of the land. I don't know anything else all my life. I have no parents. I lived with an aunt. She was glad to see me married. So it wasn't so hard to leave. But still, America is so different. It's hard to get used to. Why don't you speak English?"

"I have to learn. In the valley nobody spoke English. *Ach!* The coffee! It is ready now. I believe it's warm in the front room. Suppose we take it in there."

"Well—whatever. But it's so nice here in the kitchen. You mustn't make company of me!"

"No, no, of course not. But—" Savina looked shyly at Lena. "You're the first visitor, and I have never used my front room. Let's go in there!"

"Why, of course. I'll help you. Here, I'll take the plates."

Lena looked about the front room. "This is very nice—very nice. *Gott!* It is like a rich house, I can tell you!"

Savina made deprecatory signs, and Lena continued her frank admiration of each object in the room. She was clearly so free of envy and any other feeling than congratulation of Savina's high fortune that Savina found herself relating the history of a chest or a chair with something more of heartiness and open cordiality than she had before experienced even among well-known neighbors.

She had never known anyone quite like Lena. The women of her home region were for the most part hard and secretive, self-righteous and bigoted. Even her mother had not been a generous person. If it had not been for her father, she would never have had any other standard of judgment. But her father was more open-handed and more openhearted than most men. Her mother had often mourned his "too-free" ways.

Now that she sat here talking with this open, glowing peasant woman—for she could tell that this was indeed an *echte landsfrau*—she was able to make estimate of the contrast. Lena was handsome in her husky, blowsy fashion. Her hair was thick and dark, her eyebrows heavy and high arched over clear hazel eyes. Her skin, even in pregnancy, was creamy, with spots of color in her cheeks. She seemed to give off warmth. Savina felt pale and slight of being beside this laughing, earthy woman who spoke as frankly of her body, her appetites, and of her love for her man as she would speak of flowers or vegetables, or the fowls in her chicken yard.

Savina warmed more and more to her visitor. It was like stretching out chilled hands toward a generous fire.

"You are a rich lady and I'm just a country woman—"

"No, no—" Savina protested, but Lena continued.

"—but I think we will be friends anyhow."

"Why—of course," Savina answered with a shade of embarrassment. She was not accustomed to any references to such emotional subjects as Lena juggled in her conversations. She sat, wide-eyed, but admiring, in spite of her misgivings concerning the orthodoxy of this kind of talk. She had almost a guilty feeling. She could not imagine what Peter would think of it.

As it happened Peter did not leave her in doubt about what he thought of Lena Janek and her visit.

"What did she want, *die Janekie?*"

"Want? She didn't want anything."

"Then what did she come for?"

"Just to visit." Savina puckered her brows in a bewildered expression.

"I'm glad they don't live any nearer."

"Why, Peter. What is it?"

"I want people to let us alone." He sounded like a petulant small boy.

"She will not bother you." There was rebuke in Savina's tone.

"Well, I hope she doesn't come running here too often."

"No danger. She lives nearly two miles away, and she works hard. Like a man, I gathered from her talk. They are just lands people, Peter."

Peter was mollified by this last sentence. He was trying to think of himself as a man of the soil.

"I'll go to see her before long," Savina continued. "It looks to me as if she ought to have some help now."

Peter grunted and no more was said about the Janeks, but he went out of the house with a troubling sense of having met with a minor defeat. He could not quite define it, but the feeling persisted and he was vaguely irritated with Savina.

Several days later Peter hitched his fine gray horses to his new farm wagon and drove in to St. Stephens. He was pleased with the horses. They were perfectly curried and brushed and were satiny smooth. But they were hard to manage. Peter was not sure he had

them quite under control, but his excitement arose with their resistance. Here was something that tested him. He cracked his whip
over their ears and sent them on at a gallop. By the time he drove
into St. Stephens they were ready to stand quietly at the hitching
rack in front of Niles Tipton's general store.

Peter responded to the exhilarating sparkle and tang of the
day. St. Stephens looked less shabby than usual. He spoke with
something like cordiality to several people.

By midafternoon he had made his purchases and had left some
orders with Niles Tipton.

"Guess I'd better be getting on back to the place. Dark comes
early now."

"Yep. Days are getting short. Winter's right on us."

The two men stepped out on the high platform in front of the
store.

"Clouding up a little." Peter looked speculatively at the thin
streaks of gray scudding from the northwest.

"Snow—likely."

"Think so?"

"Might." Niles paused at the bottom step. "Come on up to
Finley's and have a drink, Peter. Keep you warm on the drive
home."

Peter hesitated. "I ought to be starting on." He did not wish to
say to Niles that he did not drink, and that he had never been in a
saloon in his life.

"Oh, come on. Just take a minute."

"All right."

The warm darkish interior of Finley's saloon seemed pleasant.
Peter glanced about curiously. The bar was wet and shining, and the
rows of bottles glittered in the light of two big kerosene lamps with
tin reflectors.

"Howdy, Niles. Howdy, sir." Al Finley wiped the bar. "What'll
it be?"

Niles said something which Peter did not hear, but he nodded at Finley as if repeating the choice. Finley set out a bottle and glasses.

Half a dozen rough-looking men stood at the other end of the bar. They had been talking and laughing noisily when Peter and Niles entered. They quieted immediately and looked curiously at Peter. It made him a little uncomfortable. Niles filled the oversized glass and handed the bottle to Peter. He glanced at the other customers.

"How're you, Mason? Hello, Dodd. How's Camperville treating you?"

The men nodded, but they were not cordial. Niles glanced at Peter, and emptied his glass.

The man Niles had addressed as Dodd banged his glass on the bar. "Guess I'll go along. I don't think I'll ever get to where I can stay around a damn Yankee no more."

He stalked out rather unsteadily. There was a minute's silence. Peter's face went dark red. Then the group broke into a loud laugh. They clapped each other on the back, beat on the bar, and appeared quite overcome with the humor of the situation.

"Have another drink, Peter. Don't pay any attention. Dodd's drunk."

Peter filled his glass but his hand was unsteady. A big fellow with a short beard moved toward the door. "Me neither! Me neither! By God, I spent four years trying to kill 'em out, but I guess they breed too fast." He stopped and turned. "I remember how a Yankee squeals when you've got a bayonet in his belly."

Peter whipped around. He looked the big man up and down. There was an instant silence in the saloon. He felt a quick drumming in his ears. His clipped words came without volition.

"I've seen a good many rebels squirming on the end of a bayonet, and they all—er—squeal, as you say, in exactly the same way."

Niles had laid his hand on Peter's arm, but as Peter finished the sentence, the hand dropped quickly.

The thick stocky figure before Peter seemed to gather itself into a tense knot.

Al Finley knocked on the bar with a thick glass. "Go on now, Streeter. None of that in here!"

But the man lurched at Peter.

"Why, you—you—goddam—" He swung his fist in a wide, awkward arc at Peter who stepped out of his way. He rushed at Peter again, and this time Peter struck him hard on the temple. The man grunted and rolled over on the floor. He stumbled to his feet, his hair and beard thick with sawdust. He brushed at his clothes in a slightly dazed fashion. Something in Peter arose to singing pitch. He laughed. He had not intended to laugh. He scarcely knew that he had.

"Look out there, Mister!" Finley warned.

Streeter was struggling to extricate a big pistol from his pocket. Peter snatched it and struck Streeter a smashing blow across the hand with the heavy butt. He flung the pistol on the bar and seized Streeter by the collar. His terrific strength must have have surprised Streeter, who, for one startled instant, made no resistance. Peter rushed him to the door and threw him into the street.

"I'll take that pistol," he said quietly to Finley. "Save somebody being shot in the back sometime."

The silence hung heavy in the room. Peter turned slowly to Tipton.

"Another drink?"

Tipton looked straight at Peter. Then he turned and walked out. Peter, astounded, stared after him. There was a half laugh from the group of men, but Peter looked up quickly and the laugh died. He poured himself another drink.

"How much?" he said shortly to Finley.

"Six bits."

Peter laid the coins down, buttoned his coat, and walked toward the door. His head was whirling. The realization that he was not sober went over him like fire. He came back to the bar.

"Who was that—that man? What did you call him?" he asked.

Finley hesitated a moment. Then he answered shortly. "Vane Streeter. Runs a freight boat. And if I was you, Mister Kettring, I'd keep out of his way."

[80]

Again Peter laughed without intending to. "Hardly seems necessary, does it?"

Peter unhitched his horses, mounted to his seat clumsily, and drove hard toward the hill road. A hurricane of emotions tore across his brain. Astonishment, fury, and shame.

He reached home, unharnessed the team, and fed the stock. When he had finished he sat down on an overturned box. He held his head between his hands and leaned against the feed trough. He was shaking from head to foot.

How did this ridiculous thing happen? What on earth made him take part in a saloon brawl? How could he lower himself in such fashion? He clutched his hair and pressed his face hard against the rough boards. The veins stood out on his forehead, and a heavy pulse beat in his throat.

After a long time he arose. He felt stiff and a little sick. He decided to say nothing about the afternoon's mishap to Savina. He stopped quite still as he made the decision. Why did he not wish to tell Savina? He must be honest and know why. It was—well, partly that he did not wish to trouble her with any talk of the village and of the hostility that he now knew it had for him. Not that he cared what St. Stephens thought about him. And yet—was he sure about that? This very day he had gone openheartedly into the little town. It had been like patting a strange dog on the head and having it snarl and bite. Then, too, he was ashamed. It had been undignified, not in keeping with his withdrawal from the life about him. This —this *yokel* life, he found himself saying. Damn them all.

And Niles Tipton!

Tipton had actually turned his back on him, had walked out without speaking. What did Tipton expect him to do in the face of open insult and attack? That was what came of association outside of one's known and familiar ways. But here he had no known or familiar ways. This was the first time he had actually paused for one moment in the single business of fitting himself into his own place.

But maybe it was a good thing that he had. Now he knew what

the people about the village and the river front thought of him. That tragically stupid war! It had not been of his making—or theirs. What had it to do with today and a man who simply wished to live on his own place and attend to his own affairs? So, this was how matters stood. If so, very well.

He went slowly into the house.

That night Peter's barn burned to the ground and destroyed his horses. A quantity of farm tools were lost, and Peter had difficulty keeping other outbuildings from catching fire.

The next morning Peter stood looking at the heap of ashes, still smoldering and sending up a drifting cloud of gray-blue smoke. Savina stood beside him, a heavy shawl over her head.

"How could it have happened, Peter? You didn't leave a lantern burning when you went out late, did you maybe?"

"No. Somebody set it on fire." Peter's voice was harsh.

"Peter! Who would do that?"

"I don't know, but I think I can guess." He related briefly his encounter with Vane Streeter.

"*Ach,* Peter. I shall be afraid the house will burn down over our heads."

Peter looked hard at Savina for a moment, as if he did not quite understand what she was saying. "I think I'll walk into town." He laughed shortly. "I'll have to walk."

Savina shook her head. "Those beautiful, helpless horses!"

"Yes. Somebody is going to pay for that."

"You will be careful, yes?"

Peter did not answer.

"It seems that some people have taken a misliking to—to us. Why is that, Peter? For what?"

"I don't know, quite. But there are, well, certain kinds of people who always do—such things as this."

"You *will* be careful?"

Peter flared. "What are you talking about, Savina?"

Savina looked a little frightened at Peter's sharp tone, but she spoke firmly. "About fighting. It is not right to fight."

"What should I do when people do something to me?"

"I—I don't know. But fighting just makes more trouble."

"I'll get something to eat at Mrs. Miner's, I suppose. I'll be back as soon as I can."

"What do you do in St. Stephens?" Savina was manifestly uneasy.

He spoke quietly. "I'll have to have horses, and a new wagon. *That* I will not buy in St. Stephens. I will buy nothing else in St. Stephens. No one is going to profit there by this kind of doing. I'll buy in Jefferson or in Kings Row. And this time I'll build a stone barn."

"Yes, all the barns at home are stone."

Savina stared wonderingly at the smoking ashes. She made little sounds of dismay, but the look she sent after Peter was all commiseration and pity. He looked so puzzled—so *outdone*. Surely he had done nothing to anyone to deserve this. A little of Peter's bitterness and resentment came into her mood. They were good enough people—she and Peter—they did no harm to anyone. They bought and paid: that was being right and useful. There must be some very unworthy folk about to so resent their presence. A new loyalty and devotion to Peter filled her. She straightened her back. She could help in many ways. And she would not be afraid.

"My man is a good man," she said aloud.

She watched him out of sight. For several moments she was uncertain what it was that stirred in her so strong a feeling of tenderness and resentment.

Already Savina had settled into the way of her people. She had heard the precepts of proper conduct for so long a time that she automatically followed the pattern. One did not stand silent, thus, given over to soft emotions. She wondered. Of course she was angry as Peter was at the destruction of property, but—yes, she suddenly knew what it was. Peter was walking! A farmer *drove* to town. He did not walk—like a hired man. It was as though his wounds were there, visible to her eyes.

She drew her shoulders up in a long shrug. It was an unaccustomed gesture—a gesture curiously expressive of dismay and rejection. She pinned the shawl more securely under her chin and wrapped her hands in the dangling folds. Then she walked across the yard to the front of the house and stood looking at the river.

The moving water was a bright hard glitter shading to gray, and to the east, a pale bluish lavender that merged with the dim lines of the uncertain banks. She looked and looked, straining to see farther and farther down the fading distance. The river was beautiful, she had to admit, but its size and the weight of its ponderous swing appalled her. It lay there as impassable as an ocean. There, before her, a close, almost mocking barrier. No, it was too big and too indifferent to be mocking. It just *was*.

She looked back. There were the hills, shutting out all view toward the country itself. What might be back there was wholly unknown, mysterious even as anything unknown is likely to seem in such half contemplation, though her common sense instantly corrected her fancy. Back there beyond the hills—well, doubtless just some more of this same kind of country, though it was all strange enough. Wilder, no doubt, as you went inland. Everything compelled her view toward the river. The whole vast window of her daily outlook was toward the river.

She had fallen into a way of looking down the river—back in the direction of home. If ever—but there was no use dreaming such dreams as that. She was here with Peter. This was home. This was their place. When one made a move it was made, and that was all there was to it. From there one did not look back.

It came to her suddenly that she often stopped in her daily rounds to look at the river, and now that she thought of it, she knew that she always faced that direction. If she was inside of the house she always paused at an east window to look out, never a west one. She turned now to look in that direction. It was surprising how much less familiar that view was. But Peter always looked toward the west. She had often noticed it. She wondered if he might be dissatisfied with the St. Stephens region. Maybe he had that wandering instinct she had heard her father talk about. It had always been mentioned as if it were an ailment of the mind—something not quite seemly.

An instant recurrence of that wave of conscious loyalty swelled her heart. Savina was standing straight and severe at the highest point of the knoll that was the end of the long, gradually declining spur of hills. She was not looking down the river at this moment. She was not even seeing the hateful, slippery, sliding thing. She was scarcely aware even of her inner vision. She was given over entirely to feeling and that feeling was a swift gathering together of resolution and resistance—a protective and inclusive gesture of the mind which encircled this place and herself and Peter, and whatever of fortune, good or ill, that might come here. In some subtle and obscure way the river itself was involved. Among the things to be resolved against, to be ranged as objects of this already established resistance, was the river.

Savina took a step forward, hesitated—she had not even washed the breakfast dishes! Think! To be standing here doing nothing but looking. But she acted in contradiction. Freeing her hands from the shawl, she held her long full skirts up a little and made her stumbling way down the rough slope and on to the thick growth of willows that stood all along the water's edge. It was a miniature forest of yellow and reddish switches. Progress was not easy here. It was softer underfoot than she had expected. Her shoes were muddy, and her dress was bedraggled.

Suddenly she stopped, and listened. The air was filled with sound—rustling, whispering, gurgling, all arising from a continuous undertone that was like sighing or like multitudinous breathing. She caught her lower lip with her teeth in her characteristic expression of indecision. Then she went ahead. She felt some kind of pressure in her throat—a kind of excitement close to fright as she looked. So big! So terribly big, and fierce, and rushing! It seemed, standing here and seeing it at her own level, as if it were actually higher than she was. Out there, far out in midstream, surely that was higher. The whole surface seemed to curve upward like the humped back of a huge racing animal. And here—she stepped back as one does instinctively from a hidden movement in the grass—

here almost at her feet was a small splashing, curling movement of water—the actual river edge. And there where it touched the land, it whispered, and sighed, and seemed shaken with a furtive mirth.

Savina turned back toward the house. She tried not to hurry. That would be a confession of her terror. She knew it was terror, and she knew it was not reasonable. But in a moment she was almost running, and the willow switches struck her across the face in a harsh and spiteful chastisement.

Peter walked with a swinging stride down the long road toward the bridge. The trees were bare now and there was a continuous view of the river, glinting silver in morning sun.

Just beyond the bridge he saw something gleaming in the bushes below the road. He went to investigate. It was an empty kerosene can. The screw top was missing, but it had been recently emptied.

"So!" he said. "So! We maybe can find out something."

An hour later he stopped at the first small grocery store. Tom Richland, the proprietor, was in the cellar, but he came up presently.

"Good morning, Mr. Kettring. What can I do for you?"

"Did you ever see this coal-oil can before?"

Richland put on his glasses and looked the can over. "Well, that's hard to say, seeing all coal-oil cans are about alike. But I kinda think I do know this one."

"Yes?"

"I think it belongs to Vane Streeter, Mr. Kettring. He came in here yesterday to have it filled. I recollect he'd lost the screw cap to it, and I put a piece of corncob in to keep the coal oil from sloshing out. Of course now I couldn't say for certain. But what you want to know for? Where did you get a holt to it?"

"I found it."

"I see. Well, I think it's his'n."

"Where does Streeter live?"

"Right around the corner there. The house that's got them two big cedar trees in the yard."

It was a shabby unpainted house. Several children were playing in the yard. They stopped and stared as Peter entered the yard and walked to the door. A small, tired-looking woman answered his knock.

"Good morning. Is Mr. Streeter at home?"

"No, sir. I ain't seen Vane since yesterday."

"I see. Mrs. Streeter, is this your oil can?"

"Let me see. Well—yes, sir, it is. Where did you get it? Yes, I know that can. It's mine."

"Thank you. I'll return it shortly, or see that it is returned."

"Yes, sir. I'll need it."

"And you don't know where your husband is?"

"Lordy no. I never do know where he is less'n I'm looking right at him. I guess he's off on the river somewhere."

"Thank you. Good morning."

"Good morning, sir."

Peter went to see Carter Day at the bank. "I'd like a word with you, Mr. Day."

"Come right on back, Mr. Kettring. It's a fine day. How are you getting along on the new place?"

"Pretty well."

"Your wife like it?"

"Er—oh, yes. Yes, of course. Mr. Day, I had a little trouble yesterday with a man named Streeter."

"Vane Streeter. I know all about it, Mr. Kettring. How did you happen to be in Al Finley's saloon? About the last place I'd go looking for you."

"I'd never been there before. Tipton asked me to go."

"Streeter's an ugly customer."

"I can understand that. Last night my barn was burned—burned my horses and a good deal of stuff besides."

Mr. Day sat up with a jerk. "You—don't—say so."

"About three o'clock this morning. It was nearly gone when I woke up."

"One of the boys said there was a fire down the river somewhere. Well, now, I'm mighty sorry to hear that."

"Mr. Day, the barn was set on fire."

"Can you be sure of that?"

"Yes. There was no fire near the place. I don't smoke. I wasn't out there after dark, so there wasn't even a lantern near the place."

"Spark, maybe, from your chimney—"

Peter shook his head. "The barn's a hundred and fifty yards from the house. The wind was from the north. This morning I found this coal-oil can just outside of my place. It had been thrown into the bushes. It is still oily on the outside. It had certainly been emptied just lately."

"I see. Um—looks pretty suspicious."

"More than suspicious. The can belongs to Streeter."

"How do you know that? You'd better be pretty sure before you say that around much."

"Mr. Richland identified it. Streeter had this can filled there yesterday afternoon. Mrs. Streeter also identified it as her own."

"As clear as that?"

"Yes: as clear as that."

"You'd better turn that over to the constable, Mr. Kettring."

"All right, if you think so. But I want to find Streeter myself."

Mr. Day put the tips of his fingers slowly together. "I'd be careful, Mr. Kettring."

"Everybody says that to me, Mr. Day. I am a law-abiding citizen. I propose to make sure other people be careful."

"Well, now, Mr. Kettring, I appreciate your feelings. But, after all, you're a stranger here—still. And—"

"I'm not asking anything of anyone, but to be left alone."

"Hard to get that in this world, sir."

"I propose to get it. Who is the constable?"

"Edwards is his name. I wish you'd let me talk to him for you."

"Well—I don't want to trouble you."

"No trouble at all, sir, no trouble at all. We want things like this handled, of course, and I'll see what we can do. Matter would have to go up to Camperville if you want to prosecute."

"I do want to prosecute."

"It will be merely punitive, you understand. Streeter hasn't got anything. You couldn't recover any of your loss. And then there is his family—lot of little children, I believe."

"I'm not much interested in the sentimental side of this, Mr. Day. It has only one side so far as I am concerned."

Mr. Day stiffened slightly. "Very well, Mr. Kettring."

By midafternoon the whole of St. Stephens knew that Vane Streeter had had a fight with that well-to-do Yankee—the one who bought the old Adams place—that Mr. Kettring had pitched Streeter through the door of Al Finley's saloon—they say he's a powerful man—must be to handle Streeter, and that Streeter had gone down there in the night and burned up Kettring's barn. Burned clean up, lock, stock, and barrel, burned up them two fine horses Kettring had bought from Jess Miller last summer—awful to take out a spite on helpless animals—they'd cost the Yankee a hundred dollars apiece, but hell, let the Yankee pay. And today Mr. Kettring was in town looking for Streeter. He'd been to Streeter's house, even. They say he took Streeter's pistol away from him yesterday. Like as not he'd shoot Streeter on sight.

Opinions varied. St. Stephens had not had such a good excuse for loafing and talking since the war ended.

In Al Finley's saloon, business was brisk. Finley, moving back and forth behind the bar, listened with that magnificent detachment found only in bartenders. He did not miss a word, but he did not take sides, even in his mind.

Fred Rice, who owned the second general store, set his beer glass on the bar. "I'll tell you, I'd just as lief not run into that Yankee feller, neither."

"Yes, but Streeter would just as soon kill you as not."

"I ain't so sure that Kettring wouldn't either."

"I never seen nothing neater'n the way he took Streeter's pistol away from him and cracked him over the hand with it."

"I ain't seen anyone handle Streeter like that before, and I've seen Streeter in many a scrap."

"Yeh. He's right troublesome, always fighting."

[89]

"Streeter fit all thoo the war."

A tall, dour-looking man with a heavy sandy mustache spoke for the first time. "I was with Streeter."

Peck Faulter, who kept the hardware store for old man Call, looked at the speaker. "Doggone if I don't believe you're Roy Coughman."

"Yeh. That's my name."

"Of course, I know you. So you was with Streeter? Well, he always struck me as a big blowhard."

Coughman shook his head. "Don't fool yourself. He's no coward."

"No? Anyhow, this is the first time I ever seen him meet up with anybody his own size."

"I'll bet we ain't heard the last of this. Not by a long shot."

"I guess Streeter did burn Kettring's barn, all right."

"Ain't no doubt about it."

"Well, I call that a dirty, low-down trick even if Kettring is a Yankee."

"The Yankees burned plenty ever' time they come to this county. Don't fergit that."

"I ain't fergittin' nothin'. But that was in wartime. It's a whole lot different just ridin' up to a place and burnin' it up when you're a soldier, and sneakin' there in the dead of night. Burnin' up livestock, too."

"That's pretty bad. I couldn't burn up no man's horses."

"Well, I guess you all know Kettring's out looking for Streeter."

"Yes, I know. An' I don't want to be in shootin' distance when they meet."

"Mr. Day turned the case over to Edwards this morning. Anybody seen Edwards?"

A roar of laughter answered him.

"No, by God, and I bet nobody's going to see Edwards close till it all blows over."

"He said he was going out to look for Streeter."

"He'll look where he's sure Streeter ain't goin' to be."

"Sure, he's hoping Kettring will find him first."

"I'll bet my bottom dollar Kettring'll settle Streeter's hash in short order when he finds him."

"I'm pretty sure he ain't going to find him easy. Streeter didn't come back in here yesterday evening, you notice."

"That's right. But, comin' back to Edwards—"

Again everyone laughed. In any contest between citizens and the law, popular favor was likely to run with the fugitive. Kam Sandifer said it was an aftermath of the war. You unleashed everything that was lawless and destructive in a man for years and then expected him to step back into harness and be orderly. It wasn't human nature, he said. Bob Dawson, a big white-haired farmer, was thinking of that now.

"I guess people get used to fighting and killing in a war. Then it's hard for 'em to quit when the time comes."

"That's so, Mr. Dawson. Right now when any kind of a dispute comes up, first thing anybody thinks about is getting out a gun."

"I kinda feel that way myself sometimes." Coughman had a countryside reputation for gentleness and good humor. "Darn 'f I don't think about shootin' ever' time I talk to old man Day about the mortgage on my place!"

The group roared again. Roy Coughman was a regular sight, they agreed—a sight, that's what he was!

The door opened and John Persons came in. Persons was the postmaster.

"Howdy, John. Heard any news?"

"Nothing special. Give me a glass of beer, Al. I saw Mr. Kettring down at Franklin's saddler shop."

"That so? Talk to him?"

"No. He was just leaving when I came in."

"Phil Franklin have anything to say?"

"Well, he said Mr. Kettring was talking to him about going up to Kings Row or to Camperville next stock sales day. Said something about not buying anything more in St. Stephens. Can't say I blame him much."

"How's that?"

"Kettring's a decent man. Respectable, quiet. 'Tends to his own business, spends a lot of money right here in St. Stephens. Then he runs into that low-down Streeter and gets his barn burned down. Hell, I'd be mad, too."

"Something to that. Tipton made a nice little pile out of Mr. Kettring."

"Well, you ought to seen Tipton turn his back on Kettring yesterday and walk out."

"You know Tipton. He's a hothead himself, under all that quiet way of his."

"Yes, I know. Niles goes along easy-like till you step on his toes some way, and then he fires up and ain't got no more use for you."

"That's Niles, all right. Independent as all get out."

Fred Rich nodded. "Well, all I got to say is, if I had as good a customer as Mr. Kettring has been to Niles Tipton, he could just say and do whatever he wanted to. Hell, money's money."

"Wouldn't be surprised, Fred, if you don't get him for a customer, too. I bet he don't go back to Tipton's store in a big hurry."

"Hear anything else, John?"

"Old man Patterson told me Streeter's boat is tied up at Dawson's Point. Know anything about that, Bob?"

"Yes. His boat's down there. He's having some work done on it."

"You didn't see anything of Vane down there, did you?"

"No, I don't know when I did see him last. I had some trouble myself with Streeter last year. Don't want to see him."

"He's a tough customer."

"You reckon this here Kettring's really out after Streeter?"

John Persons nodded. "I'd stake a good deal that he's a hard man and don't forget easy."

"He looks that way."

"He's having Marvin Greenway make some signs for him."

"What kind of signs, John? If you ain't the darndest fellow, Persons, dolin' out news a snippet at a time."

Persons laughed. "Don't get a chance to talk in here! He's just posting his place, that's all."

"Oh, I see. Don't want nobody pestering round."

"I saw what he wants on them. He left it for Marvin. Written in a mighty pretty hand, too. That's an educated man."

"What did he say?"

"It said: *Absolutely No Trespassing. This Means Everybody.*"

"I'd say he means business, and I'd have to *have* business before I'd set foot up there."

"Well, he's on his rights. What do you say, Mr. Dawson?"

"I got my own place posted, but don't anybody pay any attention to it. I just try to keep hunters off so they won't kill everything."

Persons continued, sure of his effect this time. "Mr. Kettring's bought a shotgun, too."

"Yeh!" Peck Faulter spoke up. "I sold it to him myself. But I declare, I didn't think nothing special about it at the time. He bought a supply of powder and buckshot, too. Looks like he means business."

"Well, I can't say I blame him. If my barn and my stock was burned up, I know somebody'd pay for it."

Bob Dawson leaned back against the bar. "You know, boys, I don't generally believe in taking the law into your own hands, but there's times when you feel like you have to. Now, Al here was telling me who all was in here yesterday when the trouble started. Lot of bums if you ask me. They started something. Mr. Kettring is a man that's come to settle down here like most of us did, or like our daddies did before us. We need new people, need more money. Need to open up the country. Now, Streeter's a roustabout. Wouldn't any of us take off of him what he said to Mr. Kettring. I can't say I got so much use for Yankees myself, but before the war you never thought if a man was a Northerner or not."

"That's sure right."

"The war's over. And we don't want a man like Vane Streeter driving out a good substantial citizen that'll help build up the country."

"That's good sense, Bob, sure as shot."

"Well, anyway," Persons broke in, "nobody's seen hide or hair of Streeter all day."

"Ray Tinker seen him 'long about daybreak walking down toward the Point."

"That so?"

"Yeh. Tinker drove in to town early this morning. Said he seen him about three miles below the Adams place—Kettring's place, I mean."

"I guess Edwards must of heard that this morning, too. He went *up* the river looking for Streeter!"

Even Bob Dawson joined in the shout of laughter that greeted this.

In all minor matters the sporting instincts of this community favored a culprit against the law. It was all right for Edwards and his kind to keep the Negroes in their place, and to drive tramps out of town, but when men of the general run were involved it was altogether a different matter. Nobody liked Streeter, and certainly burning a barn was a grave enough crime—a sneaking, low-down kind of crime. But, as Nick Pearson said: "still and all, it was a Yankee's barn, and I'd be the last one to he'p Edwards find Streeter, even if he wanted to, which I doubt."

Toward evening as the men of St. Stephens were straggling home, Peter was seen going up the principal street. His head was down and his face was dark and brooding. He seemed not to see anyone and people stepped out of his way on the narrow sidewalk.

Peter's long heavy coat was buttoned high and his cap was pulled well over his ears. The wind was sharpening. Under his arm, the double barrel pointing down, Peter carried his new shotgun. He walked with his swinging stride on up the street, past Mrs. Miner's boardinghouse. He turned east along the street he had traversed that first evening in St. Stephens. Last spring! He thought for a fleeting moment of that evening. It seemed very long ago. He crossed the street, and turned north again, going rapidly toward the edge of town. The sidewalks disappeared now.

He stepped out into the middle of the road and quickened his step. Dusk was deepening. Only the river still gleamed, a thinning streak of light in the graying landscape. With a wholly unconscious gesture Peter swung his gun to his shoulder. The gun felt comfortable there—natural. Straightening, he marched briskly, soldier-wise, along the dark hill road toward home.

4

Streeter's boat was tied up at Dawson's Point for four days. But no one saw Streeter. No one saw Streeter all of that week. Streeter's wife said he was probably off on a spree.

But St. Stephens kept him in mind. Another week passed. People began to ask in a queer, quiet tone, "Guess nobody's seen anything of Vane Streeter yet, eh?"

"No. Ain't heard anything about it. Ain't nobody seen him anywhere?"

"Well, say. Listen here. You recollect that trouble he had with that Yankee Kettring. You don't suppose—"

"Don't suppose what?"

"Well, this Kettring fellow was a-looking for Vane. Said something or 'nother 'bout getting him on account he said Streeter burnt his barn."

"Guess Streeter did burn it, too."

"Well, now. You don't suppose this Kettring would go so far as to—as to make away with Streeter, do you?"

"*Say!* Well, now—"

Edwards went about looking mysterious.

Peter was digging the foundations for his new barn one afternoon. It was a windy, blustering day with scattered flurries of sleety snow. The ground was frozen but Peter worked hard. He already had a sizable pile of rocks hauled in, and a few tiers laid at one end of the big rectangular excavation.

He looked up from his work and saw a man at the top of the short ladder which stood where the digging was deepest. Peter's face darkened.

"Howdy, Mr. Kettring."

Peter glowered. "Did you come in here by the gate?"

"I did that, Mr. Kettring."

"Didn't you see a sign there?"

"Yep."

"That sign means everybody unless they've got some mighty special business with me."

The stranger rested a heavily booted foot on the top rung of the ladder. "Yeh, I gathered that. I *have* got special business with you. Could I have a few words with you?"

Peter thrust his spade into the ground and mounted the ladder.

The stranger was a tall man and stoutly built, but Peter was half a head taller and decidedly more massive of shoulder. The visitor looked closely at Peter.

"What do you want?"

"My name's Hall, Mr. Kettring. I'm the sheriff of the county."

Peter nodded, but his expression of angry impatience did not change.

"I came down from Camperville this morning to look after two or three things, and I thought I'd better come out and have a little talk with you."

Peter drew his heavy eyebrows together. "What about?"

"Vane Streeter."

"Streeter? What about him?"

"Seen him lately?"

"No. But I've been looking for him."

"So I hear."

"You hear? What are you talking about, please?"

"Take it easy, Mr. Kettring. I got a right to be here, you can rely on that, or I wouldn't bother paying you a visit."

Peter drew up. "Will you please be more explicit?"

"Well, I want to know if you found Streeter anywheres?"

"No, I didn't."

"Did you say, maybe, that you'd kill him if you found him?"

"I don't recall that I said it. I may have implied it. I probably would have killed him if I'd seen him that day."

"Would, eh?"

"Streeter burned my barn. Two fine horses were burned with it, a new farm wagon, and other stuff."

"You think he did it, eh?"

"I found his coal-oil can—"

"Yes. I know that. His wife said it was his'n."

"I don't take that sort of thing very lightly, Mr. Hall."

"I guess none of us do. Still and all, you don't kill a man—"

"Are you suggesting I did kill Streeter?"

"No, I ain't suggesting anything. I'm asking."

"I didn't. But I've killed a good many men who never did anything to me at all."

"Eh? Oh, yes, of course. You was in the army. You mean it'd be easy to kill a man if you got a good reason."

"I didn't say that. I don't want to kill anyone—or anything. But I do want to be left alone—by everyone."

"Well, Mr. Kettring, I guess you know Vane Streeter has disappeared."

Peter looked steadily at the sheriff.

"Ain't nobody seen hide 'r hair of him since the day you bought yourself a new shotgun."

"I'm not very interested, Mr. Hall. Since I *didn't* kill Streeter—"

"Well, I recollect now someone did say they seen him down round Dawson's Point the next day, but that was the last."

"Let's hope so. The world gets on very well without such men."

Sheriff Hall cut a chew of tobacco from a hard twist, put it in his mouth, clicked his big Barlow pocketknife shut, and looked up at Peter.

"Mr. Kettring, I don't think you made away with Streeter."

Peter bowed. The unexpected courtliness disconcerted Hall. He was not sure if Kettring was being polite, or if he was making fun of him.

"Well, you know a lot of people around here are letting on you might a-done it. 'Course, nobody's come right out, unless it was his wife. She's been a-squawking a good deal. She didn't pay no attention at all at first, but now that she thinks maybe something has happened to him sure enough, she's setting up considerable racket.

She did admit that was Vane's coal-oil can you brought around to her house, though. I guess he could-a fell in the river."

"I hope so."

Sheriff Hall stared.

"I mean that quite simply, Mr. Hall. I have no use for the kind of bully that Streeter was. I had to throw him out of a saloon because of his talk—"

The sheriff laughed. "Yeh. I heard that. I'd a-liked to've seen that! I knew Streeter."

This time Peter stared.

"Well, I just wanted to talk with you. I'd be careful what I said if I was you, Mr. Kettring, seeing you're a newcomer and all."

"Careful? Why?"

"I mean about killing people."

Peter nearly smiled. "I don't think I said that, though it's possible. But I've come here to live. This is my place. I bought it and paid for it, and I don't propose to be interfered with in any way."

"You sound mighty independent."

"I am."

"Well, you got to deal with people."

"Not more than is necessary."

The sheriff smiled good-naturedly. "Well, maybe it takes all kind of people. So, you didn't kill Vane Streeter and bury him around here somewhere?"

Peter answered the smile. "No, I didn't."

Hall looked around. "Pretty fine place you've got. I used to know it. Lonesome, though. Anything could happen up in these woods and nobody'd ever know anything about it."

"All I want in these woods is to be left in peace."

"Well, Mr. Kettring, it's my guess you'll have plenty of that. Going to build a rock barn?"

"Yes. They don't catch fire so easily."

"Um, I see. Well, guess I'll be getting along. Good day, sir."

"Good day, Mr. Hall."

Back in town, the sheriff remarked, "You all are crazy. That man never killed Vane Streeter."

"What makes you so sure, Sheriff?"

"Hell! I know a straight an' honest man when I see one."

But St. Stephens was not convinced. Their dislike of Peter Kettring, brought into being largely by cross-fertilization of careless and inaccurate talk, was shaded with respect, and certainly modified by a lurking element of fear.

The sheriff's notion that Streeter "could-a fell in the river" may have been correct. In any case Streeter's disappearance was permanent. From time to time someone remembered him, and always the question came from someone: "You reckon that Yankee made away with Streeter and buried him up there somewhere in the woods?"

And always someone made the pat answer: "I wouldn't put it past him. I know good and well I wouldn't want to get on the wrong side of Peter Kettring."

The winter was a bitter one. Savina thought of the even cold and the long still nights at home. Here the unsteady rhythms and sudden onslaughts of weather filled her with answering disquiet.

Peter worked with superhuman energy. But by Christmas he realized that he would have to employ help. Savina suggested Michael Janek. With Janek, Peter dug ditches, built fences, and worked on the big stone barn.

February was so cold that the river began to freeze. The ice crept farther and farther toward the center, crowding the flow to a swift sullen channel. One morning after a heavy snow Savina stood at the bedroom window looking out. She was wretched. All morning she had struggled with a mounting nausea. She pressed her forehead hard against the icy glass. So, she thought, as Lena Janek had phrased it, "something had happened." She was going to have a child. She did not know if she was glad or not. For this moment she was simply very sick. She pressed her hands to her temples and stared at the gray-blue day. Even the snow seemed blue under this heavy sky. It stretched level and unbroken across the bottoms and on out across the ice. She could see the streak of open water, narrow and straight and slaty black, like an obsidian blade.

[99]

BOOK TWO

I

SPRING poured over the hills and down the valley like a cataract. One day the skies were low and windy, and the hills still sleeping under gray and brown. The next all the heavens were filled with mountains of snowy clouds drifting east and casting great dreaming shadows on the hills where a thin shine of young green had come out overnight.

Peter threw himself into the activities of the season with a driving fury. He did not look well, Savina thought. His hair looked rusty, and his cheekbones stood out ruggedly.

Janek could not help any longer. His own small farm took all of his time now. Peter rushed from one task to another. He was up at four o'clock, and often did not end his day's work until well after dark.

Sometimes Michael and Lena came for a brief visit on Sunday afternoons. Lena's baby, born in midwinter, was a big-eyed, rosy girl. Peter never more than paused to give the scantiest greeting. His Sunday was like any other day.

"He works too hard, your man." Michael looked after Peter and shook his head.

"He feels there is so much to do, and, of course, he will not have help."

"Yes, I know how he feels. But you cannot run a farm in this way. It's like riding a horse, you have to give a little—or you get your teeth shaken out."

"The place is so big." Savina's words took on a defensive tone.

"Yes. It is a big place." Janek spoke with admiration. "A fine big place. But big, or little, you must be master of your land or it will surely kill you."

Lena nodded in agreement, and added significantly, "You'll have to have some help yourself, before the summer is over."

Savina glanced quickly at Michael to see if he had heard. He nodded, too, a frank smile beaming in his good, open face.

"Yes, yes!" He nodded his head more vigorously in agreement. "The first time you have to be a little careful. After that," he turned his hand over. "After the first one, it's nothing."

Savina tried to look away, but the Janeks were unaware of her confusion.

"It's nothing so much, anyway, not even the first time," Lena said firmly. "My little Taska, she came very easy. An hour or two one morning before breakfast, and there she was." She rolled the husky baby on her lap and gave it a resounding spank. Taska squirmed and seemed already to participate in the rough and hearty humor of her parents.

"When will it happen, you think?" She looked at Savina speculatively. "Not soon, I guess?"

Savina abandoned her embarrassment. It was useless with Michael and Lena. "In October."

"Oh, then I can come up and help you myself. In the fall on our little place there is not so much to do."

Savina felt tears coming to her eyes, and blinked hard. What kind of way to behave was this?

"And Peter, what does he say? Is he glad?"

Savina made an equivocal gesture. She did not wish to tell Lena that she had not told Peter anything about it.

Savina was grateful for the occasional visits of the Janeks. She saw no one else. She had not been to St. Stephens since she came to the farm. The Janeks were the only people she had spoken to through all the dark winter months. And now Peter was working so hard that he seemed too tired at the end of the day for even a few words. But the farm had taken on an ordered, well-kept look. Savina realized that Peter was doing his work well. Both of them worked at high speed through the spring and on into the summer. And so it was that sometimes days went by without the exchange of more than a few necessary words.

It was a long time before Peter actually noticed the change in Savina's appearance. One morning at breakfast he said abruptly: "You are going to have a child?"

She bent her head low over her plate. "Yes."

"So?"

He said nothing more until that night.

"I expect you'd better have somebody now to help around the house."

"I don't need anyone, yet."

"When does it come?"

"In October some time."

"Can you get the *Janekie,* you think?"

"We have already spoken of it. She will come any time I want her."

"Oh!" Peter felt that he had been ever so slightly rebuked. He made considerable pretense of looking through a box where he kept farm memoranda of various kinds.

Savina waited for him to say something else, but the comment seemed to be finished, and she went back to the kitchen. She was a little hurt, but she could not define it, and set her feelings down to her disturbed state.

The subject was not mentioned again, and both of them felt somewhat ill at ease.

Mrs. Janek went in to St. Stephens to make some purchases for Savina, and evenings after supper, while Peter returned to the barn to work at one thing and another by lantern light, Savina cut and sewed baby clothes.

All through that summer in the crushing heat, Peter labored like a man possessed. He was puzzled sometimes at his own almost bitter obsession with the work of the farm.

Travelers along the river road observed him at all hours of the day. Sometimes, in the easy custom of the countryside, they shouted across the fields to him, and waved, but he never gave any sign in return.

"Damn funny fellow, that Kettring. Unsociable as hell."

"Sure. Like all them Dutchmen."

The usual late-afternoon group stood about the bar in Al Finley's saloon.

"Well, you have to remember, he *ain't* a Dutchman. That's what makes him queer. You expect a Dutchman to act that way. You take them Dutchmen up the river a piece and they won't talk to *nobody,* less'n they have to."

"I know. Some of them people don't seem hardly human. Just work from morning till night, like slaves."

"That's why I always think of this here Kettring same as them Dutchmen."

"Kettring, all of you ought to know by now, is just plumb peculiar, and that's all there is to it."

"Well, I guess it's his business, if he wants to live to himself."

"Kind-a ties up somehow with that old trouble he had with Vane Streeter. Recollect?"

"Yes, of course. Say, nobody ever did see anything of Streeter again, did they?"

"No. Just dropped out of sight like he was drownded."

"Maybe he was. Good enough riddance, too, if you ask me."

"Yeh. Streeter was no good."

"Well, there's one thing sure, Kettring's making a fine farm out of that old run-down place."

"Old man Day says Kettring's smart."

"I heard he was some kind of a professor before he came out here. Wouldn't want him teaching my kids."

"Has he still got all them signs up?"

"Yes. He won't let nobody on the place for nothing."

"Damn funny. What's he hiding?"

"If he ain't hiding anything, he acts mighty like it."

"Gives you a funny feeling about the place, don't it?"

"It's him that gives me a funny feeling. D'you ever look right into his eyes?"

"No. What about 'em?"

"Well, I don't know, exactly. His eyes are black as coal, you know. Well, when you look into his eyes, just like I'm looking in yours, you just don't see *nothing at all!*"

"Pearson, you're a damn fool!"

"Fact. What I said. He's got a might funny *blank* look."

And so here and there about the region, as men gathered and talked among themselves, a sort of legend began growing up about the name of Peter Kettring. It was not altogether a good legend. No one could blame Peter for a single breach of law or custom. It was just that there was something about the man that disconcerted people, made them a little ill at ease, and sometimes made them avoid that "blank look" in his eyes. Peter was not unaware of this. On his rare visits to town he went straight about his errands and did not stop for a social word with anyone. But he felt rather than saw the looks directed against him, and knew by some sense other than hearing that whispers and low-voiced comments passed from one man to another behind his back.

Once or twice he wondered if the whole nightmarish atmosphere of these visits to town could not be dispelled. Perhaps if he walked quite naturally into a group of men and exchanged commonplace words as he saw others do—perhaps the whole tension would disappear and the half-sinister seeming that the world had would vanish. But he was unable to force himself to that step. He was too proud, too shy.

Peter began to realize his own solitariness. This was what he had sought, but he had not counted on having it thrust upon him. Solitariness was loneliness, and loneliness of this kind had a bitter flavor. But, he said to himself, there was something proud in a lonely thing—like a single tree standing on a headland. There was pride, too, in silence. He was beginning to love the deep silence of his place—a silence that was not really a silence at all, but a deep, many-voiced undertone of the world itself. Wind, and water, and leaves, and birds, and even the tiny insects crackling minutely as they sprang through the sun-baked grass.

Yes, he was alone. He began to know the part he was to play.

Many times Peter would pause for a moment on the height where his house stood to look down across the fields and over the river, and back again to the hills behind him. He had seen it as a mighty amphitheater, and now he began to see himself as the actor in some sort of epic drama. He would stand motionless for these few seconds, great and rugged and grim, an unconsciously tragic and impressive figure.

Savina's son was born after a night of frightful labor. Lena Janek laid the baby, washed and warmly wrapped, in the curve of Savina's arm. She smiled her fine, big smile at the weary woman lying wax white in the great black-walnut bed.

"Now," she said, "there you have your boy."

Savina's eyes turned to the strange screwed-up little face. She tried to smile, but her lips only trembled.

Lena shook her head. "I thought maybe you are like me. But you are just a fine lady. Such a time I never see anybody have with one little baby! I go now and send your man in."

Peter came in quietly and closed the door behind him.

"Savina!" He started at the sound of his own voice.

Savina opened her eyes, strangely wide and deep in her drained and exhausted face. She indicated the baby with a look.

Peter lifted the covering with a finger. He nodded. He could think of nothing to say. He went over near the window and sat down, resting both hands on his knees. There was something he wanted to say to Savina—why was it so difficult to put it into words even in his own mind? Well, anyway, he would sit here for a while. It was far more eloquent of his elemental reaction to the birth of his son than he had any idea. He was there in an attitude of sympathy, or friendship, or some kind of devotion to what he knew he and Savina were to each other. But Savina did not see him. She did not even know he was there.

Vague images—mere shadows of thoughts crossed her mind. She would have liked to dispel them, but she could not. They came in slow procession like the endless clouds always drifting down the valley. Through the moments that dragged their ponderous weight over her she was conscious of some huge and hateful feeling. It was partly surprise—surprise that the birth of this child warm against her side should have cost so heavily. She recalled briefly a phrase of Lena's about fun. Maybe in some other way of life—maybe back there in her lost Martinsgrove, in a little neat house—maybe there everything would have been different. But here where every season and every change was violent and savage, other aspects of life were violent and savage, too.

She amended this slightly, recalling Peter's strange and fiery passion. A faint tremor shook her nerves in recollection. And then something which Savina recognized as a secret and purely feminine exaltation covered and obliterated the unease. There had been times when she was afraid of Peter, when his possession of her had seemed shameful even, that was at the beginning. Now—

Her mother's canny phrase re-echoed in her half dream. "A woman can do much with her man . . ." Was it possible that her mother meant what she herself was thinking? A tinge of embarrassment colored the thought. But a slight residue of the idea remained to be caught up a moment later in an unexpected onrush of a feeling that was part loyalty, part tenderness, and a very small part something that touched her flesh like a passing flame.

Savina's attention wavered like a spot of reflected sunlight on a blank wall. And then subtly she was aware of something indefinably comforting that was creeping along her aimless dreaming. There was something—something . . . After a long effort it came through broken and wavering images of her fancy. It was—why, yes, of course, she had not thought about it! It came to her now on the echo of Lena's words—just two words: "your boy." She had a boy, hers, to grow up and be with her, here in this house.

She was going to have someone to talk to!

And so Savina lay dreaming, and as she dreamed there was coming into being in her mind a definition of the structure of her life to be. She had not felt anything of this before. She had been painfully adrift, held only by her conventional tie to Peter—her husband. Now everything was different. Her wandering thought, finding its own way without pressure or direction from herself, began to outline a pattern. It was with a faint impact of surprise that she saw herself for a fleeting instant in the place of her own mother. Her father and her mother and herself—she had never really dissociated herself from that relationship. Now she perceived the new: Peter, herself, and her own child. He was a boy. She stirred slightly. He must have a name.

"Peter."

"Yes, Savina."

"What will we name him?"

"How do you like David?"

"David. David. It's a nice name. We will call him David."

She closed her eyes again, and felt herself sinking back into the hazy and dreamful state that was so new to her, and so delicious. Yes: Pop and Mom and herself—Savina; and now Peter and Savina —and David. The faintest curve of amusement showed on her pale lips. Peter was Pop, and she was Mom. It seemed ridiculous!

Savina's picture dreaming flowed easily, effortlessly across her half-veiled consciousness. The old order of living, from which she had never been clearly separated, showed thin and transparent. The new was strong and insistent of attention. There would be so much to do! David . . . David! He would grow fast. There would be clothes to make, and—and playthings to find for him. And sometime he would have to go to school. Maybe Peter would teach him at home. Peter was so smart, and had so much education.

Everything began to fall into place, to make an ordered sequence. She could see it happen. And everything had a meaning. She guessed she had been born just for this. And others had been born—the magnitude of her vision rolled over her like a wave. It was very wonderful to happen so to her, and that she should be a part of—of everything! But it tired her to think further. She tried to stop the quick shuttling pictures and quiet their excitement. It was enough. She would not have to think about it any more. It remained now for her to work it all out. An impatience twitched her fingers. There would be so much to do! Pretty soon, in a few days, maybe, she could be beginning. Peter would be about his great undertakings, and she would be about hers.

Now, the new place was no longer strange, nor did she give another thought to the strangeness of the country. Now, the farm had become "a place." Their place—or Peter's place as she preferred to think it now—Peter's place spread out on every side, the nice, pleasant house in the middle of it, and in the very heart of it, David!

Peter, sitting stiff and self-conscious in the chair near the window, dreamed, too, or sat half thinking, vaguely uncomfortable. He should perhaps be speaking to Savina, but still he could think of nothing to say.

A curious excitement trembled inside of him. It was a troubling excitement and he did not know what to do about it. It involved Savina, somehow, and this baby. David. David Kettring. A new person in the world, and someone so curiously and closely related to him.

He wanted to go out of doors and acquire some sort of clearness in his perspective. Already Peter was finding it easier to think out of doors. But something held him here. The thought that Savina might need him for something. It was a foolish notion. Lena was here, and Lena knew what Savina needed.

He spoke very softly. "Savina!"

There was no answer. He watched the slow rise and fall of the blanket edge folded across her chest. One of her hands lay relaxed outside the cover. It was unnatural to see Savina so still. It was almost alarming.

He called her again. But Savina's sleep was deep, she did not stir.

Peter sighed and leaned back in the chair. He had never during these months thought much about feeling "at home" in the new house. There had been such a sense of novelty about every aspect of it that being *at home* in it had not occurred to him. For the first time he thought about it, and a new consciousness of anchorage came over him. Another equally unfamiliar consciousness attached to it. It was a new realization of responsibility. Savina had remained strange to him—so much so that he would not have been greatly surprised had she vanished. Now Savina had a fresh reality. She had all at once attained place and was part of this, like the trees growing out there in the yard.

Here in this small upper room, Peter and Savina were, each in a different way, growing into an unspoken unity. Either one of them would have been a little embarrassed to have heard their set of mind so designated. But it was a loyalty to a way of life, a way of being, and it was at the core a devotion—a devotion that would remain unspoken because that was their way. All of the elemental strength of their natures went into these allegiances, but neither would ever know what the other felt. The strength of these attitudes would remain separate as two trees growing side by side, each drawing the sustenance for its different needs from the same soil, and each remaining in the essence of its being secret from the other.

Peter arose and went out of the room. In the kitchen Lena was washing dishes. He noticed that she splashed water about her much more than Savina did.

"You go out now?"

"Yes. I have to go over the place today to—"

"You go on. Don't worry about anything. Savina is all right now. In a couple of weeks she'll be around like always."

"Will you—can you stay on that long?"

"Me? Oh, yes. I stay. You see, Taska is as quiet!" She pointed to a clothesbasket where Taska lay asleep.

"What—what does your husband do without you—Michael?" Peter said the name with difficulty. This necessary familiarity with the Janeks was distasteful to him.

"Michael, he makes out fine without me. He can even get

drunk a little while I'm away." She laughed and slapped the dish-cloth vigorously around the edge of the dishpan. "You go on now. I don't need you for anything."

Peter closed the kitchen door behind him with relief. Such a loud woman! He thought gratefully of Savina's quiet presence.

He went into the barn and looked about. He half expected to find some sort of change evident. His horses stamped a little and whinnied recognition.

Peter nodded. "You want out, eh? All right."

He walked through the barnyard and observed each creature carefully. All was as usual.

Some powerful impulse to "go over the place," as he had said to Lena, moved him. He wanted to see all of it today, to look at it again. A phrase came into his mind. *Tell the trees.* Now, where did that come from? He thought about it for a moment. Some tale, or legend, maybe. Maybe there was some old custom he had heard of, associated with important events. He shook the thought aside. It was doubtless some foolishness from a book—the echo of super-stition.

But there was a curious expression in Peter's eyes when he came into the woods. He looked closely at the trees. He reached out and laid his hand on the smooth trunk of a young tulip tree growing beside the road.

It was a still, warm day. Few leaves had fallen yet but the foliage seemed thinner as if it had shrunk from the summer's strug-gle with heat and storms. A few trees were already yellow, and the flaming red points of scattered gum trees thrust up from the thick green down the slopes.

High, clear spaces between the tree groups seemed to float and to be existent in some enchanted silence and to live—Peter chose the word carefully, to live apart from the commoner life on the ground.

Through breaks in the forest he could see the warm blue over the river. The south bank was withdrawn and remote behind the thickening haze.

Indian summer.

Already there had been a full round of seasons since he had come here. He would know more about them now when they reappeared. He had one full year of experience of weather and change: the sudden spring, the savage summer, the rich, dreaming fall, and the violent winter. He told them over in his mind—the mighty seasonal cycle of this region. He felt closer kin to it today just because he had seen it make its full circle back to its beginning.

He went on slowly. Gravely, his eyes observed, noted; and with equal gravity his awareness commented to the deeps of consciousness. Peter was in full communion with the aspects of his own place. He was repeating the findings of sight and awareness to the profounder phases of himself—to a faraway part of his being which neither saw nor felt.

The ferns which were so lush in spring were curled now, and browning as by fire. The goldenrod and black-eyed sunflowers were finished. A brownish weed bore tiny tufts of purple—Indian paintbrush: Peter wondered how he knew its name.

He left the road and plunged down through the thick woods toward the fields below.

A cloud of dust drifted along the river road marking the lazy progress of a farm wagon drawn by a team of mules. From time to time the driver cracked his whip and shouted unconvincingly. There was no perceptible acceleration of pace. The cloud of dust arose evenly in the wake of the steady progress, spreading and thinning slowly in the sun.

The corn fodder stood in tufted wigwams. Fallen stalks cracked underfoot as Peter made the wide circle of the bottom. Presently he came to the eastern arm of hills which marked the boundary of his farm. He stood looking upward where the coloring trees arose terrace upon terrace toward the height. He did not say to himself that this was beautiful. Other words and other phrases came to him—the glory of the hills . . . the majesty of the heavens . . . the changing wonder of the clouds. He pondered again as he had at the name of the Indian paintbrush. Where did these phrases come from? His mind echoed often with the thundering phraseology of his father's sermons, but they were echoes only, not memories. Doubtless he had read such words as these somewhere.

Peter walked rapidly, lunging over the uneven ground, but keeping no straight course. He went here and there across his fields, aimlessly. He came presently to the sharp rise of the hills. The slope was stony and sparsely patched with stubbly grass. A little farther up the scrub oak began, and haw trees, now a dull rusty red, and then the tall fine trees. Peter scrambled uphill along a sort of gully, stone-dry now, but marked and deeply cut by the headlong rush of spring rains. He turned to look at the field below. He would have to dig a ditch. This would ruin the field unless controlled. Sitting down on a jutting rock he studied the land below and began to lay out the plan in his mind.

He had been sitting there for an hour falling more and more into reverie when he heard someone coming around the curve of the hill. Presently, a tall man came through the thicket of haw trees. Peter looked at him sharply, and with a sudden stir of annoyance. The man was carelessly dressed but he did not look like a farmer. He walked with a kind of lazy grace. Coming near, he shifted the gun he was carrying to his left arm and raised the other in a half-mocking salute.

"Mr. Kettring?"

Peter arose and nodded. He eyed the gun the other man was carrying with a pointed look of question.

"Oh, it's all right, Mr. Kettring. I'm not shooting on your premises. I read your signs." He smiled slowly. "Couldn't miss 'em."

In spite of himself, Peter smiled slightly.

"My name's Sandifer, Mr. Kettring, Kam Sandifer. My place is next to yours all the way up and down on this side. I guess I ought to apologize for not having called to see you, but we're a lazy lot over my way."

Peter bowed with a shade of courtliness. Sandifer's keen blue eyes caught the unexpected suggestion of graciousness. His eyebrows went up a trifle.

Peter spoke abruptly. "I had to post the place to keep it from being overrun by just anybody. I don't like hunting on my place."

Sandifer stood his gun against a log, and sat down. "Can't say I blame you much. Mostly we're too careless around here to notice whose land we're shooting over. But I guess all that will have to change." There was a faint regret sounding in his words.

Peter went on with a kind of insistence. "I don't like killing things, or having them killed near me."

"I see. Well, well!"

Sandifer took a corncob pipe from his pocket, tapped it on his shoe, ran a stiff straw through the stem, all with the greatest deliberation. He filled it, tamping in the tobacco with exaggerated care, and lighted it. Then he darted an amused glance at Peter who was still standing. Peter wished to say to Kam Sandifer that no intruders were expected on these acres. But Sandifer's easy assumption of a right to be there disconcerted him.

Sandifer held out the small cloth bag of tobacco. "Smoke?"

"No—thank you."

Sandifer returned the tobacco to his pocket, savored the smoke from his pipe, and settled back, clasping his long thin hands about a raised knee.

"Sit down, sit down, man. I came over to talk to you."

Peter flushed a little as he realized that he had been more than rude. He sat down abruptly, and took off his heavy felt hat.

"Thank you, Mr. Sandifer—"

"Everybody calls me Kam. My father is Mr. Sandifer."

Peter smiled, more easily this time. "You—you see, I don't know anybody in the neighborhood."

"Ye-es. Well, you'll get acquainted. I guess this part of the country is slow taking in strangers."

Peter frowned quickly. The remark nettled him. "I haven't made an effort to be acquainted. In fact, I settled here with the idea of being to myself—very much to myself."

Sandifer nodded. "That's pointed enough, Mr. Kettring. I guess I ought to be going on."

"I don't mean you. I'm speaking generally. I—well, I suppose I don't take kindly to the idea that I'm waiting, or supposed to be waiting, on any kind of acceptance. I'm not waiting, and I don't want it."

Sandifer made more ado with his pipe. "Well, Mr. Kettring, I don't guess anybody's going to thrust themselves on you, but it's pretty hard to live in the open country like this and not be a little neighborly."

Peter looked straight at Sandifer who instantly caught the import of the look.

"Yes, I know. It doesn't look like I've been in a hurry to be neighborly either, does it? Well now—but first, let's get straight on this. If you'd rather, I'll just get up and take myself home!"

"Certainly not, Mr. Sandifer—"

"Everybody calls me Kam."

Peter was silent for a moment, then he said gently, " My name is Peter."

Sandifer nodded. A look of interest in his eye deepened. Certainly this was not the kind of man he had expected to find.

"To tell you the truth—Peter—I've been hearing tales about you."

Peter looked sideways at his neighbor. "Yes?"

"My God, yes! Whole countryside's been talking about you."

"I'm not sure I feel honored. From what I've seen of the countryside, excepting you, I'm not particularly interested in them one way or another."

Sandifer laughed. "Some are all right. There's white trash wherever you go, Peter, and a lot of it seems to settle in river bottoms." He laughed. "Now for God's sake, I don't mean you. You're too touchy, man, for your own good."

"Maybe."

"I'm just not going to be offended, Peter Kettring. I came down here to pay a neighborly visit, and I'll be damned if I don't be neighborly, if it takes all day!"

Peter laughed. "I'm glad to see you." He could not yet make himself say Sandifer's first name.

"Well, that's something. Now, listen, you must know the whole damn region's been talking about you."

"No, I didn't know it."

"Not even after Vane Streeter?"

"I suppose some people think I killed Streeter. I didn't."

"No? I'm almost sorry. I hoped you, or somebody, had."

"I would have, probably, if I had found him while I was mad."

"You had cause. He's skipped out, I guess, for good. But I thought you didn't like killing."

"I don't. I—I had too much of it."

"The war?"

Peter nodded.

"I knew you'd been in the army. Were you in—in the thick of it?"

"Yes, in the thick of it."

"I had a little touch of it myself. Not much. Must say I didn't like it. Can't say I ever killed anybody." He laughed. "Never got close enough to see!"

"That's something else—the main thing—you people out here have against me."

"I haven't. Don't give a damn where you come from. If you're a good neighbor, that's all I care about."

"I mean no harm to anyone. I want to be let alone."

"Anybody doing anything to you—say, except me at the moment?"

Peter found himself relaxing further each time Kam Sandifer made these mock-rueful remarks.

"No. Nobody's bothering me—yet."

"Well, anyhow, your land is here, and mine is there. We're likely to have problems enough in common. I'm late making the first visit. My wife'll be over one of these days to see Mrs. Kettring, but she's always just having a baby, or getting over having one. We've got three. Been married four years. You haven't any children, I believe."

"One."

"Oh, is that so? Boy or girl?"

"Boy."

"How old is he?"

Peter grinned fleetingly. "About six hours."

"You mean—born today?"

"This morning early."

"You've got somebody with your wife, of course?"

"Yes. The Janek woman."

"Who's that?"

"Bohemian couple down the road."

"I see. Don't know 'em. Well, I congratulate you." Sandifer leaned over and shook Peter's hand heartily. "That's fine."

Sandifer knocked the ashes from his pipe, refilled it, and smoked meditatively.

"You ought to smoke, Kettring. It's a help."

"I smoked in the army. But—I quit."

"That so? Didn't like it?"

"Well—I guess I had to shed everything that reminded me."

"I see." Sandifer looked intently at the blue smoke curling away in the still air. This man had been hard hit by something.

"Don't mind my asking you all these questions, do you?"

"Not at all."

"Well, then, tell me something 'bout yourself. You're from Pennsylvania?"

"Philadelphia."

"Oh. But you're a farmer."

"Just starting to be. I taught school after the war, and saw a good deal of farms in Martinsgrove—that's where I taught."

"Well, I'll be damned. Say, you're going to have too big a job on your hands with all this place you got."

In a little while Peter found himself telling Kam Sandifer a good deal. Sandifer listened with interest, and with deepening understanding and sympathy, but Peter did not know that. Peter talked on and on, unaware that this meeting with Sandifer was answering a hungry need in his nature. He plaited stalks of tall shiny grass into a chain as he talked. He was more than half talking to himself.

". . . I can see that a man might want to strip himself of all the useless encrustations of custom and habits, and try to get himself down to essential man—just the simple, uncomplicated man that in his innermost nature he might be.

"I found out in the army that we can exist without nearly all of the things we are used to and which we think are necessary to our lives. You move without anything but what you can carry. There's a terrible side to that. You get beastly. You get dirty. You become a thief and a robber. You're nearly a wild animal but without the clean simple nature of an animal. But on the other hand, shedding all that is false and artificial is a good thing. It's like a fresh start—"

"In the garden of Eden!" Sandifer's eyes twinkled.

Peter wasn't sure for a moment if Sandifer was making fun of him or not. He went on after a moment's hesitation.

"I believe people need to start over—every so often."

"Well, Peter, I think they do—in a way. Not so drastically as you suggest. All the pioneer movement. People leave a way of life and go out and rough it. They shed a lot of custom and habit, too, when they do that."

"I'm talking about something much deeper than that. The pioneers shed some—er—physical habits of behavior, but inside they are the same. What they really tried to do, and did, was reconstruct another world as nearly like the one they left as they possibly could."

"I don't see that people could do anything else, much. You try to keep the good, and leave out the—the unsatisfactory."

"No, no. I mean—well, ideas and words—the whole more or less abstract world that exists only in words. We're really governed by that world."

"Of course. Good thing, too. Obvious as all get out, Peter. You're word spinning yourself, right now."

Peter winced. "I hope not." He sounded discouraged.

"Go on, go on; I'm interested."

Peter looked somewhat deflated. The unconscious enthusiasm went out of his manner. "I guess I mean just start over, but more basically, more fundamentally than is—is usual."

"What for?"

Peter hesitated.

"Lord, man! You can't throw away what your grandfathers learned—"

"That's just it! They learned and believed so many things that are not so."

"For instance."

"Religion—largely."

"H'm. Atheist?"

"I think I am."

"I am, too, in a way, but I don't think it's a good thing."

"Why not?"

"Like Santa Claus for children."

"Do we have to make a world for grown-up children who haven't enough bowels to live in the hope and expectation of finding—er—"

"Well—finding what?"

"Reality."

"Not very good at philosophy, are you, Peter?" Sandifer grinned happily. He was enjoying this talk. Kind of talk that never got one anywhere, but a relief from cows and crops.

"I've read a lot of philosophy, but I have to reject most," Peter continued. "All the theological stuff."

"Don't know any theological stuff myself. Read a Presbyterian book on predestination once—written by a fellow in Kings Row—professor of something or other at Aberdeen College. Very amusing."

"Amusing?"

"Sure. Just made up, you know. That kind of a venture into a —well, I guess you'd have to call it a philosophy which extends all over fields of ethics and history, and so forth—why, the universe is too complicated for any man to lay a pattern on it."

"That's what I mean, in a way. I think, though, the universe is just too simple for the patterns philosophers and theologians invent."

"I never feel that all that has much to do with us—really."

"Oh, but you're mistaken. It gets to where it has a lot to do with us, and it shouldn't."

"Peter, I went to college, but I'm not really a thinking man a-tall, I'm just a kind of farmer fellow—so long as I can get somebody to do the work for me. I've kind of lost the thread of what we began talking about. I gather that all this is important to you in a way that I don't understand. It's got something to do with your life. Right?"

"Yes."

"Try again. I'd like to understand."

"I want to—listen, er—"

"Kam's the name, Peter."

"Well, Kam, then. When I saw so much blood, and misery, and destruction during the war, and hate—"

"Shucks, Peter. There are a lot of things a man has to hate. It's a pleasure!"

"No, I mean the senseless, corroding hate that's just worked up with—with words."

"Like what?"

"I never hated a Southerner. Never cared whether he had slaves or not. Black people were remote and incomprehensible. But I got all worked up back there, and I started shooting with a kind of religious fervor. Can you imagine anything more senseless?"

"Pretty senseless, in a way. I kind of think we had more reason for shooting than you did."

"Maybe. But that—not just the war—but all the kind of life I think of my ancestors living just doesn't seem good to me."

"Queer talk for a preacher's son."

"When I saw the Pennsylvania German farmers at work it seemed to me they were living and—*creating* as men ought to."

"I know some of those Dutchmen. There's a colony almost, up the river."

"I didn't know that."

"They seem—well, I don't understand them a-tall."

"My wife is a Pennsylvania German farmer's daughter."

"Oh, is that so? You know I *did* hear that Mrs. Kettring is a foreigner. That's what they meant."

"She doesn't know English."

"You don't say so? Where is she from?"

"She's American. Lots of those people have never learned English."

Sandifer stared. "Well, I'll be darned."

Peter scarcely noticed Sandifer's astonishment.

"Do you speak German?—well, of course, I guess you must."

"I was trained as a linguist."

"And you want to be a farmer?"

"It isn't just being a farmer that I want—"

"What then? That's what you're at, anyhow."

"I guess I'd have to say I want to be *making* something, creating something, a whole life and everything that goes with it—"

"Adam in his garden, and Robinson Crusoe on his island—all at once!"

Peter glanced quickly at Sandifer, then away. He was pleased with the description.

"To remake one's world from the bottom up," he said dreamily.

"Ambitious idea—fatiguing to think about."

Peter scarcely noticed Sandifer's remark. "That's why it has to be done in a new place," he went on. "Maybe that's why I had to come away from the East. I hadn't thought of it just that way. But —old ideas, the hampering accretions of time—these are the disadvantages of old places. Thinking and living crystallize into forms, get written into books—"

"You hate books, don't you?"

"In a way—"

"Why? Are you clear about that?"

Peter hesitated. "I may not be clear, but I'm convinced."

"But, my dear man, the best that man has ever done, or thought—"

"Yes, I know all of that! The worst, too. And the worst has a wider control."

"You couldn't prove it!"

"Look at the state of the world. From time to time, certain people have to go away and begin again. I'm not recommending the idea for everyone—or anyone. I don't care what other people do. I'm not a philosopher, not a guide for anyone. For me, this is the way I want it."

"Ever read Henry Thoreau?"

"Yes. Humbug!"

"Oh, now."

"Contemplation's not enough. A man has got to create and build."

"First thing you know he's writing some more books!"

Peter's fervor subsided. He nearly laughed.

Kam Sandifer saw this. Damn it, he thought, he ought to laugh. He's too young for all this solemn talk. He looked narrowly at Peter. This huge fellow with his set jaw was a boy hiding behind an exterior that was just a little Byronic. A little less ferocity of expression and he'd be handsome in quite a grand manner.

Sandifer was amused again. Peter was so terribly in earnest, his eyes might be those of a fanatic—or a prophet. He sat very still now, looking away toward the river. His fine big hands were turned palm downward as he folded the long stems of grass over and over in a tight woven chain.

Sandifer remembered hearing his father say that a man's eyes tell what he feels, but that his hands tell what he is going to do about it. If I'm a judge, and these are an index, Sandifer thought, he'll keep his own counsel and do whatever he damn pleases.

The talk ambled on until nearly noon. Peter had never before spoken so much to anyone. Even in uttering words about his attitude to his projected world, and his feelings about his world as it now existed, his sense of injury struck deeper than it ever had.

Sandifer felt the incongruity of so much bitterness in so young a man who had after all been remarkably fortunate; but he saw also that Peter had been hurt, and that he would have to make a slow and solitary recovery. The injury might be obscure and it might be more than half imaginary, but he believed that Peter had instinctively chosen a sound and feasible way to accomplish the cure. Sandifer was a kind man, and just now his resolution to be a friend to Peter was warm in his heart. But Sandifer was also a lazy man, and Peter was shy.

It so happened that six months or more passed before the two actually met again. But in the meantime Sandifer had a word to say for Peter wherever occasion offered. Peter, knowing nothing of this, went about cherishing a sentiment of liking, and an assurance that over the hill was a man who was really friendly on grounds that were important and of consequence.

Peter regarded Sandifer with a kind of mild amazement. Sandifer had found a way through life, a simple, direct, sunny road, and yet he talked lightly and casually of the same factors of life which puzzled and depressed Peter. For the Janeks Peter had a not dissimilar astonishment. Their lighthearted response to the world and everything in it was more than acceptance—it was a joyous embracing of the whole round of experience from weather to the joys of the flesh. The latter they discussed with frankness and with a gusto that must in itself have redoubled all such pleasures.

The Janeks, unmindful of Peter's reluctance to have anything to do with them, came frequently. They accepted Peter's dark reticence as a personal peculiarity. They appeared again and again as cheerfully as before, offered advice, and talked with a high indifference to any lack of response.

The Janeks' Taska grew and developed with the precocious independence of pure peasant stock. David looked like a secretive child before he was a year old. As a mere baby sitting in his crib he wore a preternatural look of wariness—almost of guile, Peter thought with a faint amusement.

Peter did not pay much attention to David. A child, in his mind, was a mother's affair. This coincided precisely with Savina's tenets and traditions, and so David's first years passed without the usual parental conferences and discussions.

As David began to talk, Savina realized belatedly that she must know English.

"Peter, you see, David begins to talk a lot now."

"Yes. So he does."

"But in German."

Peter stared for a moment. Of course. He hadn't noticed it particularly or thought of it as being unusual.

"And such a funny mixture, Peter, of your German and mine."

Peter nodded.

"Of course I can speak better German, too, like I learned in school, but it is not easy, and besides he must have English."

"Yes. Yes, of course."

"I must learn English. You will have to teach me."

"But I have no time for such—"

"You must speak English to me now, always. I will try to understand. And, you know there are those big boxes of books in the attic. All your books which we have never unpacked."

Peter shrugged with a look of annoyance. "They would do you no good at all."

"Anyway, someday I want them in shelves. They will look nice."

"You will have to have some books, I guess, of some kind."

"Maybe books like little children have in school—in English."

Peter looked at her for a long moment. He was surprised at the sensible suggestion. "Of course. I'll get you the regular schoolbooks."

"I think maybe I can make out pretty well myself. If you'll do that—and talk to me always in English. The *Janekie,* she talks already very well in English, doesn't she?"

"I hadn't noticed. You'll learn. You're smart, Savina."

Savina reddened. It was strange to hear praise from Peter.

"I want my David to be like other children." She spoke a little stiffly. Savina, like all of her people, became tongue-tied whenever she came upon emotional grounds.

Savina had already given up any notion of becoming any part of this river-country life herself. She was resigned to the routine of her working life on the farm. This seemed entirely right to her. In itself it was everything. She had met Mrs. Sandifer in St.

Stephens one day but the bar of language kept them effectively apart. Lena Janek, for the time, supplied all necessary incident and variety.

Letters from the East were rare, and were written to Peter in English by the schoolteacher. Savina's parents already were dim in her mind. She was nevertheless unprepared for her mother's death which occurred when David was two. A few months later her father died. Savina wept a good deal in secret, but felt it unseemly to speak much of what she felt. Peter attended to the correspondence, settling the estate. Savina named certain household effects which she wished sent on to Missouri.

It was not long after this that Kam Sandifer met Peter in Kings Row.

"Just the man I want to see!" He took Peter by the arm. "Come on over to the courthouse. We can sit in the shade. I want to talk to you about a business matter."

"Business? With me?"

"Yes. Have you got any money?"

Peter was too astonished to answer. He wondered if he had heard aright.

"I mean loose money, lying in the bank."

Peter decided that his neighbor was in trouble and wished to borrow.

"Yes. A little."

"It's this, Peter. Here's this new railroad going to run down to Dawson's Point."

"Are they building on it already?"

"Yes; and it's going to change a lot of things."

"I suppose so." Peter sighed with regret.

"There'll be chances to make money. Tell you what I'm going to do. I'm going to buy land up in here—between here and Camperville."

"Farms?"

"*Coal.* This railroad opens things up. There's better coal land over around Camperville than here, but there'll be a road into Camperville, too, before long. If you've got any money to spare, you better buy, too. You could be a rich man without turning a hand."

"I don't know anything about coal land—"

Sandifer was not listening. "I've been talking to a smart lawyer here, Colonel Skeffington. He's got a partner, Bud Montcastle, who knows every foot of land in four counties around here. I'll put you in on some of this if you want me to."

"Well, I just don't know—" Peter was bewildered and did not know what to say. It seemed to him that everyone conspired to lead him away from his seclusion. He wished he had not come to Kings Row today.

"I tell you, Kettring, I'm coming up here next week again. You go home and talk it over with your wife. Then you can see me and tell me what you want to do."

"I haven't any head for this kind of thing; I wouldn't know what I was doing."

"Well—I won't lead you in too deep. That's what I'm going to do anyhow. Think it over."

The phrase "talk it over with your wife" echoed oddly in Peter's mind after Sandifer had gone. He had never talked anything over with her. But this would be different. A thought struck him. There was Savina's money—the proceeds of the sale of the Umholz farm. A good sum.

The next day when he reached home he told her of his talk with Sandifer. She was busy with supper, and went briskly from the cupboard to the table, and from the table to the stove. She seemed scarcely to listen.

"Well, what do you think?" he asked finally.

"Me?" She stopped in surprise. "What do I think? Why, how should I know?"

"I mean this, Savina. It seems a good investment, but it's your money."

She stopped midway of the kitchen and looked at him with blank surprise. "What money is my money?"

"From your father's farm. It's a lot of money."

"It was a good farm." She returned to the stove.

"But it's yours. I wouldn't have, maybe, enough to buy much land up there, I've put about everything into this place. I wouldn't want to run a risk unless you think—"

"Peter Kettring, I never heard such foolishness! Am I the man in this house?"

Peter half laughed. "Now, Savina—"

"That I should bother my head with such things! I have enough to do without such worries as what to buy or not buy."

"But it's *your* money!"

She stopped again. "I have no money. You are the man."

"But a woman can have property, you know!" Peter laughed.

"If she has no man of her own, then I guess a woman has to look out for herself. When she has a man—*no*."

"Because you're married doesn't mean you don't or can't *own* anything, Savina."

"Listen, Peter. A married woman—she owns maybe her clothes, or her special chests. But it is her right that her man should own things and be responsible. I would be ashamed if my man couldn't look after property and money, that he should come running to me to ask what about this, and whether that! Think now!"

And the discussion got no farther. Peter ended by buying land near Camperville, and smaller tracts near Kings Row. Sometimes he wondered if he had been foolish. Money in the bank was safe. He was troubled that he had allowed himself to be talked into doing something he knew little about. He disliked the entanglements with so many people. But all together it proved simpler than he had anticipated.

By the time the railroad from Camperville to Dawson's Point was completed, the lands he and Sandifer had bought greatly increased in value. But Sandifer advised holding on for an indefinite period. The county was going to see better and better times, he insisted.

3

Life began to change rapidly along the river with the coming of railroads. Many new people came to Dawson's Point and St.

Stephens. There were new subjects to think about and to talk about so that gradually Peter Kettring and his eccentricities faded somewhat from public attention.

The farm itself was pointed out as an object lesson. This was what you could do with a farm in the river bottom "if you had the git-up-'n'-git" to do it. It was a shame and a disgrace, many people agreed, that it took an Easterner to do it. The river-bottom people were all lazy, they said, each one feeling as he made the accusation that thereby he excused himself.

Peter Kettring's corn was taller than anybody's and produced more bushels to the acre. His watermelons were the biggest and the sweetest. His cattle had a groomed look, and the butter from Kettring's brought five cents more a pound than any other.

Peter had as little to do with the town as possible. He delivered butter and eggs and other produce from the place, ordered what he wished in a peremptory tone of voice, and passed along the streets speaking only when he was spoken to first. The people of St. Stephens disliked him. The tales that had been told long ago had become set into a belief with the passage of the years.

Passers-by saw him plowing and working on Sundays as on any other day. Neither he nor Savina went to church. The big white house on the hill always had its curtains drawn and its twin front doors closed. It had become something of a mystery house.

Peter sometimes asked himself as he hurried through his daily round of heavy work, if he had found the things he had sought. He was not sure that he could give himself an answer. He had sought seclusion, but he had not planned to have it thrust upon him by a hostile neighborhood. He had sought seclusion: yes, but he had not expected loneliness. And there were times when this loneliness was harsh and weighed upon him like a garment of iron.

He had wished for an exaggerated kind of privacy—perhaps only in so far as he might have protection while he found a new path for himself; he had not expected isolation. But when he found that loneliness and isolation had come upon him, he did not move to change the conditions. He met them with pride and disdain.

There were times when he half welcomed Michael Janek, and

other times when he wished mightily to see Kam Sandifer, but there were always unfinished projects and the endless complication of chores, varying only with the seasons. He undertook more work than any two men in the region, and accomplished it through fierce stubbornness—a stubbornness that was like a defiance. Every object and every animal on the farm seemed a kind of challenge, and Peter arose every hour to that challenge, working with a speed and an intensity that reminded Savina again and again of her father's relentless and almost senseless fury of endeavor.

Savina did not ask questions of herself. She was too busy, and besides everything seemed simple and without the need of either question or answer.

She understood what she had to do and did it thoroughly. She, too, accomplished an incredible amount of work.

Little David grew rapidly. He promised to be large-framed and strong like Peter. From the time he was two years of age he developed a strong attachment to his father. He followed him as best he could, imitated him, and was miserable when kept in the house. At the age of five he was an amusing small double of his father in looks and action. Just after David's fifth birthday Savina bore a second son. He was named Robert but Savina called him Robby from the beginning.

That fall a small schoolhouse was built a half mile below the Sandifer farm, and David went to school there. Each morning he waited on the river road until Taska Janek joined him. Savina often watched from her front window until the two children were out of sight.

David Kettring was a lean, darkish boy, with a thick brush of hair always falling across his brow. His eyes were deep and appeared black, but as light struck into them they showed an almost reddish brown. He talked a good deal, his intonation and accent an exact echo of Peter's fine, careful English. In company he was quiet and watchful as if he, too, had something of his father's suspicion of people. But this air vanished instantly when he spoke. A quick, rather foreign sort of vivacity was tempered only by the child's precocious earnestness.

David was an interesting contrast to Taska Janek. Taska was as warm and richly colored as a late summer peach. Her skin was velvety, her braided hair heavy and brown, her eyes as bright and keen, for all their liquid beauty, as her mother's. She was a chubby, solid little girl, enormously vital and healthy. Her laugh was nearly constant as if an inextinguishable comedy played always before her sight.

It was a curious friendship in these small children because it was so established and secure, as if long community of interest and understanding bound them together. Often during the school day some incident sent them into simultaneous giggling fits. Often they exchanged their comments on the playlot behind the school in their dissimilar German dialects to the discomfiture of other children.

They lived in a small private world of extremely free exchange. Even at that early age Taska had her mother's frankness of speech. What she thought she said, and in the fewest words of direct import.

Year by year this intimate companionship grew. David took on something of Taska's utter lack of reticence, but this was only in his association with Taska herself. With other children, and at home, he was uncommunicative.

David continued to stay as near to his father as possible while he was at home. He began to have small tasks assigned him, gathering the eggs from the chicken house and from the stray nests about the barn, feeding the young turkeys in late spring, and helping to carry the milk crocks to the cellar. He prepared his lessons without help. Savina was always eager in her inquiries about his progress, but Peter took it as a matter of course that David should learn quickly and well.

In the summer David saw little of Taska aside from rare Sunday visits, but each September they resumed their companionship as if it had not been interrupted.

When they were ten they were somehow aware of their own attachment. They knew it was out of the ordinary. The children at school teased and called them sweethearts. This they accepted as a fact. They were aware of the significance of being boy and girl.

On this ground they had made material comparisons and drawn conclusions. Any authentic information about such recondite matters was furnished by Taska who found out anything she wished to know by the simple expedient of asking her mother.

David and Taska settled some of these questions and thereafter said no more about them.

David, more thoughtful than Taska, did dwell from time to time on the hours spent on the road to and from school. It seemed to him that the very happiest part of his life existed just there, on that stretch of the river road from his gate to the little schoolhouse set back in the grove of tall sycamores a half mile away. It was a very special world, with just the two of them in it, and all of its aspects and all allusions to it were the special and secret property of Taska and himself.

These were good years. The farm prospered. Peter and Savina worked hard from early morning until full dark. Nothing happened in the valley or in the town to make any apparent break in the even progress of the times.

But Michael Janek shook his head. "Things don't go so good with Peter Kettring." He made the remark to Lena one Sunday evening as they were returning from a visit to the Kettrings'.

"What in the world do you mean by that?"

Michael shook his head again. "I can see it," he said.

"You can see what, now?"

"I just told you. I think things don't go so good with that Peter."

Lena laughed impatiently. "You!"

"It's so."

"So? Peter Kettring has a big farm, all paid for. He has a nice, hard-working wife—healthy, too; children growing up. He has the best crops anywhere around. He has luck like the devil himself, and you say things don't go so good. I could wish they would be that bad by us."

"We got it better."

"Yes?" Lena made scornful sounds, but she looked covertly at her husband. He had a way of being right about things she never noticed. "Yes? Well, what is it then?"

Michael took his pipe from his mouth and pointed with the stem as if the subject of the discussion stood before him. "This Peter, now, he hasn't got just what he wants."

"That I have such a fool for a husband!"

"No. I am not a fool. It is that you can never see anything until you fall over it."

"So." Lena plodded along. She knew that Michael would say what he had to say in his own way. It might take half an hour for him to get it said, or it might require days. Michael would drop fragments of his thoughts, disconnected, apparently unrelated to the subject. The listener would have to piece these observations together as best he could. It was Michael's way. He felt things—he received impressions in many ways, and it mystified him that Lena did not understand him without all of this talk which was so hard to put in order.

Lena did understand him better than he knew. But she was a clear-eyed realist, and she liked to have things expressed in small, hard, concrete words. She would call Michael a fool, and declare him a nuisance with his imaginings, but she had a secret respect for his intuitions, and she was overcome with curiosity whenever he began one of his disjointed revelations.

Michael pointed again with his pipe stem at the invisible presentment of Peter. "Yes, it is indeed so. It is very plain."

Lena quickened her step through irritation. "You are just like the peasants in the old country. You never can say anything straight out and have done with it."

Michael opened his eyes very wide. "Now what is this about peasants? Of course I am like a peasant. I am one. So are you. What—"

"What about Peter?"

"Peter, yes. I have seen the like before in the old country, and I have heard my father talk much of people. It is the way Peter is with his land."

"As far as I can see, he works with his land like anybody else—only harder."

"No, it is not that. I work hard, too, but I do not fight with my place."

"There you go. That's peasant talk again about land. You would think a landsman was made out of soil."

"He is. We all are. You are mistaken about the way a peasant is to his land. It stands so in the books, I have read it, but I do not believe the landsman loves his land that way. It is a poetry that is made about us by people who would like to feel we belong underfoot."

"What, in God's name, are you about?"

"Just what I say. I would rather do something else than work in the field."

"So? Maybe you would like to be a lawyer and sit in an office!"

"Yes. I would like that, but since I have not that education, I work in my field. But it is you now that runs away from the subject. We talk of Peter. When you must work with the soil, and that is your lot in this world, then you be friends with the soil. It must be so. If you fight with it, it strikes back."

"Michael, maybe you know what you say. I don't understand one word of this. The land it strikes back! What is that?"

"Well, as with me, Lena. I take certain things easy—"

"Too easy."

"Keep still, while I explain."

Lena laughed. "And I shall sleep on my feet before you come to the end."

"You, Lena, you have seen those other farmers, those Dutchmen who live above St. Stephens on the way to Camperville. They fight with the land, some of them. By and by each one becomes no more than a handle to a hoe."

Lena made no reply.

"It is something like this with Peter. He becomes set toward everything and everybody and that is to be hard, and when one is hard all over like that, nothing comes out of the heart any more, and nothing goes in." Michael held out his hand, palm upward. "The hand becomes hard, but the heart should never be so."

"How does one prevent that? I suppose you are so wise you know that, too."

"Of course. My hands struggle always with things, with tools and with animals, with wood and stone, but I keep the heart to its own work."

Lena regarded him with a strange mingling of tenderness and irritation.

"The work of the heart, Lena, is to thank God, and maybe to sing to itself about—"

"About what?"

Michael made great ado with his pipe, knocking out the ash and refilling it. He looked a little sheepish.

"About what?" she repeated.

"To sing to itself, maybe about you, sometimes, and Taska, and the good seasons passing over our heads."

Lena took a deep breath. "You, now!" she said gently.

Kam Sandifer also concerned himself somewhat about Peter. In his easygoing fashion, he was given to rather extended musings about anything that came of itself across the field of his attention. Underneath he had considerable curiosity, but he was too lazy to grant much play to it. Consideration of his neighbor's behavior became a sort of pastime.

Driving down from Kings Row one day with Dawson, Peter passed them in his shiny spring wagon. As usual his big gray horses were tearing along at high speed. Peter half raised his hand in greeting. Dawson grunted to himself, whether in question or disapproval it would have been hard to say. He slapped the lines on the fat back of his plodding horse.

"How are you and—and that Kettring fellow making out on your investments up here, Kam?"

"Oh, fine. Good as we could have expected. Better."

"How do you get on with him?"

"Perfectly. Why?"

"Nobody else seems to be able to get on with him a-tall."

"Nobody tries, I guess."

"Well, damn it all, Kam, it oughtn't to be so hard to get on with a fellow."

"Doesn't seem to me Peter Kettring asks anybody to get on with him."

"Yeh. That's so. Damn queer sort of a man, though. Say, he's really well fixed, isn't he?"

"Yes. He's made a go of his place. Done a lot better with his than I have with mine. At it all the time. Early morning till night. It's not worth it. Life's short."

"What does a man like that get out of life anyway, Kam?"

"Damned if I know. I suppose he gets what he wants—maybe."

"Well, what does he want?"

"That's hard to answer. I think Kettring is different from most of us—quite different."

"Looks to me like he's got something on his mind."

"If you mean a deep, troubling secret, you're wrong. But I do think he has something on his mind, as you say. He talked to me pretty freely once or twice. He came out here looking for something—some deep satisfaction that he couldn't find where he came from. I guess we're all doing the same thing to some degree."

Dawson nodded. He was a man of considerable depth and understanding.

"It's a funny thing, Dawson, but I like Peter Kettring."

"Do you, sure enough?"

"Yes, I do. But I'll be damned if I think he likes me. I don't believe he likes anybody."

"D'you know his wife?"

"No—not to say know her. Pretty as a picture, though."

"I've never so much as laid eyes on her."

"I keep on thinking about the man, though it's none of my business what he's like, or what he does. He's a good neighbor, keeps up his fences and so on."

"Yes. You know it's right funny how often the fellow pops up in conversation. Nobody seems to know anything about him but you, and still you'd swear everybody's got something against him."

"That's not right or fair. Peter never has done anything to anybody."

"Less'n it was Streeter. Remember that?"

"Nothing to it."

"Maybe not, maybe not."

"No. It's just that most people can't stand for other people to be independent."

"That's right, Kam. I've seen it a thousand times."

"Well, that's all that's the matter with Peter Kettring. Absolutely independent. Doesn't give a damn what anybody thinks about him. Plows on Sunday." Sandifer laughed. "Now how's that for something to hold against a man? You know all of us work one way or another on Sunday—"

"Except you!" Dawson laughed and slapped Sandifer on the knee.

"Yes; I don't work any day I can get out of it; but the whole river bottom talks about how terrible that fellow is. *Plows on Sunday!*"

Dawson chuckled.

Sandifer settled back in the seat and pulled his straw hat well over his eyes. The buggy creaked sleepily, and Dawson's horse trotted along with a noisy clop-clop. Sandifer was still thinking about Peter. It was a little troubling the way he felt about Peter, as if he, himself, were in some way responsible. He smiled as he realized how thoroughly Peter would resent such a feeling in anyone.

He had thought, several years ago, that Peter was just young and maybe hurt in some way and that sooner or later he would mellow and adjust himself. Solitude, and—well, just nature around one, and work in the fields had a way of taking any kind of bitterness out of a man's system. Did not look as if it were doing it in Peter's case. He did not like the look he saw in Peter's eyes at times. A keen, bright fire of some kind—like a wild man. Fanatic. That was it—fanatic. God, it must be uncomfortable to feel burnt up like that all the time! He could not imagine Peter sitting down quietly some afternoon and just looking out over the world, taking it in, and sort of dreaming about it. Too bad—some of the best moments of life came that way.

Yes, he thought, Dawson was right: Peter Kettring was peculiar as all get out. He wondered what in thunder could be out of gear in the man, anyhow. He felt impatient, even at having to think about it. The doggone fellow ought not to be that much of a bother!

Peter did stop sometimes in the fury of his driving work to look out over his place and to think. Perhaps thinking did not exactly describe it. It was rather that he gave himself up to a sort of burning. At such times he was likely to go to the hills, to the densest wooded places, where he could not be seen, and from where he could scarcely see out in any direction. It was an instinct to hide, he knew that. And he had to say to himself that he was hiding from the sight of men because such waves of misery swept over him that he could not bear to meet anyone, or have anyone see what must show in his face. When he could say this to himself he was also driven to ask in all sanity what was wrong. Why was he flung down and crushed by so strange an unhappiness? And here, alone in the woods, as on that afternoon long ago, above the valley of Martinsgrove, he was overwhelmed by what he felt. He could not define it. Here was his little kingdom, his independence—independence of body, mind, and spirit—here was that isolation he had dreamed of where everything deepest in him was to reach out and establish a mystical union with the security and simplicity of—of what? He brushed the back of his hand across hard, dry eyes—so hard in their staring and searching, so dry that the pain was physical and actual. Of what? Of what? What was it he had to reach out for? What was it he sought to touch? He did not know. He could not find it.

These moods had been coming over him more often of late. He was not even sure what it was he was trying to think about. He passed everything in his present life in review. There it was as he had wished it to be. The material objects—the things that belonged to him—these were inside a clearly perceivable boundary: they were his possessions. People were outside of that circle and, so, out of relationship to him.

He thought of Savina and the children. The boys seemed more of her than of him. David used to be with him so much. There had been something comforting in that shadowlike companionship. He wondered vaguely why it no longer existed. Of course David had lessons to attend to. He would have to have enough education to take care of himself and his property. He would see that his children had plenty—land and equipment. Soon David would have enough of school. He would give David a farm, a good one.

Savina? Apparently Savina had quite what she wished to have. He had never heard her complain since those first uneven days when she did not know how to cope with new and rude ways. He had not known either, but he had learned, and he had learned well.

Always when Peter withdrew like this to the shelter of his woods there was something that swirled about him—an invisible tempest—just beyond and outside of clear perception. It was a stinging, evil tempest that was somehow held beyond the range of injury. In it were the people of this region and the near-by towns. They did not like him. Very well; he did not like them, either. They did not need him, or speak to him. Very well; he did not need them, and he had no word for a one of them.

Today he leaned back against a tree. It was good to feel it there—his own good solid tree. He wondered why he was so tired today. Now that he thought of it he was always tired. Savina had said once—but that was long ago, two or three years ago—that he worked too hard.

Peter did not realize how deep this chronic and constitutional weariness reached. The poison of fatigue had settled little by little deep in his being. He was in a constant state of irritation. All of this spoke in the increasing harshness of his speech and manner.

He sighed deeply. Several times Kam Sandifer had suggested that he have help. That was precisely what he did not wish to have. If he was to round out the making of a little world that was to replace what he had cast off, he must make it himself. David was growing bigger and stronger every day. David would have to take over here and there.

Peter did not realize how much he had added to the regular heavy work of the place. He shod his own horses. He made hinges for his gates. In the winter he carved and put together wooden rakes. He manufactured new tools. With each small creation he felt an exultation of a separate small victory. He had won just that much more freedom. But he looked old.

Michael's description of a man becoming "the handle to a hoe" did not exactly apply to Peter. Peter was too dominant a being to be described by such a figure. But this huge place seemed to be alive with demands—it reached up and held him in the myriad throes of its needs, and against it Peter was himself the only implement for conquest and control.

These insistencies were never far below the plane of his acute attention. He used the best he had of intelligence and talent to organize his labors and direct himself to best purpose.

Now he was again in the mid-current of all their pressures. He had to arise and go down to the fields and work to make up these moments he had wasted here. He shook himself as a massive dog shakes away annoying gnats. He went almost falling downhill with a heavy, inelastic step.

Peter was thinking again about David. It would be good to have him along in the fields more often. A few more years . . .

David went uncomplainingly to school. He was careful with his lessons and his "grade card" exhibited a commendable record— much better than Taska's. Taska was indifferent about lessons.

Savina had succeeded in having Peter's books unpacked and David was beginning to be curious about them. But he felt that his father did not approve of this. Whenever he had a book in his hands Peter thought of some piece of work for him to do. Gradually an unspoken conspiracy developed: David took books to his room to read, but no mention of this passed between him and his mother when Peter was present.

The books were difficult, and for the most part incompre-

[139]

hensible, but there was an inescapable fascination in the strange pages, and David read sometimes for long stretches without understanding anything of what he read.

Once Savina asked him what he was reading.

"It's about places, a kind of history, I guess."

"Do you like it?"

"I don't know. I—I guess I don't understand much of it."

"Why do you read it, then?"

"Well, I have to read something, don't I?"

"Maybe there are some easier ones. You must look."

"I did. They're all hard."

"I tell you. I'll give you some money along and maybe sometimes you can buy some books you like."

This indefinite prospect angered David, but he said nothing.

"Would you like that, David?"

"Oh, of course."

"Well, we won't say anything about it."

"I wish Pa would tell me about what's in some of these books. He's smarter even than my teacher, but you can't make him talk."

Savina sighed. "Yes, I know. He doesn't like all that."

David considered his mother's phrase. What did she mean by "all that"? He felt that he should not ask. There seemed to be some kind of grown-up difficulty about it, and grown-up troubles were things you did not talk about.

"Pa is—is kind of funny about some things, isn't he?"

"No, David. He just has his ways." That was Savina's explanation of anything that was individual or peculiar.

"Come now, David. You're getting to be a big boy. I show you now how to make your own bed and straighten up your room. I've got so much to do."

"All right. What do you do first?"

Savina was pleased with the way David answered. He was a good boy. Always when she asked him to do anything he was quick and cheerful in his response.

She glanced at him out of the corner of her eyes as he awkwardly tried to smooth the wrinkles in the sheet. He was not a handsome boy, she decided with her habitual honesty of appraisal. But he looked like a good boy. She amended this quickly. David did not always look like a good-humored or willing person. It seemed to be when Peter spoke to him that a sort of heavy look came across his face. That was very strange, now that she thought of it. David had always been so strong for Peter—followed him everywhere, talked like him, walked like him. Just lately, maybe— yes, it had been only of late that David . . . Savina broke her meditation.

"Here, David. I show you. Put this straight across the top first, then pull the middle tight toward the bottom and fold it under. Like this—look."

"It doesn't do very good for me, does it?"

"You'll learn. Right away you will see how."

. . . What was it that made the difference? It was just the way David looked—not contrary, exactly, but certainly not as willing as he used to be. Maybe it was just the way his face was changing— the way his thick, black eyebrows grew together in a straight line across his brow. It made him look as if he were frowning all the time. She had to remind herself that Peter was a silent man—more and more so as the years went by. He had little to say about anything. It would be natural if David grew to be like that, too, since he was in many ways so much like Peter. It never occurred to Savina that there was anything to do about the way people were, and the way they behaved. It was not the custom in which she was bred to look deep into the minds of other people. The rights of self-determination and personal privacy were fiercely guarded rights. If one were peculiar, or did not get along well with others—well, that was simply a greater or less degree of misfortune. One would not be so rash as to venture any kind of reformation of an adult. She hoped that David would not be peculiar.

Savina had to rely altogether on a recollection of her mother's counsels, and upon her own common sense. She could not quite accept Lena Janek's ways, which were all, as she often said to herself, "every which a way"—easygoing at unexpected moments, swinging suddenly to extremes of loud talk and quarreling. Such a way to live!

Her attention turned back suddenly . . . She might have trouble yet with David; she would have to watch. Savina's brow drew into fine lines, faintly anxious, but her mouth, firm and girlishly pink, kept its expression of calm.

Savina went down the stairs and out to the side yard where Robby was playing. Her face changed: the tiny lines disappeared, and a faint smile touched her with transforming magic. Robby looked up and answered the smile with a shy grin. His gray-green eyes slanted upward ever so little at the corners; his blond hair was almost silver. He was tanned now, and his skin was an even goldish color. There was a deeply preoccupied air about Robby which contradicted his babyish ways. He seemed to look and to listen with an absorption that made him seem remote as very old people are withdrawn and remote from everyday disturbances.

He is my child, Savina thought, just as David is Peter's child. She loved them equally, but she felt a tenderness for Robby which David did not call forth.

"Robby," she called softly.

The child turned his eyes slowly toward her as if reluctant to abandon some vision of his own. His eyes were long, and the greenish light shining under the thick lashes seemed to add an almost audible sparkle to their natural brilliancy. He made a startling picture, sitting there with the sun glinting on his bright hair—he seemed to be naturally luminous.

"Robby."

He arose and came directly to her. She took his hand and they walked gravely toward the gate, Robby stretching his step to the utmost to match hers.

"Let's go see if the cherries are ripe enough to can, not?"

The child smiled again, a wide-mouthed smile curiously at variance with his reticent cast of countenance.

He walked with his head thrown back so that he could look at her.

"Watch now, when you're walking. You'll fall down."

He tightened his hold on her hand but he did not change the tilt of his head. They walked on down the slope into the orchard, Savina on the lookout for ripening cherries, Robby with his eyes turned upward to her face with a look of intent and rapt adoration.

David returned to the book his mother had noticed. He opened it at the place where he had carefully laid a slip of paper to mark his place, and drawing his brows into a black frown resumed his attempt at reading. After a while he looked up, blinking a little from the strain of the close print, and sighed. He went to the window and leaned his head against the frame. The river twinkled, yellow and silver—a broad speckled band of light lay directly in front of his vision, dimming a little as it passed midstream, and quieting on the undulations of the current. A faraway look came into David's eyes—his gaze followed the swift center that outran the shallows on either side. What was down there—on and on, beyond the dim waters at the distant curve? What did it look like? Who lived there? There were towns—he knew that—bigger towns than St. Stephens or Dawson's Point, and finally, there was St. Louis. But that was a city—his fancy stopped short at what St. Louis might be like—all towers and shine, likely enough, and frightening.

A lump swelled in David's breast, a hard, sickening lump. He wanted something, wanted it desperately, and he did not know what it was.

He wished . . . he wished—oh, he wished *everything,* he said to himself. One thing was clear to him: he did not wish to be here, he did not wish to help his father with the stock, or to work in the fields. He would rather—again he ran into a blank in his imaginings. What would he rather do? Surely he wasn't just lazy. That would be disgraceful! His mother said so. He had talked it over with Taska, too, and they had agreed that real, sure enough laziness was very bad. It made you like those people who lived along the river above St. Stephens. White trash, he had heard them called.

He had heard with wide-eyed wonder that his father had been a schoolteacher before he came here. How could anyone leave so exalted an occupation to work in fields? A daring thought came to him and with it a wave of relief—doubly a relief because it was a grand dream that included an aspect of loyalty to his father. His father had been a teacher! Certainly, his father must have thought it a good thing to be or he would not have done it. Why could he not be a teacher sometime? It must be wonderful to read all the difficult books and to understand them.

David sat down and opened the book again. He turned back to the first page and began to read. He said the words aloud, pronouncing them syllable by syllable, hoping that the sound might reveal their meaning. He glanced again at the title: *The Decline and Fall of the Roman Empire,* by Edward Gibbon. He said it aloud. It had a beautiful sound. He looked out of the window and repeated the words: *The Decline and Fall of the Roman Empire* . . .

When David was fourteen he finished the classes at the little schoolhouse down the road. That fall he went to school at St. Stephens. It was his turn now to start earlier and call for Taska. There had been no discussion at the Kettrings' about David continuing with his school although Savina had anticipated objections from Peter. Peter, to her surprise, seemed absent-minded about the change and only nodded as David explained it to him. But at the Janeks' there had been lively differences. Michael thought Taska had enough learning. She was a big, strong girl, he said, strong enough to relieve her mother of much, and to do some field work besides.

"Field work she shall not do." Lena was firm.

"Why not? You have no silly ideas that she is too good to work as you and your mother and all your grandmothers worked, have you?"

"It is not that. Life is different over here. She must be like the American girls. They do not work in the fields."

"The fields are the same and the necessity to live is the same."

"We live already better than our people ever did."

"Then—"

"That is why. Taska shall have much schooling."

"What would she do with it?"

"She might even teach school."

Michael was stunned. "Taska? Taska Janek teach a school?"

"Why not?"

Michael could think of no good reason. It was evident that Taska was smarter than he would have believed possible. The things she talked about already. But he felt that he must not give in too easily. He blustered for several days whenever the subject came up. Lena was practical. She related the wages earned by teachers—actual money—dollars.

But it was not the wages that convinced Michael. It was the glory. That maybe sometime his girl could teach in a school and sit in the place of authority. Ei! That would be something to write letters to the old country about. The money, that was all very fine, but he could make money himself, certainly all Taska would need. Gradually, his muttering died out, and it was not long afterward that he mentioned ever so casually in St. Stephens that he purposed training his daughter to be a schoolteacher.

David and Taska went rather shyly to St. Stephens. They expected that the children would be different, better dressed, too, and maybe would not receive them well. But the children were the same, only there were more of them.

David was attracted by two redheaded boys whom he heard addressed as Paul and Timothy. They were twins and that interested him greatly. It must be very strange, he thought, to be precisely like someone else.

They spoke to him the second morning.

"What's your name?" one of them asked.

"David Kettring."

"Where do you live?" The tone of the question was a shade insolent.

"Down the river."

"Far?"

"About two miles."

"What does your father do?"

[145]

"He's a farmer."

Both of them said, "Oh!"

David was slightly annoyed. "What's your name—your last name, I mean? I know you're Timothy and Paul."

"Nolan."

"And where do you live."

"Here in St. Stephens."

"Where's your house? Can you see it from here?"

They hesitated and both of them reddened slightly. "We live down the street there."

"What does your pa do?"

The red deepened. The twins looked at each other. "He keeps the saloon—the one that used to belong to Mr. Finley."

This time David said, "Oh." It was expressionless because he did not know what he thought about this.

"It's all right to keep a saloon." One of the twins was very red now, and looked belligerent.

David shrugged. "I don't care if you own a saloon or not."

"Well, some people look down on us because of—because Pa is a saloonkeeper."

"Some people look down on me, too, because I'm a Yankee."

"Wasn't you born here?"

"Yes. But my pa's a Yankee."

"You ain't a Yankee if you was born here."

"I'd just as soon be. It's all right to be a Yankee."

The other twin broke in. "Sure it is. I bet you don't know which one of us is Tim and which is Paul."

"No, I don't."

"Can't hardly anybody tell us apart." The boy seemed highly pleased with his.

"Well, which one of you—is which?"

"I expect it won't do any good to tell you, but I'm Paul, and he's Timothy. Everybody calls him Tim—when they know it is Tim. Look! I got bigger ears'n him. That's the way you can tell us."

Timothy had been looking across at the girls' side of the playground.

"Say, is that your sister I saw you come to school with?"

"No. She's just a neighbor."

"What's her name?"

"Taska Janek."

"Is she a foreigner?"

"Her father and mother are."

"What kind of foreigners?"

"I don't know. Just foreigners."

"They have to be some kind."

"They talk German."

"Then they're Germans, you dummy."

"So do my father and mother talk German, but they're not Germans."

"What are they, then?"

"Just Americans."

"Why don't they talk American, then?"

"*English,* not American." It was Paul correcting Tim.

"My father used to be a schoolteacher."

"Gee! Wouldn't you hate to go to school to your pa?"

"Yes, I guess I wouldn't like that."

"Are you a Catholic?"

"No."

"What are you, then?"

"Not anything, I guess. I don't go to church."

"Sure enough? That must be awful nice."

"Taska's a Catholic."

"Is she?" Timothy Nolan looked with interest at Taska who stood talking to a group of older girls.

"Gosh a' mighty, but she's a pretty girl. Is she your girl?"

David flushed. He did not know what to say.

"Well, is she?" Paul laughed, but Timothy did not.

"Why, I don't know."

"Aw, come on. Of course you know."

"Well, we're—I've always known her. I've played with her since I was little."

Paul looked wickedly at the sadly embarrassed David. "Oh! *Played with her?* And you don't know if she's your girl or not? Say!"

David's flush vanished. "Say, you shut up your mouth about Taska Janek, you hear me?"

The twins looked at each other. There was a question in Paul's eyes. Timothy shook his head. He turned to David. "He didn't mean nothing. If you like her a whole lot we won't talk that way about her."

David subsided suddenly. He realized that he had been ready to fight. He was appalled. Suppose he had gotten into a fight? Like as not they would not have let him come to school at all. Then, what would he have done?

Timothy covered the awkwardness. "What are you going to be when you grow up?"

"I don't know—yet."

"Well, I want to be a lawyer—"

"And I want to be a doctor."

"Will your pa let you be?"

"Of course, he wants us to be."

David looked respectful. "Gee, that's wonderful."

Timothy gave David a clap on the back. "I expect we're going to get on fine together. Let's—just us three—be friends and not let anybody else in."

"In what?" David was mystified.

"Into—well, whatever we're going to do. We'll get up some secrets."

It sounded marvelous to David. His heart expanded and he loved the whole world. He could hardly wait until he could tell Taska about his wonderful new friends.

It appeared, as David and Taska sauntered along the dusty road, that her day had not been remarkable. She showed little interest in the girls she had met. Yes, they were nice, but they were just girls. She was much more interested in the twins, and asked many questions.

"They're awful nice-looking boys, I think. Don't you think so, David?"

David was suddenly unhappy. He did not know for sure why, but he suspected.

"They asked a whole lot of questions about **you, too.**" He was apparently bent on making himself as miserable as possible. He had definitely planned not to tell this to Taska.

"Oh, they did? What did they ask?"

David scarcely recognized her eager, **coquettish voice.** It filled him with rage.

"They asked me your name."

"Is that all?"

"Well, that was part of it."

"What else? Go on, David, tell me."

"What do you want to know for?"

"Just 'cause."

"But what for?"

"Wouldn't you want to know what anybody said about you?"

"No. Depending on who it was, I guess."

"Well, I just want to know. Go on, tell me, please."

"You sound so silly, Taska. Like a baby."

"I don't."

"You do, too. Well, if you got to know, one of them said you were an awful pretty girl."

"Which one?"

"What good would it do for me to tell you that? You wouldn't know which was which, anyway."

"I'd like awful much to know." Taska spoke quite humbly, and David softened.

"It was Timothy."

"Timothy." She said the name dreamily, and David felt the tightness in his chest again.

"They asked me something else, too."

"What?"

"I don't know if I'll tell you that or not. It might make you mad."

"Not unless it was something not nice."

"They wanted to know first if you were my sister. And then when I said no, they—they asked me if you were my girl."

Taska stopped and looked hard at him. "What did you say?"

"I said first, I didn't know."

"What did you say that for?"

"'Cause I didn't know."

"Oh."

"Then I said you were just a friend."

Taska made no comment on this, and David felt uneasy. He kicked the dust, and threw a small flat rock far out into the river.

"Looky! That skipped five times!"

"Um!"

"Taska."

"What?"

"Then I nearly got in a fight about you."

"A *fight?* What for, David?"

"Well, Paul said something more, and I just said I'd played with you ever since we were little together."

"You didn't fight about *that,* did you?"

"We didn't fight at all."

"Well, what did you nearly fight about? You're just like your pa—nobody can get anything out of you."

"Well—he thought I meant something else when I said I'd played with you."

"Oh, he did. What did you do?"

"I was going to hit him, I guess, when Timothy said Paul didn't mean no harm."

"Timothy kept you from fighting then?"

"I guess so."

"It wasn't anything to fight about."

"Well, I guess it was, too. You're not mad, are you?"

"About what, David? For goodness sake, you are the funniest boy I ever saw."

"Mad 'cause we—'cause there was that kind of talk about you and me?"

"Gee, no, David. I wouldn't have cared if it had been so."

David stopped in his tracks. He gulped. He was sure he could not have heard her correctly. He choked so that his breath was nearly stopped.

Taska blushed red, but laughed at his embarrassment.

"Did you mean that, Taska?"

"Of course I meant it, but don't you get any idea that I'm going to, 'cause I ain't."

David could not think of a reply.

"Anyway," she added, "not for a long time. What made you tell them I wasn't your girl?"

"Well—for goodness sake, Taska—we never—"

"Next time anybody asks you, you tell them yes. You hear?"

"Of course I will. I just never—"

"Well, we're just kids. Let's stop talking about that now, only I think you ought to kiss me."

David's eyes widened and the look of embarrassment vanished. He dropped his books and took her by the arms. Then he kissed her slowly and solemnly.

"Now, you are my girl, and I'll tell anybody so that asks me."

"Look, David, we better hurry—the sun is nearly down. My goodness!"

When David left Taska at her gate he went stumbling along the road, his brain in a whirling confusion. It was not Taska who was responsible for this—not just Taska, he told himself, though he felt that she might henceforth be a troubling part of his already troubled mind. David knew that he had to make up his mind about many things, but it was not all clear to him what these things were. He knew that he wanted something out of his life—something that was not now in prospect.

He had often heard a phrase used in disparagement of some "no account" person: he doesn't know what he wants. He knew that those words exactly described his own state of mind. Teachers

were always talking about "making something out of yourself."
He had heard his mother say it, too.

He went more and more slowly along the road, falling deeper
and deeper into his restless musing.

He supposed one had to choose something and set that as a
mark. In that way, for instance, the twins were far ahead of him.
They knew what they wanted to be.

But David had no real basis from which to make a choice. He
had never heard anybody talk about the world and what people did,
or how they happened to become whatever it was they wished to be.
He had never heard anything, he thought with a surge of bitterness.
His father would not talk about things, and—his mind balked a little
at the first critical appraisal he had ever made, or felt, about his
mother. But, all the same, she did not seem to know very much,
except just about the farm, and about chickens and such things.

He was shut in, and he wanted passionately to see out.

Turning slowly he looked up and down the valley, across the
river, and back again to the long line of hills ranged in a forbidding
barrier. He felt very small, moving in the vast flat land closed off
here by the river and there by the hills. The only thing he could see
was more of just what was immediately about him. If he could only
stretch up—high—so that he could see out!

There was Taska, too. Taska understood a lot of things. She was
barely a year older than he but he felt that it made a great difference. Taska would stand by a fellow through thick and thin. But
for all that, she was just a girl and he was not sure that what he felt
had anything to do with her. This—this terrible *wishing* that was
in him, strong as—as the river itself—out there where the mid-
current carried everything along with it.

The river. It was always going somewhere—laughing and talking to itself, following its own way out. Way out! Yes—there it was,
on its bright and certain way—free as air.

It was strange the way he felt about *down* the river, and *up* the
river. Up the river was more land, more country like this, wider and
emptier and—dreadful. Down the river was—everything: cities—
and the whole world. It must be altogether wonderful there.

The day itself appeared to be running out of the valley on the current of the river. The river, David thought, always seemed to flow more quietly when the light was dim.

"Da-a-a-vid! Yoo-ee!"

He jumped. It was Robby, calling and gesticulating from far down the road. David began to run, and Robby ran to meet him.

"What is it? What are you doing out here?"

"I came to find you. It's late."

"Well, what of it?"

Robby spoke, as he always did to the family, in his mother's homely dialect German. "The Mommie, she worries herself when you are late."

David answered in English. "That's silly. I was just walking along, thinking."

Robby nodded as if that were the most natural thing in the world, but he repeated, "The Mommie, she worries herself."

"Where's Pop?"

"I don't know. Somewhere, I guess."

"Of course. Do you think he's mad because I'm so late?"

"I don't know. He maybe does not know."

"That's so. I—I was just walking along—slow."

"The Mommie—"

"You said that twice already. Can't I be late without everybody making a fuss about it?"

"I don't know."

"You sound so silly, Robby."

"No, I'm not silly. The Mommie told me to come out on the road and look for you. And I found you!" Robby laughed and walked backward as he talked. At intervals he turned around three or four times in a dancing circle, ran sideways, or hopped. His progress was silent and unpredictable. He looked as if he were moving on currents of air.

"Why don't you walk, like anybody else? You act like some kind of a thing—"

"What for a thing?"

"Something that flies."

"Yes. It feels good to go around and around. Everything looks different everywhere you look."

Robby continued his whirligig motion. David watched him with annoyance, and at the same time, with a kind of curiosity. He thought Robby was a strange boy. He was a strange color, even! In the failing day his hair seemed to shine with a light of its own. It was too long—Mom ought to cut it for him—and it flew about. All the time, turning this way and that, with his arms spread out as if he were swimming, Robby's eyes glinted with amusement and delight. He was aware of David's annoyance.

"You've got eyes like a cat!"

Robby stopped for a moment. "How? Like a cat?"

"Yes. They're green, too."

Robby rolled over on the grassy strip beside the road in a ridiculous imitation of a cat. He miaowed and spit. David laughed.

"I guess you are some kind of an animal!"

But already Robby's attention was caught by something else. The laughter vanished leaving his face utterly changed. His eyelids drooped, and all of his features seemed suddenly veiled. He appeared to be listening so intently that he scarcely moved.

David was used to these strange transitions, and said nothing. Sometimes he wished he had a brother who was more like other children, but there were other times when he was moved to a tender and protective attitude, and when he was fascinated by Robby's appearance. Robby had a transparent look even under his tan, and he moved without making a sound.

David met his mother at the gate of the side yard. She was carrying a milk pail.

"You're so late, David!"

"Yes, I forgot to hurry."

She laughed. "That sounds more like Robby."

"I had so many things to think about."

"Well, right now will you listen?"

"Yes, of course." An easy affection marked the exchange.

"I'll take your books and you milk Buff for me. Quick now,

[154]

while I hurry with supper. Pop will be in any time. Robby, you come with me."

Robby danced ahead of her, going backward so he could see her face.

"Watch, you'll fall down, running backward like that!"

He shook his head vigorously. "I can *feel*," he explained. He stepped high over a stone beside the path. "See! I didn't fall over *that!*"

Savina laughed. "You were just lucky."

"No. I *feel*, because when I run around I remember all the places; then, even with my eyes shut, I can go without bumping!"

Savina shook her head with mock dismay. "Now I have a child that won't use his eyes."

"But I'm always looking—every time at something new."

"When you're carrying the eggs to the house, or the milk to the cellar, I'd rather you used your eyes."

"I could go in the dark!"

"You could break your little neck, too, and I wouldn't like that."

Robby was now the complete easement of Savina's heart. She had not felt lonely since he began to talk. Robby, as soon as he could walk, followed her every step. How he had learned English she could not imagine. Perhaps from listening to Peter and David. With her he spoke always her dialect German. That was very comforting. Savina tried hard with English, but Peter forgot to help her; it was easier for him to speak German to her. He was impatient if he was not immediately understood. Savina sighed. Peter spoke little enough, in either German or English, she thought, but she made the observation without blame or bitterness. Since she had the children, life had gone much as she understood it should go. She was busy with cooking and housecleaning and sewing and endless chores of the farm.

Savina thought comfortably of the jar of money upstairs in her linen closet, money from the sale of her own efforts, money that belonged exclusively to her, to do with as she pleased. It was true she had few occasions to spend it: Peter was a very good man in that way; the house was well provided with everything one could think of. Whenever he saw a new appliance for any use he brought it home. Most men did not think of such things. Savina noted often how much more convenient and well supplied her house was than her mother's house in Martinsgrove had been.

That Peter was more withdrawn and gruffer than formerly, she did not see. All the men she had ever known had been hard-spoken, and she never questioned ways which had long been familiar to her.

"Wash your hands now and set the table for me. Not?"

Robby made quick work at the kitchen washstand.

"No, no, Robby. I think your hands can't be so easy clean as all that! Let me see. Tch! Tch! Look."

He grinned and repeated the operation. He held up both hands with his fingers starred out wide. "So?"

Savina nodded, thinking at the same time how unusual, how downright strange his hands were. So slight and so long-fingered.

"You like to help, not?"

He shook his head emphatically.

"No? You don't like to help me work?"

"No."

"But you are so quick to help."

"You *said*."

"Oh!" Savina looked at him doubtfully. He was already beginning to make jokes. She could not always be sure.

David finished the school at St. Stephens well toward the head of his class. He would be seventeen in the fall. All through that year he had been deeply troubled. Paul and Timothy Nolan were going to Kings Row to school and were full of plans.

"You just got to come with us, Dave. Gee, we'd have a big time up there! Four years and then we could all go to St. Louis or somewhere."

David looked gloomy. "I don't know if Pa'll let me go."

"But, gee whiz, Dave, you got to go somewhere."

"I don't believe Pa thinks that way."

"You mean he don't want you to have an education?"

David nodded.

"Your pa's got plenty of money, Dave."

"How do you know?"

"Everybody knows that."

"*I* don't."

"Everybody talks about your pa as—" Timothy reddened and stammered.

"As what, Tim?"

"Well, they always call him that rich Yankee farmer."

"Oh!"

"It must be so. Look at the big place you got and all that fine stock."

"I guess I could go to Aberdeen College if he wanted to let me."

"Well, for Pete's sake, why wouldn't he want to let you?"

"I don't know. Pa's awful queer."

"That's what everybody says."

"Do they—honest? I wonder why."

"Well, you know, Dave, how people talk." The twins exchanged quick glances.

"No, I don't. I don't know anybody except the kids here at school."

"It's funny you don't, Dave. Why don't you go around more?"

"I've always got to hurry home and do so much work. Pa just keeps me at it all the time."

"Gosh, I think that's terrible. I wouldn't do it—I'd—"

Paul broke in. "Yes, you would, if you had to like Dave has to. You're just talking big. If our pa told you you had to do something, you can just bet you'd do it."

"Ye-es. I guess I would. But, gee, it's so unreasonable."

David sighed. "It feels that way to me."

"What does your ma say about it? Couldn't she talk him into it?"

"I don't know. She doesn't say much usually."

"He just has his own way, eh?"

"Of course. It's his place."

The twins stared. "Say, you want an education, don't you?"

"Of course, but that's not saying you're going to get everything you want."

"What would you do, then?"

"Work on the farm, I guess."

"Gosh. Suppose our pa said we'd have to help in the saloon!"

The twins eyed each other speculatively. Paul shook his head emphatically. "He wouldn't, 'cause he's always saying he wants to make something out of us."

"But suppose he did!"

"Oh, Paul, you make me sick. Pa wouldn't act that way. I'd run off if he did."

"Yes, you would!"

"I would. I wouldn't want to stay here in this little hole of a town."

"Me neither 's far as that goes."

"Dave, you just got to go with us. Think of the fun we'd have."

"Yes, I know."

"We've had a lot of fun here together, haven't we?"

"You bet. I never will forget you all."

"You won't have to. You just got to go up to Kings Row with us, one way or another."

"Listen, Paul!" Timothy seized his brother's arm. "Shut up talking so much! Let's think this thing over."

"Go ahead and think. What are you going to think with?"

Timothy absent-mindedly gave his brother a kick.

"Ouch! You—"

"Shut up! Dave, d'you think maybe if our pa talked to yours, it might do some good?"

David looked terrified. "Then Pa would know we'd been talking it all over, and—"

"Well, for the Lord's sake, we can talk about him, can't we?"

"Yes, but—"

"Does he think he's Jesus Christ, or something?"

David looked as if he were about to cry. Paul shot a warning glance at Timothy.

"Gee, kids, you all don't understand what Pa's like. I don't,

[158]

either. Just seems like my house never has been like anybody else's."

"The hell, David! We didn't mean—"

"Oh, you're all right, kids. Gee, I don't know what I'd have done—"

"Say, Dave, ain't Taska's folks sort of friends of your folks?"

"Well, not 'specially. Pa don't like 'em to come around much."

"He don't? Why, we thought—"

"I think Ma likes 'em all right, though."

"Then I guess they couldn't do much with your pa, could they? About helping you to go with us, I mean."

"Oh, Taska's folks don't understand anything like that. They haven't got any education. Taska had a hard time just staying in school here in St. Stephens."

"I never heard of such ignorant people!"

David flushed.

"Oh, shoot, Dave, I didn't mean *your* folks. Everybody knows your pa is smart. What gets me is why he doesn't want you to do just like he did."

"Well, I guess he thinks he ended up on a farm, I might as well start off there."

"You'd be pretty well off, 's far as money goes, at that."

"I don't know. I don't care. I just know I don't want to stay here and plow and—and do all that kind of work. I hate it."

"Why don't you just up and tell your old man that—just like you said it then. I bet he'd listen."

"You know, Dave, when you said that you looked just like him!"

"I hope I never am as—as queer as Pa."

"I don't expect you ever will be." There was something in Paul's tone of voice that made David look up. He saw the twins exchanging the same look he had noticed a few moments before.

"What are you all talking about, anyhow?"

"Nothing."

"Yes, you are. Is there something—something you know that I don't know?"

"Well—Dave—"

"Shut up, Tim."

"What for?"

"You shut up."

"I think Dave ought to know what we're thinking about."

"You better keep your mouth shut!"

"Listen, kids! Don't treat me that way!"

"It's all right, Dave, Tim just don't know when to keep his fly-trap shut."

"But *what* are you talking about? Please! Gee, I'm kind of in a fix, and I don't see my way out."

"It's just what you said about your pa being queer. You know people are always talking."

"Tell me what you're hinting at."

"Shoot it all, Tim, I wish you'd keep still once in a while." Paul was angry. "Listen, Dave, didn't you ever hear about any of your pa's experiences when he first came out to Missouri? About his barn getting burned down, and all?"

"No, he never told me anything about it."

"Well, maybe I better tell you, then. Remember it's just what I heard. Even my pa wasn't here then. Seems like people didn't like your pa much at first, because the war was just over and he was on the other side."

"Yes, I know that. They still call us Yankees."

"Well, one time your pa got in a fight in that same saloon we own now—"

"My pa—got in a fight! I don't believe that. I don't believe he ever went in a saloon, either."

The twins flushed.

"Oh, thunder, kids—I didn't mean that! I just mean Pa is so—strict."

"Well, it's so. Pa told us. A man said something your pa didn't like and he threw him out of the place. Just picked him up and threw—"

"*Who* threw who out?"

"Your pa threw this other man out. And that night your pa's new barn burned down with all the horses and cows and things."

[160]

"What did that have to do with—"

"Don't you see, this man your pa threw out wanted to get even, and he burned it down for spite."

"What did they do with him?"

Paul hesitated. "Well, that's where the story comes in. From that day till this nobody ever saw that man again!"

"What became of him?"

"They say the next day your pa bought a big shotgun and said he was going after the other feller. And, just like I said, nobody has ever seen anything of that man yet."

"Did Pa sure enough shoot him?"

"Don't nobody know for certain, but everybody says he did. The county sheriff came down here from Camperville to investigate, but they couldn't prove it on your pa, and so after a while it was just hushed up."

David looked slowly from one twin to the other. His face was suddenly haggard.

"Gee, kids, *that's awful!*"

"Well," Timothy waved his hand as if brushing the whole matter aside. "My pa said it was a good riddance."

David spoke out of a trancelike horror. "If they'd have proved it, they'd have hung Pa, wouldn't they?"

"Maybe not. Again they might have just because he's a Yankee. You know people haven't got any sense."

"Dave, didn't Taska ever tell you anything about it?"

David shook his head. Paul spoke quickly. "Taska's got brains in her head so's her tongue don't rattle round like yours does."

"Shut up. Dave had to know sometime."

"I'm—I'm glad you told me. I guess it's a whole lot better for me to know about it than to have people talking behind my back."

4

Peter felt that the fierce summer heat in the river bottoms was more than a condition of weather. It was like a manifestation of a nature hostile to man and all his works.

There was no stir of air in the fields. A steamy exhalation from the soil struck one in the face—it was like a breath from a cauldron. Above, the sun burned with a steady ferocity. In the midst of his furious labors, Peter often paused for a moment to look up at the hills. They looked cool in their green depths, but he knew well the smothering heat of the woods. Only the topmost trees swayed with a phantom motion. This mirage of refreshment assuaged his bodily torment for an instant, and then he turned again with automatic speed to his work.

This summer David was helping, and Peter felt the easement of the farm's daily, deadly pressure. David was up at dawn and went about his labors with an intelligent sense of management. Peter made no comment. From time to time David spoke to his father, asking what was to be done next, or how this or that was to be undertaken, but there were no conversations.

Savina looked at her two men with approval, but also with concern. Peter was already bent. He walked stiffly, and his face was set in lines of anxiety and strain. Surely, she thought, so much was not necessary. But she knew it would be useless to suggest that he should consider himself a little.

David was blackly serious. He worked with the same intense preoccupation that characterized Peter. Such effort set its instant mark on his face. It was no longer a boy's face.

He saw Taska rarely. Lena kept her resolution that her daughter should not work in the fields, but there were endless tasks nevertheless. Berries and fruits to be gathered and canned, milk to be cared for, butter to be made, and the recurrent sewing and mending, washing and ironing, and housecleaning.

One evening in August David went to see Taska. There was a great orange-colored moon which transformed the familiar valley into a strange and magical region. David felt the spell, but he was not disturbed by it.

Taska was sitting out of doors with her mother. "Lord, David, what are you doing out so late?"

"It isn't nine o'clock yet."

Lena arose. "It's nice you come. How is your mother?"

"She's well, thank you."

"And your father, is he working hard like always?"

"Oh, yes. I am, too."

"Yes, I bet. And little Robby?"

David laughed. "I don't see much of Robby. I guess he spends most of his time helping Ma, or just not doing much of anything."

"Oh, I think he helps your mamma a lot. I have seen. Robby is a very sweet boy."

"He's a curious customer, if you ask me. I never could talk to him much. He just looks at you like he was thinking about something going on somewhere else."

Taska laughed—her laugh was low and musical. "Robby knows what he's thinking about, I guess."

Lena nodded. "I think he is very smart, that Robby. Deep!" She picked up the small kitchen chair. "Well, I guess I go to bed. I have to get up early tomorrow. Taska, you make a cool glass of lemonade for Davy. There's some spice cake in the cupboard, too."

"All right, Mom."

"Good night, Davy. Say my hello to your mamma."

"I will. Thanks."

"Good night. Don't set too long in the night air—come around on the front porch, maybe."

"All right, Mom. Don't bother. I guess we won't melt out here."

David and Taska sat for several minutes without speaking.

"It is nice tonight, David." Taska spoke in a slightly lowered voice.

"Yes."

"What's the matter with you?"

"Me? Oh, nothing, I guess. Nothing new, anyhow."

David was suddenly aware of her compelling sweetness and warmth. He could see her clearly in the brilliant moonlight, her firm round throat and her heavy hair swirling low over her brow and her ears. She sat very still, her hands folded in her lap. He could see the slow rise and fall of her breathing. Taska gave off waves of herself, he thought—it was almost like touching her to be this near. A gusty confusion swept his brain for an instant. He

[163]

thought of that tousled head against his chest, of her strong smooth arms about him—he held his breath and pressed his hands hard against his knees. The stormy thrust of emotion passed.

Taska leaned forward in her chair. "Why don't you talk to me, David?"

"I don't know that I really have anything to say, Taska."

"What did you come down here for?"

"Just to see you. I have to see you once in a while."

"Yes. I miss you when you don't come."

He held his head between his hands for a moment. "Taska!"

"Why, what's the matter, Davy?"

"Taska, whatever do you suppose is going to become of me? Won't I ever get away from this place, you reckon?" His voice broke on the last word.

She sat very still for a full minute.

"Taska! Do you reckon?"

"Do you want to get away so bad, Davy?"

"I've got to make something out of myself, Taska. Paul and Tim are going up to Kings Row next month."

"To Aberdeen College?"

"Yes, and I want to go, too."

"Can't you?"

"I don't know. I don't see how."

"Your pa could send you."

"But he won't let me go!"

"How do you know?"

"I just know."

"Did you ask him?"

"No. I can't. I just don't think I could ask him anything."

"David, that's just as silly as it can be. You're his son. For goodness sake, if you can't ask your own father to send you to college— I never heard of anything so ridiculous."

"You don't know Pa."

"Oh, yes, I do. He's an old crosspatch, and he must be mighty selfish or he wouldn't wait for you to ask him. What does he expect you to do, anyway?"

[164]

"Work on the place!"

"Say, you are afraid of that old man, aren't you?"

"I guess, in a way, yes."

"Well, that's silly. He can't kill you for asking for something—particularly something you've got a right to anyhow."

"Taska, did you ever hear that Pa killed a man here in St. Stephens—a long time ago."

"Oh, *that!* Of course. Didn't you know it?"

"Not till the twins told me."

"Oh, I heard that long ago."

"Taska, do you think it's the truth?"

"Lordy, I don't know, David. Why should you care, anyhow?"

"Well, of course I care—if it's so. I don't like my father to be a murderer."

"Well, he killed people in the war."

"That was different."

They were silent for a few moments.

"Taska, I want to get away and do something—I want you to like what I do, too."

"Heavens, David, whatever you do will be all right with me."

"Suppose I was just stuck here—on a farm?"

"That's all right. Your people and mine are on farms."

"But I've *got* to do something different. I hate crops and stock, and everything about a farm. I'm going to do something else, some way; I don't know what it'll be, or how I'll do it, but I've got to."

"All right, David. You've got to be your own boss."

"There's just one thing—"

"What's that?"

"You."

"Well, what about me?"

"We'd have to wait such a long time. It'll take me forever to get any kind of a start, and—and be independent."

"I guess I could help, some way."

"Taska, do you like me a whole lot, that way?"

"Yes."

"But you deserve something else. You ought not to have to wait and wait—to—to get married."

"And getting married means living together, doesn't it—and going to bed together."

David was stiff with embarrassment. As well as he knew Taska, he was always startled by such frankness as this.

"Well," she went on, "if that's what it is and we think we can't wait—well, we don't have to wait."

"Taska, I wouldn't have you that way!"

"It would be all right."

"I guess I love you more than anything in the world."

"Well, then, don't worry. If you want me, you can have me—anyway—rich or poor. I can work, too. I work hard now, and I know how to manage. I've never been so bothered by—by the other thing, though I do wonder about it lots of times. We'll know some-day."

She laughed and David laughed, too. "I guess you're the very finest person there ever was."

"Oh no, I'm not."

"As long as I think so, it's so. But I have to go. There's so much work to do these days—I get so dog-tired I just fall into bed—first thing I know it's time to get up again—same thing over, day in and day out. Gosh-a-mighty, Taska, looks to me sometimes like there just isn't any sense to it."

"When it's your place, and your own work, and you're making the living out of it—"

"Well, I don't get anything out of it."

"Listen, David—" Taska hesitated.

"Well, what, honey?"

"Oh, nothing."

"What were you going to say?"

"No, I guess I'd better not. I don't want to influence you in any way."

"Lord, Taska. Where you and I are concerned, you can certainly talk out and say whatever you want to!"

"Well, listen, then. Suppose we got married and settled down—"

"But my good gosh, Taska, I'm just seventeen."

"You're old enough, I guess."

"I want to know something first."

"Well, I'm not trying to make you marry me, don't get that notion."

"Taska! You know I don't mean it that way. I just keep thinking that when we get married we're not going to slave on a farm and be nobodies."

"Nobodies! Farmers—"

"I know everything you're going to say. When that's what you want to be, why then that's what you are, but I want to know something. I want to see things and read lots of books."

Taska sighed. "I guess when that's what you want, that's what you want, and I hope you get it. If you want books and such things more than you want anything else—"

"You twist up what I say. I want other things first so we can have a more important kind of life. I don't want you to work like your mother and mine do."

"They seem to like it. I never heard either one of them complain."

"They don't know any better."

"And maybe you're mistaken. Your father wasn't—he was a teacher, you told me, and he wanted *this*."

"That's for him, not for me."

"Well—"

"Taska, do you want me to stay here and be a farmer?"

Taska hesitated. "No, David. Not if you don't want to. I'm just trying to tell you it doesn't make any difference to me what you are. I'll wait until I'm an old woman as far as that goes. Only, it does look like a long time. Here we are, and—and we have to go and be separated for ever so long a time. It looks so unnecessary." Her voice shook a little.

"Taska. I don't know what to do!"

He sat down on the ground at her feet and laid his head on her knee. Putting his arms about her legs he held them close to him.

"Gosh, Taska, what ought I to do?"

She rubbed his cheek. "Whatever you want to. Whatever you want most in this world, you should go after it."

"But, I guess it's not fair to leave you stuck here alone for a long time while I'm out doing things and seeing things."

"You're probably right to go away. I shouldn't have said what I did. A girl hasn't got the same kind of sense that a boy has. She can't see very far."

"What do you mean, Taska?"

"A girl just knows what she wants right now, and if she can't have that, she can't see over the top of it to anything farther away."

David laughed quietly. "Do you mean, Taska—"

"I mean what I always have meant—since we were little kids. I guess we kind of agreed on it way back there, didn't we?"

"Yes, I guess we did."

He pressed his face against her and absently stroked her ankle. "Goodness, Taska, you haven't got any stockings on!"

"No, it was hot."

With a quick impulse he lifted her skirt and laid his flaming cheek against the smooth soft skin. She pushed him away a little.

"Don't stop me!" He moved closer and kissed her knees.

"Be careful, David, please."

"I don't want to be—I don't want to be careful."

"Sh! You're talking so loud!"

"All right then. Come on, let's go somewhere."

"What for? What do you mean, Davy?"

"You know as well as I do. I can't wait forever, either. I'll stay here, I'll work in the fields, I'll do anything—"

"Listen. Listen to me! David!" She held his hands. "You know, so far as I am concerned, you can have anything you want—but—"

"But what—what?"

"Not this way."

"How do you mean? Why not?"

"It's not right—for you, or me."

A sudden chill swept over him. "Then you don't love me, like you said."

"Of course I do; I can feel just like you do—"

"Well, then—"

"Not now. Not this way!"

"I don't—"

"Tomorrow you'd be sorry."

"I would not! Why on earth do you say that?"

"Because you're just all worked up now—"

"Is that all you think it is?"

"You've got to listen to sense. I said you were just all excited—so am I, but tomorrow when it's all over you'll feel that I'm in your way. You'll feel like you've *got* to stay, then, and tomorrow you will want to go away just as much as you do now."

"I don't see—"

"I know you don't, not just this minute, but I see, and tomorrow you'd be sorry."

"Why? Why? Why?"

"Because tomorrow you would have had—what we both want now, but the other thing, the books, and whatever you want, that would be in our way. Then maybe you wouldn't want to go, or you'd feel like you ought not. *I'd* be in your way, and I couldn't bear that, Davy."

"I just want to—I want to—"

"I know." She spoke with a strange, wise tenderness. It didn't sound like the ardent, pulsing voice of a minute before. "There's something else—"

"What?"

"If this happened, tonight, and then you found a way to go off somewhere—I just couldn't stand it!"

"I don't know what you mean, Taska, exactly."

"I mean—oh, you—I couldn't begin—and then do without you for a long, long time afterward."

"Oh." He kissed her hands gently.

"What do you think I'm made of, anyway?"

"I didn't think, Taska."

"It'll be hard enough with you away for goodness knows how long."

"Taska!"

"Yes, Davy."

"Suppose—suppose there should be somebody else come along while I'm away?"

"Well, suppose somebody else came along *your* way, while I'm sitting here waiting?"

"There couldn't ever be!"

"Well—"

"I know both Paul and Tim always have been in love with you—"

"Stuff."

"Honest."

"Did they say so?"

"See! You want to know more about it!"

"David!"

"Oh, Taska, I'd go crazy. I know now I would. I don't know if I can leave you or not—for anything."

"That's the way you feel tonight."

"Do you think it's no more than that?"

"It's a warm summer night, and here we are all by ourselves, and me half naked with your hands under my dress—what do you expect?"

"Do you want me to stop?"

"No—yes—no!"

Both of them laughed, she kept her hand on his face, and they sat without speaking.

After a while he stirred uncomfortably. "Do you mean, honest, you don't want to—tonight?" He felt her shiver slightly.

"Stand up, David—please!"

He arose and held out his hands. She swayed a trifle as she stood up and David held her close, crushing the breath out of her as he kissed her eyes and cheeks and mouth.

"Do you still mean you don't want to?"

"I wanted to all along, but don't beg me to. It's not right to me —to either one of us. Please."

"All right." He dropped his arms and looked out moodily at the river.

"You know, David, I don't care what anybody says is right or wrong, or anything like that. I think my own way, but—"

"Taska, sweetheart—you *are* my sweetheart, promise me that."

"Of course. I always have been. I don't know how to say what I want to."

"What is it? You can say anything to me, now."

"I guess I mean that we're decent people, and I wouldn't want you to go away and think maybe I wasn't. You'd be away off in some other town and see lots of other people, and you'd remember about all this, and you'd say something to yourself about *that Janek girl.*"

"Taska, do you think I'm that—that low-down kind of boy?"

Taska began to cry. "Oh, I don't know! I don't know what anybody is—or might get to be. I—I'm miserable, that's all!"

"Please, honey, It's all right. I guess you know best. I ought to go on home now."

"I'll walk down to the road with you. Is that the way you're going?"

"Yes."

She put her arm over his shoulder, and he put his about her waist. It didn't make for convenient progress, but they scarcely knew that.

At the gate, he held her close again. "Taska, you're still crying!"

"No, I'm not."

"There are tears on your face. What's the matter."

"I'm afraid."

"Of what?"

"Of the time you're away."

"But I don't even know I'm going, or how I can."

"You'll find a way."

"Do you think so?"

"Of course. Oh, David—if you still want to—I—I'm ready—"

He seized her arms and sank his fingers deep into her soft flesh. Then he shook his head.

"You were right the first time, when I lost my head. I know you

[171]

were. Sometime—and I hope it won't be long, but we'll be married, and we won't have to sneak, or lie—"

"But you'll forget me."

"Taska, for heaven's sake, I haven't even gone anywhere yet!"

"But you will, and maybe I'd like to have that to remember!"

They stood, close in a desperate, heartbreaking, questioning embrace. Only the faint sound of the river across the road, and the dry tremolo of the frogs broke the silence.

Presently she drew away. "I'm all right now. Maybe we've both been a little crazy tonight. It's all right. Go home now."

"I—I love you, Taska."

"I love you, David."

"Forever and ever—I—I swear to God."

She kissed him lightly on the mouth and turned away.

David stood watching her until she reached the deep shadows about her house. Then he drew a long, shaken breath and walked rapidly down the river road. He struck his hand across his cheeks. There were tears there, but he did not know if they were Taska's or his own.

On the way home he was aware of the oppressive heat. He slowed his step and looked at the sky. The full moon, more orange in color than was usual, was high in the east. It must be pretty late. He hadn't realized that he was staying so long. Taska! Beautiful, wonderful Taska. His heart jumped, and then seemed to lie heavy again in his breast. What was he going to do? How would he ever get out of this? What would become of him and Taska?

David walked more and more slowly. He wiped his forehead on his sleeve. Surely this must be the hottest night he had ever felt. The river gave off a barely perceptible coolness, but the current was really rather far out now. The river was low, and there was a wide stretch of sand and rocks and mud. It smelled pretty bad, he decided. He dreaded going home. The house would be close. The bedroom would smell of heated varnish, and the bed itself would be hot from the day's baking heat. And yet, he'd better hurry and get some

[172]

sleep. Pa would be up early and would have a thousand things for him to do. It was strange about Pa. Most of the farm people called this the "slack season." They drove up to Camperville, or Kings Row, or even took the boat and went for a day in Jeff City. They idled about the stores in St. Stephens and talked, told stories, and compared their season's experiences. But not Pa. He could think of more things to do than anybody.

All of that week was what the older men in the bottom called a "record breaker." The sun came up in a flaming haze and sank in a blood-red welter of thin clouds. The day was a blazing arc of fire.

David considered his father curiously. It seemed as if Peter were fighting with the weather. He went from one place to another with his head down—a lowering, threatening look. His eyes were red-rimmed and sunken.

Savina was uneasy about him. "Peter, maybe you better go a little easy. This weather is fearfully hot."

"And what can I do about it? The work doesn't do itself."

This was a species of logic that Savina knew very well. She used it herself. Work had something imperative in its nature. It arose before one, an event, a sequence of events. It was more than a challenge; it was a command. Only extreme illness or death itself slowed the urgent and immediate fulfillment of duties. But she shook her head and made small sounds of mingled distress and com-miseration. She was also faintly surprised. It was natural enough that she herself should think as she did about the day's work. She had been brought up that way. But it was surprising that Peter felt and acted in the same way. Perhaps it only proved the inherent rightness of the whole attitude. She remembered hearing outsiders say of her people that they didn't know anything but work. She wondered what else there was to know. Of course some people shirked, but that was sinful and shiftless, and so not to be considered. Still—in such hot weather! It was almost more than she could bear to keep a big fire going in the kitchen stove and to cook so much.

The summer kitchen was supposed to be airier and cooler, but the thin walls were nothing more than a division between the furnace outside and the furnace inside.

Peter was suffering more than anyone guessed. He hated the heat. His heavy blue work shirt and overalls irritated his skin which for the last few days was a mass of prickly heat. He had kicked off his shoes and socks, but this gave him little comfort, if any. The hard-baked clods hurt his feet, and the ground burned like a hot iron.

In these days of acute discomfort, his defenses fell lower and lower. A thousand old tormenting questions came rushing through at him—questions which he had thought answered and settled long ago. He felt that he was confronted with a thousand specters of himself. Specters, he imagined fantastically, of his many selves—one for every day of his life. They stood in tormenting attitudes of question, or flickered past in a flurry of mocking. All of his old disquiets suddenly visible and felt, as if they had never been laid at rest.

Peter's bodily anguish and his ancient chagrins fused in a nagging sort of torment. He, like David, paused to look up and down the great valley, feeling as he did so that he was smaller and far more helpless against it than he had ever dreamed. Here he was, struggling day after day with a whole inanimate world that remained as viciously opposed to him as it had been on the first day of encounter.

Always, in making this place—"making his world over from the bottom up"—he had unconsciously viewed that process as a means to an end. Now, he seemed no nearer that nebulous and retreating goal than at the beginning. Means to an end. What end? Some kind of peace, maybe. Well, did he not have that? And here, in his undirected thinking, so much of his mere discomfort and the long accumulation of hideous fatigues confused directly with vaguely defined mental states that Peter saw them as one.

His head dropped lower, like the head of some stubborn, fighting animal which does not and cannot count the odds against him. His eyes were wide—burnt-out-looking—and his lower lids drooped a little.

Savina, passing from the summer kitchen to the cellar, caught sight of him as he came out of the barn.

"*Gott!*" She was startled. All at once she saw him as he was at this moment, set sharp against the picture of the way he used to be.

Peter was bent, far more than his years could warrant. His arms hung heavily, but his hands were clenched. He was still barefoot, and his trousers were rolled nearly to his knees. Shaggy, heavy-moving—he looked worse, she thought, than any farm hand she had ever seen at home. But it was the air of ferocity which disturbed her. Like a bull, she said to herself. Yes, like a great, angry bull!

"*Gott!*" She watched him out of sight and a look of trouble gathered in her clear young-looking eyes.

"What has become?" she said aloud, thinking again of the way he used to look. The tall, straight, proud man that he was, just those few years ago, and now this grim and embattled figure—"like an earth-man," she added as she hurried on.

"Like an earth-man; what has become?"

Peter, in another way, and without articulate words, was asking the same question. An overwhelming certainty of tragic destiny reached through to the last guarded cranny of his mind, to be instantly rejected. No, he thought. There was no certainty about anything having happened, or ever happening to him. What could reach him? What, out of all this indifference surrounding him, could injure him? There was no question of destiny, no question of tragedy. He saw himself again for a moment as the central and important actor in this wide theater. The same great white clouds drifting east—always east—always more and endlessly more of them. The same river—like that in—in—he shaded his eyes from the blinding glitter of the river—something he had read about a river—all light—oh, yes! —a whisper of words sounded faintly through his mind—like the hollow echo of a footfall in a long-unopened house . . .

E vidi lume in forma di riviera . . . fulvido di
fulgore . . . intra due rive dipinte di mirabil primavera . . .

He remembered now—the river in Dante's Paradise . . . *lume in forma di riviera* . . . and then, again . . . *dipinte di mirabil prima-*

vera . . . the soft words lay for a moment on his aching mind like the touch of cool flowers on a fevered hand . . . strange that he should remember.

A little, a very little, of the turmoil in him quieted. The jibing specters withdrew a little. For a moment the struggling nerves and muscles released their tension. Peter looked up as he always did in times of stress to the hills. The huge masses of gleaming white clouds arose beyond and moved into the intolerable blue of the sky overhead. Peter's thoughts were as changing, as formless, and as relentless in their eternal drift as those great clouds. He blinked and looked back again. As always, those distant treetops swayed with a faintly perceptible motion . . . tantalizing, beckoning, dreaming . . .

He brought himself back sharply—hurried to make up for this moment of reverie. This river did not run "between banks painted with the miracle of spring"—it ran turgid and yellow in a false dance under the ceaseless quiver of heat. But something persisted in his mind as he gathered some overripe melons and heaped them in a wheelbarrow. If he did not feed them to the hogs, they would rot here in the field.

E vidi lume in forma di riviera . . . what was that now, which followed? Against the background of his eyelids when he closed his eyes he could see a picture, but the words were uncertain . . . *faville vive*—yes, that was right—*faville vive* . . . and then something he could not recover . . .

Poi come inebriate dagli odori . . .

Peter shook his head. He tried to translate—light like unto a river, running between banks painted with the wonder of spring . . . living sparks . . . drunk with perfume . . .

He said the fragments over and over. A too-ripe muskmelon squashed as he dropped it on the heap. The sick smell struck him with horrible irony. Some of the half-liquid thing had splashed on his hand. He stooped and wiped it vehemently on some dry grass and then on his trousers.

He fumbled for his bandana handkerchief. A quick physical revolt covered his face with renewed sweat. "In God's name," he mumbled. "In God's name . . ."

That night at supper the long misery of the day had silenced even Robby who usually managed to keep some sort of mealtime conversation in halting motion. David scarcely ate. His eyes were big and excited. His searching look never left his father's face.

Peter was about to push his chair back from the table when David spoke.

"Pa!"

Peter paused and looked inquiringly at him. David cast a wild and appealing look at his mother but she merely looked puzzled.

"Well, what do you want?" Peter spoke absently, but to David's strained hearing it sounded cold and hard.

"Pa—you know it's the last week in August!" David swallowed hard and the excited look in his face changed to something desperate.

Savina broke in. "David! What is with you? You look so—"

"Yes, quick." Peter was impatient. "What is it about the last week in August?"

"Well—well—Paul and Timothy—uh—"

"Who are Paul and Timothy?"

"Oh, you know, the Nolan boys—the twins."

"Oh, yes, I know now. What about them?"

"Well, they're going off next week."

"So? Where?"

"To Kings Row. They're going to Aberdeen College."

"David—what are you talking about? Try and get to the point, will you?"

"Can't I go, too?"

"To Kings Row? What for?"

"I want to go to Aberdeen College, too."

Peter stared at David without speaking.

David stood up and backed away a few steps. His face was working as though he was about to cry, but there was a terrible at-bay expression mingling with his fright. Robby slipped quietly out of the room.

"Now, David," Savina interposed gently. "You talk to your pop another time about all this. He's tired. It's been so hot today."

David flung an accusing look at her. It was both accusing and dismayed. He knew that he was standing alone.

"I want a good education," he said slowly.

Peter heard, but at the same time his mind was running back over the day. Somewhere in his struggle with the heat and the hard undertakings had been a half-formed thought that he had an ally. That ally was David. He had not thought it clearly, or definitely, nor had he thought precisely what he expected David to do. But it had been as though he had been fighting his way alone through long-encompassing opposition, and as if at the far point of vision he had perceived help—help to "make a world all over new from the bottom up." The refrain struck at him like a lash. Now, after so long he was still saying it. And the unexpected intrusion of all that he thought he had driven out as inimical to simplicity, and honesty, and hope for—his brain went spinning away in an angry confusion. He felt the uncontrollable upsurge of anger—even in the scalding impact of his overflowing temper he knew somehow that he was passing beyond reason ... as that time he had thrown Vane Streeter into the road ...

David was wide-eyed, but he looked stubborn—he looked as rooted as a tree, Savina thought in a flash. "Now, David—"

"Keep still!" Peter roared the words, and Savina blanched.

Instantly David's features became still. The high color of excitement gave way to a stony gray look.

Peter turned toward him. He banged his fist on the table until the dishes jumped with a grotesque semblance of gaiety.

"You mean I can't ever—"

"*No!*" he yelled. "*No! No! No!* Do you hear me now? And never ask me again!"

David stared back stonily.

"Do you hear me?" Peter demanded. David looked at him curiously. He had never seen his father's face look like that.

He spoke with an effort. "I don't want to stay here."

"Well, you will."

"I won't do it."

"David!" Savina stepped between the two. "You must not say that!"

"I mean it."

Peter was breathing heavily. Savina motioned him back. "David does not mean—"

"Yes, I do, Ma. I want to be somebody, and do something."

"So!" Peter exhaled the word on a note of utter scorn.

David's flush returned. His voice rose and fell to a hoarse animal sound. *"Yes!* And I'm going to."

"We'll see if you don't do what I say."

Savina tried to push David toward the door, but he was insane with rage and grief. This had been much worse than he had expected.

"Yes! Yes, I will do something. You can kill a man for burning up a barn, but I haven't done anything but—but *work, work, work!* You can't kill me!"

"David! You—child, what are you saying? What—"

But Peter thrust her aside and struck David with all of his strength. The boy went down, crumpling into the corner with a faint whimper that was instantly still.

Peter turned and slammed out of the room.

Savina was over the unconscious boy instantly. She was making strange little sounds in her throat but she did not know it. She reached for the water pitcher and dipped the hem of her apron in it. There was blood on David's mouth.

Late that night Savina went softly into David's room. She closed the door behind her, and lit the lamp. There was a stir from the far side of the bed, and a startled whisper. *"Ma?"*

"Yes, it's me."

David sank back on his pillow. His face was swollen and discolored.

"Davy!"

"What, Ma?" His voice was tired and indifferent.

"I want to talk to you, quick. Are you good awake?"

[179]

David sat up. "Yes. What's the matter?"

"Nothing is the matter. You want to go away, not?"

Once more he sank back against the pillow. The despair in his face and in the movement seized at Savina's heart so that she could scarcely speak.

"Oh, Ma!"

"All right, you listen, now. You go, if you want to."

"Where—where can I go if he won't let me?"

"You go somewhere far from here and get you some work to do."

"But I can't—" His voice wailed.

"Sh! Look. I brought you this." She held up her jar of money.

"Your money—oh, no, Ma, it's all you got!"

"Oh, no. Anyway, I don't need it. It's enough so you won't have to go hungry or anything until you can find some work. You hunt a job, and make a little money, and everything will work out some way."

David sat up again.

"Get up, quick now, David, and dress. I'll help you put a few things together."

"You mean, now, tonight—right away?"

"Yes." The desperate intensity of the whispered word frightened David.

Half sobbing, the boy arose and pulled on his clothes. Savina fastened a roll of clothes with his old schoolbook strap.

"Now, listen, David."

"Yes, Ma!"

"I put the money in this little leather bag. Your—your father brought gold from the East in it when we first came out here. You wear it under your clothes. This goes around your neck. When you settle down somewhere, you put the money in the bank."

"It looks like a lot."

"It's more than two hundred dollars." She stopped and thought a moment. "I'd say you should go to that college in Kings Row—I could help you later on—but I guess your father would find it out, and maybe come after you."

"Pa never did hit me before."

"No, David. Maybe he's got the right, but he won't ever hit you again. You go, now."

Savina was white and tense. David flung his arms awkwardly about her. He was in a panic of fear and pity. He knew this was costing his mother heavily. Why—he had never known she liked him so much.

"Aw—aw, Ma. I can't go and leave you."

Savina was dry-eyed. "Yes, you can. That you must do. There comes a time—yes—there comes a time when everybody has to go—away."

David was near to crying. "Ma! Maybe Pa'll be mad at *you*—for this!"

"That does not matter. Now, listen, David. When you get to wherever you're going to stay, you write to Taska—she'll tell me what you say."

He looked wonderingly at her.

Savina nodded. "Taska is a good girl." As she said the words she remembered something. Somewhere else, an eternity ago, someone had said that about her—her mother talking to Peter. Her calm expression broke a little, and her habitually firm mouth quivered.

David hugged her again, his face an agony of bewildered indecision.

Savina read the look. "No. You go now."

David was as white as the whitewashed walls of his room. "I can't go!"

"*Yes*. It is best for you. If you want later on to go to that college—or some other, maybe—I guess you will."

"Oh—good-by, then."

Savina nodded. She shut her teeth tight together so that she would not cry out. She nodded again, her eyes straining at David's drawn, scared face. Then he was gone.

She waited unmoving until she heard the latch fall on the side gate. Then she brought her hands slowly together and closed her eyes. She moved to the window and looked out. Very far away a rooster crowed. It would soon be morning. Other people were sleeping in their beds, she thought, as if nothing had happened. Other mornings the world looked just this way before dawn—days when nothing had happened.

She turned to close the closet door, then quickly she stepped inside of it and pressed her face into some old clothes hanging there. She pressed hard as if she might so smother the choking sounds that shook her from head to foot. With her clenched hands she beat softly against the wall.

David ran frantically along the yard fence, keeping low in the high weeds in an irresistible desire to hide. He could not keep small half sounds from coming past his shaking lips. He was going away —alone—he did not even know where he was going! He was horribly frightened, both at running away from his father, and of a huge unknown world. Why!—he did not even know where he would sleep tonight. But he had some money—so much money, it seemed —had he thanked his mother? He could not remember. He knew in this instant of dreadful revelation that he really loved this place. He looked back at the house. He wanted to say good-by once more to his mother, and to tell her not to worry, but he dared not go back. He thought of Robby. A sudden rush of affection for his strange young brother struck through him. He looked this way and that— he must somehow say good-by to this home of his, say good-by to someone, or something. He dashed hurriedly into a low door in the side of the barn away from the house. It was so dark that he had to wait a moment to regain sight. There was Buff. He could see her blinking in sleepy surprise. He put his arm over her neck, and his face close to her head. "Good-by, Buff—good-by, Buff." He said it several times. Then he gulped hard, and ran out of the barn and down the slope toward the road through the woods. He ran like a frightened creature, stooped.

A faint, watery green light filled the woods. It would be morning before long. He slowed suddenly. Where was he going? Maybe he should have gone to Dawson's Point and taken the train there for Kings Row; but he could not turn back now. He would have to pass the house again, and that he dared not do. The river road, too, led past the house. His father might be up and see him. He knew if his father called him he would have to obey and go back. No: he must go on this way. He would go by and call Taska! He could not leave without seeing her. He broke into a run again, and did not slow his pace until he reached her house.

There was already a tall shaft of blue smoke rising from the kitchen chimney. He stopped in dismay. He had not counted on the Janeks being up so early. But he must speak to Taska.

He came through the backyard just as Michael Janek came up from the cellar.

"Good morning, Mr. Janek." David tried to make his voice sound natural.

"Why, David! My goodness, what are you doing around so early?"

"I—I'm going away, Mr. Janek. I—I've got to speak to Taska. Is she up yet?"

"N-no. I don't think she could be up so early."

"Do you think maybe—maybe if you'd call her, she'd get up—just for a minute. I've got to speak to her."

Lena came to the kitchen door, dressed, but rather tousled and sleepy-looking.

"Mary, and the saints! What's up, David? You look like somebody pulled you through a knothole. So early! What goes?"

"He says he's going away. Is Taska up yet?"

"No, I don't think so. What's the matter, Davy?"

"I'm going away."

"Where to?"

"I don't know—I'm—I'm running away from home. Ma knows I'm going. She gave me some money to help me."

"David, what is with your face?"

"Pa hit me."

"You and your pa—"

"I just asked him, Mrs. Janek, to let me go to college."

"Oh, so! So, that's it, eh?"

"I want to see Taska, and—and say good-by to her."

"Of course. I'll call her. Have you had your breakfast?"

"No, ma'am."

"Well, you have to eat some breakfast."

"I'm afraid I haven't got time. I've got to hurry."

"Listen. You must eat before you go. Where are you going?"

"I don't know."

"*Gott im Himmel!* You don't know?"

"No, ma'am. I'm just running away, that's all."

"But you got to run somewhere when you run away!"

"Anywhere. Some other town—pretty far away, I guess. Then I'm going to try to get work."

Lena shook her head. "What a wrong thing! What a pity! You go out there on the front porch. I send Taska out, and then you eat a good breakfast."

"Oh, I can't, Mrs. Janek—"

"Listen." Michael wagged his finger. "Tomorrow I was going to Camperville. I just as soon go today. How is it, maybe, if I hitch up right away, and we go to Camperville in the cool part of the day. By eleven o'clock we be there and you can take a train to Kings Row. From there you can go anywhere you want to. I wait and come back in the cool of the evening. Eh?"

Lena nodded. "Yes, that is a good idea, not, Davy?"

"Are you sure you don't mind? I'm putting you to an awful lot of trouble."

"Trouble, nothing! I got to go anyhow tomorrow."

"But we'll have to hurry."

"Don't worry, Davy. Your pop, he won't come after you. Go now and set down. I call Taska."

David sat on the edge of a chair, hardly conscious of the brightening dawn. Presently Taska came out. There was something intimate and warming about this ready acceptance of his wish to see Taska. It approved, and it guaranteed something.

"Taska!"

"Oh, David, your face! Mamma told me!"

"Yes—let's don't talk about that. Taska, will you wait for me?"

"Wait—yes, David, forever, if I have to."

"It won't be forever, I promise you. I'm going somewhere and

I'm going to work, then I'm going to send for you to come, too. I'll show him!"

"That's all right, Davy. What will I do without you, until then?"

"Can't you just sort of trust in me, Taska?"

"I told you—forever."

"Oh, Taska, I love you so."

"Yes, David, and now you're going away. I—I wish we'd gone ahead the other night!"

"Oh, Taska—do you, honest?"

"Yes. I'd have had that anyhow. David—I'm so afraid you won't come back."

"Maybe I won't ever. Maybe I won't want to. But you are going to come to me."

She put her arms about him.

"I will. I promise I will."

"It might take me a long time to—to be able to make a living."

"I'll come whenever you say. I wish I could come with you now."

"That wouldn't be right."

"No, I guess not. Will you write to me?"

"That's one thing I want to talk to you about. I'll write to you and you must tell Ma what I say. She can't read English very well, and I guess I couldn't write in German. Anyhow—it has got to come through you."

"Of course. I'll go to see her as often as I can. David—have you got anything to go on—any money?"

"Ma gave me all she had. It's plenty."

"Well. You can take care of yourself then for a while."

"Yes. Kiss me, Taska."

She tightened her arms around him and lifted her face. Her eyes looked straight into his. They were deep and warm and steady.

Savina set the coffeepot on the corner of the breakfast table, and gave a quick look about. She pressed her fingers hard against her eyes for an instant. It was hard to collect herself.

Peter came in from the barn and washed his hands and face.

"Breakfast is ready. Come now." Savina's voice sounded muffled.

Peter glanced at her, but she was sitting quietly at her place, her face composed and tranquil as always.

"Where's Robby?"

"He's overslept, I guess. I thought just let him sleep."

"Um."

Peter was not exactly at ease. He waited for a moment, then he asked casually, "And where's David? Why isn't he up to breakfast?"

"David is not here. He has gone," Savina answered quietly.

"What do you mean, Savina? Gone where?"

"I don't know. Away."

"Savina, will you please tell me what you are talking about?"

"I told you plain. David has gone away. I don't know where."

Peter sat silent for a moment. Savina buttered a slice of bread.

"Was he—just gone when you called him? Was that it?"

"No. He went in the night. I helped him to go."

"You—I don't think I understand this."

"It is not hard to see. He wanted to go somewhere—away. I told him to go."

Violent color swept across Peter's face and then subsided leaving him pale.

"I guess he won't go far."

"Yes, I think he will go far—and not come back."

"He can't make his way on nothing."

"I gave him money. All I had. It will take care of him until he can make his way somehow."

"So?"

"Yes." Savina's voice arose a little in pitch. "And he will not come back."

Savina saw anger flare in Peter's eyes, but she was possessed of the same kind of desperation now that she had felt last night. She felt that she must say what pressed so hard in her throat.

"Maybe it is better," Peter said thickly.

"Yes—it is better. It is right now that he should go."

Peter laid his fork carefully on his plate.

Savina held up her hand. "No, I will speak now, this once. Maybe it is not right for David to run away; maybe it is not right for me to help him leave his home, but it does not seem wrong to me. When you thought it right to leave everything and come here you did what seemed right to you, not? I did not ask. I was your wife, and you are my man, and I go with you wherever and whenever. That I will always do. But David, he is somebody, too. It is not wrong to wish for an education. He does not like the farm as you did not like the school—"

"Neither you nor David know what you are doing—"

Savina arose with an abrupt and angry gesture.

"David is my son, too. I know some things that the heart tells me. I have maybe a poor head, but my heart—that I can trust. David is a good boy."

Peter pushed his plate aside. He was about to speak, but Savina gave him no time.

"You, Peter—I do not understand you. I do not know what it is that you want, but I have seen my people in the East make slaves of their children. I have thought very much about that since I have been here, and I think now that there is not right in that. No."

"So, you and David, you talk it over behind my back in the night, and he sneaks away—"

"No! He does not go as you say—not in that way. He is afraid, yes, and that is not right. Why should a child be afraid of his own father?"

"He seems to think his father is a murderer!"

Savina stopped; she had been moving aimlessly between the dining table and the stove. "That I forgot! I thought me I must tell him he has heard wrong, that this is not true. I forgot."

"Are you sure it isn't true?"

"Don't, Peter; don't make foolish talk now at this minute. I know, of course, it is not true."

"Thank you, Savina."

"You must not talk to me in that polite way—the way one talks to a stranger one does not like!"

"I did not mean it that way."

[187]

"There has been that talk, I guess, among the people since that time. But what is that? Nothing."

"It seems to have been enough to help David make up his mind to run away."

"That is not it."

"Then what in the devil made him go?"

"He wants something different. It was wrong that you would not even talk to him. Maybe you could have changed him. You are smart, you know so much—and David he wants to be smart, too. I guess it's just that he wanted that way to be like you."

"Hm!"

"Not like that, Peter! I cannot bear that you should—"

"I know what is best for my family. I have worked like a slave to give them what I know is good."

Savina looked at him very steadily. "No one knows altogether what is good for anybody else."

"I guess parents haven't any rights at all—"

"Peter. You have little enough respect for all your forefathers. You yourself told me—long ago—back in Martinsgrove. You did not ask anyone to tell you what was right for you—"

Peter hated this talk. It had been a long time since anyone had ventured an argument with him. This morning he felt that his mind was as tired and injured as his body. There was no place to turn, no one who cared how he felt. Suddenly he saw the vast work of the place here for him to do alone without David's help. Discomfort and deadly fatigue and a sense of guilt all fused suddenly in an unreasoning anger and resentment.

"I'll go after him," he said grimly. "I'll teach him."

Savina moved a step nearer. "You will not!"

"What do you say to me?"

"I say you will let him alone. David is my child, too. I gave him his life—in blood and suffering. You cannot spoil it—I will see to it!"

"Are you crazy, Savina?"

"Yes! Yes! Yes! All these years I am here on this hill with nothing to see but that river out there! I think during this time. Many things are clear. I do not ask for me—no. Nothing. But for my child—if he wants to go away, he must go. And you cannot stop him—"

She flung out her arm in a wild gesture. Her hand struck the coffeepot and flung the scalding contents over Peter's arms and hands. He did not move, but the underlids of his eyes seemed to sag, and he compressed his lips tightly.

Savina stood for a moment, then she turned to a shelf and took down a small jar.

"Turn back your sleeves. I put some mutton suet on. It is good for a scald." She applied the suet carefully. Peter did not speak.

"Wait now, I get some clean cloth."

She returned in a moment with strips of an old sheet, and bandaged both arms. "It will be better tomorrow. I send Robby now to get someone to help you with the work."

Peter arose and walked out into the yard. The day was already hot. He stood under the thinning foliage of the tall sycamores and stared out across the bottoms, across the river, and on beyond the murky haze that lay thick on the south bank.

Savina went upstairs. She was curiously numb and still inside. She knew that after a while she would feel the full shock of this terrible night and this terrible morning. It was—it had been like a fight! It was unbelievable!

She went to the front window of the spare room upstairs and raised the blind. She could look down and see Peter where he stood leaning against a tree. "Ei!" she said softly to herself. There he was —and how old he looked, and battered. His hair was rough and straggling. His work clothes were shabby and old. Why did Peter allow himself to go so? It was not becoming in a good and prosperous farmer to look so like—like something beaten down. She noticed that he held his bandaged arms cautiously. She shook her head. Such a thing!

She wondered if Peter was maybe taking it hard—different from what she had expected—that David had run away. Maybe, after all, Peter might have shut up inside of him some feelings about his family that she did not know.

She laid both hands against her chest. She felt as if she had nothing but ashes there where her heart should be. Had she been wrong in something all along, maybe? Was there something she should have done that she had not done? It was not right that her family should be broken up so soon. It was not right that her man should stand there looking like that. He was—he was like something thrown aside by the river!

Somehow she must do something. What?

Now for the first time a wind of fear blew across her mind. Poor David! How would he fare? Perhaps things would go badly. She quickly thrust the fear aside. No: David would manage. He had all of his father's pride and independence. He would make out. And yet—Peter himself was not making out too well. He had made money—yes. But—Savina's thought reached out slowly, cautiously, along unaccustomed ways. She was uncomfortable and insecure in these paths of analysis and speculation. She only knew that things did not look too well for the man—her man, Peter—standing down there looking like a beaten and cast-off person of no consequence. Her loyalty and her devotion—she did not even have words to name these deeps within her—something that she was and must always be to Peter, these were unchanged, of course. It was not to be thought of that any happening whatsoever could make changes there—no, it was that she must try some way to help him in his troubles.

"Ei!" she said again. It would be good if she could cry a little, but she could not. She suddenly thought of something else, and a hideous alarm ran along her nerves. She reached out and steadied herself against the window frame. *Robby.* Yes, she had work to do— a careful, a so careful work that further trouble should not come. Unconsciously, she was standing between the two—Robby, shy and timorous as a squirrel, and Peter, down there—Peter! How horrible that she should have to feel herself so ranged.

The alarm would not quiet itself, and yet it seemed preposterous —out of all reasoning—something like a bad dream just before waking. There—just there—Peter! Did he look as if he meant to harm anyone? In God's name, did he even look at this moment as if he *could* harm anyone?

What have I done, she thought, what have I done that all this should come to me?

Peter, his whole thought blurred and confused, still stared out across the water and the land.

5

The small schoolhouse down the river from the Kettrings' was always referred to as the "Sandifer school," because Kam Sandifer gave the land and a good part of the lumber. He said it was really because there were so many Sandifer children.

The little Sandifers were a noisy, happy-go-lucky, laughing crew. They were clannish only when one of their number was attacked. At all other times they went their several ways with amazing independence, pausing only to conduct healthy fights among themselves from time to time.

The Sandifer house was a characteristic expression of the family itself. It was a big two-story frame house with a double gallery on three sides. Its front doors were always standing open, and one could see through to the back porch which ran along an extension ell. A half-dozen hunting dogs lay in the wide cool hall in summer or were casually tolerated about the open fires in the winter.

Kam Sandifer's father, who was "Mister" Sandifer, sat on the gallery through the summer, moving only to follow the shade around the house, and by the fire in the winter. He was a tall, thin, sharp-tongued old gentleman, the typical rural Missourian with his tangy speech and his pithy remarks. Kam, himself, in spite of his incurable laziness, managed to maintain a stock farm of good local reputation, but he seemed to observers to spend most of his time hunting or fishing, or driving about the countryside to gossip with whoever had time for him. Mrs. Sandifer presided over this helter-skelter household. She liked her children, was entertained by them, and they in turn adored her without giving the slightest outward sign of it.

Tred, the oldest boy, was already talking about being a doctor.

"You'll end up raising cattle and hogs," Mr. Sandifer assured him.

"I don't want to, I'm sure of that, but if I have to—"

"You're the oldest boy. The place ought to go to you." Grandpa was strong on English tradition. "How can you ever have a family that *is* a family if you keep splitting up homesteads? The oldest boy keeps the place and the family going."

"What about the rest of us?" "Nate"—short for Nathan—was the next oldest boy.

"Get out and scratch—like I had to. I had seven brothers older'n me. We all got out and left the place to my oldest brother."

"Is it still in the family?" Katherine, the oldest daughter, knew the answer, but she liked to hear her grandfather talk and splutter.

"No!"

"No?" Her mock surprise did not deceive the old man.

"No!" He shouted. "I've told you a thousand times. You know as well as I do, the damn fool split up the place amongst his children. Now, I guess none of 'em has anything."

"Well," Nate dumped an Irish setter out of a rocking chair, "I'd just as soon raise hogs and mules. Anytime Tred wants to hand over to me, I'll be satisfied. Gee, I'd hate to get kicked out of my own home. I like it here."

"There's adventure everywhere. Whyn't you go out to Wyoming or some such place as that, when you're old enough?"

"I might."

"That would be fine. I might go with you when you're ready."

Mrs. Sandifer came into the room. "Supper'll be ready in a few minutes. Where are Laurel and Jane?"

"Upstairs—studying their lessons."

"Without anyone telling them to? I wonder what they've been up to now." Mrs. Sandifer smiled.

"Laurel's a smart child." Grandpa made the remark with great firmness.

Kam opened the door at that moment. "All my children are smart, Father. Take after you."

The old man grunted. "They'll do well enough. But I never did see a child like Laurel in all my life."

Katherine winked at her mother and father. "Well, if you had to deal with her like the rest of us do, you'd change your tune!" Everyone knew that Laurel was her grandfather's favorite child, and that criticism of her always put him in a temper.

"Now, Katherine!" Mrs. Sandifer leaped for the breach, but too late.

"What's the matter with Laurel, I'd like to know?" Mr. Sandifer glared furiously. "And why have you got to *deal with her* in any way at all?"

"Oh, she's just hardheaded."

"Hardheaded? What's the matter with that? It's character, Laurel's got—character. That's what it is. She's exactly like her great-great-grandmother Witherspoon, and there never was a finer woman in the world!"

"Gramper, you make me feel so sorry for the rest of us."

"And I know what you're up to all the time. Just riling me, that's all. All the Sandifers are all right."

"But Laurel is special, eh?"

"Yes, Laurel is special. There always is one—"

"Who is her grandfather's pet," Katherine broke in. "If I'm not mistaken, I hear the little paragon on her way downstairs now."

There was the sound of a terrific bumping, some half-muffled screams, and a pell-mell clatter of feet on the uncarpeted stairway.

The door was flung open, and Roy, who was about nine, dashed for safety, but Laurel caught him before he could reach his mother. She pried his hand open to an accompaniment of lusty screams.

"Laurel!" Mrs. Sandifer called ineffectively. "Don't hurt the child!"

"Let her alone!" Mr. Sandifer was watching with shining eyes.

Laurel retrieved a piece of crumpled paper. She quietly tore it to bits and threw it in the wastebasket.

"Now, mister," she said, "you let my things alone."

Roy bent his fingers back and forth experimentally. "I think you broke my hand—that's what you did!"

"It'll teach you to keep 'em out of other people's business."

"Laurel!" Mrs. Sandifer protested absently. "What could be so important as all that?"

Roy danced. "I'll tell—"

Laurel looked steadily at him, and his threat faded out. "You'd better not."

He essayed another halfhearted Indian dance. "I'll tell! I'll tell!" His tone was unconvincing and he knew it.

"No, you won't," Laurel said with quiet confidence.

"There you are, Gramper." Katherine had been sitting on the arm of Mr. Sandifer's chair during the fray. "See what I mean?"

"Hm! Spunk, that's all."

Everyone laughed, except little Jane who had watched the brief skirmish with a disinterested look. Jane was not quite eight but she liked a good fight. She turned away as if she had known from the beginning how it would end.

"Laurel, you ought not to fight your little brother." Mrs. Sandifer spoke mildly.

"I have to," Laurel answered indifferently.

Laurel, just past thirteen, was the family beauty. She was tall and straight and her black hair curled crisply. Her eyes were hazel and heavily fringed under winglike brows. Her full mouth pouted, and her face wore a perpetual flush as if she were sunburned. There was a contagious vitality about her whole appearance from her quick, springy step to her low-pitched, jerky speech. She seemed always to be tumbling in or out of a room, down the stairs, or out of a chair.

"A tumultuous child, my daughter Laurel," Kam remarked to no one in particular. Laurel flashed an inquiring look at him, and then laughed.

"A tumult, just so, is what you mean." Mrs. Sandifer laughed, too.

Katherine looked quizzically at her young sister. "A cyclone, a thunderstorm, and a general catastrophe, I'd say." She arose and Laurel took her place.

Roy began to dance again. "Laurel's got a secret—and I know what it is!" He sang the words, taking long steps right and left as if he were executing a motion song.

"You'd better be careful, Mr. Roy Sandifer!" Laurel half arose, but her grandfather pulled her back to his knee.

"Laurel's got a secret, and I know what it is!"

"Well, go ahead and tell it. I dare you!"

"Double black dog dare me?"

"Yes."

He was still undecided about Laurel's temper, but he had gone too far to retreat with honor.

"I'm going to tell!"

"Go ahead, and if it's something I don't want you to tell, you better watch out!"

"I'm going to tell, Laurel's got a secret—"

"Oh, hush, Roy." Kam picked up a paper and sat down.

"*Laurel's got a sweetheart.*" Roy backed toward the door, but Laurel made no move, so he came back a step or two. "*Laurel's got a sweetheart.*"

"Pshaw!" Laurel made no other reply. But Katherine was looking at the slow color that deepened on Laurel's face and neck.

"Who is it, Roy?" Katherine's tone was casual.

"I know who it is!" Roy began his song and dance again. "I know who it is, and I'm going to tell."

Laurel sat up suddenly. "Well, tell and shut up, you little fool!"

"Laurel!" Mrs. Sandifer was not smiling.

"Oh, well, I'm sorry, but he makes me so mad."

"He's just teasing."

Roy felt encouraged. "Laurel's got a sweetheart, and I'm going to tell who it is—who it is—who it is."

"Who is it, Roy?" Katherine persisted.

"His name is—" Roy backed toward the door. "His name is—Robby Kettring is his name! Robby Kettring is his name!"

There was a moment's silence, and Kam laughed. Katherine

giggled softly, and Roy, holding the door half open, began his chant again, but Laurel interrupted him.

"What of it?" she said coolly.

The family exchanged amused glances, and Laurel sat up.

"What are you laughing about, all of you?"

"Nothing at all, Laurel." Kam was quick to see Laurel's flaring look.

Katherine sighed. "Well of all the funny people to have for a sweetheart!"

Laurel leaped to her feet, her eyes in a blaze. "He's the most beautiful person in the whole wide world."

Roy did a pirouette of sheer ecstasy, and Laurel dashed for him, but her father caught her arm.

"Laurel! What in the world is going on here? What are you trying to do?"

"Kill him, if I can catch him."

She was breathless with rage, but she did not try to loose her father's firm grip.

"Laurel! This is no way to behave. A little scrap is one thing, but you can't fight like this with your little brother."

"Then make him let me alone."

"You made him tell, really."

"Do you think I care who knows?"

"Then what are you so mad about?"

"At all of you—I'm mad at everybody in this house!"

"Why?"

"Because you laughed."

"We didn't laugh at you."

She blazed again and tried to pull away.

"Laurel!"

"Yes, sir."

"We were not laughing at Robby Kettring, either."

"You were so."

"Laurel Sandifer!"

"All right, I'm sorry again, but she did—she laughed at him!"

Laurel pointed at Katherine. "She's a nasty, stinking, mean, old—old fool!"

"Laurel—" Kam shook her slightly, but he laughed a little in spite of himself. "You've got to apologize to Katherine, right now."

"Will you make her apologize for what she said?"

"Maybe—I'm not bargaining with you."

"Make her apologize first."

"Laurel!"

"She said what she said first, and she ought to apologize first."

"Oh, Laurel, for heaven's sake!" Katherine gave Laurel a friendly push. "I'll apologize. I didn't know it would hurt your feelings. Have anybody for a sweetheart you want—"

"Well, say he's all right!"

"I don't know anything about him."

"Say it anyhow."

"I'm sure he's all right. Will that do?"

"Yes. And I'm sorry I called you all that."

Kam released Laurel's arm, and she rubbed it abstractedly. "You hurt my arm." She looked at him with heavy accusation.

"You pulled to get away."

"You held awful tight."

"You pulled awful hard."

Laurel grinned, and her father gave her a loud flat spank.

But somehow ease was not quite restored. Laurel stood very still looking at her fingers. Her father looked up after a moment and saw that she was half crying.

"Why, Laurel!" He spoke softly, but Katherine, too, saw.

"Oh, Lord, Laurel, have you gone crazy?"

Laurel wheeled on her sister, bit her lip, and did not speak.

Mrs. Sandifer reached for her sewing. The silence upset Laurel again. She stamped her foot and began to cry in earnest. "I want you to let me alone, everybody—*let—me—alone!*"

Kam arose, put his arm about her shoulders, and led her to the door. "You better run upstairs and wash your face."

He closed the door after her and turned back toward the room. "Well!" he said half laughing.

"The child must be sick." Mr. Sandifer was instantly defensive.

Katherine sniffed. "Sick! She's got a bad case of puppy love."

"Listen, Kathie." Kam spoke very seriously. "Not one of you is to mention the subject again. Just let Laurel alone." He glanced quickly at his wife, and was reassured by her face. "The first one that starts teasing Laurel again is going to be in trouble."

Mr. Sandifer chuckled from his corner. "Laurel will take care of them herself, I think, if nobody's around to stop her."

Kam arose. "I want to speak to Roy a moment."

Mrs. Sandifer shook her head. "Never mind now, Kam. Better let me talk to him."

Kam hesitated. "Well, now, Martha, no soft-soap about it. I want that young monkey to understand—"

"He'll understand. You'll fly at him, and then all of his Sandifer stubbornness will come out."

The notion that Kam dealt quite severely with the children was an old fiction in the family. Even the children half believed it. They were convinced that some time or other Father must have been pretty hard on Tred and Kathie, but no one had ever seen this parental ferocity in action. Martha Sandifer kept the legend green, and Kam was near to believing it himself.

"Well," he agreed reluctantly, "I might not handle him too gently."

Martha smiled slightly over her sewing. "I don't see why all this hullabaloo over such a little thing, anyway. Heavens, Laurel's just a baby."

Mr. Sandifer spoke up suddenly. "How old is Laurel?"

"Laurel? Why, she was just thirteen last March. Why?"

"Her great-great-grandmother Witherspoon was married at that age. She had four children before she was twenty!"

"Oh, that's horrible, a baby of thirteen!"

"Baby? They were great people in those days. They were trained for responsibility. Knew what they were in the world for, and set about being that. No foolishness about it."

"Well, anyhow, Gramper, I'm sure she didn't marry a little boy of fourteen."

"No-o. I guess he was all of seventeen. Is that how old this neighbor boy of ours is? Fourteen?"

"Just about. He was born less than a year before Laurel."

"H'm!" The old man shifted his chair. "Kam, what are those Yankee folks like, anyhow? I've seen him, of course, but I've never laid eyes on her."

"They're all right."

"Yankees, though."

"That has nothing to do with—with anything. Good people— just as good as we are."

"H'm!"

"Kam! You and Father talk as if you were arranging an alliance for Laurel."

Mr. Sandifer pointed a long finger at Martha. "Listen, daughter, I bet I know your children better'n you do."

"I don't doubt it. They certainly run to you with everything."

Gramper sat up straight. "I'm proud of that. The confidence of children—why, I'd rather have it than be governor of the state."

"What were you going to say?"

"Oh—about Laurel, now. I remember her great-great-grandmother—well—my grandmother. Laurel's exactly like her."

"And? Go on."

"If she is just thirteen—don't let that fool you. If Laurel Sandifer sets her heart on anything, she'll get it. You mark my words."

Mrs. Sandifer leaned her head against the back of the chair. "You are a silly pair, you and Kam. I tell you she's a baby."

Kam interrupted. "I don't know why you say 'you and Kam.' I haven't said anything about all of this. It's just Mr. —"

"I know you agree with him."

"Oh, you do?"

"Yes. Don't you?"

"I think maybe I do."

"Do you two grown men actually believe that Laurel's fancy for this little neighbor boy means anything—or is to be even *thought* of?"

"Martha, I don't think Laurel at thirteen is going to run away with a little boy of fourteen. But all things taken together, I wouldn't be surprised if Laurel didn't hold on tight to whatever kind of an idea gets into her head—well, until she's a whole lot older."

"I think you're crazy, Kam."

"No, I'm not. Did you look at her today—just now when all this rumpus was going on. She acted older than Kate."

"It's just her way."

"I know her way."

"Nonsense!"

After supper that night Kam sat by the window watching the slow twilight darkening across the land. Martha rocked slowly in her chair near the table.

"I declare, I ought to light the lamp and get on with my sewing."

"Wait a little. I like this time of day. When you light the lamp it's all gone."

"I think I'm just getting lazy."

"You do enough."

"What were you thinking about just now? You looked so serious."

"I was. I was thinking of the children—partly—and I was thinking about Father, too."

"He's devoted to the children—he's wonderful with them."

"Yes. He's been better for them than I, I expect."

"I don't know sometimes how I could have brought them up, or go on bringing them up if it wasn't for the two of you."

"You—oh, now, Martha—"

"Well, go on. You were going to say something else."

"It's just that—I was thinking how important events are when you are very young."

"Yes, they seem so. Children are—"

"No, no, Martha! I mean they *are* important—just as important as they seem. We think they aren't, because we think children forget. At our age nothing seems too terribly important. And then, when you're old, like Father, the same things are important again."

"That's foolishness, Kam. Your father takes on a lot about the children's little troubles. That's just because he hasn't anything else to occupy him."

"I don't believe that's it at all. Of course one gets busy making a living, and all that kind of thing, and you are intensely absorbed in it, but those matters don't shape and color your life."

"I'm afraid I don't understand you. You're pretty funny, Kam, and I guess I'm the only person that knows it."

Kam nodded. "So you just indulge my wandering, eh? My dear Mrs. Sandifer, you are listening to a philosopher!"

"I was afraid that might be it."

"But seriously, Martha. We smile about Laurel's outbreak. I don't take a childhood attachment seriously in the way you think I do, maybe, but in other ways, yes. It's a new color of life that's come into the child's mind. You could be rude and careless with it and spoil everything. It's terribly important to her."

"Well—"

"And do you notice how important it is to Gramper?"

"Oh, that's just because he loves Laurel so much."

"I don't think so."

"Well, you know he idolizes her. I think he loves all of the children—but Laurel—my goodness!"

"Yes, I know all that. But Father sees just as the children do. It's a kind of clairvoyance that comes with the years. And then, too, he's got a long experience as a sort of reference."

"Great-great-grandma Witherspoon!"

"There might be more to that than just something to laugh at, Martha. History—especially in a family—has the darnedest way of doing itself over and over."

"Kam, we're doing all the talking about Laurel. What's this little boy like, do you suppose?"

"You've seen him, haven't you?"

"Oh, yes, passing. He comes by here sometimes after school. He walks home with Laurel, always has since they started to school. It looked to me as if she had him under her wing." Mrs. Sandifer laughed again. "Laurel's always been the same, since she was a tiny little thing. She's a protector. I heard the other children say Robby Kettring was very shy."

"I don't know much about him."

"But you've been over there from time to time."

"The boy is entirely different from his older brother. I don't know anything about him."

"He talks very well. Lucy's always giving them bread and butter or cake or something after school. He seems very well brought up. Talks rather peculiarly, though, almost with an accent."

"He speaks German to his mother, I believe."

"Do you mean to tell me that woman hasn't learned to speak English yet?"

"Oh, I think she can, in a way. But, for heaven's sake, where would she learn it? Nobody ever goes there to see her, and she never goes to see anyone. Kettring always speaks German to her, I think."

"Isn't it a funny way for people to live?"

"They like it well, enough, I guess. If they're satisfied—"

"I ought to go see Mrs. Kettring sometime, I suppose, but I seem to have so much to do."

"But now, to go back to what I was saying—when you get along to our age, nothing seems important."

"I'm surprised to hear you say that. I'd say—"

"Oh, yes, of course. But you and the children—all of us—our lives are already set on the road they are to go. I don't think there's much to do about it at this late date."

"Presbyterian predestination!"

Kam gave his wife a humorously rueful glance. "Wouldn't it be terrible if those old theologians should be right, after all?"

"It would, but they're not."

The next morning Kam went for a walk. He went slowly through the lower pasture glancing appraisingly at the stock as he passed. It had been a bad year. Pasturage was poor—and the cattle showed it—corn crop had been bad. He would have to sell off a lot of the cows—mules, too. He would not be able to keep them through the winter. Expenses were piling up these days with two of the children away at school. He sighed rather heavily.

Kam Sandifer was not as impractical as the countryside thought. He was merely lazy. A prize procrastinator, he called himself. He knew a number of people with stock farms who made out better than he did. But there was always some small thing that got in the way of larger enterprise.

He thought uncomfortably of his neighbor, Peter Kettring. Peter's farm was the talk of the river bottom. There was nothing like it far or near. Even the Pennsylvania Dutchmen on beyond St. Stephens had not done so well. He is intelligent and he works like hell, Kam thought, and that is the combination that does it. He knew he could not do it. Still, with help as cheap as it was, he could get fine results if he would only plan a little. He resolved that he would do that—he must. But just now, there were pressing needs. He supposed he would have to sell some of the property up about Camperville or Kings Row. Tred would need a decent allowance. Might not be so easy to find a buyer, either. Darn funny, the luck some people had. There was Peter who had bought land up in the county at the same time he had, bought it practically sight unseen, and Peter's property had turned out to be better located than his own. Strange fellow, that Kettring. At the same time Kam felt a kind of pity for Peter. Ever since that boy had run away—more than a year ago—Peter had been grimmer, and harder to talk to. Kam could not make out if the man was grieved, or hurt, or just mad about it. Kam thought it might be a combination of all of these. Anyway, Peter had been hit, and hit hard somewhere in his peculiar make-up.

Kam pushed his hat forward over his eyes, and thought for a moment. Maybe Peter would buy some of that coal land up there, or a piece of the fire-clay property at Kings Row. He could count on a decent price. He squinted at the long hill that stood between him and the Kettring place. He would have to climb the hill, and that would be arduous, or take the long way around by the river road.

He decided on the hill. It would be pleasant to be in the woods for a little while.

He crossed the pasture, noting the dry short grass underfoot. Yes: he had better get Bill Edwards and Clem Worrell to drive a lot of the stock up to Kings Row next stock sales day. He would not get a fair price, but it would have to be done.

He swung over the zigzag rail fence halfway up the long slope to the woods. The goldenrod was fading to a dusty, sneezy-looking brown, but there were bright flecks of purple where the stiff-stalked field asters held out against sun and drought. Spanish nettle all gone, long ago. He liked the bright gold things, but they were a sign of poor farming.

At the crest where the disused pathway turned down toward the old Adams house, he took off his hat and sat down. The hazy sun was warmer than he had thought. But there would not be much more really good weather. Already a brushing of color showed along the face of the hills, here and there a bright-red point, or a shattering of lemon-yellow leaves. It was so still—not a sound, unless you listened carefully for the faint echoes from below. The smoky Indian summer blue seemed to muffle sound as it veiled and obscured clear sight. The river flickered with an almost copper reflection of the sun. There were wide, stony stretches on both sides. It had been low last year, but this second terribly dry year had narrowed the channel still more. It looked scarcely wider than a big creek.

Kam loved the river. He had fished there, gone swimming in it when he was a small boy, he had explored venturously in a crazy canoe, and at all times he had watched it. It was like a living pulse in the landscape. He felt now, as he looked at it, that it must be dull to live inland where there was no moving water.

He arose, brushing the grass and leaves from his clothes. He shaded his eyes and peered across the bottoms. That looked like Peter, far down there. Yes, it was. The man was clearing fence corners, piling brush and weeds to burn. Lord, what energy! It might have been easier after all to have gone around by the road. But he had had a look at the river from up here and that was always worth the climb. He did not wish to go. Somehow when he was alone like this he was so intensely conscious of the world about him that he hated to break the spell. He stood quite still, looking and listening, with a keen, terrestrial awareness, like that of a fine hunting dog.

The mellow October tints of the fields and trees blended into a harmony that laid instant quiet on his mood. The hills—those ancient symbols of strength—back of him always—like the hand of God, he thought, surprising himself by the piety of his fancy. He heard now the many faint sounds coming each one with its tiny clarity through the still air. A few clouds, summerlike, round and white, moved slowly toward the east. High, very high, and far over the south bank two or three buzzards drifted in slow concentric circles. This was his life—this was the time and the sight of his own one life—he must look hard, see it well, hear it, touch it. At this moment he felt so close to the earth and sun and river that it seemed as if he might melt into it, and fade from being on these currents of light and air. What a pity that men could not die in some such fitting way, instead of shutting themselves away in a house and battling for one last breath.

Kam sat on the fence. It was hard to talk to Peter Kettring. The man would not hold still long enough. He seemed so fearful of time. Kam watched him as he pulled the weeds up from the loose, sandy soil and threw them into heaps. The man had certainly paid heavily out of himself for this fine place. There it lay, all about him, well kept, rich, and—*young*. It looked as though it drew its own splendor and strength from the man who was its master. Peter looked spent.

"Kettring, I didn't come by just to pass the time of day."

Peter looked up.

"I've got two or three things I want to talk to you about."

Peter nodded, but went on with his work.

"Can't you stop pulling up those damn weeds long enough for me to say a few words?"

Peter half smiled. He relished Kam Sandifer's rare visits. "Can't you just say what you want to?"

"No, not with you weaving back and forth there. Jesus, sit down a minute!"

"All right, all right." Peter sat down on a pile of brush.

"You don't look much interested!"

Peter gave Kam a look that was as near to camaraderie as he could achieve. "Mostly when you want to talk to me you want me to do something."

"What? What's that?"

"Yes: I have to hitch up and go to Kings Row, or Dawson's Point. You have many projects."

Kam laughed. "I've got several this time. First, I think you're a bad citizen. You don't take any part in the life of the community."

"You came to tell me that after all these years? I don't wish to have anything to do with the—the *community*." Peter said the words with an emphasis of scorn that startled Kam.

"Oh, thunder. I don't expect you to give a dance."

The hard look vanished again, and once more Peter half smiled.

"Tell you one thing I want you to do."

"Go ahead."

"I want to put you on the school board."

"What for?"

"You have children that go to school, don't you?"

Peter stared unblinkingly at Kam who flushed a little. Dammit, he had forgotten about David for the moment.

"You're an educated man. You must have good ideas about schooling. We've got a lot of clodhoppers and village politicians."

"Naturally!"

"Eh? Well, you could be a help."

"Frankly, I don't even care if you have a school or not."

"That's not sensible."

"It's how I feel."

"Well, you ought not. Tell you what—"

"I won't do it."

"You're sidestepping your duty as a citizen."

"I am not a citizen of this—this St. Stephens region."

"How do you make that out?"

[206]

"I live here. I have a place here. I ask nothing of anybody, and I do not give anything to anybody."

"You send your son to school."

"I pay school taxes."

"Guess you've got me there! But we ought to have better schools, and—"

"*You* make them so. You are a good citizen. People like you, they like you, I imagine. You probably understand all that is necessary."

Kam shifted his position. He took out his pocketknife, cut a section of tall dry weed and whittled at it.

"We're going to get a new teacher at the Sandifer school next year."

"Yes?"

"I'm going to put old man Janek's girl in there."

"Taska?"

"Yes. She's away this year at a normal school. She can handle the kids. Besides I like her. She's got a lot of her old man's heartiness."

"She may be good."

"She will be. I can tell from the way my own kids talk about her. She's smart, too."

"How did you happen to think of Taska Janek?"

"Her old man talked to me about it. Say, Peter. It's none of my business, but what do you hear of your boy?"

Peter did not answer.

"I mean David. Where is he?"

"I do not know."

"You don't know?"

"I do not wish to know. It is—nothing to me where he may be."

"Now, listen, Kettring—that's no way—"

"Please!"

"Going to tell me to mind my own business?"

"Not in those words."

"But that's what you mean?"

Peter looked Kam straight in the eyes. "Yes."

"All right. All right. Hoe your own row! It's going to be a long, hard one the way you're going at it."

"It has already been a long and hard one, but—it is my own row."

"Well, Peter Kettring, you're a hard man. I am still your friend any way you look at it."

"I am glad for that, but some things I must do my own way."

"I guess so, Peter. But I guess, too, you're some kind of a darn fool."

"I do not think so." Peter spoke so judicially, as if he were speaking of something quite outside of himself, that Kam laughed.

"Well, go it, old man. Go your own way. Now, another thing. Would you agree to be on the board of directors of the bank? Day is going to retire. He's getting old. We're going to get a new man, Cooper, John Ball Cooper."

"Don't know him."

"From up about Lexington. He's all right."

"But why me on the board?"

"You own stock. You've got business sense."

"That I have not."

"You could at least have a say in looking after your own interests."

"I bought those interests on your advice. I believed Day to be competent. And as long as you are on the board I can rest easy about my interests. I leave them to you."

"Thanks. You won't come on?"

"No."

"Well, I don't seem to be having a very successful trip today."

"What else do you want?"

"Money!"

"That I can do for you."

"Whoa! Not so fast. You don't know what I want."

"But you know what I have."

"Peter, that's damn fine of you. I swear—"

"You did not expect it, you are about to say?"

"I was not!"

"I think you were. You know very little about me."

"I don't want a loan, Peter. I want to sell you some land."

"Why?"

"I've got to pay for my children's education. Tred is at Aberdeen—"

Peter interrupted. His words came quickly—harsh and short. "I have no interest in what you do with money—that is your own business. What do you want to sell?"

"The tract at Camperville."

"How much is it worth?"

"I'll be darned if I know. You know what I paid."

"Yes, I remember."

"I'll take what I paid for it."

"But you lose that way. Taxes and interest."

"I need the money."

"Go ahead and fix up the papers. I'll pay your price."

"Thanks. It gets me out of a tight spot."

"All right."

"And I don't mind telling you that takes a load off my mind."

Peter nodded.

"Say!"

Peter looked up. "Yes?"

Kam did not speak for a moment. He was deeply troubled, and perhaps a little shocked at what he saw in Peter's eyes. It was not easy to define. God, he thought, the man looks as if something were consuming him! I wonder if it's that boy. Hardly likely. He never acted as if he knew his children were alive. He checked his speculations suddenly. David Kettring had run away from home because his father would not send him to Aberdeen College. And now Peter was furnishing the money to pay for his own son's education! The sharp irony of this was almost too much for Kam. Words burned on his tongue. It had never been easy for him to refrain from speaking his mind. Just now it was especially difficult. It was a damned injustice. Almost he felt that he should not take the money for Tred. It was like a betrayal of that strange, dark brooding boy who had run away. How in thunder could a man do that to his own flesh and blood? What did Peter hold against the world that he was so bent on going against the grain of common sense and ordinary justice? And what, especially, could he have against learning—against education? He was, himself, a man of exceptionally good education. It showed in his speech and in his occasional unusual references.

Peter spoke again. "You were going to say?"

"Oh, yes. I noticed something when I was sitting on the hill back there." Kam turned around to look out at the river.

"What was it?"

"That big sand bar out there. Notice just how it lies?"

"N-no. I see that it is bigger this year—and much bigger than several years ago."

"Well, I took a good look at it."

"So?"

"I guess you've never noticed the river currents much."

"No. Not at all. Why?"

"Well, I know this old river pretty well. I've watched it all my life. You never can *know* it, not really. It's unpredictable as the devil. But if you watch it long enough, and keep checking up on the way it behaves, you can sometimes, not often, mind you, but sometimes you can tell what it's going to do next."

"I must say it looks pretty bad sometimes, in high water."

"You've never seen a real flood yet!"

"No? Three years ago—"

"Nothing to talk about."

"You have seen—yourself—"

"Yes. Once when I was a young boy." Kam half closed his eyes and nodded. "All these bottoms under water. People got caught. Cattle drowned everywhere."

"Can't you prepare—when you see—"

"The river does freak things overnight. It'll take a hundred acres off your place and plaster them up against Tom Hill's place across on the other side. Fact. Just depends on the way the full weight of the currents gets to swinging. You see that long tongue of land of yours that runs out up there?" Kam pointed to a narrow grassy strip that jutted out into the river. Peter nodded.

"Well, sir, that was an island forty years ago. Water used to come in back of it. During the flood the whole damn river swung over this way and just washed everything on the Adams farm down into Louisiana."

"But now it is—well, no longer an island."

"Old man Adams—I guess it was Adams' father—yes, it was— went to work and built this up. They blasted and dug away an old sand bar out there—government helped—and got it straightened out again. Adams filled it in pretty well. There's a half acre up there a little way that's just made land. For a while the river actually helped. Piled up against it. But you know, Peter, that island was twice as wide as the strip of land is now."

"What happened?"

"River's gradually cut it away. If you'll go out there and look at the upper side you can see how it cuts under, then the bank falls in a little, then the currents cut under again. Of course the strip of land isn't worth anything, but I expect to see the river wash the whole thing away some spring freshet."

Peter shrugged slightly. "I guess that wouldn't make much difference."

"N-no, it wouldn't."

"But what have you on your mind—about the sand bar?"

"Come on out here with me. I'll show you what I mean."

Kam led the way over the rocky river bed to a point nearly a quarter of a mile above the little neck of land he had been discussing. He stopped and pointed.

"See the way it lies?"

"Yes." Peter's tone was doubtful. He did not understand at all what Kam was driving at.

"That sand bar wasn't anything much a few years ago. They come and go, you know. But some willow stumps, likely, got lodged right at the upper point. Sand built around them, other things lodged. Pretty soon the sand bar was a substantial obstacle. Now the way it lies is the real point. It's diagonally across midstream, cutting the main current in two, deflecting most of it this way."

"Yes."

"You can see for yourself. Look how swift that water is on this side."

"I don't see what—"

"I know you don't. You don't know anything about the river. That current on this side is bound to sweep out in a wider and wider arc when the river rises again. It's going to cut right into that strip down there on your place."

"Well, what if it does?"

Kam shook his head. "I could guess all wrong, of course. I'm not a river expert, but I'd bet a good deal that it'll wash that strip away someday."

"Well, just as we said, it's not worth anything. Nothing but willows on it."

"But suppose this sand bar got to be a real island, willows take on and hold out against the rise, you'll have the river turned this way."

"Then—well, of course, I don't see much difference one way or another. The general look of the river currents has changed a good deal since I came here."

"I know—but *back* of that place there's lower ground, and if a real flood came along some spring, you might have the whole confounded river running right down through your bottoms—and mine, too, for that matter."

"What's to be done about it?"

"Go over to Jefferson and see if we can get some government help and blast that sand bar out now while the water's down. They don't give a darn up there at the capital as long as a few boats can get through, and the railroads hope the boats *can't* get through, and there you are. Then, too, I'd get me some men and a few teams and do a little filling in all along that low dip—right along your line I guess it is."

Kam was full of enterprise as he talked. He was always good at planning. What he said sounded logical to Peter, but he doubted the danger. He had watched the river rise and fall all of these years. There had never been the slightest threat to his place.

They went slowly back along the way they had come. Kam was happy in any chance companionship, but he felt particularly well today. It had turned out to be a good day after all. He was glad Peter had agreed so readily to take those lands. He would be free of any financial worry for the next year. He could sell only such stock as seemed really unpromising. The children could go decently through the year without embarrassment. He decided he would go up to the county seat tomorrow and arrange the sale, have deeds made, see a few old friends. Maybe Mr. Sandifer would go with him. His father always enjoyed a day in town.

And so, light of heart, whistling softly under his breath, he went back over the hill.

Peter returned to his work, hurrying to make up for lost time. Kam Sandifer was a terrible time waster. It seemed to him that every time his neighbor came to see him there was nearly a half day wasted. That sand bar now! It had seemed interesting enough, almost important as long as Kam was actually talking about it, but now it receded along with the suggestions about the school board, and the board of bank directors. No, indeed. He would certainly not make the mistake of involving himself in the general affairs of the community. If they could not run their own affairs, all the worse for them. They were certainly not to be considered as affairs of his.

Nevertheless, he had been glad to see Kam. There was only one thing: he wished Kam had kept his mouth shut about using the money to send Tred Sandifer to Aberdeen. He almost wished he had not been so ready to agree to the purchase of that land. The recollection of the whole matter lay like a bitter and corroding taste upon his tongue. He fought against remembering. He turned upon his work with fury, but the picture of David persisted in his mind. He did not ask himself at this moment if he had loved his son. He had never asked himself that question. He had thought of his son as belonging to him, as being a part of himself, just as these acres and trees and buildings were his. The dark and troubled face of David—that night when the boy had been so frightened—and so desperate. Why should his own son be frightened? Why should he act like that? He disliked the thought of anyone being afraid of him. He half thought that he disliked timorous people. But that would include Savina. Savina seemed to be afraid of a good many things. He could not really understand that. Perhaps the children got it from her. But David had not seemed afraid, ever, of anything. He did not permit himself to wonder what had become of David. He clamped down with iron rigidity upon any movement of his thought in that direction. David was gone—he would not consider might-have-beens, or wander through vague and sentimental recollections. David had chosen to go—somewhere. He knew that Savina heard of him through Taska. He was not quite certain how he knew that. But it was their affair. Savina had helped him to go. If she was troubled about it, it was her own fault. She had bereaved herself of her son. It was decidedly their affair, David's and Savina's, and somehow Taska's, though what in the devil Taska had to do with it—wait! Was it possible? He had not thought of anything so obvious. Of course the boy and girl were in love. And now Taska was to teach school! This seemed vaguely ridiculous to him, though he did not know why. Taska, child of those Bohemian peasants. But that was the way of this new country. Maybe that was the real good of it. You could do what you wished, become what you dreamed—again, an unwelcome thought returned—again like a palpable bitterness upon the tongue. David! But David could not understand that he had wanted to save him from the complicated and worrisome life that lay along that difficult road. He would have given him any of this—all of this if he had been willing to accept it. And if he wanted that girl, too, that Taska Janek, that would have been all right. Taska would doubtless have been a good wife.

Peter did not allow himself to know that there was one small area of ease in his mind about David. He did not consciously say to himself that since Savina must hear from him she must know that he was not in trouble, or that in such case she would either help, or ask him to help. But the feel of the thought was there. It was something else that troubled him sorely: the knowledge that rather than live life as he, Peter, saw it and thought it should be,

David had chosen to leave, to go away, to throw away a world—this world which he had dreamed of and built in its security and completeness.

Peter's face was hard as he thought of these matters. There in his faded work clothes, soaked with sweat, unkempt and rough-looking, Peter was the full likeness of a man who burns with a zeal beyond all measure of reason or control. Just once, in this morning of gnawing question, did he ask himself what satisfactions his life and world here had given him. And there, banked against that question, was his feeling about the people of this place. He did not, however, ask himself how it was that his careless dislike of St. Stephens and its people had changed into this deep-lying and moving hatred. There it was, black as a subterranean lake, cold and poisonous. He spat. People!

As he worked his way around the field his shoulders sagged. The old fatigues, crushing as a weight of stone! He straightened, and moved his shoulders painfully. Wiping the sweat from his eyes his glance flared across his wide acres, along the hills—it had been a struggle, a long, keen struggle—why must he feel his own place arrayed against him, like an enemy? But he was winning. *Winning.* Some sort of query, from the rim of an alien logic, teased and nibbled at the word. Winning? Peter refused the question. Yes, by God, winning all he had sought when he came here years ago! . . . No, he had not counted on the hostility and dislike he had met. Curious that it had been so. But even that had come to be a sort of tonic.

And, as he had seen himself, long ago, a solitary actor in this great amphitheater of hills and woods and fields and river, he saw himself now, harder pressed, but still unbound.

He had created! Digging and planting, reaping and storing, sowing and reaping again, and by the ingenuity of his hands and mind he had created—yes, tools and ways of accomplishment. Out of the earth and out of his mind . . . will, and long determinations . . . and soon he would be a rich man. Not that it mattered greatly. He had not sought that, but he had not been blind to the consideration it had brought him—a consideration he swept out of his notice with a biting contempt.

But there was a breach in that wall of protection he had built stone by stone, a breach from the inside where he had least expected it. David . . . David, who had broken through and gone. He must needs build it up again. He must build so well that he would not even remember that it had been there.

If Robby—but Robby was still a child. He knew nothing about Robby. He had not known anything about David, either, but David had seemed like a man—even when he was very little he had been an individual. He had stood up so! Robby . . . Robby had a child's look in his eyes . . . certainly there was no way to understand a child. A child was as mysterious and otherworldly as a creature of the woods, seeing as men do not see, hearing as men cannot hear, and living in a thin air of utter strangeness.

Was there anything he should do about Robby? No: that would be Savina's business. Robby had always seemed peculiarly to be Savina's child, anyway. He thought now how they had always talked much together, Savina and Robby . . . Savina was not too unlike a child herself. It was better so—yes, he was sure of that. David—David must have been like many of his forefathers, cloudy and brooding—maybe, even, a little like he, Peter, had been when he was young. He could not remember well what he had been like. It seemed to him that he had never been young. He was glad he could not remember. There must be much in all youth that is too foolish to recall with comfort or with pleasure.

Robby—yes, he was like Savina. Savina was . . . the hard, stabbing angularities of Peter's thinking changed whenever the picture of Savina crossed his mind. Sometimes the thought of Savina ran along his nerves like a streak of fire. He pressed the back of his hand to his brow, trying to steady the vertiginous rush of feeling. Savina! It was curious, he thought, that after all of these years she was still the same to him, an unrest in the blood and almost a confusion in his brain. It was so that the thought of her and the apparition of her had broken through to all of his senses that afternoon on the mountainside above Martinsgrove.

He knew that all she had been to him through these many nights and days lay like a close-woven snare upon his inmost being. He knew she was like a flare in the obscure places of his mind, fitful, but inescapable. She was like those fires that crept along the hillside under a thick fall of leaves, slow and secret, blazing out again and again, troubling the nights and threatening far unexpected places.

Peter shook his head. The headlong eloquence of his reverie embarrassed him. Savina—he tried to think calmly—Savina existed on two widely separated planes. This one, where a part of him which he did not really know was intricately rooted in a passion that bewildered his thought and burned his senses, and on another, quite different, where he saw her moving about her prosaic routine, saw her and thought of her in the commonplace terms of ordinary day.

He wondered suddenly what she thought of him. Was there a secret world in Savina, too?

Savina had seemed to find all she needed of companionship and conversation with Robby. And with that Janek girl. He remembered now that Taska came often since David had left. Fetching news of David to Savina, no doubt. Something raced across his quieter thoughts like a sudden wind across wheat stirring an intricate commotion. He was not jealous that Savina should hear from David and tell him nothing of it. That was natural enough. He wished no news of David. Certainly not. But he hated this talk that must go on behind his back . . . this secret, half conspiracy! How much of that there must have been between David and Savina he could not guess. But they—they had something in common which they kept from him. Why did they not talk to him, too? Why could they not come out in the open and *say* what they had to say?

There would not be such a thing as conspiracy in Robby. No: he was sure about that. When he thought of Robby there fell across his attention the same quieting sense that he sometimes felt when he thought of Savina. It was like a lull between gusts of contrary winds.

The dinner bell rang and Peter went to the house. He ate hurriedly, and did not stop for even a moment's rest afterward.

The mists of the earlier part of the day had cleared, and the sun beamed down with summer strength. Peter gave himself over wholly to his work. He had forgotten the meditations and questions of the forenoon. He had fallen now into that self-induced suspension of thought and feeling by which he temporarily escaped consciousness of fatigue and the needless, vexatious mauling of his own mind.

The sun kept up its steady heat; the day was still. No one passed, or called to him from the road. Once or twice he was momentarily conscious of a recurrent beat, like the tramp of a horse, or the faraway sound of a river boat. He looked up once but saw nothing. Later it came again, elusive—not really a sound, but a rhythm. He thought it might be the regular motion of his own labors that set up a counting in his brain, but he found himself fitting words to it . . . trying to remember words . . . some words that belonged to this rhythm, this beat . . .

. . . *therefore I tell* . . .

Peter brushed his ear as if to drive away the hum of gnats.

. . . *therefore* . . . *therefore I tell my sorrow to the* . . . He stopped as if to listen—oh, yes . . . *to the stones,* . . . *though they cannot answer my distress, yet* . . . *yet in some sort are better* . . . No, that was not quite right—not quite . . . *are better than tribunes!* . . .

Peter started. He put his hand to his eyes and stepped backward as if he had come suddenly on an abyss. He muttered unclearly to himself.

Now what the devil was that? Where did those words come from, and what did they mean?

Peter stood still. Down in one's mind, deep down as in the bottom of a well, there must be many strange, unexplainable things, half memories, incompleted experiences, what not, in God's name! what might not be there? All of a man's life that he knew least about, maybe the shattered fragments, the inescapable souvenirs of other lives than his own—his father's—his father's father's! A chance drift in the imperceptible currents and a broken reflection comes to view.

. . . A word out of this mysterious catchall . . . a scrap from a rag bag . . . The derelicts of discarded wishes . . .

He stopped again to shake his head savagely. He hunched his shoulders. The fighting-bull look, misshaping the tall gaunt figure . . .

A man could be betrayed in this way! Those words, those fool words about sorrow! *Tell the stones!* Some sort of abominable poetry, more than half forgotten, sunk away beneath the years, and rising now to mock at his peace, to sound a lie—as if—as if there lurked somewhere in him distractions and tragedies. Poetry! He used to read a lot of it. A useless ingenuity with words to make some small thing seem great. A trick to talk to the senses instead of to the mind.

There had been another time . . . perhaps that was not so long ago, when he had found himself saying lines from Dante. He remembered that someone had called Dante a Methodist parson howling amid the tombs. He did not know who had said it, but it was not inept, even if it did fail to perceive—fail to perceive what? Peter frowned as he caught one part of his mind disagreeing with another part. For even now in this moment he felt again the curious sweetness of those words. He straightened himself, took off his floppy old hat, and walked to the fence. He leaned there for a little, resting his arms on the top rail.

He thought again of the unknown part of a man's mind. Deep, dark, hidden away beyond reach or inspection. The deep well, as he had said to himself a few moments ago, the black, deep well of a man's past. It could be a threat—against peace, against sanity, even. The sweat stood heavy on his brow. He turned his attention inward, far inward, seeking—listening, but there was no response. It was silent back there and dark.

Peter tried to tell himself that this was not healthy thinking. The mood was morbid, shadowed by a senseless fantasy. But something else persisted—an unmistakable sense of pressure from that unknown, a sense of mounting pressure. Presently, presently, it seemed to say . . .

He cleared his vision with an effort. Out there the narrowed stream stirred the white sunlight, breaking it in a million sparkles— *faville vive*—like something moving in the brilliant silence of a dream.

"Pop, oh, look, Pop, what I got!"

It was Robby coming hurriedly along the road. Peter's heart jumped a little. This was certainly strange. He had never known Robby to break upon him like that—so gaily—so—so unafraid.

"Looky, Pop."

"What have you got there?"

"It's a dog!"

"Yes. I can see that much." Peter smiled, but his brow knotted against the glare looked frowning and heavy.

"It's a little bloodhound!"

"Where did you get that?"

"Laurel gave it to me. They've got five."

"Who is Laurel, Robby?"

"Laurel *Sandifer!*"

"Oh, of course. I'd forgotten."

"She gave me this one—it's the nicest one. It's a she."

"A bloodhound, eh?"

"Yes. That's a wonderful kind of a dog. You can track anything with a bloodhound."

"Yes?"

Robby looked anxious. "I can keep her, can't I? You don't care if I have her, do you?"

"You'd better ask your mother."

"I don't think she would mind, if you don't."

"You think not?"

"No, I'm sure. Can I keep her?"

"Yes; as far as I'm concerned."

"Goody!"

"Do you like a bloodhound?"

"I like Jude's mother. This one is Jude. I named her."

"Where did you get that name?"

"I don't know. It just sounded like she looks. Looky, Pop. Jude looks old and worried already."

Peter laid his hand under the puppy's velvet jaw and lifted its face. The deep creases, as of age-long sorrow and anxiety, lay in a symmetrical pattern across the high, domed head. The topaz eyes, tragically set, were in ludicrous contrast to the puppy's friendly eagerness.

Peter laughed outright.

"What's the matter, Pop?" Robby drew back a little.

"She—looks so serious."

"I expect she is a very serious dog."

"I wouldn't be surprised."

"Do—do you know very much about dogs, sir?"

Peter stared at Robby for an instant. "What did you say just then?"

"Me?"

"Yes—you, of course."

"I—I said, do you know very much about dogs—sir?"

"Do you always say 'sir' to me, Robby?"

"I don't know. I guess I don't speak to you very often."

"Why not?"

"You're busy all the time, and I don't like to bother you."

"I see."

"Laurel said I ought to say 'sir,' when I speak to Mr. Sandifer, so I—I thought it would be right to say it to you, too—sir!" He laughed, a shade more at ease. A flash of amusement, like an instant of lightning, set his green eyes alight, at the same time half hiding them in the mesh of his thick lashes.

"Well, that seems all right."

"It's polite, isn't it?"

"Yes; you don't have to overdo it, though."

"Just often enough so it sounds like you know how?"

"Yes, I guess that would be it."

"The Sandifers have lots of dogs."

"So I've heard."

"All kinds of dogs to hunt with, and—and other kinds that you have just to lie around the house."

"How did, this—Laurel child happen to give you a dog?"

"She is my special friend."

"Oh."

"I guess I'll run now and show Jude to Mom."

Peter nodded. He watched Robby as the boy galloped sideways, taking the corn rows as a horse takes a hedge. Peter was puzzled. He was not sure what it was that was puzzling. But, whatever it was, it had to do with Robby. Come to think of it, he could not remember when he had ever taken a square look at the boy. Nor could he recall Robby ever speaking to him of his own accord before. Peter's face crinkled a little at the picture of this preposterous dog. He had never had a dog when he was a small boy—or a pet of any kind. He had never really owned a living thing until he bought a team of horses. That dog, now. She seemed to have taken up with Robby at once.

The next afternoon Laurel burst into the Sandifer living room. She gave her father a quick hug.

"Where's Mother, eh? Where's Mother, Daddy?"

"Heavens, give me time to answer!"

"Where is she?"

"Well, first of all—good afternoon, my daughter."

"Oh, don't. Where's—"

"She's upstairs, I fancy. What is so urgent?"

"Robby's out on the porch."

Kam sat up in mock surprise. "No!"

"Yes, he is—oh, you're making fun!"

"Well, the news was so startling."

"He comes by here every afternoon. We're hungry. There's some pie in the kitchen cupboard."

"Yes." Her father answered dreamily. "Currant. Canned currants, of course, but delectable."

"But what?"

"Good, darling, good."

"D'you think it'll be all right—"

"I'm sure you and Robby are welcome, but it might be discreet to ask your mother."

"All right."

"I think I hear your mother—"

Laurel dashed out into the hall.

"Mother!"

"Hello, darling. Home already?"

"Yes, we hurried 'cause we're hungry."

"Roy?"

"Oh, goodness, no! *Robby*. He's out there on the back porch. I saw some pie—"

"I'll come with you. I think I'd better save a wedge for Roy—"

"Hurry up, please—"

"Are you starving? Hello, Robby."

"Hello, ma'am."

"How are you?"

"All right, ma'am."

"I hope the—er—dog was a welcome visitor over at your place."

"Yes'm."

"What did your father say?"

"He said Jude seemed to be a very serious dog."

Mrs. Sandifer laughed. "I dare say."

"Can I get the pie, Mother?"

"Yes, run on if you're starving. Are you hungry, too, Robby?"

"Yes'm."

"Well, I suppose we can find something else if the pie doesn't fill the void."

She stood considering Robby who looked back at her with the bright frankness of a bird.

"Your hair is all every-which-a-way, Robby! In your eyes!"

"I guess I'm pretty *strubbelkupfich!*"

"What's *that?*"

"Hair all every-which-a-way!"

"Oh!"

Mrs. Sandifer reached out and ran her fingers through Robby's gold tousle of hair that seemed to float away from his head.

"Your hair is thick!"

"Yes'm."

"You should brush it back more. Here—" She took a comb and brush from the porch washstand. "Let me see what I can do with it."

"Mother, what are you doing to Robby? Here, Robby, here's your pie."

"Just fixing his hair. Now, isn't that better?"

Laurel considered it. She nodded agreement.

"I think Robby is very handsome that way." Mrs. Sandifer looked sideways at Laurel.

"I told you the other day Robby is the most beautiful person in the world!"

"Oh, yes. I had forgotten."

"No-o, you didn't. You're trying to tease me. Don't you let her em-embarrass you, Robby."

Mrs. Sandifer laughed. It would be about as easy to embarrass a robin, she thought. Robby was certainly an odd one. She had never seen so unself-conscious a person—like a little creature, or—or a savage!

He is beautiful, she thought. Laurel is right. I have never seen a boy's face like that. Robby was busy with the pie, but his eyes seemed to go on with the conversation. It was clear that an unusual understanding existed between him and Laurel. Mrs. Sandifer sat down on the long bench against the wall and watched the two children. Heavens! Laurel was growing up fast. Her long legs were no longer a little girl's legs. They had a grown-up look, and, oh, dear—allure. Laurel's skimpy gingham dress was tight across her chest. The firm little breasts were sharply outlined. Laurel ate silently, watching Robby as she gulped.

The boy and girl were a striking contrast. Laurel was all flush and color, all movement and exuberance, all warmth and eagerness. Robby was like—well, Mrs. Sandifer thought, he's as much like a young tree as anything. His complexion was slightly pink under his even tan, and his soft young mouth was cut like a girl's. Robby had

[224]

the same look of almost unearthly purity that transfigured Savina.

"Are you through, Robby?" Laurel brushed the crumbs from her dress.

He nodded.

"Where are you going, Laurel?"

"With Robby."

"But where?"

"Up through the woods."

"But you'll have to come back alone."

"No, ma'am. I go nearly home with him, then he brings me nearly back to my house again."

Kam sauntered out on the gallery. "A very nice arrangement. Could be prolonged indefinitely, I should say."

Laurel looked at him doubtfully. "I don't know what you mean by all those long words."

"I'll bet you do."

"I just know I like to walk home with Robby, and that he likes to walk back with me."

"I thought you understood me in the first place."

"Kam!" Mrs. Sandifer gave him a warning glance.

Laurel flung her curly head about. "Don't bother, Mother. He doesn't hurt me any by all that. I'm just in love with Robby, that's all."

"I see. That's all—just so!"

Mrs. Sandifer looked quickly at Robby. He was listening to Laurel and her father as if the conversation had nothing on earth to do with him.

"Well," she said under her breath, "I never!"

"He's in love with me, too, of course," Laurel continued airily.

"Naturally, well I hope so, Laurel."

"Aren't you, Robby?"

Robby nodded briskly.

"Well, come on, let's go, then."

The two started up toward the hill in an easy dogtrot.

Kam looked after them. "I wonder if we are right in permitting those children to run around in the woods like that—alone."

"Well, I'd wonder, too, if I were considering Laurel alone."

"What do you mean?"

"Can't you look at her and see what I mean?"

"Great-great-grandma Witherspoon!"

"Yes, but Robby—"

"Well, he's a boy, isn't he?"

"No. I think he's an elf."

"I doubt that."

Mrs. Sandifer looked thoughtfully after the two figures just disappearing into the old path over the hill. Her brow shadowed a little as she thought of her passionate-eyed little daughter. She knew that no inept hand could guide the child, who was scarcely a child any longer. But there was a clairvoyant reassurance in her mind. And that was Robby himself.

Kam knocked the ashes from his pipe on the porch rail.

"I hope to God they'll grow up and marry each other."

"Why, Kam?"

"She'll need somebody like that, I imagine. Besides he'll be a rich boy someday."

"Well, I don't know. I don't know anything about them."

"Don't worry. They're all right."

"Are they?"

"Yes. I was over to see Kettring yesterday. Sold him my land up at Camperville."

"Why, Kam! You said it would be a good thing to hold on to that."

"It would have been, my dear. But I have to pay bills. And this does it—for one more year, anyway."

"Are things pretty bad, Kam?"

"Bad enough. But Tred and Kate will have everything they need this year."

A few moments' silence fell. A rooster stepped cautiously onto the gallery. He cocked his head first to one side and then the other, ventured farther, and picked up a crumb. Reassured by the inactivity of the human dangers, he pecked rapidly.

"Kam?"

"Yes, honey."

"Didn't that other Kettring boy run away from home because his father wouldn't let him go to school?"

"Yes."

"And he let you have the money to send Tred?"

"Well, that isn't why he let me have the money. He just bought the land, that's all."

"It's perfectly outrageous. I wish I had a chance to give that man a good dressing down."

"Wouldn't do any good. He'd just look at you with those impenetrable black eyes of his, and you'd stutter and sputter, and quit in confusion."

"You must have tried it!"

"In a way, yes."

"Well, what's the matter with him, anyway? Why can't he act like other people?"

"I wish I knew. Whatever has happened to him—to his real, inside self—must have been more than serious. He's in some sort of horrible misery."

"Goodness, Kam!"

"I think that. But I'm not sure that he knows it himself. Sometimes when he looks at you—like yesterday, for instance—I was sitting on the fence and he was sitting on a brush pile, so he had to look up, he—well, he looked like a man down in a snake pit. He gives me the shivers sometimes."

"You couldn't be imagining a lot of that?"

"I don't think so."

"You don't think it could be plain ornery meanness, do you?"

"Like the Pennsylvania Dutch, you mean, Martha?"

"Yes."

"He's not of that breed. Not at all."

"Then I don't understand the first thing about it."

"Neither do I. But I'm sure of one thing—"

"Yes?"

"We haven't seen the last of tragedy over at the Kettring place."

"Oh, Kam—you—"

"It's just a feeling, but I'm usually right about that kind of a presentiment."

Robby and Laurel rounded the curve of the hill, higher on its face than the way of the old trail which formerly led from the Sandifer farm to the Adams. There was a group of magnificent trees just above an outcropping of great, gray boulders. The foliage was so thick and the shade so dense that the ground and the trunks of the trees were covered with a heavy pile of green velvet moss. There was a peculiar quiet prevailing here, as if sounds of the outside world were muffled, and as if birds silenced their singing. The two children came to this place often. It was their favorite spot of all the wooded hills. At first they called it the "haunted place" and provoked shivers in each other recounting imaginary happenings of the past which might have left this strange spell in their wake. Their imaginations reached little beyond ghosts and robbers in the beginning, and then as their fancies grew they created stranger beings and darker happenings. For a while they called it "the church" until Robby discovered the word cathedral.

"What's a cathedral, Robby?"

"A very special kind of church."

"Special how?"

"I don't know. Just special. Very big—with popes and cardinals, and altars and things."

This was vague to Laurel, but she accepted one set of words as an explanation of another set equally mysterious.

So it was "the cathedral" for a while, until Robby fancied "the temple" as less restrictive on the imagination. A temple could be anything.

Just outside this grove of great trees stood a thicket of cedars. They devised a pathway through these which they invariably followed. Two tall ones were the columns of the gate. The way through to the temple was a circling, mazing route which doubled on itself and entered the inner precinct finally from the opposite side. Neither of them would have dreamed of varying this procedure, even when alone. It was one of the many rituals which they called "sacred." They used the word first in the belief that it meant very secret, later as a mere form of evocation.

This afternoon they entered the temple with their accustomed solemnity.

Laurel had perhaps a little more than the usual fancifulness of children. It might have been because she had been stimulated by Robby's flying imagination.

Make-believe, fancy, mounting to a kind of clairvoyance, was the natural air of Robby's confined world. All of his fourteen years had been spent inside the small range of river and hills. These were the physical boundaries of his material journeyings. The village of St. Stephens did not interest him much. Camperville and Kings Row and Jefferson confused him. There were too many houses and too many people.

But here, with the flow of the river leading out to infinity, and the hills leading one's eyes toward another infinity, Robby lived with an intensity that perhaps no one but Laurel saw or realized, though she was far from understanding it. Laurel perceived that Robby's way of being was a way of seeing. It seemed to her that he saw more than anyone, that he saw through and into the objects before him. To some extent she followed his mind as it went its unpredictable way—like a dragonfly making a pattern of a wayward flight.

"Can you see into a rock, Robby, into the inside of it?"

He looked at her rather dreamily. "Of course," he answered airily.

"What's it like?"

"Just like it looks when you think about it."

Laurel nodded thoughtfully. She accepted this as explanation.

Laurel sat down on the soft moss. Robby stood leaning against a tree. They had spells of talking—sometimes both at once which never seemed to confuse them. Now, as often happened, they had little to say.

With Laurel, Robby was as completely himself as it was possible for him to be with anyone. With his mother he was a simple, natural, and affectionate little boy, chattering gaily of commonplace things. At school and with the people he met he retired to a bright-eyed reticence. He was not really shy because he was not self-conscious. He was not really timid because he had no impulse to project himself in any way. But here, the look on his face and the manner of his bearing were different. Sometimes Laurel was amazed because she did not seem to be a necessary or a living part of his mood. But there were other times when she felt as if she and Robby were simply two aspects of the same person.

Then she usually broke out with an exclamation. "I just *love* you, Robby."

Robby would glance at her and go on doing whatever engaged him at the moment. He would nod, or say something in agreement as if he could not understand the necessity of saying what was so obviously true.

Here in the temple they were as quiet as chipmunks. But they were aware of each other with an almost abnormal sensitivity of eye and ear. They looked at the same things, they were sure that their responses were the same, and they almost breathed as one. The subtle, indefinable currents of apprehension and appraisement of their own special world flowed back and forth between them weaving an ever-deepening understanding, an ever-increasing unity, and an ever-strengthening devotion.

They were curiously untouched and uncolored in mind by their experiences. Their contacts with adult talk and behavior they left outside, as the faithful leave their shoes outside the door of a shrine. All they saw and heard from day to day seemed to have nothing to do with them. When they were together they were as much alone down there in the valley as they were at this moment.

This was the peak of their childhood, the last high reach of a golden period when all the seasons of their minds were spring.

Robby's eyes were as limpid as a forest pool, but faint shadows were encroaching upon Laurel's steady regard of him as he stood there looking out through the drooping branches to the light moving on the river. The first far tremors of the alarms of adolescence made obscure passage along her nerves.

She stirred restlessly. She recognized a new mood, a new feeling for Robby, but she did not know what it was. A picture flashed into her mind: once when she and Robby were high up in the hills on a late summer afternoon they saw a phantomlike flash of heat lightning far down the west. The sky had seemed cloudless but in that instant of lightning a whole company of thunderheads stood revealed, towering and threatening across the horizon. She frowned and pondered for a moment. There was no lightning, no thunderclouds. The day was silent and serene.

She looked up at Robby. He was looking at her and his quick smile crossed his face with a transforming light. She caught her breath, and then, on the instant, the curious mood of tension passed.

"I guess we'd better go," she said involuntarily.

"All right."

He took her hand and swung it back and forth as they threaded their way through the cedars.

BOOK THREE

I

ANOTHER year passed with all of the characteristic violences of changing weathers, and another October lay dreaming over the valley.

Men gathered as usual in St. Stephens to talk over the events of the year. All of the scattered fragments of news were brought together—stitched and quilted into that patchwork of legend which was the valley's own story of itself.

Many of these people who assembled at the general stores, saloons, at the post office, or on the platforms of the feed exchanges saw each other only once or twice a year, but they met and took up comment on the county happenings without the necessity of pre-amble or explanation. It seemed almost as if the news itself traveled on the wind and waited only for examination and criticism at some time, when casual encounters took place.

Small talk—all of it. It was made up of half statements designed to draw the listener out, of sly half questions to which a nod or a grunt or silence might make significant answer. To the uninitiated it might sound like the idlest of comment, but, like rustic gossip the world over, the actual gist of the exchanges lay between the words, in the tone of voice, the assumed lack of interest. It was an old art—this gossip—developed through long periods of caution and indirection. No one committed himself in words too outspoken. All preferred the suggestion, the oblique inquiry, each rich with inference and implication, each sounding with a complication of rewarding overtones.

Such talk was rooted in shrewdness, in cold curiosity, in keen social awareness. It was practiced as one of the rights of communal interchange. It was conscious, and calculated, and each man savored it carefully and critically according to his character.

"I hear Kam Sandifer's got three of his children off to school this year."

"Yep, that's what I heard."

"Public school not good enough for 'em, heh?"

"That's not it. They're the older ones, done finished down here."

"Don't say so? Well, ain't that enough schoolin' for anyone, less'n they goin' to be lawyers or doctors or somethin'?"

"Well, you know the Sandifers. Always was a little tony in their ways."

"Yes! Even old Mr. Sandifer always thought he was a shade better'n anybody else."

"Got a passel of children, ain't they, the Sandifers?"

"Whole houseful. About seven—maybe nine—I don't know exactly."

"Takes a heap to provide for that many these days."

"Yes, everything's changin'. Used to be a man had a lot of children and as soon as they growed up a little they began to help."

"That's right. A man with a heap of children in them days was lucky. He had his own farm hands."

"The children are different now. They got a lot of new ideas."

"Ain't one of Kam's oldest a girl?"

"Yes."

"Send her off to school, too?"

"Yes, sir. Up to Columbia. There's some kind of a female seminary up there."

"Well, I'd be doggoned if I see the use in sending girls off for schoolin'. Just makes 'em dissatisfied."

"Well, that's the way things is a-goin' nowadays. *Ever'* thing's changin'."

"So Kam's got three of 'em off? Must cost a heap."

"I heard him say right down there at the bank one day that it was going to cost him seven or eight hundred dollars a year."

"You don't mean apiece, do you?"

"Of course."

"Lord! Kam Sandifer can't afford that. Where's he get the money? I bet everything he's got's mortgaged to the roof."

"No, it ain't. I happen to know. I guess Kam's right smart. He's been in some kind of partnership with that Kettring feller—they bought a lot of land, you know."

"Yes. Done well at it, too. Maybe Kettring furnished some of the brains."

"They say he's smart as all get out."

"He's a rich man, but he sure gets out and works like anybody else."

"Well, I wouldn't say he was anything special. No reason why he *shouldn't* work just like anybody else."

"You know how it is, though. A man gets a little money and first thing you know he thinks he's too good to work."

"Like Colonel Middleton up round Kings Row."

"Yeh—like Kam Sandifer, too, 's far as that goes."

"Kam ain't got ideas like that. He's just lazy."

"Kam's really a good practical stock farmer."

"Maybe so."

"Old Mr. Sandifer was lazy, too."

"Well, he had slaves. God, in them days if a man owned a few slaves he didn't have to work."

"The Sandifers owned a lot of 'em."

"Them big slaveholders never did learn to work, neither."

"They all seem to make out somehow."

"Doggone if I ever can understand it. I always had to work."

"Me, too. Ain't found no way out of it yet!"

"Them Nolan twins is in town today."

"Where they been?"

"Oh, they've been up to Kings Row, goin' to college. Didn't you know that?"

"No. I guess I just never asked nobody. Come to think of it I ain't seen 'em for a long time."

"They've been up there going on three years, I guess."

"Nolan don't figure on 'em takin' over the saloon business, I guess."

"They're goin' to be doctors or something like that. Old man told me so himself."

"I guess keeping a saloon pays pretty well, from the looks of that."

"You ought to know. I guess you've contributed as much as anybody!"

The other laughed this off. "Sho! All of us just get together and pay for Nolan's boys to go to college, eh?"

"That's about the size of it."

"It's pur near enough to make me lay off drinkin'."

"But not quite enough, I bet."

"Well, what's the odds? I guess Nolan's got as good a right as anybody to educate his boys."

"Sure, sure, he has."

"What's the boys doin' home then?"

"It's Saturday. I guess they come down to stay over Sunday with the old man."

"I think there's another reason. You know old man Janek, down the bottom a piece?"

"Yes. Some kind of a foreigner."

"He's got a girl."

"I know. I know. Named Taska."

"That's the one."

"She's a schoolteacher now. She's got the Sandifer school— below Kam's place."

"Well, I think the Nolan boys, one or the other of 'em, 's after her. I saw them around with her two or three times."

"H'm. Nolans are Catholics, ain't they?"

"Yes. So's old man Janek."

"What's his girl doing teaching school then? First thing you know she'll be turning all them school children into Catholics."

"Well, anyway, she's teaching down at the Sandifer school."

"I'll be doggoned if I think that's right. Don't believe in havin' no Catholic teachin' in the public schools. Let 'em go teach in their own schools."

"Old man Janek's a right nice old fellow."

"Don't make no difference. That's all right 's far as it goes. But a Catholic's a Catholic. You can't change 'em."

"As I said—I think one of the Nolan boys comes down here to see her."

"Nolan's got plenty of money. Be a good match for her, wouldn't it?"

"You know, I did hear once—last year, I guess—that she was settin' her cap for Peter Kettring's oldest boy."

"But he's young, ain't he?"

"Same age as the Nolans, about. But of course you remember he ain't here any more."

"I forgit. What happened?"

"He run off—or his daddy run him off, I don't know which."

"Well, I'll be doggoned. I guess everybody has his troubles. Take all the pains to raise up a boy, and he gets some kind of fool notion in his head and runs off."

"Children ain't dependable like they used to be."

"Parents ain't strict enough."

"The schools have got a lot to do with it. All kinds of new notions goin' round."

"Yeh."

"What do you hear of the new railroad, Bob?"

"Well, Mr. Day was down to St. Louis the other day. He says it's certain."

"Well, now. That'll change a lot of things, won't it?"

"Yes. It'll be good for St. Stephens."

"Bring in lots of new people, I guess."

"When they think it's comin', Bob?"

"I don't know. There's been a lot of surveying going on last three or four years. Another gang of 'em went through here about a month ago. Let me see, now—yes, it was; just about a month ago—maybe six weeks."

"You don't know any particulars?"

"I hear there's talk of putting the depot up about the Sanderson lots."

"Why that's 'way out on the edge of town!"

"Town'll grow to it, don't you worry."

"Cut right through the bottoms, I guess?"

"Pretty much along the old river road, I believe."

"River'll wash it away ever' spring. Mark my words."

"They'll build up the roadbed, like they did on the south side."

"But we get all the floods over here. We're lower."

"They can fix it."

"Hear any more talk about a bridge?"

"Not now. That's kind of died down."

"Costs too much, I guess."

"Doggone if I believe they could build that big a bridge!"

The Nolan twins were still as much alike as the proverbial two peas, but even two peas exhibit differences on close examination. Most people were still confused by their resemblance, but Taska was not. Timothy was the more aggressive of the two. Paul was a little shy.

The three of them sat this Saturday afternoon in Phillip Bachman's Ice Cream Parlor. They had a table just inside the window where the stiff-starched lace curtains were tied back with blue watered-silk ribbons. Phillip was very proud of this effect. The three attracted some attention from the people passing by, but they were not aware of it. Timothy's eager manner was evident enough to cause some comment, but no one noticed Paul's hovering watchfulness.

Taska was enjoying herself. She had her father's talent for simple enjoyment of trivial pleasures.

"Taska!" Timothy looked straight into Taska's eyes.

The girl's warm color came and went in quick response to every slight emotion. Just now she felt a more serious tone in Timothy's voice and a more purposeful look in his eye.

"Taska, I bet I know why I can't make any time with you a-tall!"

"Do you?" Her smile was teasing, but her eyes shadowed a little.

"It's David."

"Do you think so?"

"Yes. It is, isn't it?"

"Maybe, Timothy."

All at once they were serious. Their easy confidence and understanding carried into seriousness as well as in casual encounters. Taska knew that Timothy liked her—that he liked her more than was comfortable for her to think about. Curiously, she knew that Paul did, too, but she was not considering that just now. Paul was so clearly making way for his brother. No one of them thought it peculiar that this tentative courtship should be carried on in trio. There was no separating the twins in any relationship. For one instant Taska wondered how they would ever manage marriage.

"What are you smiling at, Taska?"

"I don't know. Nothing important."

"Maybe you think I'm funny?"

"No."

"You've got the darnedest way with you! I just can't make you out!"

"There's nothing to 'make out.'"

"It *is* David, then?"

"I guess so, Tim."

Paul laid his hand over Taska's. "It's a darn shame—his going off and all that."

"Say!" Timothy spoke in a half whisper. "Where is David, anyway?"

"You won't tell?"

"Well, for gosh sake, is it a secret?"

"He doesn't want Mr. Kettring to know. He's afraid the old

devil might come after him or make trouble for him in some way."

"What's he doing, Taska?"

"He's working in a newspaper office."

"He is? How's he getting along?"

"Pretty well."

"David's all right."

"Tim, you were going to say something."

"Yes, Taska. Gee, you know we like Dave a lot—even if he has got a hold on you—" Tim hesitated.

"Go on."

"I thought maybe he'd come up to Kings Row and stay in our room. We got a big room."

"What good would that do him?"

"Well, I know he wanted to go to Aberdeen—"

"Yes—he did: more than anything in the world, I guess."

"It's a doggone shame," Paul broke in like a timed chorus.

"Well—this is what I was thinking about. I bet my dad would lend him enough money—it doesn't cost much, just tuition, and board, and he could stay with us for nothing."

Taska looked hard at Timothy, then at Paul. "I think you are the grandest kids I ever heard of."

"Do you think he would do it, Taska?"

She shook her head. "No. I know he wouldn't. I offered to help—myself."

"Well, of course, he couldn't take anything from a girl!"

"Why not?"

"Oh, thunder, Taska, don't you understand anything?"

"I know that I—I love David enough to do anything for him."

Timothy drew his shoulders up as if he had been sitting under strain. He let them down again, and whistled softly.

"Bad as that, Taska?"

"Yes, Tim. I wouldn't say that to anybody else."

"Well, I certainly do wish you felt that way about me—or—or Paul, but since it's David, all right, that's the way it is."

"That *is* the way it is, Tim."

"You won't change your mind? Ever?"

"Never. I couldn't." Taska was completely serious now. The twins had never seen that expression on her face. "It's for life, Tim."

"Well, all right, Tass—and good luck. I wish you'd write Dave and see if—"

"He won't, Tim. I'll have to thank you for him. He has to go his own way. I guess he's that much like his hardheaded old daddy."

"Dave'll do all right."

"You bet, Taska. That kind always does."

"Do you think so, Paul, honest?"

"Sure I do. Of course."

"I believe so myself, but I like to hear you say it, too."

"You never did say where he is. We could write to him, anyway."

"He's at a little town called Crawford. 'Way down the river in Arkansas."

"Good gracious! How'd he happen to go there?"

"He met somebody in Camperville who had a brother in Crawford. That man—the brother—owned a newspaper and a printing shop. It's a bigger place than St. Stephens. About like Kings Row, I guess."

"I bet old David'll be owning the newspaper first thing you know."

"Well, I'll tell you a secret."

"Come on, I thought there was something!"

"I'm going down there next year—"

"Honest?"

"Yes. I might have to wait two years, but I'm going to him."

"And all the time I've been making up to you, you've been engaged to old Dave?"

"No. We're not engaged. It's just been understood ever since we were kids—"

"Gosh, I remember Dave was ready to fight one day—first day we ever saw him because—because we said something pretty fresh about *you!*"

"Yes. I know about that. He told me that evening."

"Say—did he, really?"

"Yes. But he doesn't know I'm going to come to him just as soon as I've saved up some money. I don't see any use in David fighting everything out by himself. I'm going to go help him."

The twins exchanged looks. Concertedly they reached for her hands and gave them a hard squeeze.

"Good old Tass!"

She laughed. " 'Good old Tass'—that sounds exactly like an old family horse, or something."

"No: just good old Taska Janek—Dave's luck."

One of the new teachers at St. Stephens that year was Perry Eastman. He was a good-looking young man, fresh from Aberdeen College, and with a leaping enthusiasm for teaching. The students took to him at once, but the townspeople were not sure that anyone so casual could possibly be all that a teacher was expected to be.

Perry Eastman looked like a Missourian, tall, rangy, and rather pungent of speech, but he was a Pennsylvanian. Savina had the surprise of her life when he walked up to the farm one afternoon in early winter and spoke to her in her dialect German.

She was flustered for a moment, and then the quaint, homely familiar speech of Martinsgrove established an immediate ease.

"How did you know I spoke so?" She felt as much at home with this young man as if she had seen him for years. All of the hard years here in the valley rolled away and she felt again the very airs of her old home.

"Robby." Eastman smiled.

"Robby? Did he speak to you so?"

"No. I heard him one day—sort of half talking to himself when he was working something out at the blackboard."

"But Robby speaks good English, not?" She asked the question anxiously. Eastman sensed at once the depth of her concern for Robby.

"Oh, yes—but he does his arithmetic in Pennsylvania German!"

"Think now!"

"Yes, it's a little odd. Does Robby always speak this way to you?"

"I believe always, yes. I never learned English much myself."

Eastman opened his eyes very wide. "Do you mean you *can't* speak English?"

"Not much. It shames me always when I think about it, but I never need it, anyway. When we came out here from Pennsylvania, Peter—that is my husband—was going to teach me. I have some books—I learned a little, but there is always so much to do. It seems I never had time."

"But your husband—"

"Oh, he is very smart. He has much education, and he speaks fine high German—even to me—he knows other languages, too."

"Oh, really?"

"Yes. Come in to the front room. Let me show you his books."

Savina led the way to her best room, raised the curtains, and indicated the bookshelves along one side of the wall.

Perry Eastman glanced at the volumes, carelessly at first, then with surprised interest. He ran his index finger along a line of titles and whistled softly.

"I didn't know there was anything out here like this, except in the Aberdeen Library."

"They are very fine books, not?" Savina sounded a little breathless, as if she feared Peter might not appear in a sufficiently favorable light.

"Oh, Lord, yes! What—you will excuse me if I ask questions?"

"Why, of course!"

"What was Mr. Kettring doing with this kind of a library?"

"It belonged to his father—and his grandfather."

"Oh!"

"But to him also. He studied and read—"

"But there's Latin and Greek and French and Italian and—"

"Yes!" Savina spoke proudly. "Robby told me. I taught Robby his German letters and already he reads German very well."

"Well, I'll be—"

"I don't know that Peter could read in *all* of these languages, but I think maybe so."

The young man was still so bewildered that his questions showed in his face.

Savina laughed a little. It was wonderful to be so at ease with a stranger, to be able to talk and make herself understood.

"You wonder. Oftentimes I have wondered me, too. Peter was, too, a schoolteacher like you, in the beginning. Then he wanted to come out here and make a farm for himself. It was not exactly that he wanted a farm—he was looking for something else. He told me once!"

"Yes?"

"He said—maybe you should not mention this ever—he said he was looking for reality."

"Reality?"

"Yes. I remember exactly. I did not know even the word, I was so dumb, he had to explain it to me."

"I see." Perry spoke slowly in a tone which said he did not see at all. "And—and did he find the reality he was looking for?"

"I do not know. *Ach!* Sit down—we are still standing!"

"Thank you—I just want to look a little more."

"I think I will start the fire. It is cold here—and you will stay and eat supper with us, yes?"

"Thank you, Mrs. Kettring, I will. I'd like to meet Mr. Kettring."

Savina was suddenly uneasy, and Perry saw it at once. "Maybe another time it might be more convenient?"

"Oh, no, it is not that!"

He looked inquiringly at her. She was a surprising person to him. She seemed much younger than he had expected Robby's mother to be, and she was amazingly pretty.

"Mr. Eastman, maybe I better tell you something. Mr. Kettring is—rather strange in his ways."

He tilted his head to one side in polite question. He did not wish to say that he had already heard that much.

"He is—he is not friendly. You must not mind if Peter does

not speak much, or maybe—even—not at all. It is that he is maybe thinking of something else, or has something heavy on his mind."

Perry Eastman smiled gaily. "That sounds like my grandfather back in Lewisburg!"

"Was he so, too?"

"Yes. But he was an old devil!"

"Oh—Peter—Peter is not an old devil."

"I'm sure of that."

"Wait now, I light the fire. It will be nicer when it is warm. Look! Already it is beginning to be dark. I light the lamp. So. Then I will hurry with the supper. I know you have not had any Pennsylvania cooking out here!"

"No, I haven't. But if you tell me you have *pannhass* and *lattwarick*, I won't be able to bear it!"

Savina laughed outright. "Better than that. Tonight I have chicken pot-pie—made, you know, in a big iron pot. An old hen—she has been cooking all afternoon."

"With dumplings cut in squares and dropped in?"

"Yes, with a few potatoes."

"But no onions?"

"Oh, dear God, no! Who ever heard—"

"That's right. Onions there should never be!"

"Of course not. Then—oh, I hear! Robby, is that you?"

"Yes."

"Come in here. Come. I have a surprise for you!"

Robby came through the door shyly. He had heard voices. "Oh, it is my teacher." He spoke, childishly, to his mother.

"Yes. And he is going to stay to supper."

"How are you, Mr. Eastman?" Robby was suddenly stiff and formal.

"Oh, all right, Robby. I was out for a walk, thought I'd drop in to meet your folks."

"We are very glad."

"I was just looking at your father's books. You've got a fine library here."

"Is it? I like many of them."

"Do you read a lot?"

"All the time—all the time I can."

"Excuse me now, Mr. Eastman, I fix supper. You and Robby talk. Make yourself at home. Robby, watch the damper in the stove. When it gets too hot, turn it off, yes?"

"Yes, Mommy."

Savina went hurriedly to the kitchen. Robby remained standing. He was looking unblinkingly at Eastman.

"Robby, what do you read, mostly?"

"Oh, anything. Pop, I guess, wouldn't like it if he knew."

"What?"

"No, sir. I think he would tell me I couldn't. But I take the books upstairs. Mommy, she knows."

"Well, why in the world?"

"Pop, he—I don't know." Robby looked hard at his teacher. He blinked a little, then something in Perry Eastman's eyes reassured him.

"Did you know I had a brother—sir?"

"No. I didn't. Older than you? Where is he?"

"Yes, older. He ran away."

"Why?"

"I don't know for sure—but it was something about books and reading, I think. Pop didn't want—" Robby stopped suddenly. "That is Pop, coming in. Don't tell I said—"

"Oh, of course not."

"Maybe we better not be in here when he comes."

"Your mother—"

"Oh, yes, she said, didn't she? O-ee! The damper! I forgot. The stove is red-hot now!"

Peter Kettring came in followed by Savina.

"Mr. Eastman, this is Peter, my husband."

"How do you do, Mr. Kettring."

"How do you do." Peter bowed. Perry Eastman stared. That bow was not of this region. People here nodded.

The two men stood in a rather awkward silence—at least it felt awkward for Perry, but he suddenly realized that it was not

[246]

awkward for Peter. Peter was standing quietly considering the young man. He was perfectly at ease.

"Won't you sit down?"

"Thank you—sir."

Peter stood drawing his gloves through his fingers. The gesture caught Perry's attention. It was a gentleman's gesture.

"Mrs. Kettring tells me you are having supper with us."

"She was so kind—"

"We are pleased. It is very seldom that anyone comes here who can talk to her."

"I am a little rusty in that speech myself."

"Yes? It's a curious speech. But you know it well?"

"Oh, yes. My family—"

"I see. It has seemed to me that Pennsylvania Dutch, as everyone here calls it, bears about the same relation to German proper as the Scottish dialect does to English."

"Well, perhaps. I'm not philologist enough to estimate it properly. But you—" Perry indicated the bookshelves. "You must be a linguist."

Instantly Peter's face darkened. "If you will excuse me—I must wash. I have just come in." He bowed again.

Perry Eastman caught his breath. He was thoroughly uncomfortable, and realized that there must be innumerable conversational pitfalls ahead. There was something very strange about all of this. These books! That manner of Kettring's! Mrs. Kettring—Robby— the boy who ran away. It just did not make sense.

Robby nudged him and pointed at one of the shelves.

"I like the poetry."

"Poetry—oh, you do?"

"Yes. I can't understand all of it, but I like the way it goes."

"I see."

"I read some in the Latin books, too, but I don't know a word of that! But it *goes* the same way, doesn't it?"

"Ye-es, I guess maybe it does. What of all there do you like best?"

"You guess it might be all right to talk about the books?"

Perry considered the strange, intense face before him. There were a wariness and a tension beneath the somewhat debonair exterior. Heavens, what a beautiful boy! he thought. Then he answered firmly. "Yes, it will be all right. I intend to talk about books to your father, myself."

"Honest? Do you dare, you think?"

Perry Eastman was not clear at that moment what was happening to him, but he knew that if Robby did not take that devouringly eager look from his face, he would not be able to endure it. What was happening to this boy—this extraordinary, this abnormally sensitive boy? What was being done to him? A fierce determination arose in the young teacher—he would find out! Somebody had to stand by him. It was curious that he had never noticed anything. Robby had attracted his attention because of his amazing, clear-chiseled features, but he had been a difficult boy to get at. He seemed normal enough on the playgrounds, and, of course, there was that engaging attachment to the Sandifer girl.

"Yes, Robby," he said after a moment. "Yes, I dare. You and I will talk a lot about books, too. Do they mean a lot to you?"

Robby looked uncertain.

"I mean, do you love them a lot?"

Robby shook his head. "No, sir."

Perry was so astonished that he did not speak for a moment.

"No? You *don't* care for books? I thought you said—"

"Oh, I like them, but you said—"

"Yes. I said love them a lot."

Robby shook his head again. "No, sir."

"What do you love?"

Robby was obviously embarrassed or puzzled by the word "love."

"I don't know."

Perry realized he was losing the ground he had gained in the first few moments. Robby was clearly in retreat.

"Well, I love a lot of things myself."

Robby was silent a moment—and watchful. Then he nodded slowly. "So do I."

Perry busied himself with a book. He spoke with a carefully disguised carelessness.

"What, for instance?"

Robby answered softly. *"Everything in the world."*

"What? What do you mean?"

Robby swept both arms in a circling gesture. "Everything."

"Do you mean nature, for example?"

The boy hesitated. "I guess so," he answered indifferently.

Savina came in hurriedly from the kitchen. "Are you all right—comfortable? Pretty soon now, we have supper. Peter, he will be downstairs in a minute. He is dressing. Don't let Robby talk you to death."

"Robby and I are just getting acquainted."

"Well—he is a chatterer—like a jaybird!"

Savina hurried away.

When Perry looked up, Robby was staring at him with a curious light in his eyes.

"What is it, Robby?"

"You—you can talk—like the Mommy!"

"Eh? Oh, you mean that kind of German. I learned it when I was a little boy."

"Did you learn from your mommy?" The soft-spoken dialect sounded unexpectedly musical on Robby's tongue.

"Yes—all my folks."

"It's easier to say, isn't it?"

"Is it for you?"

"Yes, it's the way—oh, I guess I never thought of it—"

"What, Robby?"

"I talk this way always with the Mommy. I guess it's just natural for me. But I say everything *easier* this way."

"I—I see. All right, let's speak that way, you and me."

"But—" Robby drew back.

"What now?"

"Not in school?"

"Well, no, of course not—but, why did you say that?"

"I guess the others would laugh."

[249]

"Listen, Robby, it's a fine thing to know another language—any language."

"Sometimes Pop smiles at the way the Mommy talks."

"It's only that it's quaint. It's a dialect."

"A what?"

Perry explained.

"Oh!" Robby sounded disappointed. "Then it's not as good as German—real German the way Pop speaks?"

"That's a hard question. We'll have to go into that sometime. Did you ever read any of Robert Burns?"

"Yes, sir."

"Have you Burns' poetry here?"

"No, sir. I read it over at Laurel's house. They've got books, too; but not a lot, like Pop."

"Well, anyway—"

But Perry did not have a chance to say much. Robby did indeed chatter like a chorus of jaybirds. He rattled on so fast that Perry, somewhat out of practice with the crazy syntax of this dialect, followed with difficulty. But the way was open to all of Robby's mind and heart. Perry found himself somewhat breathless with surprise. The barrier had actually been language! The place of Robby's abode lay there beyond that entanglement of idioms which were as difficult as they were curious.

But even as he struggled with his astonishment he was able to note that Robby spoke with exceptional skill. He had a way with that outlandish gibberish, a deft, light handling of the heavy words that gave them a quality of flight.

And now the sensitive, sympathetic young teacher was beginning to see into this boy's particular world—a shy, trembling, dawn-like world. He laid his hand over Robby's delicate fingers, but Robby did not notice the protective gesture. Savina had to speak twice before they heard her invitation to supper.

Perry Eastman had a lively intelligence. His perceptions were quick and keen and they communicated with a responsive imagination.

All through that strange supper he observed the Kettrings with increasing amazement and bewilderment. This, he kept saying to himself, just doesn't make sense.

The talk was fragmentary and was sustained even at that by Perry himself. Peter answered readily and easily, but he took no conversational initiative. It was difficult to make any kind of estimate of the man.

Savina was comprehensible in herself, but not in relation to Peter, or even to Robby. Eastman had seen her like at home, though seldom so pretty.

And Robby. Now, where did that Ariel child come from?

One would have said the three had met only by chance. Perry amended that at once. There was an understanding or a sympathy between Robby and his mother. It was apparently not a conscious exercise of any kind. It did not appear to be related to ideas, or even to words. It was like some charge that flowed back and forth between them—like a silent lightning exchanged by two lonely clouds.

After supper Perry determined to find out something about Peter's curious attitude to books, or whatever in thunder it might be that Robby had darkly hinted at.

He took a flying leap into a discussion of the school, of Robby's lessons, of his own studies at Aberdeen, and then, directly, of Robby's fluent use of Savina's dialect German.

Perry felt the sudden tension in the room but he was resolved not to be silenced by it. After a few moments, Peter took up the discussion, easily and naturally. The tension relaxed. Perry felt it, and saw it in that same indefinable exchange between Robby and his mother.

But when the evening was over, he was sure of but one thing, that the whole enigma of Peter Kettring had only tightened. He understood that shaggy, rough-cut man less, if possible, than at the beginning.

"I've had a wonderful evening, Mrs. Kettring. I hope you'll let me come again, soon."

"Whenever you want, Mr. Eastman. You must make like this is home."

"And Robby—"

"Yes, sir."

"I'm mighty glad to see you here at home. I'll know what to expect of you now."

Robby looked his question.

"You've a lot that most of the boys haven't. Books—smart parents."

"Yes, sir."

Perry turned to Peter. He was a shade anxious. "I've enjoyed this a lot, Mr. Kettring. I hope we can have some more talks."

Peter bowed.

Again that unexpected, disconcerting inclination that seemed so out of place here.

"Thank you," he said gravely.

Perry decided he should not let the matter rest at that. It was not the answer he wished.

"You see, Mr. Kettring, I'm just out of school, and I miss some of the teaching."

"Indeed?"

"Yes. Some of the men up there were very good."

Peter did not reply to this. He waited politely.

"It would be—well, an intellectual stimulation, if I could chat with you now and then."

"Thank you—very much."

"I expect I'll be running in to ask if I can borrow some of your books, too."

"Savina—Mrs. Kettring—is always here. She will be glad to oblige you, I know."

A long moment of silence followed.

"Well, I'll get along now, I guess."

Savina spoke quickly. "Can you find your way, do you think? Maybe you'd better have a lantern. Robby, run get a lantern for the teacher."

"Oh, I think I can make it. There's some moon—enough, I believe. There's a way down to the river road, of course?"

"Not a road, just a path, but it's plain—"

Peter interrupted. "Robby will take you to the gate. You could lose the path. But by all means take a lantern if it will help."

"Maybe I'd better."

Well, now, I'll be darned if I expected to find anything like that around St. Stephens. Perry half talked to himself as he walked along the river road toward home. The lantern, swinging from his right hand, made giant divergent shadows of his legs off to the left. The shuttling motion of these lancelike shadows caught at his attention. Absently, he tried to relate their motion to the rhythm of the lantern, but it was too intricate.

Like what? he asked himself. What had he found at the Kettrings'? He'd be darned again if he knew.

Peter Kettring had obviously had some sort of queer education, but it existed alone in a complete absence of relation to his life. It was, well, rather like a vaccination that did not take—something like that. But the man had a mind—a dynamic one. Original at times, independent. There was something—Perry searched for a word—something a bit valorous about the sudden forays and on-slaughts that Kettring had made during the talk—a little wild, too, like the surprise charge of a normally gentle creature.

Savina returned to the kitchen to make some small prepara-tions for the next morning. She had been so glad to see Robby's teacher that she had skimped her after-supper work.

She was still excited. Company! Not something like the visits of the Janeks, which were always much the same. This was real company—and he would come again. She slowed her hands—held them poised for a moment in their automatic performance of familiar tasks—a thought like a physical pain shot across her mind. *David.* David would have enjoyed this. He would have liked to see Mr. Eastman and talk like this—of things she understood not at all—of books and such matters. David—David—David. Yes, she heard of him and his work. He was pleased enough, though he made very little. The small amounts she had sent probably helped, but he said she should not send more. He would make his own way. That—that was like Peter! The thought crowded down, hard—heavy, on her running thought. What was it that she should not have David here—that Peter should make this great difficulty out of nothing?

Company! Real company! A visitor to whom she could talk, who understood all the little references to her old ways and habits.

The evening and the little homely chat at the table had stirred a forgotten kind of laughter deep in Savina's heart. Laughter. It had been a long time . . . the quiet movement of that laughter flowed out and out on the secret currents of Savina's blood. It was like a tonic—it stirred, and it awakened.

Peter was disturbed.

He thumped about the unfamiliar room, pushing the chairs into place, lowering the blinds, opening the damper in the stove pipe and closing the draft so that the fire would burn itself out.

He shook his head, a bit heavily. He paused for a moment at the bookshelves and tapped one or two volumes with his thick, clumsy fingers. He noted the incongruous relation of his worn, battered hand to the smooth leather bindings.

Peter was aware of what troubled him. He had been forced to talk about things he did not wish to talk about. Useless, fruitless discussion of questions and trivialities that had nothing to do with—he groped a bit—what was it he was about to say to himself? Nothing to do with reality? No: that was not precisely what he was thinking—nothing to do with practicality, maybe, or with life, though that, too, was a vague and doubtful way to say what he felt.

That young man, now. Clever, doubtless—and how much he disliked and distrusted cleverness. He himself had not been able to answer properly—several times he was confused. That young man used his words too quickly. He was too—too slick about it all. Peter was no longer easy with that kind of talk—abstract ideas and the like, and yet he was disturbed by the almost embarrassing realization that he had, nevertheless, enjoyed himself.

Yes, he had enjoyed himself, but he had not acquitted himself well!

This unexpected thought and its attendant emotion came like a sudden flash of lightning. Why should he care whether he acquitted himself well or not on these questions he despised? Still— he was sure that Eastman had been wrong about two or three things. All that Darwin business, now! He had read Darwin himself that summer in Martinsgrove, and he believed every word of it. Eastman had said the thought of the world was being transformed by Darwin—but that it had *gone too far!* Jackass! If a thing is true, the ultimate conclusions are not too far! They are the legitimate and proper goals! Too far!

But he had not been able to argue. He recognized with an utterly inconsistent dismay that he handled his own mind clumsily. He was no match for this boy out of college. He hated that. He wanted to prove Eastman wrong. He wanted to confound him and chase him, intellectually, from his jaunty security.

Doubtless Eastman had gotten these objections from the preachery, religious surroundings of Aberdeen. The same musty, beclouding kind of religious influence that had surrounded Peter himself at home. Always muddled one's thinking.

Peter opened the stove door and threw on a knotty chunk of wood. He readjusted the damper, turned up the light, and went to the shelves. He ran a finger along the titles. Presently he took down a thick green volume, and sat down by the table.

He turned the pages quickly . . . jackass! Of course the youngster was wrong. . . . He read slowly, blinking a little against the unaccustomed difficulty of the small, close print.

It seemed to him that there was a hazy blurring between him and the words. He just was not used to fine print any more. He shifted impatiently in his chair and squinted, trying the book at various distances. Odd, how habits were lost . . . this, now . . . having to try out distance to read—like some of these country jakes who were only partially literate.

He read, his mind fumbling against the thick, twisted prose. It was like fighting one's way through thorns and brambles.

Savina came to the open door. When she saw Peter with a book in his hand she backed away instinctively and closed the door softly. Peter did not hear her.

There was no sound in the room but the subdued whine in the stove. It was a sound that fitted itself instantly to the occupation of reading. Peter remembered that when he was a boy the stove in his little third-floor room used to whine like this. An oppressive instant of recollection lay on his attention . . . the presence of his father . . . he could almost feel the weight of that difficult personality on this moment . . . it vanished as he brought it to the fore of his mind . . . no, he was free of that—a sense of lightness followed. . . .

The thudding impact of the words he read was hard against his flying thought. It had been a long time since he had forced himself to the discipline of anyone's words or thoughts. The close reasoning fell about his own ideas like a snaring thread . . . the flight became a falling flutter . . . now—slowly . . . slowly . . . Peter's attention almost hobbled . . . he was tired—that's what was wrong! He had been going hard all day. He read on a little. . . .

Curious how these pages brought back to him the feeling of those days when he had first read them. Martinsgrove . . . the close, stuffy room which Mom Hummelfelder assigned him, the occasional puff of the freshening night coming through the window, the splashes of moonlight on the vegetable garden outside, and on across the wide orchard . . . he came back with a start. The illusion had been strong for a moment. He had felt and breathed the summer . . . here where the red glow of the fire shone through the isinglass stove door—here—here . . . he shifted in the straight, stiff chair.

Now that other tack of young Eastman. He had never heard of that poet. Whitman. Unlikely-sounding name for a poet anyway— Walt Whitman! Affectation, no doubt. From what Eastman had said—his description of the stuff—he was convinced that it was an affectation, the whole of it. Eastman had said he'd bring a book of it along the next time he came. Why couldn't he send it by Robby if he was so determined to have it read? He was not at all sure that he wanted that chap hanging around. Talk, talk, talk! It was deadly oppressive to think how much talk went on in the world, all of the time, everywhere, and about useless subjects. Running one's mind around and around in circles like the overflowing activity of colts.

He mused—the sound of falling ash in the stove came distinctly through the crystal silence. There were minute creaks in the floor, along the ceiling as if the infinitesimal settlings of the walls had become audible. From time to time there was the sound of the fire itself, muffled, like the flutter of a moth's wings. The sound of his own roughened fingers over the binding of the book came magnified and clear, separated itself into small, hard grains of sound.

Peter was aware of a motion in his mind. It was like the motion of the river out there in the quiet landscape. Once you took notice of it, it broke into small details—a flash here, a sparkle there, a rippling succession of shining links. . . .

In such wise a word would rise to visibility, then another, then a phrase—the sudden, smiting music of a rhythm. . . .

Peter thought again of the well at the bottom of his mind—the figure that had occurred to him the day when a meaningless phrase—an unrelated image had struck into his mind. . . .

Again and again he found these floating fragments come to consciousness. Some he could identify; most of them he did not recognize. He would not have been more surprised had his shovel turned up a Corinthian capital, or a sculptured head, in the sandy river bottom. . . .

Into their hands . . .

. . . bound with two cords—but cords to me were threads
touched with the flame . . .

Those words had come often. Poetry of some kind, but he could not identify it. He said them over softly to himself—all at once they seemed to thunder at him.

Another fragment added itself . . .

They only lived who fled . . .

meaningless, annoying, but somehow ominous. Sometimes these sounding puzzles were more like the first distant tremolo of a summer storm—threatening the peace of the wide sunny day.

Whatever made him recall to the clear light of consciousness these useless scraps of memory—whatever it might be had in it a premonition of disaster. Peter twisted about in his chair, trying to elude the devising of his own imagination.

He nodded. His eyes burned from the long day in the wind and from the unaccustomed reading. He was tired. Too tired to prepare for bed.

He thought of Martinsgrove again. He used to be tired in those days, too, but it had been different. The work was new and he was unaccustomed to labor, but he had been hard and vigorous. Then he had looked forward to the work of his own place—the plans, the constructive order of effort, the act of creation. Sometimes his muscles had ached, almost unbearably—like toothache, but this—this was different.

He pondered, sleepily. Old Anton, for example, had not suffered from the—the counterattacks of the land. Maybe because back there in the long-disciplined and long-controlled farm lands there was no longer that kind of fight left in the soil. This was still somewhat wilderness.

Sentimentalizing, wasn't he? He asked himself half dreamily. Dramatizing! Making a seeming in a place where there was nothing—nothing at all. Maybe that was just it! Once he had thought of the soil as friendly. Maybe it was not an enemy, but certainly it was no friend.

No one seemed to count up all the dreadful total of such toil—how cold one could be, and how many times—day after day, year after year; and then the heat that seemed literally to strike at one; the million gestures of spading, chopping, shoveling; the weeds—the damned weeds that grew with a kind of ferocity, a gleeful ferocity—how hard they were to pull up, to root out. Wet, and cold, and hot, and dry—these were states endured over and over in continuous and battering sequence—like the varied torments of a skillful inquisitor!

Peter aroused himself. This was a new and strange kind of experience—to add to mere discomfort with the personalizing of the very elements—making bogeymen for himself.

Unexpectedly, without volition, he said aloud:

"*Cords to me were threads touched with the flame . . .*"

He stood up, thrust at the draft control on the stove plate with his foot, and pushed the chair back to its accustomed place. He cupped one hand about the lamp chimney and blew. Then he stood for a moment in the sudden dark until the faint glow from the stove door brought the objects in the room dimly into view.

Cautiously, heavily, he made his way to the door.

The next day Peter went about his work with less energy and less interest than he had felt in a long time. Very seldom during these years in the West had he really paused to take stock of himself. A brief stop now and then to consider—to consider the relationship of some one phase of his life to some remote and rather fantastic pattern or plan already half obscured, half lost in the complexity of actuality. Even today he was not precisely taking stock. He was merely remembering with a decided accompaniment of irritation that he had tried last night to talk to another man, and later to think a little, and that neither of these efforts had been satisfactory.

He thought back and forth over these simple facts, tallying the score against himself.

Perhaps, during all of this time, one of the strongest reliances of his pride had been his faith in the superior workings of his mind—a sturdy belief in the correctness of his intuitions, and a secure repose in the rightness of his courses. He tried hard to veer away from this—it related too directly to something he would not look at.

Peter walked around his great stone barn. Solid—a concrete evidence of what he had planned. He touched the wrought-iron hinges on the big doors—his handiwork. He passed his fingers over the polished teeth of a hickory hand rake. He had made it. He looked around at this little collection of buildings, smokehouse, tool house, chicken house, summer kitchen, corn cribs—almost a village of them. He surveyed the fields, carefully fenced, the pruned and corrected orchard, the tight hayricks, and the neatly piled supply of winter wood.

All of this was what he had planned—what he had made. It was at once the symbol and the fact.

Very slowly, very carefully and cautiously his mind stole about that thought. It was—it was the visible body of what he had come here to seek and what he had found. *The visible body.* His wary thinking fell unknowingly into an old sequence—it moved in some long-disused pathway of his brain.

This was the visible body. Where was its soul? What was its soul? Which was real? Which was imagined? Was this the shadow, merely, of a more important reality?

Now where, he asked, had he read *that?* Some mystic or other. That was, indeed, the very essence of the senseless and fruitless speculations he abhorred.

Immediately, he turned with his accustomed speed to the day's work. He was somewhat eased again, but not completely. The foolish questions continued to scratch at his attention.

He went to the tool house and took out a long-handled grubbing hoe. There was a patch of brush in the orchard near the house. It would be a good time to dig it out.

Peter found Jude, Robby's bloodhound, sniffing about the spot. In summer it was Jude's favorite retreat from flies and gnats. Now on sunny days she curled up in the midst of the leafless switches. Jude was an unaccountable dog.

Peter leaned on the handle of his grubbing hoe and looked at her. She promptly sat on her haunches and returned the look.

Robby had said Jude was a serious dog, but this was a considerable understatement. To judge from her appearance Jude was the very embodiment, the complete sign and signal, of the world's longest sorrows. Her high narrow forehead was more deeply seamed and furrowed than ever. Her sagging eyes looked mournfully at the hopeless plight of all that lay before her. Peter laughed. Jude acknowledged the unseemly sound by a shamed droop of her head.

"Jude!"

She raised her beautiful topaz eyes in mild question. This was surely unusual. No one but Robby ever spoke to her.

"Jude, I think you a fraud."

Her head sank again.

"Nothing could be as Godforsaken as you look—nothing. Have you had something to eat this morning?"

Jude sagged a little. Peter repeated the question in German, and Jude promptly stood up.

"Oh, you speak German? Well, it seems to suit you."

Peter laid his hand on the high, pointed head. Jude submitted, but politely, as one who submits only to oblige. She lay down suddenly as though the props of courage had failed her.

"I wonder what that boy sees in you? I never saw anything less like a boy's dog than you. Discouraging, that's what you are!"

Jude seemed to shrink and cower as if she lay under a cold rain.

"I don't believe you can be intelligent . . . all the sense you have is in your nose, isn't it—eh, Jude?"

Jude's incredibly sensitive nose was lifted toward Peter as he talked. It appeared to be eye and ear, so expressive was it, as it twitched and quivered, assorting and identifying innumerable simultaneous impressions.

Peter reminded himself that he had come out here to uproot this busy growth. He considered it. Maybe Jude liked the place especially. In summer it might be a real comfort to her. After all it did not harm—just a little untidy. Might as well leave it.

"Want to come along, Jude?"

But Jude was not responsive."

"*Willst du mit gehen?*"

She arose and achieved a wag of her tail.

"Come, then."

Jude ambled along with Peter who started to the tool house to replace the hoe. Jude hesitated at the barn-lot gate, then turned slowly and retreated toward the orchard without looking back.

Peter watched her until she disappeared.

Peter went into the house. Savina was ironing. She looked up, surprised.

"What time is it?"

"I don't know. Ten, maybe. It's not near dinnertime yet."

"Oh, I thought maybe I was forgetting."

Peter went upstairs. He could not remember when he had ever gone over the house before. Not in a long time. He only came up here to change clothes, and to sleep.

He looked into Robby's room. It was bare, and entirely un-communicative. Nothing here could possibly suggest what kind of person used it. That other room over there—that had been David's room. Peter opened the door. It was dark. Savina kept the shades closely drawn so the rag carpets would not fade.

"Peter!"

"Yes, Savina."

"Are you hunting for something?"

There was a moment's silence.

"No. I was just looking around."

"Oh."

He came down presently, and went into the front room.

It was dark, too, but he raised the blind and looked about. It was a gray and cheerless room—stiff and uninviting. The books in the shelves looked as dead and cold as the stove.

"Peter! Are you—in the front room?"

"Yes."

"What *are* you looking for, Peter?"

"Nothing."

"But you shouldn't go in there with the dirty shoes on."

"Oh. I forgot."

"I'll have to sweep again."

"I'm sorry, Savina. I was just looking around."

"Are you sure there isn't something you want?"

"I don't want anything. I'm going out again."

"Is it getting colder?"

"No. It's not cold."

"It looks cold."

"There's no wind."

Peter suddenly found that he was thinking of the front room again. It would be rather nice, he thought, to build a fire in there . . . and sit down . . . and read, maybe. But Savina would think he had lost his mind.

He went out hurriedly. That manure pile back of the cowsheds. It would have to be moved—to make room. It was not a pleasant job. No, by God, it was an abominable job, a mean, stinking, abominable job. It wasn't a job for—for—he stopped his crowding thoughts, cut them off short.

In a few moments he was hard at work with a pitchfork.

. . . A mean, stinking, abominable job, that's what it was. . . .

2

The day darkened. The clouds which had been blue in the forenoon were a deep slaty gray by three in the afternoon. They hung heavy and low, closing the day in, crowding it, seemingly, into a smaller and smaller circle.

Peter glanced at the sky a few times. Still no wind. There would doubtless be snow. The feel of snow in the air was unmistakable, as if the very consistency of the atmosphere thickened. Ordinarily Peter looked at all weather as a spectacle. Today he looked at this sky, and regarded this gloom as a mood and a malicious manifestation—directed against him.

The day was small, he said to himself, small and mean. As it bent down and narrowed, he felt himself enclosed by it—a prisoner of that lessening space. He, himself, was made smaller by it, and the odious task of the hour, meaner, less appropriate to the dignity of a man.

He corrected his own feeling, setting himself again in clearer perspective. He was not compelled to do this. He could stop whenever he chose. He could thrust this pitchfork into the manure pile and walk away if he wished. He could hire someone to do the job— or he could leave the damned thing as it was.

He *would* walk away, too, this moment. He stuck the pitchfork in the ground, leaving it vibrating from the violence of the thrust.

Long ago he used to go up in the hills when encroaching waves of black threatened his inner fastnesses. He had not been up there for years, except to search for some wandering heifer, or to chop up a fallen tree.

He bent a little to one side as if he listened for a distant sound, or as if he tested some uncertain sensation inside of himself.

What was the matter?

Why did he feel like this?

What was he questioning?

Above all why was he suddenly moving inside his own world as if, mentally, he trod upon a viscous and uncertain soil?

Peter glanced at the corner of the barn where a long crack showed in the masonry. A crack like the representation of a river on a map, wider at the bottom, weaving its way up and across the face of the wall, branching at the top. At one spot, the force of the stress had broken a stone in half.

Curious! A settling or shifting underground in the foundation, moving so slowly, so slightly, so stealthily—and there the riven stone showed graphically the direction and the power of the hidden movement. It was at this moment as if he saw clearly such a fissure across the tight structure of his own fabric of existence—only, as he thought of it, and looked at it with the vision of fancy, he seemed to see it move, appear suddenly alive, to flick out in small, deadly lesions. . . .

Peter was staring so hard at the actual crack in the wall before him that he confused it for a moment with the fancied image in his mind. He watched the wall with a tense fascination, expecting to see the thin lines crawl and flash and widen.

He shook off the thought and walked up the slope back of the barn. The ground was strewn thick with dark-brown leaves. He looked back. Brown, and ocher, and gray. It was a somber beauty—like the word November itself.

Just then Jude came slowly along the yard fence, moving toward the road that led into the woods. She paused and flung up her head, sniffed—snorted softly to clear her nostrils of confusion, and sniffed again—her long thin muzzle pointing straight before her. Then with a whimper of delight she streaked along the road and disappeared into the woods.

Robby, of course! He did not usually come home that way, but her amazing nose knew him afar off.

Peter went on up the hill.

Robby sat huddled against the trunk of a tree in the very center of his and Laurel's "temple." He snuggled his chin deep in a knitted scarf wound close inside of his coat collar. He sat very still. In the windless afternoon every twig, every clinging dead leaf hung motionless. The silence and the quiet were like a spell, like a waiting.

Slowly and carefully Robby surveyed every detail of the scene about him, earth, sticks and switches, the varied pattern of bare trees, the olive green of the river. His overbrilliant eyes moved quickly as he observed first one detail and another, then his lids drooped a little as his attention turned inward where he compared the picture outside of him with its apprehended counterpart within.

He moved a little, thrusting his hands into his roomy sleeves. It was cold—the kind of cold one did not notice at first, but which crept treacherously along one's very bones.

Jude sat quietly beside Robby. Occasionally long tremors shook her brown body, but she seemed to be contemplating the same scene that held her master. She lifted her head from time to time and, half closing her eyes, took quick successions of small delicate breaths. She, too, was accounting for what was about her, assorting it, considering it.

Robby sank deeper into his abstracted state. He was watching the slow formation of those other pictures inside of his head, and with a detachment, half curious, half passive, he felt the pictures turn into words—a process like those incredible metamorphoses which occur without effort and without surprise in the depths of a dream.

High up in the hills, on the very crest, Peter, too, sat watching with dark and troubled eyes the landscape beneath him. He did not see Robby far below him, nor did Robby ever look up to where he might have seen the bulky figure of his father outlined against the sky.

Neither was aware of another presence in the woods.

But Jude turned her head toward the rise, alert and watchful. She had known when Peter first came over the ridge above them. She stirred uneasily, and made small muttering sounds in her throat.

Robby reached out absently and laid his hand on her head. Her sibylline eyes were intense with communication.

"Goes someone, yes?" Robby spoke softly, and Jude lifted one foot, holding it poised.

"So? Well, it's all right, I guess."

Robby listened. The hush was absolute.

Jude stood up. She breathed daintily of the cold air settling from the hilltops. Then she sat down again, and the two remained silent and unmoving in the deepening twilight.

3

Lena Janek sat down heavily in the creaky rocking chair on her front porch, and wiped her face with a corner of her apron.

"Tomorrow is the first of June, and already it is so hot a person can hardly stand it. What will the summer be?"

Taska came to the door. She laughed. "Mamma, you say that every year!"

"No. This is terrible. Me, I don't really mind the heat. You know I don't complain."

"Ever since I can remember, you've complained of both the heat and the cold."

"I do not do so. My, my! Already the first of June. And next week you go away!"

Taska came out and sat down on the step. Her crinkly hair caught the late evening light, showing a deep glinting copper, and her face, shadowed a little as she sat resting her head on her hand, was warm and rich with glowing color. Her blue dress was open at the throat and the creamy curve of her breast rose and fell quickly with a sudden excitement.

"Yes. Tuesday."

"Have you told *her* yet?"

"No."

"Why not?"

"I don't know how glad she will be. Maybe it will make her—remember—everything."

"She is Davy's mother, and she knows already anyhow, don't she?"

"Oh, yes. It's just—oh, can't you imagine, Mamma? She's never seen Davy in all this time, and then when she looks at me and knows *I'm* going to see him, she'll feel bad, maybe."

"Taska—you have not told me. Is Davy glad you're coming?"

"Of course. He's afraid, though, that we'll be awfully poor."

"He has a good job."

"It doesn't pay much, but he's getting on. Someday David wants to have a newspaper of his own."

"Then he should have a wife to take care of him. If he has to pay board as it is, you two can make out some way."

"He doesn't know I have saved any money."

"That'll be a nice surprise."

"It will help. Maybe I can teach school there, if necessary."

"Not long, I guess. You'll be having children."

"Maybe." The color deepened in Taska's face. "I hope so."

"Lots of them, Taska, I hope."

"*You* didn't have lots of them, Mamma, only me."

"That was God's will, not mine."

"Oh—I didn't mean—"

"That's all right. You are a grown woman. Something happened, and—it's all right. You were trouble enough!" Lena laughed and leaned over to lay her hand on Taska's shoulder. "You've been a nice child—a good girl—I—your papa and I will miss you."

"I hate to leave you."

"It'll be lonesome. But it's right. It's time you have your man and all."

"I'll be glad to see David. Mamma, do you suppose he might have changed a lot? Maybe he might not care so much for me now as he used to."

"Foolishness!"

"We were just kids when he left."

"Davy's kind are still water—deep. He would never change."

"Poor David!"

"Why do you say that?"

"He was so upset, so hurt."

"Yes, yes. I have never understood."

"It was wrong. There's Mr. Kettring with lots of money, and it would have taken so little for what David wanted. It was wicked."

"You should not say so. You cannot know everything—only when you know everything can you blame. God alone can blame."

"I can't be that good, Mamma. I've hated Mr. Kettring ever since that morning when I saw David's face, all black and blue!"

"Yes, yes. It is hard sometimes—"

"I would never have set foot on the place again if it had not been for her. She's David's mother, and—"

"She always loves him, not?"

"I think she's been half brokenhearted all this time, but she never shows anything."

"He—of course—"

"I never speak to him more than to say good morning or good evening."

"He is David's father."

"He is a selfish, self-centered—beast."

"Taska!"

"He is!"

"I think you are wrong—somehow. We never can see all there is inside of another person's heart. Maybe he is sorry."

"If he was he could find out how to reach David. She told me he has never spoken David's name since that day."

"Tch! Tch!"

"David wouldn't have accepted anything, of course. David is as hardheaded as his father. And he's too proud. He'd never take a nickel."

"You will make up to him, Taska, for everything."

"I mean to. That's what I want to do."

"You *are* happy that you are going to him? You're satisfied that it's Davy, not?"

"What do you mean?" Taska raised startled eyes.

"Timothy." Lena said the word softly, but her eyes were steady on Taska's face.

"Oh, Timothy!"

"Or—Paul?"

Taska shook her head. "Not while there is David in the world."

"I wondered sometimes. They—I couldn't tell which, were—they liked you *very* much."

"Yes, I know."

"They said so?"

"Oh, many times!"

"Which one?"

Taska laughed. "Both of them!"

"So? That was something now!"

"Yes. You couldn't quite separate them in your mind."

"I can imagine. They are nice—and so droll—those twins."

"They're as fine as anybody can be. If—sometimes I think if there had never been David—I—I could have liked—"

"Timothy?"

"I don't know. One or the other—or both of them."

"Ei! I never thought how hard it would be that way. I never knew which was which."

"Timothy laughs more."

"They know about David?"

"Ever since we were in school. But they've been fine. They said tell David they'd keep trying till they were sure it was too late."

"So? They know you go?"

"Yes."

"Tomorrow you must go to see Savina."

"I will."

The next day as Savina listened to Taska's account of her plans a change came over her bearing. It was not easy, Taska thought, to say just what it was. It did not really seem to be so much a change as the appearance of something that had always been there, but hidden until now. Savina straightened in her chair.

"On Tuesday?" She said the words with a faraway look in her eyes.

"Yes."

"It takes you a long time to go there?" Savina spoke slowly. Taska, she knew, did not understand her speech very well.

"Two days."

"Two days?" Again she looked across the top of Taska's head as if she saw something on a distant horizon.

"Two days and two nights—really."

"On Friday, then, you will see David?"

Taska's heart was heavy with pity for the suddenly hungry look in Savina's eyes.

"Yes," she said gently.

"I will be thinking about you at that time. Say—say everything for me to David. You will?"

"Of course. David will have a thousand questions."

"You are going to be married right away?"

"Yes."

"He will have a place?"

"There is a little home David thinks will do at first."

Savina thought for a moment. "Could David have money enough, do you think, to buy things?"

"I guess so. I have some money. I saved it from teaching, for this."

"Listen, Taska. Upstairs I have so many things—towels, sheets, pillowcases, covers—so many that I brought from back East. They are in chests. I have never used them. My mother's things, too, were sent to me, many of them—patchwork quilts—you should see!—oh, the pretty ones. This afternoon I send them to you. Peter will bring them—"

"Mr. Kettring?"

"Yes. I send them by him. It will help you to have these ready."

"Oh—are you sure—"

"I do not need them. Even if I did, I send some things to my son's house. That is *right*."

"I can't thank you enough."

"I am glad you go to him, Taska."

"Are you honestly?"

"Yes. You will be good for him. He must be lonesome. I hope he is good to you."

"David? Why, of course—"

"He is in many ways like Peter—and one must understand."

"But, Mr. Kettring is good to you."

"One has to understand much, and then there is peace."

"I see." Taska had to say something, but she wondered deeply. She was just a bit ill at ease. But Savina went on.

"It was hard to see David go—that way. Of course, in some other way, later, he would go away, anyhow—but so—it was hard. And I do not see him again."

"We'll come back to visit when we can."

"David will not come, I think."

"Oh, yes—"

"And, Taska!"

"Yes."

"I want to send David something special. I always have a little money, you know. Will you take it?"

"Of course, if you want me to."

"You tell him from me to buy a nice new suit—to be married in—it is from me."

Taska knew that she was looking straight into the deep of Savina's heart. It stirred her to see how simple, and good, and sweet it was.

"I'll thank you now, from David."

Taska arose. "I must go—I have a good deal to do yet."

"You will write—often?"

"Yes—Mamma will tell you—"

"No. Now it is different. You write to me, and you tell David to write, too, and to *me.*"

"But, you know, I can't write German—"

"In English! Robby—he will read to me. And I will have him write for me."

"Oh, of course."

"I think I won't be lonesome when I have once a letter of my own."

"I will write often—I promise."

"Taska, you are so pretty. I am glad."

"Thank you—but never so pretty as you—"

"Me! I am an old woman!"

"You are so pretty."

"If it is so, I—well, I guess that is nothing I have done."

"Yes—you are so good."

"No. Often I think terrible thoughts, Taska."

Taska laughed. She placed her firm warm hands on Savina's shoulders and kissed her.

That afternoon Savina collected a great heap of goods from her chests.

"What is?" Peter looked at the heap, the neat packages carefully tied, small boxes, and a pair of silvered glass vases—the kind that hold bright witchbells.

"I want you should put these carefully in a big box and take them to Taska Janek."

"Well—what for, Savina? Are you giving them away?"

"Yes—to her. On Tuesday she goes away, to marry David. These are for her house. Hurry now."

Peter, like Taska, noticed the change in Savina's bearing. It was a manner and a speech he had never seen. Neither of them realized that this was simply Savina in another relationship. In all matters pertaining to Peter and Peter's plans, she was the pliant, docile, obedient wife that was proper. In this—which was as much her own domain as the disposition of her bread pans—she exercised her appropriate rights.

She watched Peter go toward the wagon carrying the last of the bundles.

He is a hard man, she thought. Hard. Can he not say one word when his son marries? Not even one word to me—not even the name?

And Peter . . .

Peter placed the packages in the wagon bed and climbed to the seat.

Couldn't anybody talk to him? Why did no one ever tell him anything?

So David, the runaway, was going to marry Taska. She would be good for him, doubtless, wherever he was. Why had no one told him where David was? Was it a secret? If they knew, couldn't someone have mentioned it?

An image of David came back to him. It was the same troubling image that always returned whenever thought of the boy crossed his mind. David with a frightened face, his mouth working, his eyes wide, his voice whimpering and cracking as he tried to talk.

His own son frightened of him like that! What had been the trouble?

Now that he thought it over he felt that he had never been really hard on David. He had not driven him. Perhaps he had paid little enough attention to him, but he had thought of David as a boy, still the charge of Savina. Savina could have talked it over with him.

But no! They had planned behind his back—connived as though he were an ogre. He had been completely unprepared.

There had been that ugly flare-up about Aberdeen. Certainly, he would not have had David go *there!*

And the next morning David was gone. The black-browed boy who was so like him. Maybe it was too bad he had struck the lad—

so. Actually, he liked things which resisted—like these fine gray horses. Whenever they tamed he was bored, and bought new ones. He did not like things that were afraid.

Doubtless he had a bad temper. So had David. Clashes were inevitable; but they could have fought it out.

What was the boy doing, anyway? If they'd only tell him what was going on, maybe he could help. He was rich.

Savina sending these things! *She* knew. She was informed. Those Janeks, of course. But everything behind his back. Even Savina. Stuff for the new house. Savina was sending David these things as a sort of wedding present.

In God's name, why didn't someone speak to him? Say some word so he could send something, too? He'd give them a house— he'd give them anything they wished! But they kept him in the dark! They told him nothing! He was not even supposed to know!

Pain and anger mingled oddly in Peter's heart. He cut viciously at the horses with the long ends of the lines. They leapt, tearing down the winding hill road at top speed.

Peter stood up, bracing himself in the swaying wagon bed, holding the lines tight while he swung the lash. "Get up! Get up! Damn you! Get on! Hi-e-e-e! Run, damn you!"

His shouts arose above the rattle and crash of the wagon.

The horses were foaming and heaving when he drew up at the Janeks' side gate.

Michael and Taska came out.

"Something or other that Savina sent." Peter was curt.

"Oh, yes, Mr. Kettring. Won't you come in? Papa can bring the things in."

"N-no . . . thank you." The words came gruffly, grudgingly. The girl was a beauty, really. Good . . . David.

Michael quickly laid the boxes and packages inside the gate.

Taska looked up at Peter, shading her eyes from the sun.

"Thank you for bringing them, Mr. Kettring, and thank Mrs. Kettring again."

"Um."

Taska turned abruptly and went into the house.

"Well, well!" Michael took his pipe from his pocket. "Looks like we're going to be kinfolks!"

Peter stared. Michael and Lena! He had not thought of it. A strange warmth went through him. Kinfolks! Why—he had never had kinfolks. Even the simple Janeks . . . he had not thought of it!

But Michael looked angry. Misinterpreting Peter's silence, he stooped and picked up some bundles.

"Good day," he said shortly.

Peter stared again. Then he drew the lines tight.

In a few moments Michael heard Peter shouting at his galloping horses as they smashed along the upper road. Peter was standing again, teetering from side to side. "Old fool! Stuck-up old fool! He'll kill himself with those wild horses yet. And not many will mourn if he does."

4

"Papa says I have to go away somewhere to school—after next year when I've finished at St. Stephens." Laurel spoke slowly as if she were saying over something difficult to herself. She looked away, not wishing immediately to see Robby's face.

A long minute of silence followed. Robby snapped the stem of a leafy stalk growing near him. He pulled the leaves away, one at a time, and scattered them. He answered presently in precisely the same detached tone of voice Laurel had used.

"I wonder what I'm going to do—then."

Laurel and Robby were sitting in the grove of their favorite hillside retreat. The full tide of summer filled the valley; thick leaves almost obscured the view. The heavy, warm day pressed close. Its seeming stillness was vibrant with innumerable small sounds— the thin whine of insects in the air, tiny rustlings in the grass, and the muted flutter of wings in the trees above them.

Laurel lay on the mossy slope, resting on her elbow. She had removed the ribbon that bound her hair, and her face was half hidden by the cascading curls. Robby could just see the curve of her cheek, flushed and warm. Laurel had lost her chubby look. She was tall, slim, and rounded. Her old noisy manner had gone, too. She moved and spoke quietly, but there was a sultry look about her that was eloquent of the quick temper, the headlong impulsiveness, that lay just beneath the surface.

Robby was scrutinizing her as closely as if he had to memorize her. Her full lips pouted with a look of discontent and impatience, but this look was contradicted by the resolution and clarity of her level gaze.

"You look tropical, Laurie."

Laurel looked up without moving. "Are you being a poet this morning?" The words sounded like a rebuff, but the nuance of her contralto speech was a caress.

Robby smiled. "Yes—but I'm a poet because I love you so much."

"You do, really, don't you?"

"Altogether—every how in the world."

"Do you ever write poetry about me? Ever?"

"No."

"Why not?"

"I don't know. When I see you—that is everything. I have you in my head—inside everywhere—all the time. Other things I write about to hold them—so they won't get away and be forgotten."

"I wish you'd write so I could read it."

"I—I can't, Laurie."

"Everything in that funny talk you use with your mother?"

"Yes, everything. It's beautiful, not funny."

"I guess anything you would say would be beautiful."

"It's strange, isn't it, Laurie, the way we are—you and me?"

"I guess people who love each other always think so."

"No—it is different—altogether different. Do you know anybody else—any other two people who are like us?"

"No. But we don't know anything about other people any more than they know about us."

Robby considered this for a moment. Then he shook his head. "No. You can see in their eyes—you can see on into the middle of them—what is there. It is different."

"What did you mean by tropical?"

"Warm, and rich, and lots of color, and everything all glowing, and big stars, and wonderful great moons, and strange flowers, and dusky—"

"Oh dear!"

"—and velvet, and soft, and—"

"Robby!"

"What?"

"Your face! It looks so smooth today—like a little girl's complexion!"

He smiled. "I shaved."

"Oh!"

"I was getting rather fuzzy."

"I know, now that I remember. It didn't show much because you're so blond." She sat up and touched his face with her fingers. "Your face is like satin. My goodness!" She touched her own cheeks. "You're as smooth as I am."

Robby leaned over her and brushed his lips over her cheeks, her brow, her eyes. He kissed her lips lightly, but Laurel put her free arm around his neck and held him close.

She released him suddenly and caught her breath.

"That is so nice." Robby might have been speaking of a plum, or an apple. "You are so sweet."

He moved close to her, drew her head to his shoulder, and kissed her again on the cheek, on both eyes, then all across her brow and back to her cheek, and suddenly, on her parted lips.

"Goodness!" Laurel pulled away.

"What's the matter?"

"Nothing."

Robby turned his head on one side like an inquiring sparrow. "You—don't like—"

"Oh, Robby, of course I do."

"I love you, and I love to kiss you—forever."

"Yes. So do I." There was a suspicion of dryness in her reply. Robby looked puzzled.

"Robby—don't you know—anything?"

[277]

He looked at her a long time. Then he nodded. "Of course." He said the words with utmost naturalness—casually, even.

"Well?" Laurel sounded cross.

"Well, what?"

"You asked me why I pulled away."

"Oh." Then after a moment he nodded again. "Oh."

"I guess we aren't children any more, Robby. We'll have to be —sort of careful, I guess."

Robby considered this. "I never have thought about it, Laurie —not much. Of course—sometimes."

"You are not like other boys."

"What about other boys?"

"Oh, boys—they're always trying—"

Robby thought for a moment. "Did anybody—ever—"

"Talk like that to me? No. I guess they wouldn't."

"No. Not you. I guess they'd be afraid."

"Why?"

"You've got a bad temper—sometimes."

Laurel laughed outright. "Do you think that's the only reason?"

"Laurie, I tell you I never thought much about it, until now."

"And now—"

"I *am* thinking about it."

"Isn't it funny? You and me—we've always been sweethearts, since we were little—oh, Robby, I love you so much, and I've always loved you, and I had to fight with my brothers and sisters about you—"

"Why?"

"They teased me. And I just loved fighting for you."

"That's funny, too."

"Yes, I suppose."

"I guess I am just what Mr. Eastman said I was."

"A dreamer, he said."

"It wasn't altogether as nice as that. He said my head was in a fog—he didn't even say clouds. I guess I never have thought much about anything, Laurie. Somehow I never *had* to. I—I just went

[278]

around looking, and sort of feeling about everything, and—maybe once in a while the—the fog cleared and I thought."

Laurel listened. Her expression when Robby talked about himself was always a mixture of tenderness, indulgence, and respect.

"Just now—I thought—hard."

"What about, Robby?"

"When you said you would have to go away. We've never been separated! Sometimes I don't see you for—a lot of days, but I know you're there, over the hill."

"Yes, Robby." Laurel was listening with a new look of eagerness.

"But if you went away . . . then what would I do?"

"Don't you suppose you'll go to school somewhere? Hasn't your—your father ever spoken about any plans for you?"

"No."

"That's curious, I think."

"You remember about David?"

"Yes. Of course. I was thinking."

"It was about that—"

"Robby!"

"Yes—what?"

"You wouldn't run away, would you?"

"From you?"

"That's what I wanted you to say."

"Never, never in the world!"

"Maybe, after all, I won't have to go. Maybe Papa can't afford it."

"Oh."

"You don't understand that, do you? Your father is rich."

"Maybe—somehow—we could go to the same place."

"There aren't any schools for boys *and* girls."

"I mean the same town."

"There's Kings Row. They're going to have a new girls' school there."

"I don't think I want to go to school, though."

"Why, Robby Kettring! Why not?"

"I just want to read a lot, and—and go around—and write."

"All your life? Like a poet?"

Robby smiled. "Not *like* a poet, Laurel! I *am* a poet—I mean I will be."

"But, Robby, what can you do with—with what you write in that funny language? Nobody can read it."

"Lots of people can. In other places. I've got a secret to tell you."

"Goodness, what?"

"Well—Mr. Eastman sent some of the things I wrote to a paper in Pennsylvania. It's a paper printed in Timmonstown, and they have a whole page every week in Pennsylvania German—poems, and funny stories, and translations, and the like. There are lots of people there who can't read anything else."

"Go on—and—"

"And they're going to print them—my pieces."

"Oh—Robby! I'm so glad. You'll be famous!"

"Well—hardly. Mr. Eastman said—well, what he said, exactly, was that there wasn't much of an audience for dialect writing, but you know, Laurie, the first time he ever talked to me about—about all this he mentioned Robert Burns—"

"Oh, yes—we had him in English class, I remember."

"Yes. He was a great poet and he wrote in a dialect. Why couldn't I?"

"And you could be—be like Robert Burns?"

"I don't see why not."

"Why can't you write in English so I could read it, too?"

"I can't, Laurie. I've tried that. Everything in my mind says itself the other way."

"Well, I guess you have to do it your own way."

"Now, this is what I've been thinking about. After, maybe, they have printed a whole lot of my things in that paper in Pennsylvania, I could show them to Pop, and then maybe he'd let me go away off to some great school like a big university, or—"

"Robby! *You* were planning to leave *me!*"

Robby looked blank. It took him a full minute to understand her.

"Oh!" He said it weakly, still seeking logical ground to stand on.

"And you were just about to make such a to-do about *me* leaving *you!*"

"I don't know, Laurie. Somehow it doesn't seem to be the same thing."

"Well, it most certainly is!"

"A man always has to go somewhere."

"Does he?"

"Yes, like my Pop came here."

"Mine was born here."

"Yes, but—"

"And your father brought your mother with him!"

"Maybe you could go with me."

"Robby—you're a simpleton."

"Well, for goodness sake, Laurel, we have to get married *sometime!*"

"What made you think of that?"

Robby flushed. "A while ago when I was kissing you. I was telling you that sometimes I do think. And I thought that I couldn't live without you. I know that more and more I'll feel that way, until—"

"Yes, Robby, I guess I understand you."

"—until I can't be away from you—day or—or night."

Laurel's high color deepened, and then receded. She looked a little pale and sounded short of breath when she answered.

"I know, Robby. I've known that for a long time. I feel the same way—and—it's troubling sometimes. We've always been such happy kids—"

"We always will be."

She shook her head. "It's already different. It had to come sometime. Mamma talked to me about it."

"She *did?*" Robby's eyes were wide.

"Yes, Mamma knows everything. And she likes you a whole lot."

"I'm glad. I like her almost like my own mommy."

[281]

"Robby, you're too big to say *Mommy*. You should say—well, you ought to say *Mother*. It's more dignified."

"But—I don't know, Laurie—she just is the Mommy."

Laurel laughed and patted his hand. "Say it your own way. But what I was going to say is that we're getting grown up; we aren't kids any more."

"Do you mean because of this morning?"

"Not just that. It's all right for you to *think* what you want to. But I guess we've got to be good—as long as we can anyhow."

"It's funny about all that, isn't it, Laurie?"

"Not funny, no—not even the way you mean. I guess we could go all to pieces mighty easy."

"I guess so, too. But it doesn't look like it could make any difference to anybody. You and I—well, we've always been—each other's sweetheart. It's just *us*—"

"Oh, Robby—sweethearts have always talked like this, haven't they? You know you read it in all the books."

Robby thought for a moment. "Yes. And of course they were right."

"I don't know. I think we ought to try—not to."

"We never have tried one way or another, Laurie, and nothing has ever happened."

"I know, but it's different now. We've talked about it, and everything feels different already."

Robby nodded gravely. "Yes—but I guess things have been getting different all along and we just didn't notice."

They both sat up. Robby drew his knees up and rested his chin on them. Laurel smoothed her stockings, snapped her elastic garters into place, and leaned back against a tree. They did not speak for a while, but each followed the thoughts of the other with the effortless communication that had been theirs for a long time.

Robby was thinking over what Laurel had said. Yes: it was true. He could not quite say in words, or think concretely what it was he felt, and knew. It was maybe that now—this moment— childhood was over. The little changes had come so gradually that they were unnoticed. One by one the little shelters and defenses of childhood—the accepted protections and freedoms—had gone. Now —just now—the last one had fallen away.

He recalled the day he had laid both hands over Laurel's hard little breasts, saying unself-consciously, "You're changing, Laurie." He remembered that she had said, almost with unconcern, "Of course, I'm thirteen." Nothing more had been said on the subject.

BOOK FOUR

I

A RICKETY buggy drawn by a fat sway-backed horse moved slowly along the river road toward St. Stephens. It was a Sandifer turn-out, the general utility one. In it were Laurel and Robby. Characteristically, Laurel was driving.

The horse clop-clopped softly in the beaten center of the road. The buggy twisted and rocked from side to side as the wheels ground through the wide sandy ruts.

Both Laurel and Robby were subdued, and as nearly sad as was possible for them.

"It's hard to believe that school is over." Laurel looked sidewise at Robby who was slumped in the seat.

"And we'll never go any more at all." Robby added the awkward, hesitant phrase in the same gloomy tone Laurel had used.

"I didn't think school would *ever* be over."

"No. I thought, too, we'd go on forever—you and me together."

"And now it's all over."

They relapsed into silence. Laurel cut skillfully at a horsefly that was annoying old Bob.

Robby spoke after a while, listlessly. "What do you suppose Mr. Eastman wants to see me about? It can't be about any kind of schoolwork."

"Do you think it might be about going off to school?"

"No, I don't think so." Robby slumped farther down in the

cracked cushions. "I guess he knows as well as I do I'm not going away anywhere."

"It's a darn shame."

"I keep thinking, though, somehow something will happen."

"Well, I certainly hope you're right. Lord, I wish I could talk to your father just once."

"It wouldn't do any good."

"It would do *me* a lot of good." Laurel's color blazed as always at mention of Mr. Kettring. "You haven't said anything more to him about going off to school?"

"*More?* I've never said anything to him at all!"

Laurel squared about in her seat. "Never? In all this time?"

"No."

"Well, for goodness sake—why, maybe he'd say yes."

"You don't know Pop."

"Yes, I guess I do. I know his reputation, anyhow."

"That's why David ran away."

"But maybe he's changed since then."

"Nothing could ever change Pop."

"Have you talked to your mother about it?"

"Well—just a little—a long time ago. I don't know if Mommy just exactly realized what—how important it might be. She hasn't got so much education herself."

"I see."

"But she said what she always says—let's wait and see."

"Well, why don't you get her to ask?"

"I don't know. I don't want to—somehow."

"I know what's the matter. You're all just afraid of that old bear!"

"Of course we are."

"That's terrible."

"Of course it is."

"I don't understand anything over at your house."

"What, for instance?"

"Well, you think your father is pretty hard and all that. But you

[286]

never have had to work hard like other boys on a farm. Even my brothers have to do a lot."

"I know. Pop never asks me to do anything. I help Mommy, though. I'm pretty busy when I'm not doing my schoolwork."

"But you won't have any schoolwork now."

"I guess I'll work on the place."

"It's all wrong."

Laurel slapped the lines vigorously, and old Bob hastened his pace for at least a dozen steps. He cocked his ears backward, and as soon as conversation resumed he seemed to know that he could proceed again at his usual comfortable jog.

"That's Pop, isn't it, coming toward us, now? Yes, it is."

Robby straightened up in his seat.

Peter's big gray horses attached to a spring wagon swept along with a great wake of dust trailing out behind. As he passed, Laurel raised her hand in a half salute. Peter lifted his hat.

She turned to look after Peter but there was nothing to see but a thick cloud of dust. "That's curious. Your father always tips his hat to me—raises it 'way up."

Robby frowned. "Doesn't everybody do that?"

"No, dummy, don't you ever notice anything? Your father's manners are—well, totally different from what you'd expect."

"You mean—"

"I mean they're better—he has manners like Mr. Sandifer, and you know *he* thinks all the rest of us behave like savages."

Presently they drove into St. Stephens. They ambled up Main Street and stopped at River House. Robby jumped out and hitched the horse. Then he held his hand out for Laurel who gathered her skirts carefully together and swung over the wheel, ignoring the step.

She looked up toward the second floor where Perry Eastman lived.

"I certainly hate to leave *him*."

Robby nodded. "Me, too. He's been the best friend I ever had, except you."

They walked into the cool office. Mrs. Miner came out from the darkened parlor. She walked with a cane.

"Well, well. It's Laurel Sandifer. How-de-do, Laurie! How's your folks?"

"Very well, thank you."

"And—well, hello, Robby. Out of school now, eh?"

"Yes, ma'am."

"I guess you all want to see Perry Eastman."

"Yes'm."

"You might as well go up there—he's expecting you and the room's all straightened up."

"Thank you, Mrs. Miner."

"Robby!" Mrs. Miner wagged her head.

"Yes'm?"

"I'm going to tell you something I bet you don't know. When your pa and ma first landed in St. Stephens they stayed here at River House."

"Sure enough?"

"Yes, they did, for a fact, all the time your pa was looking for a farm. But what I was going to tell you, they lived right up there in that same room Perry Eastman's got now."

Robby half closed his eyes as he always did when he was trying to visualize something. "That—that was a long time ago, wasn't it?"

"Not so long. Seems like yesterday. Your pa was a mighty fine-looking man, and your ma was the prettiest little thing you'd want to look at."

Robby flushed. He was pleased to have Mrs. Miner say that.

"Give her my regards when you go home. Tell her to stop in to see me. Yes, sir, that same room. You can think about that when you go up. You better go on, too, I think Mr. Eastman was looking for you."

Perry Eastman opened his door at Robby's knock. "Oh, it's you. Been expecting you. Come in. Laurel, I guess the two of us can chaperone you up here."

Laurel smiled her crinkly, impish smile. "Mrs. Miner seemed to think it was all right. But I guess she thinks I'm still a baby."

"Well, anyway, sit down. Excuse the confusion. I was just finishing my packing."

"When are you leaving?"

"This afternoon."

"Oh!" Robby's exclamation sounded his dismay.

"Yes." Perry spoke briskly, as if he feared he, too, might reveal his feeling. "I'm going to school this summer."

"You!" Laurel laughed.

"Yes, I've got a lot to learn, Laurel. I've just started. But I had something special to talk about."

"We were wondering, but we didn't know you were leaving right away. Mother hoped you'd spend a few days with us before you left."

"Will you thank her for me? But I have to go. And—you know I won't be coming back next fall."

Robby leaned forward. His face drew a little as if he were bracing himself. "Oh—"

"I hate to leave but I'm going to the university for a year or so."

Robby seemed to shrink into his chair. "It'll be awful—here—without you."

"Well, that's what I wanted you to say. I'll miss you, too, both of you. Now, here's the next thing. Those pieces of yours which we've been publishing in the *Timmonstown Bugle*—I had a letter from the editor—several letters, in fact. I'll turn them over to you. I'll see him when I get back to Pennsylvania, myself, but in the mean-time, I'll tell you what he says."

Laurel edged forward in her chair and looked anxiously at Robby. She was fearful of bad news of some kind. Vaguely, she knew that these verses of Robby's meant a great deal to him.

"It's this, Robby. These little pieces are pretty good. In fact, I'd say they're really good, as far as you can go in a dialect like that. It's such a severely limited language."

Robby kept his eager look fixed on Eastman's face. Perry wished the boy would not be so intense. It got into him, somehow.

"Well—the short of it is that they've attracted some attention. The editor, Mr. Strenger, has had a good many letters from readers.

You see, mostly, they've just had translations, funny stories, and the like. This is the first time there's been any original work sent in of any merit whatever. There's a man at the University of Pennsylvania, some sort of philologist, or maybe a folklore man, I don't know which, saw these things and said he thought you had talent, and that there was poetic value in the poems—I guess we can call them poems now."

Robby squeezed his hands together between his knees like a small boy. Laurel leaned over and laid her hand on his arm.

"So—here's what the editor suggests. He thinks they ought to be made into a little book."

"Robby! Robby! Did you hear that?"

Robby turned his eyes slowly toward her and nodded. He swallowed hard, but he did not speak.

"Now—" Perry Eastman was so touched by the naïve delight of these two children, so differently expressed, that he scarcely trusted his voice. "Now, here's his plan. Getting a regular publisher is out of the question—"

"*Why?*" Laurel was shrill, and instant to the defense.

"So little market—the language—"

"Oh."

"But this editor, Mr. Strenger, says he'll get out a small cheap book himself at their printing plant. He says that as a—a sort of literary curiosity he might be able to make back what he puts into it. But that's just a poor country newspaper. He thinks it would cost about a hundred dollars to print some copies and place a few advertisements."

Robby waited without saying anything. He felt his heart sink.

"This is his suggestion. He'll put up half the money, but you'd have to put up the other half."

Eastman waited. Laurel and Robby exchanged looks.

"Oh, gee." Robby's voice quivered this time. "I haven't got any money."

Eastman laid his hand on Robby's knee. "Yes, I know, Robby. You don't suppose you could get it, do you?"

"Where?"

"Your father wouldn't be interested, I guess?"

"Oh—I don't—oh, no—I'm sure—"

"Well, well, maybe that wouldn't be the right way. How about your mother?"

"I don't know, Mr. Eastman. I've showed Mommy the little pieces, and she was glad, of course, but I—I don't guess Mommy's got any money of her own."

Perry Eastman sighed. This was pretty much what he had expected.

"Well, Robby—here's what I had in mind. I know you want to go away to school—and you ought to. I'd talk to your father but I'm afraid he doesn't like me very much and we might make matters worse than they are now. But I thought if we could get the book printed this summer, with maybe an introduction or a preface by this man at the university, maybe we'd impress Mr. Kettring with the importance of seeing you through to—to whatever you want most to do."

Two hard red spots burned in Robby's cheeks. Eastman saw the boy could not speak. Then he said what he had not at all intended to say.

"It seems to me there's a way to work it."

Robby looked up—there was the same look in the deep eyes Perry had seen there the night he had resolved to help this boy to self-realization.

"I—I thought I'd go by Timmonstown and—and arrange for this publication. I'll advance the money to Strenger—"

"Oh—I couldn't borrow—" Robby was clearly frightened at the mention of it.

"It's an advance—that's all. When the book is published they'll make that much back and—well, I'll collect mine from Strenger—or you can pay me yourself—how's that?"

Robby was much too choked up to answer. He looked at Laurel.

Laurel spoke quickly. "That's wonderful of you, Mr. Eastman, and we—Robby won't ever forget it, and you'll get paid back, too, somehow."

"Well—it's a bargain then!"

"Yes, sir." Robby stood up and held out his hand. Perry East-man was embarrassed at all of this seriousness and emotion. He had not meant to offer the money. Heavens above! He certainly could not afford it. Fifty dollars was a month's salary, but he was glad he had said it. It *had* to be.

Robby stood very straight. "I'll make some money some way and pay you back in a hurry. Don't you worry."

Eastman laughed. "I shan't worry. When you're famous I'll ride along with you."

The young teacher, laughing now, and looking almost as excited as his pupils, went down the stairs and out to the buggy with them. He stopped. "Oh, Robby, will you do me a favor? Will you run over to the bank and get my bankbook and statement for me?"

"Of course."

"I'll wait right here for you."

Eastman turned quickly to Laurel. "Just two or three things I want to tell you that might help. I never think of you two separately. I guess you're pretty fond of Robby, aren't you?"

"Yes."

"Not just school-day sweethearts?"

"Not a bit."

"I thought not. Now, listen. Robby has to learn to write in English."

"He says he can't do it in English."

"He's still young—he can change even basic thinking like that. But it's important."

"Why—exactly?"

"There's no public for one thing—supposing what he writes is good enough *for* a public—"

"But it *is* good, isn't it?"

"In its way, yes. You see, Laurel, I don't know myself. I only know that dialect in a general way. Back East they seem to think something of it, but even that might be because he's just a boy."

"I see." Laurel spoke slowly.

"Now don't jump to conclusions, but talent, Laurel—talent is a big word, and genius is a very big word. I don't know what Robby has but I know he has something. Anyway, he ought to have all the cultivation he can get. I'd write to his father if I thought it wouldn't get the boy into trouble."

"It's terrible, isn't it?"

"Yes. It's ridiculous—all the worse because there doesn't seem to be any kind of explanation. You've got to help Robby."

"Me? I mean, I?"

"Yes. As I said, maybe he's a poet, maybe he's just a lonely boy supplying something to fill empty places in his life and heart, but he's a—a rather unusual kind of boy."

"I think he's wonderful—"

"Yes, I dare say."

Laurel blushed.

"It's right that you should, Laurel. I think it's fine. You realize, maybe, or you will, that I'm not much older than you two, and I can understand pretty well."

Laurel considered this. "You've been wonderful to Robby."

"I wish he were my brother."

"I'll do what I can—here—if I only know how to do it."

"Just love him."

Laurel sat very straight in her seat. The trace of girlish coquetry and confusion fell away. "I shall always love Robby just as I do now —and—and that's with all my heart."

"Good. Remember about the English, now. I insist on it, and if it happens that he doesn't get away to school, maybe he'll work out anyway—maybe even better. Schools have ruined fine talents sometimes—still, it may be that if he's any good he will weather anything, even the English department!"

"Here's Robby now—I'll remember."

Eastman took the papers. "Thanks, Robby."

"Welcome, sir."

"Now, good-by, you two. I think I'll just kiss you, Laurel—if Robby doesn't object!"

Robby laughed, easing over the tightness in his throat, and shook hands.

"I can't tell you—sir—"

"Don't try. We'll write—not?"

"Of course."

"You'll hear from me. And listen—hold on to each other."

Laurel nodded. "You bet!"

On the way home Robby fell silent again.

"What's the matter, Robby?"

"I was just thinking."

"You're not discouraged or downhearted, are you?"

"No. I was just trying to think what I can do."

"About that little money, you mean?"

"It's a lot when you haven't got any."

"I bet if you'd walk right up to your father and ask him for fifty dollars, he'd give it to you."

"I couldn't."

"He might be so surprised."

"I've no doubt." Robby spoke dryly.

"Robby—"

"What?"

"I've got some money."

"You have?"

"Yes."

"Well, what?"

"Would you take it?"

"Laurie!"

"Now, what?"

"You know I wouldn't."

"Well, it's mine."

"I didn't say it wasn't."

"Papa and Mr. Sandifer gave it to me for a present."

"That's nice."

"It's twenty-five dollars."

"Listen, Laurie. If I could ever pay *any*body, I'd borrow money —even yours, but I just can't. You can see that."

"Robby, didn't your father give you anything for a graduation present?"

"No."

"He didn't even come, did he?"

"Mommy came."

"Yes, I know. Did he mention your graduation—what did he say?"

"He didn't mention it at all."

"Robby, did you *ask* him to come?"

Robby turned his eyes slowly toward her. "Why, no."

"Why didn't you?"

"I just don't know, Laurie."

"Maybe you should have."

"We never ask Pop anything. I don't know, but he does whatever he wants to."

"Do you have to ask his permission—for—for anything?"

Robby shook his head. "No. I ask Mommy. She always tells me."

"Maybe you ought to talk to your father more."

"You can't talk to him. He never answers."

"How do you know, if you don't try?"

"Oh, you don't understand, Laurie. Pop is—is just *completely* to himself."

"I certainly don't understand anything about the whole business."

"I don't either, Laurie. I've tried to think things out, but there isn't any place to begin—I haven't got anything to begin thinking with where he is concerned."

"I guess he's always been a mystery."

They drove on in silence for a little while.

"Laurie, maybe I could work somewhere for a while."

"Where?"

"Well, there's the threshing gang, it's starting around a little later."

"But that's awfully hard, Robby. I don't believe you could stand up to that."

"Some of the kids at school have—other years."

"But you don't look strong."

"Of course I'm strong. I'm just thin."

"What would you do—all that heavy work?"

"They use boys, sometimes, to cut the binding on the sheaves, and help around generally."

"Could you get a job?"

"I'd ask Mr. Dawson. He sends out two or three gangs."

"I expect Papa would speak to him for you. Would it pay enough?"

"I think they'd pay as much as a dollar a day. I'm going to talk to Mommy about it as soon as I get home."

"I'll miss you if you go away."

"It's just about three weeks."

"I'd miss you no matter how short a time it might be."

Robby had no difficulty about the threshing gang. Kam Sandifer spoke to Mr. Dawson for him. Dawson made inquiring eyebrows.

"Is that *Peter* Kettring's boy you're talking about?"

"Yes."

"I know him. Spindly-looking kid."

"He's strong enough, I guess, to do something."

"Oh, we'll give him something to do if it's only carrying water to the men. But I was just wondering."

"Yes, I wondered, too. But the Kettrings are beyond me."

"Old man's rich as all get out, ain't he?"

"He's got a lot. That's a fact."

"Why do you suppose he lets the kid go out with the threshers?"

"Robby wants some spending money for something or other, I guess. My daughter told me he wanted a job with you."

"Laurel? How is she?"

"Oh, fine."

"Saw her 'bout two weeks ago. Pretty as a picture, Kam."

"Thanks. Laurel's a fine little girl. Spoiled, but—"

"I think I saw this Kettring boy with her at the time."

"They're always together."

"Oh—I see."

"Yes. I let my children do their own choosing, s'long as they don't go entirely wrong. This Kettring boy is about as good as they come."

"That so? None of the old man's funny quirks, eh?"

"Not that I can see."

"Well, you tell Laurel I'll do anything she asks. What's the boy's name?"

"Robby."

"Tell her to send him a week from next Wednesday. We're going to start one gang out on the Murfree place."

"Season's a little late, isn't it?"

"Yes. Everything's late this year. And everybody wants us at the same time—it's always like that."

"Well, much obliged, Dawson."

"Not at all, Kam, not at all. I can use him."

The drive leading from the main road to the Sandifers' was long and winding. Halfway between the gate and the house it turned sharply and skirted a small knoll. At a much earlier time a flower garden had been planted on this rise, probably because it afforded a fine view of the river. It had been neglected, and little remained of the original plan. There was a thicket of lilac bushes surrounding a sagging summerhouse; straggles of white and purple flags, a few stoutly determined clumps of peonies, and a swirl of honeysuckle almost hid the entrance to the summerhouse.

The luxuriant growth of flowers, vines, and weeds, the look of age, and the hint of a past of elegant leisure gave the spot a nostalgic charm.

Robby and Laurel sat close to each other on the step of the pavilion one afternoon. They had fallen under the spell of the hour, and neither spoke for some time. The shadows stretched across the grass and long shafts of sunlight slanted through the trees.

Robby sighed. "Tomorrow, this time—"

"Robby, maybe you ought not to go."

"Why?"

"I don't know. I guess I just don't want you to."

"I'll be back pretty soon. Mommy will give me some money, too, and then—"

"Well." Laurel sighed. "It's not so long until fall and then I guess I'll have to go away."

"Maybe I'll go, too."

"I'd just rather stay here—and not break up all the wonderful times we've had together."

They were silent again. The thought of the future dismayed them. Theirs had been a special world—and the premonitions of changes to come were for them intimations of disaster.

Robby laid his arm across Laurel's shoulder.

"Laurie!"

The tremor in his voice disturbed her. She stiffened against his next words. She tried, mentally, to ward them off, but she knew that she could not. She knew herself as helpless against the swift passage of the moment with all its portent as a piece of driftwood in the power of the river.

"Laurie!"

"What, Robby?" She was surprised at the sound of her own voice. It was veiled and unnatural.

"Listen. Meet me here tonight—after supper—will you?"

His words shook a little—uncertainly.

"Please, Laurie."

She reached for his hand and held it tight.

"All right. If I can—I might be late."

They stood up at once, as by secret accord, and went down the weedy path to the drive.

After supper Robby went upstairs to his room. He stood for several minutes looking at himself in the small square mirror that hung over his washstand. He touched his cheeks and brow and lips with his fingers as if to reassure himself that it was indeed his own reflection that he saw.

A heavy dread—compound of throbbing nerves and dangerous excitement—effected a curious detachment in his mind. He looked at his own bodily habitation as if he had met a stranger.

He turned to the window. The river was like a tide of dark gold under the afterglow of sunset. While he stood looking at it, the burnished surface dimmed, and with a magical swiftness seemed to stand still—a vast arc of smoky purple and blue.

Robby moved like a ghost. He seemed scarcely to touch the floor as he left the room. At the corner of the orchard he whistled softly, but Jude was already standing beside him. She appeared as suddenly and as noiselessly as if she had materialized from the motionless air.

The two went through the orchard and across the bottoms to the road. In the west, fading copper and green streaked the horizon. Two or three stars appeared like early arrivals in some enormous gallery of witnesses.

The soft dust of the road lay pearly gray in the half light. Neither Robby nor Jude made the faintest sound as they went on into the dusk.

Robby waited, standing in the black doorway of the pavilion. Jude sat facing him. The eastern sky showed a faint greenish light. It was almost time for the moon.

Jude moved and stood up. She made a familiar muttering sound in her throat. Robby leaned forward and touched her head with his fingers. She was instantly silent.

Several minutes later Robby saw a shadowy movement on the path.

"Robby!"

"Yes—I'm here."

Just then the moon cleared the crest of the hill. Laurel's face came suddenly out of the dark, unsmiling and white.

Peter glanced absently at Robby the next morning at the table. He continued with his breakfast, but vaguely aware that some question was teasing at his consciousness. He looked up again, a bit more closely this time, at Robby. A curious expression the boy wore. His face looked shattered, Peter thought, and then modified the word in his mind. But certainly he did not look well. It might be the hot weather. Robby did not seem to be strong. Savina should look after him a little.

Presently Robby said, "Excuse me, please," and went upstairs. A few minutes later Peter saw him go out of the side gate with a bundle under his arm.

"Where is Robby going?"

"He didn't want me to tell you until after he had gone." Savina smiled a little.

"Well, but, where—what is?"

"He is going to work for a few days with Mr. Dawson's threshing gang."

"*Robby?*"

"Yes."

"But—it seemed to me just now when I looked at him that he did not look well."

"No. He is well. He said nothing."

"But his face—it looked *alles aus einander.*"

"Oh, that is imagining. He has been well."

"It is hard work with the threshers. Why is he doing it?"

"He wanted a little money for something."

"Spending money?"

"Well—for something he wishes to do—maybe for a surprise." Peter knew Savina was evading his questions.

"If Robby wished to have some money, why did he not ask me for it?"

"Ask you—just for money to spend on some idea?"

"Well, for heaven's sake, I'm the boy's father, am I not?"

"Yes, Peter, naturally, but I think Robby maybe did not even think of asking—"

"Well, I still want to know why not?"

"Whatever he wants a few dollars for—to throw away like boys do sometimes, I guess—he could have been afraid you might not like."

"*Afraid?*"

"Yes."

"You said *afraid,* Savina?"

"Yes—yes."

"Why should Robby be afraid of me?"

"You are his father, and fathers are so strict always."

"Why in God's name should anybody be afraid of me? Have I ever done anything to—to Robby?"

"Of course not."

"I still want to know why he couldn't even tell me he planned this ridiculous business."

"He thought he should do it alone without asking. Mr. Sandifer, he spoke to Mr. Dawson and it was so arranged."

"And nobody could mention it to me."

Peter's tone was so bitter that Savina was astonished.

"Are *you* afraid of me, too, Savina?"

"Me? *Ach,* no. But you see it was best that Robby did not speak to you. You are displeased and you maybe would have said no, and whatever he has set his heart on—it is all right, yes, Peter, that he should do a little work for it and earn it himself. There is nothing wrong in that."

"That's not what I'm talking about. I don't want my—my son to be afraid of me."

"That is not his fault, maybe." Savina spoke so innocently that Peter was uncertain if the dryness in her voice was intended or not.

"And I don't like the idea of my son going out like—like a hired man!"

"Peter!"

"I mean it."

"No one should mind a little work. Work is right, and no one should be too proud to work."

"You talk like all of the damned Hummelfelders, Halterwancks, and Umholzes!"

"I am Umholz. And the Hummelfelders and Halterwancks are honest people—you have said—"

"I'm not talking about honesty. I'm talking about common sense. I've got money. If my son wants some money for whatever, why can't he speak up and ask for it?"

Savina stretched her eyes to their widest. "You would give it to him without question what he does with it?"

"Haven't you raised him to have any sense of his own?"

"Of course!" Savina would have been indignant had she not been so utterly surprised.

"Well, then. I guess we could trust him with some spending money."

"Peter, you have never—never even looked at Robby to see what he wants—"

"Stop that talk! I will not be accused! Always it is that I have *never* done this, *never* done that, *never* done the other thing! The truth is that I have never done anything that there should always be secret talk behind my back, secret arrangements—"

Peter pushed his chair away from the table and stared darkly out of the window.

"I do not understand, Peter."

"No. I guess not. But neither can I understand why no one talks to me about anything. Perhaps I should like to plan, too—plan something besides the running of this God-damned farm!"

"Peter—you are swearing! That is a sin!"

Peter laughed, mirthlessly at first, and then genuinely.

"Very well, we shall see. I think Robby will not stay long in the fields these days. If he doesn't come back in a few days, I'll hitch up and go after him."

"Peter—you must let him alone in this little—"

Rage contorted Peter's face again. "I tell you I will not have my son be a hired man working in the fields of men I do not like, of men I think are no better than trash! But I will let him alone—yes, I'll let him alone until he has enough of heat and dirt and sweat. Then— *then* we'll talk, Robby Kettring and his father! We'll talk *then!*"

Peter went out, slamming the door behind him. Savina shook her head.

"It is Peter, I think, that is not well these days. It is again the heat. He does not stand it well. It goes to his head . . ." She went on speaking to herself as she cleared the table. She examined her cups and saucers. *Gott!* Peter could have broken them with all of that hammering on the table.

Peter, too, went on his way muttering.

So. Nobody wanted to talk to him, eh? Afraid. In God's name, afraid of what? Had he ever killed anybody for speaking to him? He stopped—remembering. There might actually be people who did believe such a thing. A picture flared suddenly . . . yes, that terrible morning! David. David said . . . *"you can kill a man for burning up a barn"* . . . surely, surely David had not believed that. He had heard the old, senseless talk, and then, at that moment, because he was enraged he had said it—just for spite—just to hurt him. David must have known better. . .

And Robby was afraid. That must not be. How he hated things that were afraid! Timidity, cowardice—they were the real sins. But he had done his part, he had made a home and a place for them—David had chosen to run away from it—anyway he had some spirit, but he could have wished that David had come back . . . it would have been possible for both of them to say they were sorry, or even not to say anything at all, just ignore what had happened that morning.

They would have to speak first. He had done nothing to anyone. He was the father, the husband, the master of the place, they would have to speak first, or, by God, he would hold his tongue until he died.

They wouldn't tell him anything, but he knew a lot of things anyway. There were ways a man found out. . . .

People dropped careless remarks. He could piece them together. Yes, he could do that because he was a damned sight smarter than these yokels in St. Stephens. He knew some things, even if no one wanted to tell him. He knew about David and Taska—far more than anyone guessed. They had moved—gone away down to the far tip of Texas where David had bought a newspaper. A little place, a county weekly paper. He bought it on credit. Foolishness! All David had to do was write a letter. He would buy ten newspapers if that was what David wanted. But they'd have to ask.

Savina had not said a word but he knew about the baby. A boy. They had named it Jan. Jan Kettring, his grandson. Doubtless Savina would like to go and see it, and see David, too. Well, why didn't she go? There was plenty of money in the bank. All she had to do was to say she wanted to go. She knew the money was as much hers as it was his. He had told her so. Often enough. He had shown her how to write a check, but she wasn't even attentive. She had never drawn a dollar. Even Savina was afflicted with all the foolishness of those Pennsylvania Dutch. He should have tried to change her in the beginning, but it had seemed unnecessary to change anything then. Now it was too late. Poor Savina—she could not see far.

He had seen that old fool Michael Janek smirking around St. Stephens with a letter in his pocket. He had gone about showing the letter to everybody, bragging about *his* grandson. *His grandson!* Damn it, the child's name was Kettring, wasn't it?

Peter went to the barn and attended to various small after-breakfast chores, but he was absent-minded. Robby was still in his thoughts, and confused with his uncertain opinions about the boy were all the corollary irritations of that inconclusive argument with Savina.

He thrust an empty box out of the way. It fell from the feeding floor into the cow stalls with a clatter that startled the young gray stallion near by. It lunged sideways and kicked violently at the heavy wooden bars. Peter shouted, and the stallion subsided a little, trembling and rolling his bad-tempered eyes.

Peter had been working with this young thoroughbred with the intention of breaking him to the saddle. Each day for a few minutes he had tried first saddle, then bridle, then the two together.

"Ho, you—still now—quiet down." He stepped down to the adjoining stall and reaching through the bars laid his hand on the dancing creature.

A handsome devil, Peter thought. Fit for a crusader. Peter grinned. "Your name is Saracen," he said aloud. "Saracen."

Cautiously, talking quietly all the while, Peter went in and adjusted a bridle and saddle and led the newly christened Saracen out into the stable yard. For fifteen minutes or more he walked him back and forth.

"Quiet, now, Saracen, quiet, now!"

Peter swung quickly into the saddle. Saracen was too surprised for a moment to move. He stood trembling violently. Then he began to plunge. For ten minutes the contest went on. Then Peter dismounted, patted him gently on the neck until the convulsive tremors quieted. He decided this might be enough for today, but something in the watchful look of Saracen challenged him. Peter's eyes narrowed a little. An old, familiar excitement shook him, crowding his chest until he could scarcely breathe. He noticed that Saracen's mouth was bleeding a little from the sharp bit.

Peter sprang into the saddle again. This time Saracen did not hesitate. He leapt and Peter was nearly dislodged. Seating himself firmly he plied the short double-lashed riding quirt. Saracen flung wildly to right and left, and after a few bucking jumps threw Peter headlong.

Peter arose, brushed the straw from his clothes. Then he carefully maneuvered Saracen into a corner. He seized the reins and drew them through a ring on the saddle horn. He pulled with all of his strength until Saracen's head was drawn sharply back against his side. Peter tied the reins tight and stepped back. Saracen turned around and around wildly until he fell. Then Peter walked over to the barn and returned with a heavy whip. He brought it down on the quivering animal who struggled under the fiery punishment, but could not rise. Peter struck furiously. Saracen's satiny coat was crisscrossed with welts; here and there flecks of blood showed. The stallion struggled and made strange strangled sounds: Peter lashed and shouted and swore.

Out of breath he flung the whip aside and loosened the reins. Saracen arose uncertainly, and stood shaking. His head drooped a little, and blood streamed with foam from his mouth.

"Now, tomorrow—we try again."

Peter unbuckled the girth, and lifted the saddle. Patting Saracen again on the neck, he removed the bridle. All the time he talked, softly, reassuringly. But he was unable to coax Saracen back to his stall.

"So, so now! Tomorrow it goes better. By and by—"

Peter broke his horses, as he did everything else, in his own way. He had watched others with methods more patient and humane, but he was short-tempered. He liked everything that resisted, but at the same time he could not brook that resistance. His horses were well fed, well kept, and of the best. He broke them quickly, drove them hard and fast, and when they lost their fire and spirit he sold them.

He stopped at the stable door, turned, and looked long at the still-quaking Saracen. He nodded. A magnificent horse. He walked back again.

"Come, Saracen, come come—"

Saracen flung his head high, and quick as the movement of a leopard, he reared and struck at Peter, who barely escaped the flashing hoofs.

"You damned devil—" Peter backed away, but Saracen was after him at once, rearing, striking, stretching his head forward, his ears laid back, doing his best to bite.

Peter yelled and cursed, and finally reached his whip. When Saracen felt the white-hot streaking of the lash he retreated.

Peter smiled. "So! A little fight, eh?"

2

Throughout that first day with the threshing gang Robby moved in a haze of detachment. He was scarcely aware of even physical contacts. He did not feel the heat. The flying chaff did not annoy him. The clatter and noise and loud talk of the men passed over him like the shadow of a cloud.

That night his head buzzed a little—an echo of the daylong sound of the machines—and he slept lightly. He tried in waking moments to remember yesterday and the night before, but they seemed to float away from recall like elusive fragments of a dream.

The next day and the next night were the same.

Bill Jackson, in charge, spoke to Dawson about Robby. "I think that kid's half sick, Dawson."

Dawson glanced at Robby. "Looks a little peaked, doesn't he? Keep an eye on him. Send him home if he doesn't get on all right. Wouldn't want to get on the wrong side of old man Peter Kettring."

"Me neither."

"Think you'll finish up here Saturday, all right? I just saw Mr. Anderson. He wants us Monday. I guess we'd better use Sunday going up there. It's a long trip, but we can work back this way and over to the Clinton Creek places."

"All right, Mr. Dawson."

Outside of this passing notice no one paid any attention to Robby. Threshing was high-pressure work. The men worked from sunrise to sunset in a race against threatening rains.

Robby was placed at the feed table with another boy. Placing the sheaves in position and cutting the binding was considered a light job, but it permitted no letup. The heat was terrific, and the noise deafening. The air was thick with chaff and dust.

Robby felt his knees shake with fatigue from time to time but mostly he was so dazed by the general violence of the activity that he felt little or nothing. At night the buzzing in his head was worse. But, when it subsided a little, he thought with a faint exhilaration that he was piling up the precious dollars.

This hint of lightheartedness came like a refreshment. Vaguely, Robby realized that there had always been an uncertain and indefinable uneasiness lurking even in the best of days. It was a kind of shadow. He knew now what that shadow had been. It was some kind of fear of his father—fear that the future was to be of his father's making, and not of his own. Now—here—in these few days, despite the grueling work, that shadow had lifted ever so little. And—maybe, after all, it had been an unnecessary apprehension. Maybe everything would be all right. Pretty soon he would be at home again. He would talk it all over with Laurel. The thought of Laurel came like a sudden drench of ecstasy.

It was the second week. Work had settled down to a steady grind. The men talked less. The heat was staggering.

During a momentary lull Jackson stopped to speak to the two boys.

"How you making out, kids, all right?"

"Yes, sir." Tom Baker was the boy working with Robby.

Robby nodded but did not answer.

"What's the matter, boy? You ain't sweatin' a-tall!"

Robby looked curiously at his dry blue shirt. "I don't know."

"You better go down there to that grove of trees for a little while. Lay down in the shade. Don't want you having sunstroke around here."

"Yes, sir."

Robby went without hesitation. He reeled slightly. Jackson looked after him and frowned. "I think that kid's pretty near wore out. I'm going to send him home tonight."

Robby went down across the stubble field toward the trees bordering the creek. His stomach hurt, and he thought the sun did not seem as bright as it had been. Maybe it was going to rain.

By the time he reached the creek he had forgotten what he had come for. He had forgotten the threshers. He was not at all sure where he was.

He stopped at the creek edge and dipped his hands in the warm, stagnant water. Then he washed his face. He stared dizzily at the little waves he had set in motion. He rocked slightly on his feet and almost fell in. He was not feeling well, sure enough. Maybe he should go to see Laurel—and tell her—tell her what? His head was buzzing again, and he could not think what it was he wanted to tell her.

He forgot what Mr. Jackson had said about lying down. It did not seem any cooler here than it was up there in the field. His face burned. He looked at his hands and arms. He was certainly badly sunburned.

He walked on absently. He splashed through the shallow water. Oh, gee! He had forgotten he had his shoes on! But the wet was pleasant. He stumbled up the opposite bank and pushed through the blackberry bushes. They clawed at him, cut his arms, pulled, and fought against him. Robby whimpered a little—they were hurting him, those blackberry bushes!

Then he felt the soft thick dust of the road under his feet. It would be easier now . . . perhaps he'd better go on to the little summerhouse. It would be pleasant there after the sun went down.

Laurel would tell him what to do about—about this heaviness in his head. It was weighing him down. His head was so heavy it made his feet drag in the deep dust. . . .

The long shadows fell across the road, but Robby did not notice the change. He plodded on, his head down. His throat was dry but he did not know what to do about that . . . just as soon as he saw Laurel . . . or, he could go home first . . . the Mommy . . .

Twilight settled. Robby heard a dog bark. He smiled . . . poor old Jude . . . tied to her kennel so she would not follow him . . . he would untie Jude the first thing . . .

A late moon came up, a broken piece of a moon, and somewhere at his right there was a sudden staccato chorus of frogs. There were other sounds, too, insects . . . thin, hard, high sounds that cut into his ears.

Robby stumbled; twice he nearly fell.

He stopped still and listened. Oh, that was his own breathing—that rasping, choking sound. Of course, his throat was terribly dry. He half turned around—the water jugs under the trees, back there by the creek—but that was . . . he could not quite set his wavering thoughts to words. He would go on—he would get a drink of water at the Sandifers'. . . . He pulled at his floppy straw hat, like a child, dragging it forward. He dropped it after a few steps but he was unaware of it.

The moon was higher now. It had changed from gold to silver.

Robby went on more slowly. He rubbed his eyes with both hands and tried to clear his vision. He must be awfully tired—and sleepy. He wanted to sit down, or to lie down just a few minutes, but he held stubbornly to his way . . . he might be late . . . Laurel . . .

Oh . . . oh . . . why!—he must have fallen and did not know it. . . .

He tried to rise, but it was difficult. He crawled a little distance on his hands and knees. Then, with all the strength he could summon, he got to his feet. He brushed the dust from his knees. He must be terribly dirty. . . .

He walked on but he could not go straight. He felt himself going from side to side . . . first this way . . . then that . . . as if some wide-swinging rhythm sent him this way . . . and that . . . it made him dizzier, too . . . and sick at his stomach. . . .

There was something beside him . . . walking along with him . . . making some sort of sound . . . like—like . . .

Laurel stirred in her sleep. Somewhere there was a loud noise. She waked suddenly. The dogs were barking. All the Sandifer dogs at once! She turned on her pillow, uneasy, though it was not unusual for the dogs to go crazy like that. Anything set them off.

She raised herself on her elbow and looked out of the window. A lopsided moon sagged toward the west. There was a feeling of dawn in the air.

The clamor of the dogs broke out with renewed intensity. She heard Mr. Sandifer shouting from his bedroom window. She sat up and stretched. "Oh, dear—"

Then Laurel sprang to her feet. She listened, incredulously. One sound arose above the bedlam in the side yard—a deep, lamenting voice that lifted its poignant call over all the outcry and warning of the pack.

Jude!

Laurel tore across the hall, and pounded on the door of her father's room—

"Come out, please, oh, come on—quick!"

"Laurel!"

"Oh, come on—*quick!* Please!"

"Laurel, what on earth is the matter with you?"

"Listen—don't you hear that? *It's Jude!*"

"Jude? Well—"

"Something's happened—I know. Robby's out there somewhere! That's Jude!"

They found Robby clinging to the fence. His eyes were glazed, and he could not answer. Kam loosened the boy's desperate hold, and Robby slumped into his arms.

Mrs. Sandifer was on the side porch with a lamp.

"Heavens! What's the matter, Kam? What is it?"

Laurel answered. "It's Robby, Mamma. He's sick."

Mrs. Sandifer raised the lamp. "In here, Kam, to this room." She opened the door.

Kam placed the boy carefully on the bed. "He looks pretty sick."

"Is he unconscious, Kam?"

"I guess so." Kam went to the back stairs. "Nate!"

"Yes, sir."

"Come down and build a fire in the kitchen stove, quick. Laurel, you help. Heat some water. We'll have to wash him up a bit. Call Tred, and tell him to saddle up and go to St. Stephens for Dr. Jennings. You better stop by and tell the Kettrings—no, Nate can go soon as he's got the fire going. Hurry now."

Mrs. Sandifer came out on the porch. "He's got a burning fever. I'm going to get a nightshirt. Start getting those clothes off of him, Kam."

She hurried on. Kam glanced for an instant at Laurel standing in the light that fell through the open door.

"Don't worry, daughter. We'll have the doctor now shortly. He'll be all right. No, I wouldn't go in there—Laurel!"

"I've got to see if—"

"Laurel!"

Laurel stood quite still beside the bed. She looked steadily at the grimy, flushed face. Robby tossed restlessly.

"Robby! Robby!"

"He can't hear you, Laurel."

"I see. Oh, hurry—do something!"

"Go now—see about some water—"

"All right." Laurel went hurriedly across the long porch. Her father looked after her and shook his head.

Robby had been unconscious for four days.

Dr. Jennings called Peter and Kam out to the side porch. The noon sun was just rounding the house. Midday stillness hung over the place.

"Well, Doctor?" Kam looked tired and worn. Peter merely stood. He did not speak. His face was stony.

"I'm afraid this is bad news."

Peter's hands clenched slowly, but he did not move.

"There's an internal hemorrhage—is Mrs. Kettring here?"

Peter nodded.

"You better take her in for a few minutes—"

Peter turned quickly and went into the house.

"The boy won't last an hour, Mr. Sandifer."

"God!" His thought went instantly to Laurel. She was upstairs. He wondered if he should tell her. He decided not to.

Those four days and nights had worn everyone out.

Robby must have had the beginning of typhoid when he went out with the threshers. How he had gone through so many days was hard to understand.

Kam sat down on the long bench and rested his head on his hands. He was in a panic of fear for Laurel. She had been so strange. She had slept very little, and barely answered when she was spoken to. Pity for his tempestuous, headstrong child was like a knife in his heart. He would have to go up to her . . .

Kam started violently. The hushed moment was torn by a long, tremendous howl—a deep, shattering sound compounded of terror and inextinguishable anguish.

"Tred—*Tred!*"

"Yes, sir!"

"Hurry out there—Jude—quiet her, somehow."

Kam dashed up the back steps to Laurel's room. He opened the door. Laurel was standing at the window facing him. Her eyes were wide and expressionless.

"Laurel—Laurel, darling!"

He crossed the room and put his arms about her.

"Laurel, dear—I have to tell you—"

She nodded slowly. "I know. I heard—"

The shabby little procession moved slowly along the river road toward the Kettring place. Two surreys with the pallbearers, the hearse from Camperville, and then a few buggies, surreys, and spring wagons.

Laurel sat beside her father. At the curves of the road she could see the hearse with the shiny walnut coffin inside. The vehicle swayed and bumped sickeningly as they wound their way along the road, around the Kettring house and to the grave. Peter had chosen a spot in a clump of cedars at the upper edge of the timothy field beyond the orchard.

Laurel knew she must go through with this somehow but she knew she dared not listen or look. Across the grave stood Savina, bewildered and stricken. There was a timid look in her eyes, almost a look of question.

Peter was as motionless as the tall slender cedars behind him.

Laurel felt her knees shake, but she held grimly to her father's arm. She must not look—she must not—

Her lips moved, almost imperceptibly. She was talking to herself.

. . . But it is so. *It is*. It is Robby who is in that coffin. . . . I saw him this morning . . . it is happening now—*now* . . . they are going to put him down in that grave—bury him away out of my sight, and I won't ever see him again, or hear, or talk to him. . . . I must not believe it . . . I must not see it happen, or—or . . .

Laurel knew that she must hold herself back from that verge of tears—she must not cry. She knew if she slipped even the tiniest bit on that declivity, she would be lost—she would have to run, crying and screaming across the field.

. . . I must not think—I must not. I've got to think about something else—quick—I've got to remember something else— there'll never be anything else in the world to think of. . . . I'll have forever to cry and remember yesterday and today . . . as soon as I am alone, but not now, not now. . . .

. . . But it's true. Robby is dead. . . . I saw him . . . they are lifting the coffin now . . . oh, God, what are they doing? I must not look!

She felt her father's arm about her, but she stiffened and did not lean against the support. She must not yield—not the tiniest bit.

. . . Think about something else—quick! Remember something else. Remember the walks together . . . pretend . . . just for these few minutes . . . try to pretend. Remember the summerhouse—just two weeks ago—the summerhouse . . . God, dear God, please —please let me have a baby. . . . I've got to have something . . . I can't just let him go—I can't let them take him—oh, God, what are they doing now?—I must not look! Robby, Robby, you understand, don't you? I can't look, or I'll do something terrible—I'll fight and scratch—I'll tear it away from them, that shiny coffin with you inside of it—oh, dear, dear, God, please let me have a baby! . . . I'll be good—I'll be good all my life, and make up . . .

No—I've got to look! I *have* to! I must see the last of this bright, living day go into the grave with you. . . .

Laurel swayed slightly. Kam's arms tightened around her. Peter glanced at her curiously. Something near to pity crossed his dark enigmatic face.

Someone was saying something. Oh, yes—the minister.

Laurel raised her eyes slowly. She fixed her gaze on a grove of trees that stood out on the high hill, clear in the heartless, indifferent day—a grove of trees that neither knew nor cared what was happening here in this field—their own special place—they called it "the temple."

"Come, Laurel. We can go now."

She brought herself back with difficulty. Fearfully she looked at the dusty mound, covered with cedar branches.

Robby . . .

3

That summer was dry and unusually hot. Grass everywhere was brittle as straw. Leaves yellowed and thinned. By late August a look of premature autumn lay over the land.

Laurel walked slowly through the Kettring orchard toward the house. She had not been here since Robby's death and her feet felt more leaden with each step.

The big house seemed to loom above her and she stopped at the beginning of the long slope. The shutters were closed and the spotted shadows of the sycamores lay motionless against the white walls. It seemed to be deserted. It is, she thought. No one is alive here any more.

With careful resolution she held all recollection at safe distance. She dared not, even now, remember too much.

Her breath came quick and short as she rounded the house. Savina was crossing the yard from the enclosed vegetable garden.

"Good morning, Mrs. Kettring."

Savina turned her head a little to one side. It was a characteristic gesture—timid, deprecating, gentle. It was curiously touching.

"Good morning—Laurie. Come in."

"I won't bother you long. I—"

Savina waved the apology away. She chose her English words with conscious care and effort.

"*Ich*—I am so glad to see you."

They entered the house. Savina raised the shades in the front room a little. The sun falling through the shutters made a ladder of light across the prettily colored rag carpet.

"You will sit a little?"

"Yes. I—I—"

"You are well?"

"Yes."

"It has been very hot."

"Terrible."

"I do not like great heat."

"We should be used to it—here."

Savina looked at the floor. This girl—Robby's girl—she was pretty, but she did not look well. Savina was suddenly terrified at her confused emotions. She had no direction to her mind at this moment. She could not muster even an effort to arrange her thoughts. All summer—it had been like this all summer. Laurel was about to speak when she saw tears on Savina's face.

"Oh—Mrs. Kettring—"

Savina lowered her face still more, but her hands lay quiet in her lap.

"Mrs. Kettring—maybe I should go. I can come back another time."

Savina shook her head. She held her apron to her face and cried silently.

"I am so sorry, Mrs. Kettring. Did my coming—"

"No, no. Excuse me. I cry—so much. All summer I have done nothing but cry. Every day—all day. Every night—all night. I cannot stop."

"You must—"

Savina looked up quickly. There was an odd flash in her soft blue eyes. "I must not cry, you will say! But I must! Is there anything else to do? It is everything—everything that is gone from me! I do not know how to say—my people—we do not cry or say much. I—now I am different . . . when *everything*—" She held her apron to her face again.

"I know Mrs. Kettring. I lost just about everything, too."

Savina seemed not to hear.

"Mrs. Kettring—I came to ask something."

"What you will."

"You know the little pieces Robby wrote? Are there papers here—his writing?"

Savina nodded. "Upstairs. Do you wish to see?"

"Please. May I?"

Laurel had not meant to say this. She had not wished to go upstairs, or to enter Robby's room, but she knew now that she must. Perhaps that was one of the reasons for coming here.

"Come."

They went through the half light of the hall to the enclosed staircase at the rear.

"You can see?"

"Oh, yes."

Their steps sounded loud on the uncarpeted stairs. Laurel felt that they should go on tiptoe and speak in whispers. It seemed, this hushed and darkened house, a kind of dedicated quiet.

Savina opened a door. The room was completely dark. She raised the shades, lifted the window, and tilted the slats of the shutter. The atmosphere was stifling.

Laurel leaned against the door frame and gasped a little.

Savina heard her. "Wait, I open the windows some more." She flung the shutters back, and then opened a door into an adjoining room. "So. Now it will be better. I come not much in here."

Savina's voice was matter-of-fact, steady—almost indifferent. Laurel knew that her habitual self-control had reasserted itself.

She looked about the little room. It was utterly impersonal. The bed was covered with an orange and white patchwork quilt, a hit-and-miss rag carpet was on the floor. The paper shades were brown with gilt stripes. There were no curtains. A small square table stood near the window. A kerosene lamp with a flowery paper shade was the sole object on the table.

Savina pointed. "There. In the drawers of the table."

Laurel opened the two drawers. One of them stuck a little. There were some composition books, some loose papers, and a few stubby pencils.

"Is this all?" She turned to Savina who was looking out of the window.

"Yes."

"Listen, Mrs. Kettring. Robby told me about his writing. He—"

"Yes, of course." Savina's voice was muffled but shaded with an undertone of understanding.

"What I want to ask—is—"

"Whatever you will."

"May I have some of these?" Laurel gulped. It had been hard to say. She felt she must have something that had belonged to him, and yet she feared possessing anything that might have too great a power of evocation.

"Take them—all of them. He would like, I know."

Laurel stood without answering. This room! He looked out of these windows . . . he slept there with his dear, blessed head on that pillow . . . he sat there . . .

"Come. I wrap them up for you. We go down now. It is very warm in here."

"I—I want the pencils, too. May I have them?"

"Of course. I know—you want something. There is nothing else."

"Isn't there—even a picture of him?"

"No. We never thought—I guess."

"Maybe you want these yourself."

"I do not understand them. I have looked. The pieces from the papers, too, and the letters. They are for you now."

"But you—you must keep something!"

"There is nothing. Everything . . ." Savina closed her lips tightly.

"Come now, we go down."

Savina closed the windows again, and lowered the shades.

Laurel was curious about Savina. Mrs. Sandifer had visited the Kettrings several times this summer, and Laurel had heard reports from various sources. All were the same. Peter was silent as usual, withdrawn, uncommunicative, and unrevealing. But Savina, they said, had cried day in and day out.

Lena Janek made commiserative sounds whenever Savina was mentioned.

"I was never so surprised. Always Mrs. Kettring has been so quiet—nothing to say but just the little talk there is always when women come together. She never let on about anything. Now she cries all the time. It's like she's making up for all the years she never showed no feelings. You just can't do anything with her. Seems like as soon as she hears a body's voice she begins. Except when her man is around. She goes all different. Just shuts up completely. She don't seem to have a word to say to him—not that the

[318]

Kettrings ever did talk much, goodness knows. But it's all kind of unnatural and I just don't know what to make of it."

Laurel's mother said much the same. "The woman is desperately broken up. Something inside of her is all to pieces. Of course, I never did know her very well or see very much of her since she speaks so little English, but there's something alarming about her."

Laurel realized on such occasions that her family were making a point of trying to be as casual as was possible so that her own grief might be lessened.

Savina walked around the house with Laurel. Her face was still again, but strange—stricken as if from within somewhere, as if the very fibers that bound her together had somehow been loosened.

"Come again—Laurie." Savina managed the familiarity with some hesitation.

"Yes, I will. Thank you—and thank you for these."

Savina almost smiled. "There's Jude behind you. She comes out of her bushes there to see you."

"Oh!" Laurel turned quickly. Jude with uplifted nose was at her side. "Hello, Jude, old girl."

Jude wagged her tail halfheartedly.

"I thought me Jude would die—often. She would not eat for a long time. She stayed—all the time—up there." Savina gestured toward the upper timothy field, but did not look in that direction. "Peter coaxed her away after a while. She don't eat much now."

Jude was thin. Her ribs showed and her hips stuck out in sharp angles. Her grand head was as eloquent as ever of sorrow and foreboding.

"Maybe she will go home with me for a while." Laurel spoke with a questioning inflection.

Savina considered Jude thoughtfully.

"Yes," she said after a moment. "Maybe it will do her good to see someone."

"Come on, Jude, come on."

Jude stood undecided.

"*Geh'! Geh' mit, Jude!*"

Jude started obediently.

"Good-by, Mrs. Kettring. I'll bring her back pretty soon."

Laurel crossed the orchard, skirted the timothy field, and went straight to Robby's grave among the cedars. She had not been here since the day of the funeral. The mound had been sodded but the effort had failed. The squares had shrunk and the grass was yellow and dead. She stood for a while, trying at first to think, then trying not to. The thoughts and feelings she tried to order in her excited brain refused to appear. She wanted to recall Robby, as he looked and as he spoke when they used to walk across these slopes and uplands, but the pictures and the recollections of Robby's words and voice would not come. Instead there trooped in from unsuspected hiding places in her memory other pictures—inconsequential and disjointed fragments—other recollections of phrases and sentences which seemed but drifting wisps of sound. These unexpected and unrelated trivialities struck through her with a frightening poignancy.

She had come here to find some noble and perhaps comforting aspects of her own grief and loss, something that would enable her better to endure the onslaught of each day's awakening. Instead, she had come upon those very memories she had hoped never to arouse.

When she had stood here last she had had one faint hope threading the blackness of that day's agonizing sorrow. She had hoped she might have a baby. She had faced, resolutely, all the attendant dilemma of such an event. Now, of course, she knew that she no longer had even that small dream. Here, surrounded by the scenes, and the great landscapes which had been the setting of happy days, the full realization of loss lay in her. It seemed to Laurel that she had been wasted and desolated as a field is wasted and desolated by ruinous seasons.

Maybe, she thought, maybe I have died, too.

She was brought back to the moment by Jude's familiar rumble of warning. Jude was lifting her feet and putting them down again with that odd look of abasement which is a dog's apology.

Laurel looked up quickly. Peter was standing only a few feet away.

He raised his tattered old straw hat with that touch of courtliness which had always disconcerted Laurel. Today it annoyed her.

"Good morning—Laurel." The name came to Peter's lips, also, with difficulty.

"Good morning."

They stood looking at each other for a full minute.

Laurel pointed awkwardly at the grave. "You tried sodding—"

"Yes. The summer was too dry, of course."

"It has been very hot, hasn't it?" Laurel's words seemed muffled, but her eyes were sparkling and angry-looking.

Peter considered her. High-spirited, high-tempered, high-strung. He liked her. All the marks of breeding. A flashing recollection of Taska came to mind. His boys had sense and judgment. For a second he forgot that Robby lay there beneath that sun-parched grass.

"The sod was only temporary, anyway," he said abruptly.

"Temporary?"

"Yes. I think as soon as the ground settles completely I'll build a brick vaulting and have—you know, a grave-length slab—"

"Oh, you—you—" Laurel choked on her words.

Peter turned in quick surprise. "What's the matter?"

"How can you sound so—so casual—as if you were talking of building a fence—or—something like that!"

Peter answered quietly. "I am not heartless."

"Oh, yes you are! If you hadn't always been heartless, and—and indifferent, Robby—Robby would be alive now."

"What do you mean?"

"You know what I mean!"

"I do not."

"You killed him."

"Don't talk like a little fool!" Peter's tone was icy.

"A fool! A fool! Me? *You* can say that. You blind and terrible person! Where are your sons? There's your answer!"

Peter's face set grimly. "I think you don't know what you are saying."

"You drove David away, and you killed Robby—and I—I haven't got anything left! Nothing! Nothing! Nothing!"

Peter did not answer. He looked at Laurel with a strange and startled surprise.

"Miss Sandifer—"

"Oh, don't stand there and say Miss Sandifer—"

"Stop that!" Peter spoke so sharply that Laurel's sobbing ceased instantly. "Try not to be hysterical and childish!"

"I am—"

"Please. Let me speak for a minute. I wouldn't listen to you at all—that kind of silly chatter—if it were not that Robby cared so much about you—"

"How do *you* know?"

"It was in his eyes. And it is in yours."

Laurel stared.

"Now—Laurel. I haven't any idea what you are talking about. But I do wish to say that my son David ran away from home through a misunderstanding. All of that is no one's business, certainly not yours. But—Robby . . . Robby died of typhoid fever—"

"But he wouldn't have if he hadn't gone to work on that horrible threshing."

"That may be so, but no one can be sure."

"I know. I know. He was all right when he left. And for a few dollars—*a few dollars*—"

"Laurel!"

Peter's tone sobered her a little. "What?"

"What are you talking about? I think I should know."

"About the miserable little money he wanted."

"What money—and what for?"

"*Don't you know?* Mrs. Kettring didn't tell you?"

"No." This time Peter's tone was so grim and bitter that Laurel was afraid.

"Maybe—oh, I am sorry—I've just talked too much—but I'm so—so lonesome."

"I sympathize with that far more than you know, maybe. But I want to know about this money."

Laurel related the story of the poems, the newspaper, and the projected book. But she did not tell him that the book was to be published anyway. When she had finished Peter looked steadily out across the fields and across the river.

"I see," he said. His face was ashy gray and his voice curiously dead and far away. "This is the first I have known about it. There is no reason why I should explain to you—or to anybody, but for Robby—I will tell you this. He could have had whatever he asked for. He never asked for anything."

"But *that's* where you are to blame."

"I don't see that. Robby had a mother to whom he talked quite freely. There is nothing he could have wished for that she couldn't have given him."

"She was afraid, too."

"Afraid?"

"Yes. Everybody has always been afraid of you—except me. I'm not afraid of you—or the devil!"

"Which I gather you regard as about the same thing."

Laurel was not able to cope with this kind of grown-up sarcasm.

"I'm not afraid of you—but I can hate you all the rest of my life!"

"I shouldn't waste my time, if I were you."

"Don't talk to me like that!"

"You set the tone of this—exchange yourself."

"Oh—oh! We're standing here *fighting*—over Robby's grave!"

"We are not fighting. Laurel—listen to me! For your own peace of mind, you have to believe that I knew nothing of this. Not even this Perry Eastman bothered to speak to me."

"He was afraid of getting Robby into trouble."

"Why?"

"You have a bad reputation. You're hard and selfish. You never thought of anybody but yourself in your whole life!"

Laurel was in a panic. She could not believe that she was saying the words she heard, but she was beyond any control.

Peter smiled a little. "That happens to be untrue—and unjust."

"It's what I think, and it's what everybody thinks."

Peter made a disdainful gesture with his hand. "I should not have expected you to be much interested in what *everybody* thinks."

"That's where you're so self-centered. You *ought* to care."

"Why?"

"They are people, too."

This time Peter laughed. "That's generous of you!"

"There's no use talking to you. Robby always said there wasn't —that you wouldn't listen."

Laurel did not see the gathering of pain in Peter's somber eyes. His voice was slightly unsteady as he answered lightly. "You and Robby seem to have made quite a conspiracy against me."

"He was afraid of you, and he was unhappy about it."

Peter waited a moment, trying with all his strength to keep an outward calm.

"Please let me say that I am very sorry for you, Laurel."

"For me—why?"

"I'm sorry for everyone concerned in this. And you might remember that every heart knows its own bitterness."

Laurel was surprised at Peter's sudden gentleness as much as at the quotation. But Peter was more surprised than she was. He drew himself up. It was a gesture of pride defending itself against further hurt, but Laurel misunderstood it.

"I'm going home. I guess you're satisfied now. There's nobody else you can hurt."

Peter did not answer this.

Laurel walked away quickly. "Come on, Jude."

Jude made a few hesitating steps and looked back at Peter. Laurel called again, sharply, and Jude followed her. Some half challenge danced in her eyes as she looked back.

Peter snapped his fingers. *"Komm, Jude, z'rück!"*

[324]

Jude turned instantly. Halfway she stopped and lowered her head almost to the ground.

"Come on, Jude! Come on with me." Laurel was shrill.

Jude stood still.

Peter held out his hand toward the troubled dog.

"Willst du mit gehen, Jude, heh?"

Jude hesitated no longer. She came to Peter and pushed her wet nose against his hand. Laurel turned without another word and went on toward the hill path. Peter watched her out of sight.

He stood trying to arrange his torn and scattered thoughts.

After a while he crossed the fence and gathered an armful of Spanish nettle. Returning he dropped them beside Robby's grave.

"Komm, Jude."

Peter and Jude walked across the fields toward the river.

Peter had been profoundly shaken by the encounter with Laurel. Again he was certain that he did not care what anyone thought of him—not even Laurel—but he was agitated that such untruths should be spoken and such unjust attitudes maintained. It was a bit difficult to separate the feelings held against him from the people who held them. He resented one and was contemptuous of the other, but it was all somewhat confused.

He was even more surprised at Laurel's unexpected power to hurt him. He knew now that somewhere in the secret intricacies of his being he had loved Robby. The wounds he had sustained at Laurel's hands were only evidence of the extension of that love to the things Robby himself had cared for.

He thought, with a new and burning agony in his heart, of Robby's thin delicate face and figure, of his curiously deft hands, and of an indefinable spiritual awareness that gave to every slightest motion the boy made a quality of almost painful sensitivity.

And Laurel had dared to say he had never noticed Robby, or thought of anyone but himself!

Now, even in this moment of resentment against her and all others who might dare to judge him, he was startled to find himself facing an encircling attack of questions—questions that sprang into threatening and malicious life from the farthest rim of his consciousness—from the most distant extensions of the imaginary world of arranged thought and feeling he had sought through all these years to build as the certain refuge of his soul.

Soul! He could have spat out the word with contempt as if it were a tangible, ill-tasting thing. Vague, cloudy thinking! Hateful words that reached out and over attention, like a deceptive and lying twilight of the mind, transforming the cold and distinct details of fact, enveloping certainty in an obscuring uncertainty of its own devising!

But questions, new and formidable questions, possessed of a terrifying malevolence, continued to advance.

Peter's surprise at the tumult within him was wholly naïve.

Master of his own destiny—the arranger of his own days—why!—he had asked nothing more than this. And here was this fury beating over his head. In God's name . . .

He tried to evade the things that flew at him; he strove to ward them off: he retreated to generalities. But this did not avail. Laurel had been too direct, too specific, too concrete. They were *afraid* of him! Everyone was afraid of him! David—Taska—Robby —Savina . . .

Savina! Here indeed Laurel had struck deep. Savina! To Peter Savina had never changed. He had seen her through all of these years as she was when he knew her. She was a child—simple, docile. But she had been afraid! Of what? It could only be that she believed him capable of some violence or cruelty that he had certainly never committed. And that was, somehow, in the very nature of its wrongheaded conclusions, a betrayal.

Savina had talked with Robby. She had encouraged him to go on this insane enterprise which ended in his death.

He was not certain, now that he tried to analyze his feeling, just what had been, and what now was, in his relation to Savina. He had, perhaps, thought of her, felt about her, that she was something contained inside of his personality—something held, something protected, and something warming. But he had now to see her as something outside of himself, something apart, alien even, and potentially opposed to him.

Now he was indeed bereft—far beyond the bereavement of David's defection and Robby's death—now he was indeed alone. He was alone here on his own place. He was alone in the countryside, because he did not doubt that Laurel's openly proclaimed hate could alienate the slight and amiable neighborliness that had existed between him and Kam Sandifer.

He was alone in the world, and he was alone in all the room and reach of his own spirit.

Peter straightened where he stood. He squared his great shoulders, and as he swept his gaze from the river to the hills and back again his eyes flared with a fire that had not shown there for a long, long time.

This season of desolation that was now so suddenly visited upon those regions where the sustenances of self had flourished, this, too, he could sustain.

In these moments of tragic isolation, and in his desperate misunderstanding of his own nature and the nature of the whole world, Peter arose to an actuality of the stature that had loomed so darkly and so threateningly in the imagination of others since the first years of his presence here.

He looked down at Jude. She looked back at him.

In his overwrought state it appeared to him that her gaze had a supernatural eloquence.

For the first time in his life a doubt arose on the far horizon of his consciousness, a doubt so black that it was the very brother of fear.

Laurel reached the summerhouse and sat down wearily on the stone step. She was exhausted from the torrential emotions of the morning. She dropped her hands in her lap, but her fingers locked and twisted nervously. She was still filled with shame for her outbreak. It was a poor tribute, she thought, to Robby. How could she have done that, and there at that spot of all places in the world?

She opened one of the composition books and leafed slowly through it. All in Robby's strange language. Here and there some notations and corrections in English. Probably, yes, certainly Perry Eastman's work. She looked quickly through the others. All much the same. It was like having a door closed in her face. And yet, these were his. He had dreamed and worked over these pages. She would lock them away. There would be days and dark hours of the night when maybe just to touch them would be some assuagement. . . .

"Laurel!"

It was Mr. Sandifer, calling up from the road.

"Yes."

"Want to walk down to the landing with me?"

She shook her head.

"Why not?"

"Tired, Mr. Sandifer."

"Where've you been this hot morning?"

"Over to the Kettrings'."

"Oh." He waited a moment and added in a changed voice: "Oh, I see."

"Come up and sit here."

"I ought to go down to the landing."

"What for?"

"See about having a boat fixed."

"It's awfully hot for you to be out walking in the sun."

"If you say 'at your age,' I'll come up there to you."

"That's what I was going to say. Come up. It's not very cool here, but it's shady inside."

"All right."

He came slowly up the winding path. He looked very thin and white. Laurel noticed the crinkle of veins in sharp relief on his temples.

"What are you doing, Laurel?"

"Nothing."

"What have you there?" He pointed at the books.

"They are Robby's books and papers."

"Oh."

Both were silent for a few minutes.

"Robby's mother gave them to me. Robby wrote pieces—little poems."

"I see."

"But they're in a kind of German."

"May I see one, dear?"

"Certainly."

Mr. Sandifer glanced through the book and handed it back to her.

"What are you going to do with them?"

"Keep them."

"I—well, of course."

"They're the only thing I have of his."

"Laurel, child, I'd like to talk to you a little."

"All right, grand'ther."

Laurel seldom called him "grand'ther." He glanced keenly at her. She seemed bracing herself for what he might say.

"I'm a pretty old man, darling. I've been through a lot."

"You aren't going to try to tell me that I'll forget and that everything will be all right by and by—you aren't going to say that, are you?"

"You should know me better than that. You know I love you too much to be so—such a fool."

"I'm sorry."

"I know you won't forget, honey. You ought not to forget."

"It's strange to hear you say that."

"Why?"

"Oh, Mother tries to console me, and Kathie. Even Dad. They talk as if I were a baby that had bumped its head. They're just assuring me it won't hurt after a while."

"No. I think you won't forget—ever."

"But I *don't* want to hurt like this—always."

"Laurel, child, people don't realize that most of the important things happen to us when we are very young."

[329]

She opened her eyes wide in surprise. "Do you actually think that?"

"I am sure of it."

"So am I. This—this—Robby going this way—I couldn't ever have anything worse happen to me."

"Yes. There could be other things."

"What?" She flung the word hotly at him.

"Shameful things."

"Oh."

"When beautiful things die—when fine and noble love is—is broken by death—that is terribly hard to bear. I'm not suggesting that you should feel this to be less because it isn't another kind of grief. I was only answering your question. But you—oh, my dear, I wish I could be sad for you. But this is your tribute to your sweetheart."

"He was—so wonderful!"

"I'm sure of it. I'm sorry I didn't know him better."

"He was shy."

"It's a nice quality. I like shy things. But there is something I kind of want to say to you. I don't know how you'll take it."

"Say what you want to."

"Well, it's this, I guess. I just want to say that life is greater than death. It's more important. What you do from now on—"

"I don't seem to be alive any more."

"I know."

"Do you, I wonder?"

"When one has lived as long as I have, there's been everything. I've seen everything, felt everything, I guess."

Laurel did not answer.

"You have to live, you know, darling. And what you start doing now is going to shape all the time to come."

"I don't really know what you mean."

"Those books and papers, for one thing."

Laurel laid a quick hand over them. "What about them?"

"Put them away and don't look at them. You don't have to forget them. You'll know they are there in a box in a drawer. But don't make a little grave out of them to cry over. I know that doesn't sound very sympathetic or kind to you. Does it?"

"No, it doesn't."

"But I'm right. Live with what you have in your heart and in your memory. Those things will change, they will warm you, and in time will comfort you. But not inanimate objects. They are knives to open old wounds."

"I wonder if you are right."

"I think so, dear."

"I don't know what to do with myself."

"It's always hard to fill a sudden and great emptiness. But you don't have to try. I think you should get yourself ready for school."

"Oh! I hadn't thought any more about it."

"I talked to Kam yesterday."

"Isn't Daddy pretty hard up this year?"

"Yes, but we can manage it."

"Where would I go?"

"I think up to Lexington. Nice old place. Your mother went there."

"Yes. I know."

"Learning's a great help."

"I don't believe that—much."

"Yes, it is. All the great past of all the world is in it. You need great acquaintances now, Laurel, and the only place you'll find them is in books."

Laurel edged nearer to him, and leaned her head on his knee. The old man laid his hand on her head and scratched her behind the ear. It was exactly the caress he had for his favorite bird dog.

4

Winter came, and summer, and winter again.

To Savina it seemed that all motion had ceased when Robby died, and for a long time she was scarcely aware of the passage of hours, or days, or of the approach and recession of seasons. Now, she felt the world about her move and get under way again.

Very slowly she began once more to match herself against that motion, to move with it, and so to pace her thinking and her plans.

Peter knew that he and Savina had traveled far on separate roads and that now there was no authentic communication between them. Savina only guessed it.

Peter watched her with anxiety, and later with a quiet sorrow that was close kin to resignation. He knew that Savina had become more and more like her own people, and that year by year she had sealed herself away from change—away from even the thought and danger of change.

Among the questions that thronged upon him from day to day like spirits out of the wind was this very question of Savina.

He had said to himself through all of these years that he had but gone his way; he had done nothing to anyone. And now, harsh upon his inner sight, this thin defense went down leaving only a ruin of accusation.

What had he not done?

The simple, obvious, daily omissions?

What of them?

To find himself tripped by elementary dilemma infuriated him.

On such days he would mount Saracen and ride hard along the lonely hill roads. Saracen hated him and Peter knew it. They watched each other warily.

These victories over Saracen always gave Peter the reassuring feeling of having established discipline and order over rebellion.

"Kettring's a damn fine horseman for a man his age," Bob Dawson remarked to Kam Sandifer as Peter tore past them on the river road.

"I think sometimes that's the only thing in the world he really enjoys."

Dawson shook his head. "Damned if I don't think he has enjoyed all of these years of unpopularity and general dislike."

"Kettring has been utterly contemptuous of it. Just doesn't give a damn."

"Well, I don't think we're likely to understand Kettring. But he has changed since that boy of his died. I was mighty sorry that happened."

Kam made no reply to this. He was thinking of Laurel.

"Kettring's not doing so much actual farming himself now, is he?"

"No. Janek helps, and he has another fellow regularly—Laws Cantey from upcountry somewhere. He's bought up more and more property, and it takes time for him to get around."

"Nobody hears much about the other boy, I guess."

"The Janeks say he's getting on all right. Kettring did try to send Mrs. Kettring down there for a visit after the young boy died, but she's peculiar, too. Wouldn't go, I hear. Never goes anywhere. Works all the time."

"Curious people."

Dawson was partly right in his estimate of Peter's attitude toward St. Stephens and the countryside. Peter did not enjoy being disliked, but he was stimulated by anything directed against him. In his reaction he reverted unconsciously to the protection of his early training. His manners stiffened to an old-fashioned and distant courtesy which in its turn was misunderstood along with everything he did. He could pass a group of men on the street and by a casual salute or a punctilious bow leave them in a welter of rage.

But Peter rarely thought nowadays of the people he saw. He had traveled too far on the road of solitary search to be mindful of like or dislike.

He had left people out of his plans and his considerations too long to consider them now. That was why he was so angered by the constant intrusion of thought about them. There they were! A silent, questioning, waiting company.

He often recalled that day when he first went alone along the hill road to inspect his new place. He thought of all the exultations of that day, the high dreams of setting himself in some new relationship to his place and his world. He had been so sure then that he would grow into some rewarding union with everything about him. He had envisioned himself as the master of an undisciplined and untrained nature, and as a sort of godlike recipient of nature's confidence. He had purposed speaking to the earth, and the earth was to reply.

Now, if ever in the world, he must find his delayed answers and complete his refuge. He realized with cold dismay that he had not yet begun to do either the one or the other.

In all of this unrest, and uncertainty, and searching, Peter was vaguely aware of familiar emotions. He had felt like this before. He had been driven in this way long ago.

He found himself considering and appraising all that he had made and he found himself viewing it with dissatisfaction. Something was wrong with it, something was wanting in it. He was startled to find himself saying that it was not real.

More and more now he was haunted by echoes of his old learning, his forgotten reading. Bits of poetry, lines of old dramas, torsos and fragments, hints of a greatness he could not quite recall.

His inner life—that composite of dream and recollection—appeared more and more like a partially recovered region of ruined antiquity, filled with fragments. Some were heroic and troubling, some taunting and admonitory, some were shadowy and menacing.

5

November came in gusty and dark. There were heavy snows, sleet, freezing rains, and then heavy snows again. Fields and hills were buried and encased more deeply than anyone could remember.

It was a hard winter for Peter. Savina always had her occupations, rag carpets, patchwork, quilting.

For the first time since he had left the East, Peter felt the urge to read. But somehow he never came to a beginning. Savina was not used to having him so much in the house. She annoyed him with questions if he entered the front room or went upstairs. He was not comfortable. Sometimes he bundled up in his heaviest coat and sat in the barn, thinking, brooding, battling against thinking, resisting the tenebrous limbos of memory, and fighting against questions that battered from within.

Everyone agreed that it was an unprecedented winter. In February Niles Tipton made a trip to Nebraska to see his son. He said people were lucky here at St. Stephens.

"My God, the winds out there blow for a thousand miles with nothin' to stop 'em. Snow three feet deep. Zero cold."

"Yes." Nolan rested his elbows on the bar. "That's right. I know that country out there. You got a kind of sheltered feeling here that you ain't got anywhere out West."

"It's the hills."

"Sure. But I hear they've got heavy snows all the way out to Montana."

"That's what they told me in Nebraska."

"Well, boys, you all know what that means." Nolan wagged his head sagely. "It means high water in the spring."

"That's a fact, Nolan, sure's you're born. Heavy snows out that way and we always have hell to pay here."

"Someday the gov'ment's going to have to work on control of our big rivers."

"Hell, you can't get Washington to do anything—not for us out here."

"Well, watch out in April!"

Spring was late. The snow and ice lay thick through most of March. There was a heavy snow on the eleventh of April.

When the first rains came they were heavy and warm. Every creek was a torrent. Usually the local waters had time to get out of the way before the melting snows of the West came down. But this year everything came at once.

Peter watched the river a little anxiously. Kam Sandifer came over, and together they walked along the road.

"We should have done something about that confounded sand bar out there. It was just a bunch of cottonwood drifters a few years ago. Now the damn thing's an island. I'm afraid we're going to catch hell if this keeps up."

Peter said nothing to Savina about the high water. There was no danger from an overflow. The worst that could happen would be the loss of a season. Nevertheless the spreading flood had a sinister look about it.

Peter rode down along the river the next morning. The skies had lightened and there was only a drizzle but the river was rising. The road was barely above the water which stood with a deceptive stillness in fields and low places. The Sandifer schoolyard was under three feet of muddy, yellow water. A small rowboat moved off across the field looking ridiculously out of place.

Peter rode back again. Between the Sandifer farm and his own a thin stream had broken over the road. On both sides of the narrowing roadway the tall grass was nearly submerged. There was only a thin upthrust of green showing. The water seemed not to move, but Peter watched for a few minutes: tiny clusters of bubbles and minute debris on the surface turned slowly and moved steadily in toward the field. The movement was scarcely perceptible. Everywhere in unexpected slight depressions water was standing. A peculiar uneasiness pervaded Peter's feeling. It was an unreasonable feeling, a slight but stubborn animal fear. He looked out across the wide waters. The power and drive of the flood were appalling.

Saracen danced unmanageably, turning sideways and balking at every puddle. It was nearly noon when Peter reached home.

The next morning Savina raised the shade of an upstairs window and looked out. It appeared as if the whole world had turned to water. A veritable lake extended far into the bottoms.

"Peter! The river! It is so high!"

"Yes. It's been rising all the time. You knew that, didn't you?"

She turned again to the window. "Yes, of course, but never have I seen it like this—never."

Peter came to the window. Dawn was breaking, another gray day. The river was out of its banks now. As far as one could see in both directions water had crossed the road and flooded the fields. Far out, if one squinted and peered, the surface roughened— that was the channel. The press and hurry of the increasing waters sent wide shallow ripples circling out across the slower overflow.

Peter tried to see across to the south bank, but rain was falling again and the farther shore was a blur of gray.

After dinner he went along the hill road to a clearing. Mists still obscured the distance. There was nothing to see but water. It seemed to rise out of the ground.

Laws Cantey went to St. Stephens and returned about suppertime.

"She's still rising."

"Looks like it."

"Yep. You know what's a fact though, the mark is not as high as you'd think."

"No?"

"No, sir. It's all this rain that's affectin' us around here. Ground is so soakin' full of water not a drop sinks in."

"Yes, of course, but the river *is* high."

"Oh, it's high all right, and more a-comin'. We're likely to get the crest in about a couple days."

"So far away as that?"

"That's what I heard Mr. Dawson say. Water's way up under Tipton's store. You can't get to the front of the store except in a rowboat. The rest of the town's a lot higher, of course."

"Hear anything about the south side?"

"Yes, sir. They ain't no trains today. They're going to have to raise them tracks yet."

"I shouldn't wonder."

"Well, I guess I'll be gittin' on, Mr. Kettring. Nightwork's all done."

"Hadn't you better stay here tonight? It's still raining."

"No, sir. I guess I'll git on. I want to stop by St. Stephens. It's slackenin' up a little. I'll see you in the morning. Good night."

"Good night."

Savina pattered busily about the kitchen. Peter heard her moving back and forth, the faint sounds of dishes and pans, the scrape of a chair. It was nine o'clock when she came into the living room. She looked at the clock and made small sounds of surprise.

[337]

"So late!"

"What were you doing?"

"Oh, nothing much. I had to set the bread."

"I wonder if it's still raining."

"Just a little."

"Were you outside?"

"I let Jude into the summer kitchen."

"What's the matter with Jude?"

"I don't know. She came scratching at the door, and actually wanted in. I never saw her act so strange."

"Is she all right now?"

"I guess so. She was very wet."

Peter yawned. "I think I'll go out to the barn and see that everything's all right."

This was a nightly ritual. Peter never quite trusted Cantey.

Presently, he returned. Savina heard him go to the hall closet.

"What is, Peter?"

"That damn gate back of the barn is open. The cows are out."

"Oh—my goodness!"

"They'll stray down toward that lower pasture. They could mire down."

"Oh, my! Better put on your rubber boots."

"I'm looking for them."

"I put them upstairs."

"Well, for heaven's sake—"

"Now, now! A little patience. I thought you would not need them again when the winter is over. I get them. Just wait."

She hurried up the stairs.

"Just throw them downstairs. Hurry up, Savina."

"No, no! I bring them. Here. Better take the other lantern, Peter. I forgot to clean that one today."

"All right. I'll be back shortly."

Savina went upstairs, turned down the bed covers, and began to undress.

Once she went to the window and looked out, but she could see nothing. She decided to go downstairs again. Peter would be wet and muddy. He would forget and track dirt all over the house. Never could she make him remember.

She sat in a straight chair beside the table. The ticking of the clock was loud in the silent room. Once she heard a distant shout in the direction of the bottoms. She listened but heard nothing more.

Savina was tired, and her thinking moved slowly. She glanced at the clock. Ei! A quarter-past ten! She went into the front room and looked out toward the river. There was a moving light—far away—probably on the south bank.

She went back to her chair. She nodded a little, and dozed. When she awoke it was half-past eleven. She stood up—a little frightened. Instinctively, she called out: "Peter!"

She hurried to the kitchen door and looked toward the barn.

"Peter! Peter, are you out there?"

Jude whimpered from the summer kitchen. The rain had stopped.

Savina waited a few minutes, then she lighted the other lantern, threw a shawl over her head, and went out. She crossed the front yard and looked up and down the bottom. There was a lantern moving far down toward the Sandifer's, but that wouldn't be Peter. Now, what could be? Without further hesitation she set out along the orchard fence.

What could have happened? What could possibly have kept Peter so long? Nothing serious, of course, but he might have found the cows and been unable to manage them at night. Peter always said cows had no sense, anyway.

"Ei!"

Savina stopped. She had walked into water over her shoe tops. She raised her lantern. There was water ahead of her—a lot of it! She thought a moment. The long drainage ditch must be overflowing.

She retreated and circled the field. She was not quite clear about this. Where was she really going? In the direction of the road—likely Peter would be down that way.

When she came to the gate she was standing in water again. It seemed to be running fast, too. Strange!

She listened, hoping Peter might see her light and call to her. But there was only the sound of water.

The river!

Not just the river, she amended. Likely it would not sound much. No: it was all about her. A rustling, whispering, surreptitious sound. A drizzle of rain had begun again. The little drops struck wet leaves adding another whisper to the many. Whisper—whisper —whisper . . .

Savina was disturbed as she always was when near the river. She hated it still: she would always hate it. Just now, this moment, she was a little afraid, too.

She opened the gate and made her way across the road. The road was like a creek! The water was racing along—that was what had sounded so loud. It was deeper than she had guessed, but she was soaked anyway.

There was something that seemed to move—there ahead of her. It might be one of the cows. She hurried along the little ridge beside the road. It was slippery, and there was running water on both sides of it. Then she reached a stretch of higher ground. Again she raised her lantern to try to see ahead. The lantern was burning low. She shook it. It was empty! It would not burn long enough for her to reach the house.

She thought she heard a call . . . out toward the river. Yes— there was a light, small and far away. It must be Peter, though. Those cows! They had probably gone out on the little piece of land that jutted into the river. That would be difficult with the willows and underbrush. Cows could think of the most contrary things to do!

She hurried on, stepping into puddles, flustered and a little frightened now at the pervading sound of water. It seemed to come from all directions!

She paused—half out of breath. *Gott!* There was water every-where!

There was a cold rush about her feet. She turned to the left to avoid it. This was better, but low willows grew thick. It was hard to fight through. She decided she had better recross the road and try to make for the Janeks'. It would be easier than crossing the bottoms in the dark. The lantern was very dim. She shook it and turned the wick higher. There was a feeble increase in the light. She thrust the willow branches out of her way and went ahead.

Yes—yes—she had better go to the Janeks'. It did not make any difference how wet she was now. She could keep to the road. It was not far. Then, too, the Janeks would help. For now she was certain Peter was in trouble somewhere.

She would simply take the road, even if it was running with water up to her knees. She stepped boldly forward and found herself stumbling and slipping. She grasped wildly at empty air and plunged into the water. The lantern dropped from her hand. She was waist-deep in water that pulled at her with surprising strength.

Savina calmed herself with an extreme effort. She turned and after a few minutes' groping and wading reached the bank again. She could not remember that there had been such a bank. Was it possible that the water had cut that deep into the road?

She stood quite still. The dark was intense. The sound of the water was louder now. The air was filled with the increasing clamor. It confused her. Her heart was going furiously, but she made a desperate effort to keep her head. Her impulse to run was almost overpowering.

She moved cautiously, and slipped again, but this time into shallow water.

Gott! Perhaps she had better stand still until someone came for her. . . .

She pressed her hands against her eyes. Maybe when she took them away she would be able to see a little. But the blackness around her was absolute.

No—she could not stand here. It made her numb. She was chilled, too, and her face was wet. Maybe it was the rain . . . but Savina knew her face was wet with sweat.

If she could only find something to lean against. She was

trembling with exhaustion. Stumbling, and picking her way around the water that seemed to head off progress in any direction, she fought through the willows.

These willows! So many of them! Where was she, anyway?

She thought quickly. Willows . . . why, she must be on that strip that reached out into the river. This terrified her anew. If only she could see a little bit.

It sounded so! That water—that river she had been so afraid of always! It must be all about her! Listen . . . listen to it!

The rain whispered and whispered in the leaves . . . the water ran about her feet and sighed and murmured.

Savina caught her lower lip between her teeth and bit down hard. She closed her eyes, trying to think—which way—*which way!* The question ran back and forth in her brain like something trapped. She had lost her sense of direction completely.

She tried to listen. Maybe she could hear the river itself, and turn away, but there were only the many sounds all blending as one, pressing in toward her.

Cautiously she felt her way ahead, step by step. This was better now. The water was gone from underfoot. The willows thinned. She moved more confidently.

Suddenly she stopped, frozen to the spot. A gusty wind and rain swept into her face, but there—just there before her was the unmistakable sense of free open space—*the river*.

She knew exactly where she was now. She had gone left instead of right. She was far out on the tip of that narrow peninsula.

Think! She might have walked off the edge!

She listened. There was a hard thrust of the current against the banks—she could hear it—it thudded against the barrier—and she could hear louder splashes where the banks crumbled.

Careful now—careful! She must turn squarely about and re-trace her steps. But she miscalculated. Once she felt the ground yield under her feet. She barely saved herself by stumbling backward as the edge sagged and gave way.

Once more she tried to establish her bearing. She moved with extreme caution. There was water underfoot again. She stepped back. No, that was rising ground again, out toward the point which was higher. She did not remember that place—a puddle, perhaps. She waded a few steps. It was deeper. She stood still. She could feel the splashing against the side of her leg. The water was running in *that* direction—from her left to her right—then that was— *ach, Gott!*—that was the rising river. It had cut through behind her!

She dashed forward. There was no time to lose. But she heard a louder rush, felt her foothold go from under her. She saved herself by a second. She knew she was cut off from retreat. She would have to wait—to wait, maybe, until morning, before someone found her—if—if—

. . . It seemed to Savina that all of the evil spirits of that accursed river were suddenly loosed upon the air. The whole world seemed to be turning to water—as—as it had seemed to her that morning long ago when she had first seen the great onrush of the flood from the boat.

That river—that accursed river—she could hear it on every side, chuckling, whispering, chuckling, speaking openly, shouting . . .

6

Peter roamed aimlessly through the empty, echoing house.

He had no one to talk to. He could not permit anyone to see what had befallen him. But Michael Janek saw and read the devastation in Peter's eyes. Kam Sandifer saw the physical drive and the spiritual pride go out of the man in one day. But no one knew what to say. Peter still kept all approaches to his nearer self stiffly guarded.

But here—inside of the house it was different. He stood at an upper window looking down on the receding waters. There was still strength and resistance in the pose of his shaggy head; but the depth and breadth of the ruin wrought in him was in his face.

Almost fearfully he allowed his gaze to search the fields and pastures, to go out across the road to the place where the peninsula had been. The current tumbled roughly over it. The island beyond was gone, too, and the river swept back to its old channel.

There where the strip of willow-covered ground had reached out into the stream they had found Savina's lantern caught in a snarl of roots and vines. Two men who had been out in a boat that night declared they had seen a light moving uncertainly across the bottoms and out to the road, but later when they had looked back it was gone.

. . . Again and again Peter went over the house, from room to room, upstairs and down, out into the yard and back again.

It seemed to him that he had been suddenly cut off from the whole of what had been here—even from what had been his own life. He shook his head as if to clear it, and tried to think. This strange, dead house held him as one is held by the heavy oppression of a dream.

Peter felt he must reach out somehow and touch something—anything that would re-establish a contact with his own existence. He was like a man flung from familiar ways into a void where there were neither directions nor dimensions.

He sought desperately for a sign. But there was nothing in the house to give back word or hint.

Now that he must think with this burning concentration of Savina, he had to ask himself who she was and what she was. He scrutinized every detail of this place where she had lived. But there was no record, no faintest clue. There were no letters, no pictures, no trifles treasured as memorials of times or places. For all this well-kept house had to reveal, Savina might never have existed.

Nor was there trace of his children. David and Robby had passed out of his house like immaterial spirits of the air. There was no impress of simple action, no humble souvenir to move or confound the heart. This blank, unanswering, faceless house stood as an ultimate mockery.

Peter was not able to say to himself that his losses had been the common accidents of common existence. Other men lost, but not everything. He was not willing to accept, or to view, so negative a conception of his own life and way. He could not surrender to the bogey of fate his mastery of the things which were his own and his responsibility for them.

He had set out upon a journey—the beginnings of that journey were far away and long ago. Step by step he had come to this time—and to this pass. But this was not the place of his destination.

He had held his head high, and kept his own counsel. He had scorned, and rejected, and defied. He had refused partnerships and consolations.

But this was not the place of his destination.

He had stood in his mind against anything which might emerge from the mystery of fortune. Very well, he could still do that.

If penalty fell so, as justice, that, too, he could accept.

Peter held his fists against his temples as he paced the confines of Savina's best front room. He realized that he was not equipped to think beyond the elementary notions he had chosen as guides and as a plan of life. But he must think. And now he had only the faultily remembered intellectual training of a boy—the boy he was when he left home for the war. His stature as a man existed only in a special world of his own—of his own making. His questions approached from other regions than these, and the answers were not in him.

At this moment, Peter did not think, or reason. He was scarcely conscious of his next act. It was instinctive, or else linked to the broken sequence of deeply buried habit. All of his world was a blur of pain . . . he reached absently and blindly toward the shelves. Like a man under hypnosis, or under the compulsion of a remote and mystical control, he sat down near the window, and opened the book in his hand. The print was small in the yellowing paper . . . he began to read slowly—almost like a child—his finger following the line across the page.

7

The flood had cut a wide arc across the lower fields of the Kettring place, spreading sand and gravel over the acres lying between this arc and the river. Fences were down, and drainage ditches obliterated. Peter surveyed the damage with indifference. A month later little had been done about it. The county gangs repaired the roads. Laws Cantey relaid the rail fences where the rails had not been carried away. But Peter remained indoors. No one saw him, except Cantey.

"Mr. Kettring, we might as well put up bob-wire fences now. Nobody's got rail fences no more."

Peter stood on the kitchen steps listening. He had a small leather-bound book in his hand and kept his place with a finger between the pages. It was evident that he was only half hearing what the hired man was saying, and that he had no interest in it whatever.

"All right," he said. "All right."

"Well, shall I go ahead and order the stuff?"

"Yes."

"Where you want me to get it?"

"I don't care."

"Tipton's all right, but you ain't been tradin' there."

"Get it wherever you wish."

"I could git it at Sanderson's."

"Very well."

"Which one then, Mr. Kettring?"

"I don't care."

"We-ell, all right, I'll go back to Tipton's. I'll need right smart help—"

"Hire somebody."

"Who'll I git?"

"I don't care, Laws. Anybody."

"My brother Bill ain't got no stiddy job."

"Get him."

"What'll I say you'll pay him?"

"Whatever's fair."

"We could use two or three people around here gittin' things straightened out. Seein' as you—"

"Seeing what, Laws?"

"Seein' you don't feel like doin' much yourself."

"I won't be doing much. Hire whatever and whoever you need."

"Well, now, 'bout them bottoms down there—it's going to take twenty men and scrapers and so on to fix that up."

"We'll do it in the fall when people are not so busy."

"Yes, sir. We can git plenty of help when things are slack in the fall. But what about this summer?"

"Well—*what* about this summer?"

"Ain't you goin' to do no farmin' a-tall?"

"Not much."

"Them horseweeds over in the field beyond the orchard's high as your head now."

"Handsome, aren't they?"

Laws Cantey stared. He looked away, then back again. People had always said Mr. Kettring was peculiar, but this sounded crazy.

A faint amusement showed for an instant in Peter's eyes. "I said they're handsome, aren't they?"

"Them horseweeds?"

"Yes. Quite as fine-looking as corn. Grow better, too."

Laws laughed loudly, but uneasily. "They evermore do grow!"

"Well, let 'em grow."

"Well, now, I could git somebody—"

"If the weeds are high as your head, it's too late."

"All right. Just as you say."

"Is that all, Laws?"

"Y-yes, sir."

Peter went back into the house.

Laws stood looking at the blank kitchen door. He rubbed the back of his neck, gave his trousers a hitch, and looked back again at the closed door.

"Well, I'll be danged. I'm a-goin' to talk to Mr. Sandifer. Mr. Kettring's plumb loony."

Peter was trying to think, and he was dismayed through and through by the discovery that he did not know how to think.

Through all of these years Peter had striven with nerves and muscles, under baking, blazing suns and through biting winters—he had labored and sweated and strained like a slave toward some promised land that lay always just beyond the next bitter range of obstacles. This—this which lay before him and about him was no promised land—it was only frustration and emptiness, and he had lost—incalculably—he had lost infinitely, and irretrievably.

He had to think. He had to understand. He knew but one thing: he had mistaken something of utmost importance. He must find out what it was.

Robby . . . Savina . . .

He could not say that their deaths were faults of his. He could not fall into that kind of sentimentality—but they had been lost upon *his way.*

He must think through this bitter entanglement.

Often his thoughts turned to David. But he asked the Janeks no questions.

Mrs. Janek had spoken in those days. Taska had written. She wished to know if there was anything they could do. They were grieved, and so forth. But no direct word to *him,* no word from David apart from Taska's messages.

Peter wondered, and a searching gnawed in him like small teeth of fire. Was this in the strong barriers of his mind, or merely in nerves of recollection? He did not know.

Late in the summer Peter stirred again from his seclusion. He ordered the work done which Laws Cantey had outlined. But he did not return to any of his old labors. Cantey took over more and more. He found a woman to clean the house and cook. Peter scarcely noticed her and seldom spoke to her.

In October, he had a wide fireplace built in the southwest room and ordered a supply of logs. Not long afterward he went to St. Louis.

Laws discussed this at Nolan's saloon. "You know what he brought back?"

"What?"

"Books!"

"Books?"

"Yes, sir! Books."

"Well—what for?"

"Don't ask me! He's got a room chuck-full of books as it is. Yes, sir, four big boxes of books he brought back from St. Louis—a regular library. Tell you the truth, I think he went out of his head a little when his wife was drownded."

"Never would a-thought he cared much about her or anybody."

"Well, anyhow, he just sets in the house and reads. Kam Sandifer, he comes over there off and on and they set up till all hours just talkin'. He don't take no interest in the place a-tall."

"That's darn funny. He didn't uster take any interest in anything but his place."

"I know. He's completely different now from what he was."

"Well, all in all, I guess he can afford to be cranky if he wants to."

"Sho! I hear he's worth a heap of money."

To many who looked on from a distance, Peter appeared the conventional figure of the man who had "made his pile" and retired.

Peter was not unaware of this notion by which the countryside had classified and explained him. He gave it a passing moment of attention and shrugged it out of mind.

Peter was seeing himself with a new and dreadful clarity. The curious scene of his inner life lay spread out before him, a scene as confused and ruined as his own lands had been after the flood. He was making himself view it directly.

He knew he had to begin again. This time he was without the guidance of a wishful vision, and without the support of his own confidence.

He was not taking up thought or philosophy, or life, even, where he had left off when he had turned away from all he had known.

Peter did not trouble to recall that period in detail. He did not subject it to analysis in any systematic search for the results of his trials and errors. Perhaps he refused even the figures of speech and the imagery that might have accompanied such a review and such introspection. Once or twice he thought of the river. He thought of its floods, sweeping down through this valley from a vast unknown and unpredictable land, tearing away, destroying, obliterating, and then returning again to its ancient way. He could remember that he had thought of that on the long day when he and Savina had watched the river and the marks of its destruction as they stood on the deck of the little river boat. He had thought, too, platitudinously, of the land enriched and deepened and prepared for greater harvests. Yes—sometimes. Sometimes the floods destroyed. His own rich lands lay ravaged by this one great overflow. His lands—how curiously unimportant they seemed just now.

Savina . . .

Savina had feared the river, and yet she had gone out to meet her death in it. She had always feared it, he knew, and hated it as he had loved it for the barrier it laid between him and intrusion.

Floods . . .

Floods of spring . . . of youth . . . destroying as they raged against and over the set landmarks.

8

"Breakfast's ready, Mr. Kettring."

Lottie Gross, competent, stolid, ample, stood in the door regarding Peter. Lottie was curious about this man. There had been strange stories. It was strange enough, she thought, that a man owning a great farm should sit indoors reading books, but nothing of her curiosity or disapproval ever showed on her impassive Pennsylvania Dutch face.

Peter sat down. Before him was Lottie's idea of a good breakfast—a mighty meal of eggs and sausage, ham and fried potatoes, frilly pan-size pancakes, preserves and honey, and the inevitable pie.

Peter ate absently.

"Have you been out this morning, Mr. Kettring?"

"No."

"Everything ice—all over."

"I thought it rained in the night."

"It did. Rained, sleeted, and froze. Slick as glass. I thought I'd never get here this morning."

"You didn't walk all the way from the Janeks'?" Lottie lived with the Janeks.

"No. I rode—horseback. Horse slipped and slided every-which-a-way. If I'd a-fell."

"Well, you're here."

"By the Lord's mercy."

"And good horseshoeing."

Lottie did not quite grasp this.

"I wouldn't go out today 'f I was you, Mr. Kettring."

"Why not?"

"If you fell and broke a hip at your age, it'd go hard with you. Old people are always breaking their hips and can't walk no more."

"How old do you think I am, Lottie?"

"I don't know, but old enough fur it to be bad if you broke a hip."

Peter returned presently to the front room. The logs blazed, and the air was close and warm. He sank into his big rocking chair and stared at the fire.

After a while he picked up a book and leafed carelessly through it. He had read and reread it several times lately. Thoreau's *Walden*. Peter slapped it shut with an impatient bang.

He had had an argument with Kam Sandifer last week about Thoreau. Sandifer liked Thoreau. In fact, he liked most books which did not "stir him up" as he had said at the time.

"Damn it all, Peter, you go at reading exactly as you have always gone at everything—tooth and nail. I don't want to be agitated and dissatisfied and incited. When I read I want to rest." He had smiled half gaily, half ruefully, as he spoke. "Why in thunder can't you let your soul alone?"

Peter had been amused, he remembered. Kam had a wonderful

way of sidestepping most disturbing things, and, miraculously, most of the more violent strokes of life had missed him.

"But," he said, "Thoreau is a man who set about finding, well— a key to life, or some intimation of its meaning. Seems to me all he did was turn away from it—hoped he'd shed its evils that way."

Kam grinned. "Like coming in out of the rain, Peter. Simple as that. Coming in out of the rain has always been considered evidence of common sense. Simple, effective—beyond argument as a method of keeping dry!"

He had not been much amused by Kam's way of avoiding the actual question.

"All of this rant against organized society—and factories—"

"Now, there, I should say you'd be in out-and-out agreement with him."

"—You can talk about abolishing this and that, and just go off in the woods to contemplate—"

"A man might come upon the abiding place of his soul that way."

That comment of Kam's had startled him a little. Kam had the most confounded way of revealing unexpected depths in himself— just glimpses—revelations quickly concealed by his trick of laughing immediately at his own seriousness.

"I mean this, Kam. There's been a lot of talk all along about finding the *meaning* of life. Does it have to *mean* anything?"

Kam squirmed uneasily as he always did at disturbing rhetorical questions.

"Oh, thunderation, Peter, I just think you don't talk much about such things. They *happen,* and you do something about them, event by event—I haven't any theories." He grinned again—Kam could extract some sort of enjoyment out of even his own small discomfitures. "Anyhow, other people do something. I—well, I just jog along."

Peter tried to recall more of the talk. He had been deeply in earnest. Odd, that he could be in earnest and talk so frankly of such matters only to Kam Sandifer who could not be serious about anything.

He had been talking to himself as much as to Kam, but it had been clarifying to say words aloud. "If I believe in anything, Kam, it is action."

"Oh, I do, too, oh, yes, yes—but I don't like it, Peter!"

"Life, and the meaning of life lies in the direction of living, not away from it."

"That's a damn funny doctrine to hear from you."

"Why?"

"Because you're an awful like old Thoreau yourself!"

"Me?"

"Sure; you. You've been taking to the woods, in one way or another, ever since you came here. You hated any kind of dependence on anybody else, you made as many of your own tools as you could—everything. Why, of course you're like Thoreau!"

He had made sounds of disgust, sputtered a little, in fact, but Kam was set on saying himself out.

"Principal difference is that Henry David Thoreau was a humble man and you're as stiff and standoffish as the devil."

"Yes, I feel that way a good deal of the time, I guess. Not my fault, altogether—if it *is* a fault."

Kam laughed aloud. "Confounded undemocratic cuss—"

"That's a loose word, Kam—all sorts of common fringes to it. That fellow Eastman—the teacher, you know—"

Kam nodded. "Nice chap, I thought."

"—Well, he was always talking about Whitman."

"So?"

"I read Whitman. Always going on about his love for large, rude, people. Yes, by God, that's what most of them are—and no more. You know perfectly well you can't love the general run. That's sleazy, sloppy thinking. You can theorize, sit in your room and wish the world well, but when you go out and look at them, you can't care a damn what happens to them—or how quickly."

"Peter—"

But he had not allowed Kam to interrupt. "No, no! If life does mean anything, a man has to *make* the meanings—and, well, selectivity is about the first step."

"Well, even that doesn't mean running away from everything."

"I didn't run away."

"Well, now I'm not trying to step on your toes, old man. We've kept pretty friendly, but it has looked that way to me."

"No, I didn't run away. It wasn't that there was anything—back there—that I had to get away from. No, not that, at all. I came *after* something. I was—on a search."

Kam had made elaborate business with his pipe. His keen blue glance flashed for an instant through the thin smoke. "D'you find what you were looking for?"

"No."

"What were you looking for? Mind if I ask you that?"

"I told you once. I was trying to shed the top-heavy thinking that had happened in my family, and among my kind of people—theorizing, and the like. I wanted to strip down—start over—not for anybody else, but for me, and—"

"And what?" Kam had spoken gently.

"—my children."

"I think you went at it wrong."

Now, in remembering, Peter felt his face flush. He had hated being emotional.

"Peter, a lot of what you are saying is kind of pathetic. I know it'll make you mad as hell to hear me say so. But it is the doggoned-est most egotistic kind of talk I ever heard. You don't allow for the trial and error of the whole world trying to blunder its way out. Everybody's wrong but you, and you're going to settle everything by digging in a field and shoeing your own horses!"

"I'm not such a fool as that! All of this has just been a sort of means to an end, I guess."

"And your years of hard work here—"

"Will you understand me when I say it was an exercise of the spirit?"

"No, I don't understand the first fool thing about it!"

"A kind of clean-up job first—preparing a soil—"

"For some more of the very kind of normal human experimentation you despised and ran away from!"

[354]

. . . Peter could not remember now how long the talk had gone on. But one curious result came clearly to the fore. He, Peter Kettring, with all of his pride of self-determination, was now, this day, without the equipment to cope with elementary problems in thought. He had grown older, here on his place, matured as a practical man, and by banning thought, he had held his whole mental development at an adolescent stage. That night when Perry Eastman had talked, he had been unable to keep step with the quick elusive turns of the younger man's mind. And here was Kam, no thinker at all, but making him sound like a schoolboy.

Peter bowed his face into his hands. He might be wrong—wrong about even his beginnings, but he was not stupid, he was not silly, he had always been in deadly earnest. He had tried, he had searched with all honesty of purpose for a way of life that would reward a man and his children with unquestioned values. From what he had read, he recognized in himself a creative fury that—that had seemingly come to nothing.

He closed his eyes and listened. Faint creaks sounded through the house—this dreadful, empty house.

He thought of the Sandifers, of Kam with his casual ways, and his amazing adjustment. What was that interesting thing Kam had quoted from Emerson? He arose and looked in the nearest shelf. Where was the book—it was a green one. If only Lottie would not try to straighten his shelves!

He stood tapping the titles with his index finger. Emerson was about the only one of the Americans—everything else was in the classics. . . .

He slid a volume from the shelf, and a thin, brown booklet fell to the floor. He picked it up and glanced curiously at it. He'd never seen that before.

What—what in . . .

Gläna Ernta, by—by *Robby Kettring!*

Peter blinked and look again. *Gläna Ernta*—Little Harvest—by Robby Kettring . . .

His hand shook a little as he went to the window for a better light.

It was a thin book, printed on cheap paper—almost like butcher's paper, he thought. He flipped the leaves. Dialect—all of it. *Little Harvest* . . . Peter blinked again—something stung his eyes. He began to read. It was difficult—the curiously accurate spelling of this crazy speech was baffling at first. There were no more than forty poems, all of them short—miniatures. He shifted his weight and read again.

Mostly nature poems, minute observations of shy and obscure phenomena, aspects of sun and clouds, and always the river. In almost all of them there was some reference to the river. The river in all seasons, under many lights—it ran through the pages like a voice.

Peter closed the book.

How did it come here? . . . Laurel—yes, Laurel had told him about it, but she did not say it had actually been printed. He tried to recall—to remember what she had said that day up there in the timothy field. But how did it happen to be here? Perhaps Perry Eastman had sent it, or maybe Laurel had brought it to Savina.

But no one had told him! No one had said a word about it! The thought struck through him bitterly.

This—this was what had cost Robby his life!

Slowly, carefully, he read again.

Peter frowned. What was that Laurel had said up there? She had been so angry and he—well, he did not listen very well. Perry Eastman had said maybe they were good. The editor had said they showed something—talent, maybe. Who was this man, now, who had written the half-page foreword? Edward Longwood Pace, University of Pennslyvania. And he said: ". . . a gentle lyricism, and a clear, fresh imagery . . . wringing an unexpected music from this quaint dialect."

Peter quieted the tumult that he felt rising in his mind. Careful, now! He read once more.

They were fresh, these little poems, fresh and curious, reflections of an odd and eerie mind . . . he saw again Robby's thin face with the glinting green eyes, his way of moving, silent as the smallest creature hiding itself from notice—Robby, remote, elusive—

[356]

like—like this little poem of his, *Hella Schatta*—Bright Shadow—
that was what he was like, a bright shadow. The poems were like
him.

Peter closed his eyes for a moment. These poems—they were a
little boy's poems. They were—soft and bright and musical. He
might have developed, he might have grown, he might have learned
to write. These poems were curious and interesting only because
of the strange language. To make poems of that stubborn, crabbed,
decayed fragment of a language!

Like any poet he had sung quickly with no thought of the
medium, or the possible fate of his song.

But, even as it was, young, immature, it did promise.

Promise—that these were verses of promise, saying maybe this
boy could have written interestingly or well sometime—this concerned Peter not at all. It was what his son *had been*—it was the soul
of Robby Kettring which no one had understood and which no
one had known.

Gläna Ernta—a little harvest flourishing for a little moment
only in a secret place, and garnered in secret.

Peter closed the book and laid his hand protectingly over it.

Peter put on his hat and coat and went out.

Lottie looked after him with dismay. She could not understand
why Peter used the front door. Front doors were "for nice." Doubtless he would come back in that way tracking the carpet with wet
shoes. She closed her lips in a determined line. She could at least
prevent *that*. She locked the door, and set about tidying the room.
A fireplace! In these days! So much muss—ashes and bits of bark.
She wept vigorously.

Peter paused outside the door, arrested by the breath-taking
beauty of the day. Everything was "all over ice" as Lottie had said.
Every branch and twig, every blade of grass, cased in crystal. A
magical glass world. It was dazzling, blinding, as the sunlight
broke everywhere in prismatic fire.

He walked carefully. It seemed a pity to shatter the fragile
beauty under foot. He stood for a few minutes at the yard gate.

"Mr. Kettring."

"Yes, Laws. Good morning. Beautiful, isn't it?"

"Yes. Kind-a pretty, but awful slippery. Mr. Kettring, them hounds from over to the Sandifer place have been round here again."

"Well, I guess they don't bother anything. Feed them. I expect all those dogs over there get short rations sometimes."

"No, sir. Mr. Sandifer, he takes good care of his dogs. What I was a-goin' to say was I think they been gettin' the eggs."

"Oh, I see. Chase them off then."

"I do. I was half a mind to use a little birdshot on 'em."

"Don't do that!"

"I told Mr. Sandifer about 'em, and he said blaze away at 'em a time or two and they'd stay home."

"You can't do that."

"There they are, round back of the barn."

"I'll chase them. You can't shoot at a neighbor's dogs."

"A little salt or birdshot wouldn't hurt 'em much."

Peter smiled slightly, and walked toward the stable yard.

"Get on you, go on—go home—*get!*"

The hounds stood, drooped a little, but made no move. Peter went into the barn and brought out a long whip. He whirled it about his head and cracked it at the dogs. They were not quite decided at first if this was a game or an invitation to go. Peter laughed. Just like the Sandifer hounds. He cracked the whip at them again.

"Get on now! Get out of here! Get—you!"

This time they understood and ducking their heads they loped toward the orchard and out of sight. Peter cracked the whip again, experimentally—like pistol shots. As he did so there was a loud whinny from Saracen and a series of crashes.

Peter shouted. "Saracen! Ho, now, you devil—"

But Saracen had heard the whipcracks and some half-forgotten fury stirred in his brain. In another moment the door went down and Saracen charged into the open.

"Ho, there! Ho, now, damn your hide!"

Saracen snorted and reared and wheeled. His eyes rolled and he dashed here and there in a frenzy of fright and rage.

Peter flung the long lash out toward Saracen, but lost his footing and the whip dropped from his hand and slithered away like something alive. He scrambled up again.

"Saracen! Ho, now, ho-o-o! Well, go on, run your fool head off if you want to. Go ahead—you'll fall and break your damned neck!"

Saracen charged back again from the far end of the lot. He bore down on Peter who had scarcely time to step aside. But Saracen wheeled instantly and reared, snorting and striking.

Peter realized that he must run. There was evil intent in Saracen's eyes.

He edged toward the gate, but Saracen was at him and over him in an instant. Peter saw an old singletree leaning against the fence. Maybe he could lay hold of it. He ran from side to side, dodging the slashing hoofs as Saracen pursued. Again and again he saw the sharp, shining arcs of the iron shoes flash at his head.

Saracen was in earnest—he meant to kill.

Peter grabbed the singletree and struck Saracen a heavy blow on the side of his head. Saracen charged again and backed Peter slowly into the corner. Peter struck and swore. There was no use calling for help. Laws Cantey had gone out toward the haystacks in the timothy field.

"Ho, Saracen, ho now!"

Saracen reared again as Peter reached the fence. The murderous forefeet were directly over him. He swung the singletree with all of his might, catching Saracen just below the knee. He heard the bone snap, and heard Saracen scream, but the next instant the stallion was on top of him, struggling and kicking. Peter tried to move, to escape the furious crushing attack, but Saracen caught him squarely on the forehead.

Dr. Jennings and Laws Cantey stood looking down at Peter. It was the day after the accident and Peter had not yet recovered consciousness.

"What do you think, Doctor?"

"I won't know until Dr. Capers gets here from St. Louis. I can't take the whole responsibility. I don't think there's a fracture, but certainly a severe concussion. We'll have to wait and see."

"He won't die, will he, Doc?"

"No. I think not."

"You reckon we ought to telegraph his boy down in Texas."

There was a faint murmur from the bed. Dr. Jennings leaned quickly over Peter.

"Mr. Kettring."

Peter muttered, unintelligibly.

"What is it, Mr. Kettring?"

"No!"

"Mr. Kettring, can you hear me? What is it?"

"No—no telegraph."

"You don't want us to notify your son?"

"No."

"All right, we won't. Don't worry. Just keep quiet."

Peter's mind cleared within the week. The injury to his head was not serious but both bones of his right leg were broken between the knee and ankle.

"You'll have to keep quiet a good long spell, Mr. Kettring."

"Um. Where's Cantey?"

"He's out in the kitchen. Everything's all right. Don't worry."

"I'm not worrying."

"Want to see Cantey?"

"Yes."

Dr. Jennings called Laws.

"Good morning, Mr. Kettring."

" 'Morning, Laws."

"You're a lot better, Mr. Kettring, thank the Lord. You had a mighty narrow squeak."

"Seems so. What happened to—to Saracen?"

"I had to knock him in the head, Mr. Kettring. You broke his leg, I guess, when you hit him with that singletree. I was just a-comin' and I seen you when you hit him. Both of you come down together in the corner of the lot, but I guess he'd a-killed you anyhow."

"He tried to."

"He shore did. Mighty near got you, too."

"A fine horse. Have to get another one like him."

"You won't be ridin' right away. I'd get me a horse that didn't have such a hell-fire disposition 'f I was you."

Peter smiled. "A fine horse," he repeated.

"Yes, sir; but he shore near killed you."

9

Peter's convalescence was long and slow. He hobbled about with crutches for a while, moving slowly from room to room. He did not venture out.

His battle with Saracen, his injury, and his creeping recovery had shaken him in some of his most secret defenses.

"Saracen, too!" he said to himself with a sort of wondering bitterness.

His physical helplessness was reflected in his inability to direct the ebb and flow of his thoughts. He felt exposed, as never before, to the broad rush of a hurricane of accusations. It was like living in a house from which an entire wall had suddenly been blown away.

He recalled now, as he leaned against the window frame, those first days of returning consciousness. Through all the devastating pain and nightmarish imaginings there had been an increasing awareness of something else—something which he had not been able to identify at once. It was the return of those same rhythms and echoes of fragmentary lines and phrases which had broken through to his consciousness in the hard black days when he thought he had touched the bottom of his long despair.

How little he had guessed that it was not the worst, nor even near to the full measure of disaster.

In those days Robby was alive—and Savina. He tried with the desperate evasions of a cornered animal to turn from the thought of Savina, he tried hard to think of Robby instead. But that bright and fleeting image carried him inevitably and inescapably back to Savina. And again the rising storms of accusation struck. And through that infernal clamor in his brain there ranged and cried the sound of words and lines which he could no longer silence or ignore.

The dark well at the bottom of the mind—he had named it so that day down there in the bottoms when out of it had flown the first of those new threats against his hopes of peace. Then there had been fragments only—hints and intimations. What followed was a mad symphony that sounded day and night. . . .

The dark well at the bottom of the mind—since then he had looked deep into it.

He had been able to talk to Kam about it, at what cost to his curious and intractable pride no one could ever guess. And Kam Sandifer had answered him with a simplicity that was like the artlessness of a child.

"You have denied all the greater world—actually about all we have that is worth while. Looks to me, Peter, as though you set yourself back thousands of years and tried to repeat the history of primitive man fighting his way up." Kam had smiled and looked away as he always did when he was covering up his seriousness.

"Peter, you have just been trying to establish yourself on too low a plane, and the evolutional pressure of your imprisoned ancestors would not stand for it."

He had laughed, too, but he had been more wakeful than usual that night. Yes, he had denied the reach of his own spirit. . . .

David! He had blocked David's way at some critical moment of passage and David had broken through.

Robby and Savina. His very inaction had subjected them to a kind of spiritual starvation. He corrected himself quickly. Robby *had* found what he wanted. Savina? He had never really known her. It was only that the keen tendrils of her existence had wound deeper and closer than he could have imagined. She had been there like—like the accepted presence of daylight—he had never paused to take proper count of her.

. . . Yes, she had been a fire in his flesh—and again out of the dark well came new and terrible witnesses!

Maybe, he thought with desperate hope, maybe she had understood, maybe *that* had been a requiting communication.

As soon as he was up again he went back to reading. He read in a race against the lost years. And whenever he thought of how deeply he had been struck by the discovery of Robby's verses, he stood in renewed amazement. More than anything else the pathetic little book of his son's writing had shown him what his own mind had secretly valued. His own mind, incorruptible in its stubborn integrity, had somehow stood off to one side all of these years, waiting for some other part of himself to come back to its own destiny.

All that he had wished for, demanded, and labored to possess, had always been in reach, but it did not consist of the visible furniture of this world.

"You know," Kam had said on another occasion, "practically every darned old proverb in the world is true!"

Late in the winter Peter sent for Michael Janek. Lena had in the meantime taken practical charge of the house without asking leave. Lottie sulked, but Lena's great heartiness spread a kind of cheer.

"You wanted to see my man, yes, Peter? He's here."

"Why doesn't he come in?"

"I call him right away. He sets in the kitchen."

Michael clumped into the room where Peter sat at the window.

"Good morning, Michael."

"Good morning, Mr. Kettring. How are you feeling today?"

"Pretty good."

"The leg—it works better?"

"Much."

"That's fine."

Lena stood by the fireplace, her hands wrapped in her apron. Peter noted the attitude. Savina used to stand so.

"He don't eat enough, Michael."

"You got to eat, Mr. Kettring."

Peter looked up suddenly. "Lena has always called me Peter, why don't you?"

Michael grinned. "All right. All right."

"Michael, I've got a proposition to make you. About the farm."

"Oh, you'll be around to your spring plowing—just like that!" Michael snapped his fingers.

Peter shook his head. "I'm not going to farm again, Michael."

"You ain't going to sell this fine place?"

"No. I want you to run it."

Michael looked quickly at Lena, then back at Peter.

"It's a big place."

"I don't mean for you to work it: I mean for you to run it."

"To boss it, you mean?"

"Yes. Keep Cantey and his brother. You're a good farmer; you can make it pay."

"Yes. I could do that."

"You take two thirds, or whatever you think is right."

"Oh, that—we never would fight about that."

Michael grinned. "We got news for you, too."

"For me?"

"Yes. Taska, she's coming up after a while and bring little Jan with her."

"Oh. Taska is well, I hope."

"Yes." Michael spoke soberly. He did not know what to say when Peter's manner became distant. "Yes," he repeated.

"Well. We can arrange details later. You go out and look the whole place over, make your plans."

"By golly, Peter, I make good crops. This is a wonderful farm. I wonder me sometimes how you ever did it by yourself."

"Hard work."

"Too hard for one man."

"Yes: I'm tired of it now."

Peter discarded his crutches in March. Kam Sandifer came over one rainy day.

[364]

"I brought you something." He held out a heavy cane with a gold crook handle.

"Why—thanks, Kam. I guess I could use a cane now."

"It belonged to Mrs. Sandifer's father."

"That's very nice of you. But shouldn't you keep it?"

"Mrs. Sandifer wanted you to have it."

"Thank her for me, will you? That is very—gracious of her."

"Not at all. Delighted. How are you anyway?"

"Impatient."

"Then you're a lot better."

"I guess so."

"Laurel's at home, Peter."

Peter looked steadily at Kam. "How is she?"

"Better."

"Has she been sick?"

"No. But she never has regained her spirit—quite."

Peter looked out of the window.

"She wants to come and see you. She thinks she wants to make some kind of—a—a—"

"A what, Kam?"

"Sort of an apology, maybe. I don't know."

"She doesn't owe me one."

"She thinks so."

"I'll be glad to see her, but not for that reason."

"I'll tell her."

"Kam—" Peter hesitated.

"Yes?"

"Well, Kam, most things in the world are not helped much by talk—afterward. There are things about—about my boys that no one else understands. It's all past now, and there's no use mauling subjects over, but there's been a lot that's been misunderstood in that quarter."

"That's common human experience, Peter."

They fell silent, both of them watched the coals fall from the logs, brighten in the low draft, waver, and fall to ash.

"Is Laurel going to stay in school, Kam?"

"This is her last year. I think I'll send her to my sister in Virginia for a year. To come back here—well, Peter, she's a strange child. She'll get over Robby's death in time. After all, she's just a girl. There's one of the Nolan twins, Paul, I think, has tried to go around with her a little, but she's indifferent. He's a nice fellow. Just gone into law practice at Kings Row."

Peter stirred uneasily in his chair, and stretched his leg cautiously.

"I found a copy of Robby's poems—here in my shelves. I didn't know it had been printed at all."

"Yes, Laurel told me you didn't seem to have heard anything about the whole business. I couldn't tell anything about them, of course. Couldn't read them."

"They were—not bad."

"He could have—"

"Yes." Peter interrupted harshly. "Kam, will you look in the next room there, in the top drawer of that chest—the one in the southeast corner, and bring me that green leather case."

"Certainly. Green, did you say?"

"Yes."

Kam returned after a moment. "This it?"

"Yes." Peter snapped it open. It contained a pair of old-fashioned bracelets. Peter lifted one up on his finger. A small circle of diamonds sparkled on the medallion.

"They belonged to my mother."

"They're quite fine, I should say. Beautiful."

"Savina never wore them. I gave them to her, but she didn't wear jewelry."

Kam nodded. Peter replaced the bracelet, closed the case, and handed it to Kam.

"Give them to Laurel, will you?"

"Why—I—"

"Say they are—well, tell her Robby would have given them to her."

"She'll be deeply touched, Peter. Thank you. She'll come to see you."

"Kam—"

"Yes, Peter."

"I—on second thought, I believe I couldn't see her right now. Will you try to explain? I guess I can't go through anything else this winter."

"She won't understand that, Peter."

"Don't you?" Peter's voice was unsteady.

"I guess maybe I do."

"Explain it to her."

"All right, I'll try. I suppose I can."

The April leaves were small and brightly green on the sycamore branches when Taska came.

Peter arose from his chair. He looked hard into her face. Without a word she put her arms up to his shoulders and kissed him. He kept his searching gaze on her face. He had not yet looked at the child Lena was leading by the hand.

"How are you, Taska?"

"Well—fine. You are better now?"

"Much. Almost well again."

"We were terribly worried."

"Thank you."

"This is Jan."

Taska drew the child forward, and Peter sat down. His knees shook so he could not stand.

Taska pushed her little boy toward him. "Say, hello, Grandpa."

Jan drew in his chin, but he did not speak. His big gray-green eyes looked up timidly but unafraid through thick lashes.

Peter reached out and the two shook hands gravely. But Peter's heart beat hard. He felt as if he were turning to lead.

This child—so like—so like—

Jan was the image of Robby.

Mustering the last vestige of will, Peter spoke. The words came evenly.

"He is remarkably like Robby."

[367]

Taska caught her lower lip between her teeth for a moment. Then she, too, answered calmly, "It seems so to me."

Lena broke in volubly. "Oh, he favors Robby to a tee! Taska, take off your things. Come here, Jan, let's unbutton your overcoat."

"Lena, where have you put Taska?"

Lena laughed. "Not anywhere yet. She just this minute came in."

"Give her the southwest room upstairs."

"Savina's room?"

"Yes."

Taska cleared the air of the house immediately. The old oppressive quiet disappeared. There was movement, talk, and something like gaiety.

Taska was really beautiful, Peter decided. She had lost but little of her warm color, and her amazing vitality enveloped her and clothed her with a glow and an opulence like that of a rich summer day.

"They say the river's rising fast." Taska sat opposite Peter while he ate his breakfast from a tray. He shoved his chair about and looked out.

"It is high."

"There's some overflow on the south side."

"There have been lots of heavy rains on west, I hear."

Taska looked intently at Peter. Then she drew her shoulders up and took a deep breath.

"Mr. Kettring."

"What is it, Taska?"

"I had a letter from David this morning." She waited. It was the first time David's name had been spoken.

Peter set his cup down suddenly. It clattered against the saucer. "So?"

"Yes. We—he—he is thinking of selling his paper. He has a chance to get rid of it at a profit. That place isn't exactly what he wants anyway."

"Um." Peter's intent gaze never left Taska's face.

"I hardly know what to advise him."

"Isn't his mind made up?"

"Not quite. He wrote to ask me what I thought of it. I don't know what to say. I thought maybe you'd read the letter and advise me—"

He pushed his chair back noisily. "I will not read his letter."

"Oh—"

Peter looked out of the window. Then he looked back at Taska. Her eyes were dark with tears.

"I'm sorry I brought it up—Mr. Kettring!"

Peter pounded his cane sharply on the floor.

"Taska Kettring! You tell David—" Peter choked a little. His face flushed. "You tell David to sell out that damned one-horse newspaper and come home!"

Taska stared.

"You heard what I said?"

"Y-yes."

"Well, write him that. Tell him to hurry up about it."

Taska still stared. Peter arose, thumping his cane as he moved, took up his hat, and limped out into the front yard.

Taska picked up the tray and hurried to the kitchen.

"What is, Taska, you look so excited?"

"I want to drive in to St. Stephens right away. I want to telegraph David."

"What for, Taska, is anything—"

"Mr. Kettring wants him to come home."

Lena gasped. "I call Michael. Will Davy come, you think?"

"Yes. He's wanted to for a long time."

The river continued to rise. There was talk of another flood, but newspapers were reassuring. Nevertheless, there was much anxious watching of the river.

Peter sat at the window.

Past him trooped all of the cohorts of memory. He was better now, and as he reviewed the past, assorted it and appraised it, he felt a swift resurgence of interest and energy. What was he to do now?

He had turned back, turned away from what had once seemed the one possible highroad of promise. He was—he beat softly on the arm of his chair—he was at the beginning again. So, then. So let it be! *He would begin . . .*

Taska came in and stood beside him. She fidgeted with the curtain cord.

"What time is it?"

"The clock is there, on the mantel, Taska."

"Oh, yes; I had forgotten. Three."

She returned to the window. "The water is very high, isn't it?"

"Yes. Will—this—it won't delay David, will it?"

"No. He is coming by way of Kansas City and Camperville."

"He ought to be here by five."

"Pa has already gone to Dawson's Point. He just couldn't keep still any longer."

"Where's Jan?"

"He went along."

David came through the side yard to the kitchen steps. Lena fell upon him with embraces and tears and considerable outcry.

"You go now, right away, in—in there!"

David felt his throat tighten. He pointed awkwardly. "In there?"

Lena nodded vigorously.

The house: it felt as he knew it must, as it used to be. Everything—every chair and shining pan—the same. The same clean, dry smell.

The thought of his mother arose overwhelmingly. He choked and stood still for a moment. He must not think of her—not now —later.

David opened the door into the "best front room." He stood perfectly still for a moment. This room! The fireplace. Books— books everywhere—shelves of them: books on the wide new table, and on chairs. And this man—this gray, distinguished-looking gentleman who arose from a chair by the window!

"How are you, David? Come in."

David shook hands. "Hello, Pop."

"Sit down."

"How are you, Pop? How's the leg?"

"Nearly well."

Peter was taking in every feature and movement of this tall dark man. Yes: as he should look. Black-browed, somber-eyed. Deadly serious, purposeful—yes, as he should be: strong.

That night Peter and David sat together until nearly dawn. Through all of those hours of talk David watched closely, waiting and listening for some explanation of the past years, or some revelation of what lay now behind the guarded expression of his father's eyes. Peter covered those years with the easy narrative a man might use for a casual visitor. Whatever there was, David realized, lay buried in the ashes of tragedy as inexplicable today as it was when it occurred. Peter had walked always in his own counsels. He would continue in that way as long as he lived. David saw that the changes were deeper, farther away in the secrets of personality—in the soul, he found himself saying—and that they were impressive. A strange new feeling came in to fill a painful emptiness in him. He thought again of his mother and of Robby—how unbelievable that his unreal little brother should have been a poet!—how unthinkable that his mother should have drowned out there in the dark in the wild waters of the river she had always feared. However keen this sense of loss, of useless, purposeless tragedy, might remain, there was his father, a man who loomed suddenly heroic and—he groped for a word—and, and almost legendary. The respect and the new interest he felt for this man he had never understood changed as he thought of it, changed and became affection. Yes, Taska had been wonderful, and the way he loved Taska was something clearly set apart and complete, but in spite of the welling beauty and tenderness of that love, there had always been an odd and persistent feeling of important lack. This was it. His father had not spoken words he may have hoped to hear tonight, perhaps he never would, but that part of himself which was faith was turning toward the somber presence across the hearth with the assurance that his own questing and troubled self had indeed come home.

The next day David went over the place with Michael. In the afternoon it rained again, and a chill came up from the bottoms. Lena lighted a fire in the fireplace.

When she had gone from the room, Peter leaned forward on his cane, clasping and unclasping his long fingers about the gold crook.

"David. I haven't asked you, but I'd like to know—"

"What, Pop? What do you want to know?"

"What are you going to do now? What are your plans?"

"I'm going to school."

"To—oh, I see. H'm!"

"It's this way—" David rushed his words to cover this painful minute. "They're beginning to have classes in journalism at the universities. Practical, experienced newspapermen are going to run them. I want to learn. I want to be a good newspaperman. I couldn't do much down there—alone. Too far away. Most of the population Mexican."

"You'll want a good newspaper, then, when you're ready?"

"Or else a job on a good paper—St. Louis or Kansas City, maybe, where I can put theories into practice."

"I see."

David hesitated, and stammered over his next words. "Do you think it's a good plan?"

"Excellent."

"I'm glad you think so."

"Why?"

"There's just the two of us—you and me—now. We ought to try to get along."

"We'll get along, but there are more than the two of us. There's Taska and Jan."

"Yes, of course."

Peter spoke quickly. "When the time comes we'll buy a newspaper—wherever you want it. You've got to have a good paper in the right place."

"Pop, I—"

"As you say—we've got to get along—somehow . . ."

David sat up straight. "There are some things I want to do in the world."

"Yes? What, for instance?"

David laughed deprecatingly. "You'll think I sound mighty brash, but I want to—well, it's sort of like this: seems to me the world always has to be started over, all new, all the time. Always beginning—I guess I'm not very clear."

"Maybe you are. Go on."

"I don't mean to be a crack-brained idealist or anything like that, but I'd like to work on this country right around here, go to work on its thinking, its attitude toward—toward America and the future of the country. North and South still have a long way to go to get together again. I'd like to help. You know, just begin building from the bottom up."

Peter started at the familiar words—a very echo from long ago.

"I understand," he said under his breath. "But you'll stay around for a while?"

"If you want us to."

"It's your place, yours and Taska's and Jan's. There's a lot I have to tell you, and there's a lot I need to talk out with you. I've been reading a great deal this year."

"I—I see all of these books. Lots of new ones, too."

"Yes. I was twenty years or more out of date. Didn't know what was going on outside of this Godforsaken place."

The evening came down. David had gone out with Michael to look at the stock. Taska was upstairs with Jan. Peter could hear the cheerful sound of Lena clattering about the kitchen.

Savina . . .

Robby . . .

Peter closed his eyes.

Old Jude stirred uneasily by the fire. She arose presently, stretching first her front legs, then her back ones.

"Komm', Jude."

She came, sagging in her step as she always did when she was called.

"Lie down, old girl—here, by me."

Jude collapsed as if the last spring of energy had failed. She looked up once, mournfully.

"A man's house—" Peter said the words in a half whisper to himself. Yes: a man's house—a fire on the hearth, his son, his son's son—yes, and ghosts, too—the ghosts that must forever be. They, too, were a part of a man's house and of a man's life.

It was nearly dark now. He heard Laws Cantey come into the kitchen. He and Lena were speaking. After a moment he heard the kitchen door open again. Cantey was leaving, he supposed. He heard him call back to Lena.

"Tell Mr. Kettring the river's falling."

ABOUT THE AUTHOR

Henry Bellamann has had a varied career. He has served as act-
ing director of the Juilliard Musical Foundation, dean of the Curtis
Institute of Music, and professor of music at Vassar. France has
decorated him with the Legion of Honor, and De Pauw University
has conferred upon him an honorary musical doctorate. His hobbies
are collecting stamps and translating Dante. In 1940 he published
the best-selling Kings Row. *His previous novels were* Petenera's
Daughter, Crescendo, *and* The Richest Woman in Town.